WILL OF THE STARS

FIRST CONTACT

By Pasha Kamyshev

X: @PashaKamyshev

Substack: https://pashanomics.substack.com

Will of the Stars: Derev Trilogy

1 kilosecond	16.6 minutes
1 megasecond	11.6 days
1 gigasecond	31.7 years
1 terasecond	31710 years

1 light-second	300,000 km
1 light-kilosecond	~2 * d between Earth and Sun
1 light-megasecond	~60 * d between Sun and Neptune
1 light-gigasecond	~7.25 * d between Sun and Alpha Centaury
1 light-terasecond	~1/3 * diameter of Milky way

Economic Rights of the Imperial Constitution:

1. Decitas: No tax shall exceed 10% in peacetime.

2. Capitas: The government cannot print money above population growth.

3. Habitas: You are entitled to own land which you have made habitable.

Chapter 1

Welcome to the Academy

Valor wins battles, economics wins wars, mathematics builds civilizations, and philosophy ensures they are worth living in.

The First Emperor, prior to the Unification War.

The Empire stands united. Millions of Worlds within the Human Empire, ranging from the newly terraformed to the most 'megastructured', shared a few enduring aspects. A stable Earth-like atmosphere, extended lifespan, dance parties, and unwavering respect for the Current Emperor, whoever he was. Another constant was the Academy, the most elite and often the only, institution of higher learning in a given star system.

The Academy was everything for Albert, a civilian student on Derev, a comparatively new planet of the Empire, colonized less than 10 gigaseconds [~317 Earth years] ago. Albert held the top spot in the under 600-megasecond [~19 Earth years] age category sims ladder, an ongoing star-system-wide online contest of simulated space combat. Sims combat was the most important admission criterion to the Academy. Aside from aristocratic heritage, of course.

Albert's first steps on the Academy grounds, alongside other new students filled him with joy, reverence, and admiration for humanity. As he walked among the crowd, many civilians, most of whom Albert was meeting in person for the first time, swarmed around him. Ken, shorter but with a sturdy build and a hint of ancestry from the Asia portion of Old Earth, stepped forward to greet him. He extended his hand, saying, "The legend is here."

"Thanks," Albert blushed a little. He was proud of his simulation skills, but he wished to prove himself beyond the tests. The citizen students acknowledged the group with very brief glances before passing by.

They continued on the Path towards the Academy in silence as was tradition.

The Path was a wide walkway surrounded by bushes of flowers, beginning with Earth roses. 3423 bushes grew along it. Each plant was taken from a different planet or space habitat from star systems on the path humanity took from Earth and Derev. Humanity traversed the path with generation ships, stopping to terraform planets into Earth-like environments, a process that took centuries per planet. Each plant symbolized a few centuries of their ancestor's labor, representing the effort it took to bend each planet to human will, making it habitable and productive enough to send ships further on.

Albert walked slowly. The goal of the Path was to imprint the glory of human achievement onto the new students. It worked. At the end of the Path, there was a person-sized cage sphere that contained a large space compass. The device pointed towards Earth more than 630 light gigaseconds [~20 000 light years] away. Albert didn't need a space compass because he had memorized star maps to know the direction of Earth even in broad sunlight.

The students prayed.

"Peace be upon us.

May the stars shine bright, may their Will be done.

May the Masters guide us on our Path.

May our Asabiyyah never waver.

Peace be upon us."

The classrooms and dorms of the Academy occupied a single building spanning 400 by 300 meters at the base and 6 stories tall. Half of its area consisted of a central courtyard. Above the main entrance, the roof featured stone carvings of various noble house symbols: bears, eagles, dragons, panthers, and others. Behind it stood a partially assembled railcruiser, used for hands-on instruction. Despite the railcruiser lacking two of its eight standard 200-meter railguns and missing significant parts of its frame, it still surpassed the Academy building in size.

The Academy Wall right after the Path was constructed from hexagonal bricks. Albert tapped one of them.

"Hex-boron nitride," Ken remarked, "and that's platinum silicate glass." He pointed at the window.

"Sturdy," Albert nodded his head.

"It's just the non-load bearing exterior. Standard spaceship-grade frame underneath," Ken was excited to share his knowledge.

"No wonder the building looks new after almost 10 gigas," Albert expected nothing less.

The main entrance to the building led to the Welcome Hall. Albert and Ken entered the Hall together. As Albert stepped onto the stony entrance, a sense of wonder and fear filled him. Admission to the Academy was a monumental step in his life, something many of his friends didn't even bother dreaming about. It was a culmination of his relentless efforts: daily practice of space simulation battles, coding exercises, and walking around with a weighted vest to get accustomed to feelings of high-G maneuvers.

The Principal of the Academy began greeting a new class for the 307th time with his customary motivational speech. His skin was pale and was starting to show wrinkles. His gray hair also began to show. However, his relaxed demeanor suggested he'd long stopped worrying about the passage of time.

"We are not alone in the universe. More than a hundred other civilizations look up to us. They look at the Empire of Man with respect, admiration, and a healthy dose of fear. Guided by the light of the Current Emperor and the World Unit Governors, as Custodians of the Galaxy, we have brought Order and Peace to all its inhabitants."

The students cheered. The zeal of the Principal's voice carried great energy.

Albert cheered, though he felt a strange sense along with his elation. The concept of the "Current Emperor" never sat well with him. In theory, the Emperors held absolute control over the millions of worlds in the Empire, but in practice, the world Albert was on lay too far from Earth. They recently got sub-light-speed news of a new Emperor, numbered 43,138 coming to "power" long after he had retired and passed away as counted at light-speed concurrency. It astounded Albert that the Border Worlds, such as Derev considered themselves "part of the Empire" if they didn't even know the real number of the Emperor, thus giving rise to the term "Current Emperor." The local elites and Governors of each star system ran the show within the constraints imposed by the Imperial Constitution.

Albert never knew quite how to feel about venerating the Emperor or how that differed from general cheerfulness or celebrating humanity. His family gave him confused looks when asked about this, offering only a vague piece of advice. "Just do what the other kids do," which is exactly what he was doing now. To him, it seemed the least he could do was know which direction Earth was at all times.

The Principal continued, "We have been at Peace for over 10 teraseconds [317,000 years], since we and our allies eliminated the threat of the ironbirds once and for all."

The end of the last war was the last time one of the "Current Emperors" announced minor official changes to the Imperial Constitution. Albert had not learned of any actual decisions made by any "Current Emperor" since then and for quite a while before that time. He wasn't quite sure if the more complex

Imperial history was only available for older people or if the galaxy-spanning civilization was perfectly self-managing. It was hard for Albert to get a sense of what kind of people the Emperors were. Were they as grandiose characters as the Governors or were they somehow even bigger? He knew some Early Emperors better through the long history books written about them.

The Principal continued, "We are a Border World at the very edge of our Empire. The Current Emperor depends on us to build warships, protect other worlds, and expand across the galaxy. We take barren rocks and inhospitable jungles and turn them into gardens worthy of the name ... paradise. We work with the bare minimum of what we can bring across the stars and build ourselves. How do we manage this? We do not have the technological prowess and megastructures of the Core Worlds, we do not have the production capacity of the Mid Worlds. Instead, we have you."

The Principal waved at the students.

120 students, around 600 megaseconds in age [~19 Earth years] from both planets in the star system, stared intensely at him. The citizen students sat on the top part of the hall, the civilian ones below. Citizen students wore uniforms with their respective House regalia, complete with colorful house seals, while civilians like Albert and Ken were dressed in unisex Academy gray.

"You," the Principal waved his hands at the citizens above him.

"You," the Principal waved his hands at the civilians below.

Albert felt good as the Principal's hand wave passed over him.

"You have been chosen as the top candidates for leadership positions in this star system. Over the next two years, you will expand on foundational knowledge given in your general education: quantum gravity, nano-engineering, life extension biology, programmable type theory, and Imperial history. You will learn the skills necessary to lead others in roles such as currency fluctuation management, modeling and implementation of social systems, and, in a very unlikely case, war. The most worthy men present will become warship captains. It is a duty gives significant privileges during times of peace. Once again, welcome to the Academy! Let the light of our Emperors, from the First to the Current, guide you. May your Will to Act be as strong as Theirs."

The students repeated, "May the light of our Emperors, from the First to the Current illuminate our path. May our Will to Act be ever strong as theirs."

The Principal took a less serious tone, "Considering the Emperor could not be present in person to congratulate you on your Academy admission..."

The class laughed, and Albert joined in, his tension easing. If they were going to be in this "Current Emperor" situation, at least it's good to have some sense of humor around it.

"Our World Unit Governor will come in and say a few words," The Principal chuckled, but the class stopped laughing and immediately stood up. Several students nervously adjusted their uniforms and haircuts. Albert was surprised. When he spoke to Academy alumni, they somehow failed to discuss the Governor's visit. He looked around and noticed the surprise on Ken's and many other students' faces.

The Governor walked into the room, almost as if he were gliding, his body moving with graceful steps. He stood and faced the students, "Relax; this won't be on the exams." The Governor's face was pale, similar to that of the Principal. The Governor's arms did have a gentle tan. He wore a magnificent and entirely impractical red cloak draped over his ceremonial armor.

The students politely laughed and took their seats.

'"As my ancestor, the Fifth Emperor, said more than 60 teraseconds ago [~1.9 million Earth years] when founding the Academy system and finishing the dismantling of outdated universities, 'For every student who dreams of being a spaceship captain, we need a thousand who dream of alloy logistics.'"

Albert smirked and began to make a laughing noise but immediately stopped as he noticed other civilians looking at him. He wasn't fully sure why this specific statement made him have this specific reaction.

The Governor didn't notice Albert. Instead, he looked over the citizen balcony, pausing long enough for his gaze to land briefly on a couple of students without making them feel too uneasy. He continued, "You are the future elite of our planet and this system. Your dreams, no matter what they are, are worth pursuing, as long as you're willing to take on the immense responsibility of leading the people. Speak the truth. Safeguard the helpless. And, above all..."

The Governor made the Gesture. Students inhaled, preparing to repeat the most important line of the Oath in unison with the Governor.

"Humans must come first. Now and Forever."

The Governor paused, allowing the silence to settle, and then walked out of the room just as smoothly as he'd entered. Of the ceremonies he had to do, the short ones were his favorite.

Chapter 2

The Announcement

They have slaughtered millions of their own subjects. Do not believe them to be agreement-capable.

The First Emperor when discussing Cyborg Theocracy with another human leader.

The Governor's palace stood atop a hill underneath 3 of the planet's highest mountain peaks. On the bottom of the hill were the houses of his staff, who traveled to the Palace via hill-side lifts every morning. At its base, the staff houses were clustered, accessible via hillside lifts that carried them to the palace each morning. The Governor would normally take the lift down, and then ascend the 2300 steps up with a backpack half his weight.

He missed his brisk daily walk yesterday due to travel to the Academy, and today's walk was interrupted by an urgent message from an observatory tech. This was the third "urgent" message in his gigasecond as Governor so far, with the last two being particularly serious. As he walked into the tech's office, Alexander Mishov stood next to the tech, gazing at his monitor.

The tech's office, located just down the hall from the Governor's, offered ample space for meetings. His desk featured a variety of input devices and 3 monitors 1 meter in diameter.

Alexander, the man known for having some of the widest shoulders on the planet, was the head of the military. During times of peace, this meant going through endless checklists of readiness, conducting "contingency reviews" of civilian projects, and running war games against his subordinates. Involvement with an observatory tech only meant bad news. Out of uniform, Alexander wore a casual t-shirt, signaling how urgent this meeting was. He still had his silver necklace with an orthodox cross on it.

"We have a category 1 deep space anomaly," the tech said as soon as the Governor walked in.

This was the worst news possible. Anomaly categories ranged from 0 to 10, with 0 being the most severe, a category reserved only for anomalies that contradicted the known laws of physics.

The Governor's tenure had been marked by relative uneventfulness so far, with most of his time spent rubber-stamping land trades between the Noble Houses, a task that, although dull, was necessary. Space sims practice was fun. Sirium's terraforming efforts were more standard and uneventful compared to Derev's terraforming overseen by his father and grandfather.

"Speed and distance?" Despite the frustration, The Governor was all business.

"2.16 light-megaseconds away. 8% light speed as of now. At this speed, it will be here in around 27 megaseconds [~312 Earth days]. However, assuming these are ships that will decelerate, it likely means 30-40% slower than that."

"Size?"

"Some of the objects are as large as 50 kilometers," The tech nervously glanced at the Governor, then at Alexander, and back to the Governor.

Alexander stepped forward, recognizing that the tech might be hesitant to share the information at the proper speed, "If it is a fleet of regular design, the upper estimate puts it at 10 teratons."

The Governor tilted his head back in disbelief, "Wait, what? This number doesn't make any sense. Have we ruled out sensor and computer errors?" This is not going to be the boring Governorship he had accepted as his fate.

The tech continued, "The only data is coming from our deep space observation craft. The anomaly will be in a range of closer satellites in 10 megaseconds [~115 Earth days]. I have no reason to suspect errors."

Deep-space craft are specifically designed to observe likely pathways from other systems. They are built for extreme reliability and have never been known to fail.

"Where is it coming from?" The Governor asked.

"The simplest path projections place the origin exactly in the M55.32 star system," the tech replied.

Alexander sighed, "Browly. We knew this day would come. I know this isn't quite the Governorship you wanted."

The Browly system, located 200 light-megaseconds [~6.3 light Earth years] away, has been emitting radio signals consistent with a civilization capable of reaching orbit until 3 gigaseconds ago [~95 Earth years]. There was a rapid decline in radio signals until complete silence. Since then, Derev sent five observation probes to the system. None returned. The last probe was a 'carrier probe' equipped with six internal mini-probes that it sent back at predetermined intervals. A fourth internal mini-probe was sent 2 light megaseconds [~0.06 light years] from the outer edge of the system, where it detected some orbital activity still existing in the system, but didn't pick up any radio signals. The carrier probe never returned or sent back any mini-probes. Originally, theories suggested that the civilization had suffered some cataclysm, but the disappearance of the probes and their presumed destruction may have indicated a desire to hide.

The Governor never felt comfortable with the Browly situation, despite knowing that it was unlikely anyone would dare to attack humanity. Every alien species knew what would happen or could make avery reasonable guess. He breathed heavily in and out. They were the closest human system to Browly by far. Corial was in the opposite direction compared to Browly and other human systems were even further. While he would certainly notify the others using information ships, the fastest would take nearly 400 megaseconds [~12 Earth years] to reach Corial.

"Yeah, this isn't what I wanted, but here we are," The Governor wanted to get back to business again. "And it's heading straight for us? How sure are you it's not just using the star for a slingshot?"

Alexander shook his head, "It's an invasion, buddy. Besides, those kinds of maneuvers are forbidden by our intergalactic communiques with any fleet of this size."

The Governor wasn't convinced. He countered, "M55.32, the Browly system, remains an enigma, but it's unrealistic to expect they could build a small moon's weight of warships as their first or second excursion into deep space."

Alexander raised his palms slightly up and towards the Governor. He was about a head taller than the Governor and his biceps were around the size of his head. The observatory tech flinched.

"The military section of the Imperial Constitution is unequivocal on matters of estimating the worst case," Alexander stated firmly.

The Governor raised an eyebrow, his expression skeptical, as he considered citing the laws a tad premature for the conversation, and sought to set a clearer tone.

"Alex, what's our war fleet tonnage of this star system?"

"200 million tons, give or take."

"So, by pure tonnage, this thing you think is a WAR fleet outnumbers us by a factor of 50,000, correct?"

"Yes."

This was an absurd answer.

"Given that we are a highly well-defended Border System with higher than average military readiness requirements, how many human worlds, except for Earth's Sol system, have a combined WAR fleet tonnage of 10 teratons?"

Alexander didn't like the framing of the question. War fleets outside of Sol were almost entirely a concept unique to Border Worlds, which was a small fraction of human worlds. Non-Border-World human systems relied on immobile megastructural defense platforms rather than standing fleets. Their shipyards, while civilian-ship-focused, were also significantly more numerous. Alexander crossed his arms but answered the question honestly as posed.

"Hard to tell with all the communication delays, but it could be all of them."

"Exactly. How could a single-star system produce more warships than the most successful conquerors in the galaxy? Can you imagine the energy requirements for this? Not with the power of a hundred suns can they do this."

Alexander didn't know the answer, but the question of action shouldn't have to wait for all the answers. Instead, he asked, "OK, buddy, what is your most likely estimate of the situation?"

The Governor said, "The upper estimate is wrong. It is a fleet, but these are oversized colony ships with few weapon-capable escorts. Their sensors indicated too late that this world is ours. We will invoke the standard 'mistaken colonization' protocol. We give them a small moon temporarily and tell them to fuck off to another nearby star system within a hundred years."

Alexander tilted his head. It was a reasonable guess. Civilian ships required a lot less energy and sophistication to build. Humans and other species occasionally constructed civilian ships as large as 50 km, but they were slow, unarmored, and only capable of destroying small asteroids in their path. They were very vulnerable. However, one cannot gamble the lives of humans on two planets on such a guess. He pressed on, "The average species of this galaxy generally has a non-trivial fleet escorting civilian ships. They likely outnumber us by war tonnage even in your highly optimistic scenario."

The Governor relaxed a little. Alexander understood him.

The Governor paused and gestured for Alexander to come to his office down the hall. He stepped onto the balcony, where he gazed out over the capital city, taking in the grandeur of the statue of himself at its center, before filling his lungs with a deep breath of air.

Oh, fresh Derev air. His father, grandfather, and other Governors before them had the project of terraforming Derev to be suitable for human habitation. The planet was a lush jungle planet when they arrived more than 10 gigaseconds [~316 Earth years] ago, but the atmosphere lacked the right composition to be breathable. Since then, the Governors and Noble Houses mitigated numerous dangers. They used gene drives to alter atmosphere-affecting single-cell organisms and introduced new tree species from various parts of the galaxy. They added ice to polar ice caps, and altered salt composition to shift ocean currents and mitigate hurricanes. They eradicated tremendous swarms of poisonous bugs and taught large predators to stay away from human habitation. They shifted the genomes of existing animals to better adapt to the new atmosphere. About a third of the biomass on the planet was now due to human intervention. The terraforming computer simulations showed the climate was self-sustaining and stable. It took longer than expected, but The Governor was proud of what his family had accomplished.

Yet he was most proud of the air. The air was so good, that a recent arrival from another system coined the joke "Come to Derev to have kids, stay for the air." The arrival in question has just spent more than 2 gigaseconds [~63 Earth years] on a spaceship, making him perhaps not the best authority on air freshness. Nonetheless, the Governor still liked the joke enough to include it in his mandatory report, which he was sending via an information ship to the nearby Governors every 500 megaseconds [~16 Earth years].

Before he became the Governor, he worked hard on managing the sequestration of sulfur and other chemicals from the atmosphere, cleaning the rivers from the cyanoid bacteria. However, these were always part of large teams, under the direction of his House and the previous Governors. His own rule was too late to affect Derev terraforming but too early to begin the next step of colonizing nearby star systems.

The Governor recalled his past lives. His Blood Memory revealed legendary feats carved into the stone of history. Was he worthy of his heritage?

As Governor, a part of him yearned for individual glory that wasn't tied to his family's legacy; another part urged contentment with the life he already possessed. But now, it was this second voice that was screaming at the other parts of him, "Be cautious what you wish for."

The Governor turned back to face Alexander, who stood patiently. Understanding the uniqueness of their situation, Alexander's expression softened, and he asked, "Do you want to play a quick space battle to help clear your head?"

The Governor appreciated the gesture and while it was fun to beat up someone in space sims, his anomaly decision was simple and needed to be made quickly.

"Of course, we are still taking the possibility of war seriously. We are going to DEFCON 2." The Governor said.

It was a by-the-book decision. Alexander smiled to the full extent that a man of stature could afford to, "A good decision, but I would have preferred DEFCON 1."

The Governor tapped him on the shoulder, "Duly noted. We are going to need more ships. Summon the Noble Patriarchs. It's time to build."

Chapter 3

The Anomaly

Do not put any creation of the Cyborg Theocracy in or near your body.

The First Emperor after the creation of "Virus-33" vaccine by the Cyborg Theocracy.

0.1 MS AA [Megaseconds After Anomaly]

Albert walked into his Academy room for the first time. The space, 8 m by 5 m, featured a partial wall that separated his bed from the rest of the room. In the middle of it, stood an adjustable chair across a pair of computer monitors. He was on the second floor, with his plastiglass window facing the courtyard. His closet door was open, revealing an empty droid storage cabinet within.

Albert entered his bathroom and extended his arms for a medscan. A barely visible laser moved quickly over his body, noting the heat differentials and any changes in skin coloration. Based on this information, the med-scan generated a toxicology report identifying the most likely compounds that he needed to aid cell regeneration and prevent aging. The compounds were retrieved from an in-building storage facility, mixed, and delivered in a powdered form through a tube a few minutes later.

While waiting, he took a bath. As he lay down on it, the bath adjusted to his body shape and filled itself with water. Cozy.

A tiny bit colder than his body temp, just how he liked it. The medscan prompted him for verbal confirmation of his light therapy, which Albert provided. The room shone with various light wavelengths that the medscan had determined were needed: a minute of red and two minutes of green.

The powder arrived. He mixed the powder in a glass of water and drank it. It tasted like grapes. "It always tastes like grapes when I feel anxious," he thought to himself. A quick check of his medlogs confirmed the hypothesis. Albert, like all inhabitants of the planet, had used the medscan nearly daily. It was nice to be in the Academy, which had higher purity compounds that also arrived faster.

Albert examined the room controls, noticing they had the standard temperature and airflow controls. However, noise cancellation had a setting he hadn't seen before next to a "not recommended" red warning sign.

He set the noise cancellation of the room to maximum. A screen covered the window and sound-absorbent panels slid from the walls 5 cm perpendicular to the surface. Albert sat on the floor of the room, closed his eyes, and listened to his heartbeat for about a minute. It felt slightly uncomfortable.

He adjusted the noise cancellation back to its recommended setting. He then sat in his chair, gazing at the monitor as he reached out to touch two spherical halves of a keyboard.

This was not cozy.

He pressed the auto-adjust setting on his chair, which caused the chair, monitor, and keyboard to adjust their positions subtly as it monitored Albert's muscle engagement and breathing. After a few motions, they settled into a new configuration that minimized his tension, while keeping him alert. He felt cozy again. He turned on his computer and looked over the profiles of his fellow students.

Upon admission to the Academy, the 120-person incoming class of students was divided into 15 8-person groups that attended all the smaller classes together, with a mix of 4 boys and 4 girls in each group. Albert once inquired an Academy alum about the process of selecting students and was told to "Trust the process." Ken didn't know anything either. Students were scored individually on most tests, however, each group's average score was also prominently displayed on the group leaderboard near the Welcome Hall.

Before the actual tests inside the Academy started, the leaderboard held the average admission score of each group. Albert checked it and felt pleased to see he was in the top-scoring group. He wondered how much he was responsible for this or if the other kids carried their weight. He looked at each student's test scores and was pleasantly surprised that while his average score remained the highest, his groupmates were doing well and occasionally surpassed him in some specialized tests.

"If they are just mostly grouping everyone by score, why not say that?" Albert thought to himself, but then dropped the thought and readied himself for the first class.

He felt less anxious. "Grape stuff is good," he thought.

Albert's chair adjusted itself with his room settings by the time he got to class.

Max Smith was excited to see how his Academy room turned out, situated in the Smith wing of the Academy dormitories, which had been graciously donated by his great-grandfather. As requested by Max, most of the wing was full of girls. He flipped through their photos, sorting them into categories. A couple of girls went into the 'nothing long-term' bucket, a couple who looked 'nice enough.' And then there were Sheene and Diana, in his class group, who were interesting from a political alliance perspective.

Sheene. Sheene was a proud major princess of House Li, both a key trading partner of House Smith and a rival for the title of the wealthiest House. She had a friendly smile, but did not possess the type of body he was most used to enjoying.

Diana was a minor princess of House Darien. A less significant House, though she managed to make up for her lack of familial pedigree with a pair of absolutely stunning breasts.

The room itself was quite pleasant. A full-wall holo-projector could make the room look like a tropical jungle. An aromatic mist generator further added to the ambiance. The bed was large enough for four people and featured an 'auto-firmer' mattress that could adjust firmness in at least four different sections to make itself perfectly pleasant to each person on top of each section.

Max was exactly where he needed to be. Learning about the Academy and his father's exceptional piloting skills had confirmed

Max destiny of surpassing them. This marked just one step in his journey toward claiming a place of power, a life secured by his birthright. Max recalled the brief speech by the Governor, whose gaze had lingered on both him and Sheene in a row behind him. The gaze lingered for just a little longer than he was comfortable with.

Max was also confused about how the Academy students were divided into class groups. He certainly appreciated the presence of the ladies but was frustrated that he wasn't in a citizen-only group as he had requested. His good friend Sunnak Gupta was with him, though. Max was a little late to the first class and was unexcited to find out that his only available seat in his group row was next to a civilian who introduced himself as "Albert." Max vaguely recalled seeing his name on the leaderboards.

The first-year 'Economics of the Elite' class, like all the 120-person lecture classes, was held on the top floor of the Academy building, allowing it to be illuminated by natural sunlight through the semi-transparent roof. The students sat in rows corresponding to the admission score group leaderboard. The top group sat in the front row. It included Max, Sunnak, Albert, Ken, Diana, Yezi, Sheene, and Bishakha.

Samiana, their economics teacher, began the lecture, "And so, you must understand that when payment systems are altered, it is not just a set of numbers in a machine. It affects people's hours of work, their hopes and dreams for the future, and the information about how the world's production ought to be guided. As citizens and likely future citizens, you have a duty to remember that..."

Samiana was on the cusp of excitement about the lecture when the door opened. She and the students looked at the Principal in surprise.

"Is everything okay?" she asked.

"No," he responded, "I will have the floor now."

She stepped aside. Students perked up in their chairs. They had never heard of an Academy class being interrupted, let alone by the Principal.

He spoke to everyone, "30 kiloseconds ago [~8 Earth hours], a deep space observer detected objects heading for us at 8% the speed of light. They are around 2 light-megaseconds [~0.06 light years] away. The most likely origin point is the Browly system. As per the Imperial Constitution, the Governor assumes hostile intent. The system is at DEFCON 2."

Max looked at Sunnak in shock. Albert mouthed a silent "wow". Diana leaned in, took a deep breath, and then sat back again.

The Principal continued, "As the Governor organizes the production of new war fleets and supplies, the Academy will also aid the effort. Current and future students must be ready if they are called. All your classes are canceled except those pertaining to space combat, its organization, and its discipline. Any questions?"

Quite a few students raised their hands. Principal pointed, "OK. Sunnak first."

"Do you think we will actually see combat?"

Principal smiled, "Given that many citizens have practiced simulated combat for gigaseconds, I wouldn't expect you to be ready to join the fleet by the time the anomaly arrives. Not under DEFCON 2 conditions. However, to maintain a proper readiness level for future generations, we have to act now. Diana next."

She asked, "What will happen to our other classes?"

"You will be able to take them along future Academy entrants. Max next."

Max shouted, "We are ready to roast some aliens." Many students cheered.

Principal nodded, "Excellent energy; however, not all questions are done. Ken, next."

Ken asked, "How many warships we will produce before the arrival?"

Principal said, "Our standing fleet tonnage could be increased by anywhere from 30 to 100% in 30 megaseconds [~1 Earth year], depending on strategy demands and escalation down the DEFCON levels. Albert, next."

Albert asked, "How big is the fleet coming at us?"

Albert assumed the mental posture of wanting to uncover information with the ultimate goal of solving the problem, whether or not it was his problem to solve." This mindset was both annoying to some and also the reason he got where he was now.

The Principal looked down and hesitated to answer, but continued nonetheless, "The Governor will address the system tomorrow." He changed his mind halfway through the answer, "You must understand that all estimates are very preliminary, even the estimate that this is a war fleet is preliminary. That said, the upper range puts it at 10 teratons."

The room fell dead silent. Samiana sat down.

"We are still going to win, right?" Sunnak asked nervously.

"The Empire of Man has," the Principal paused for an uncomfortably long time "NEVER lost a large-scale space engagement in its over 60 terasecond [~1.9 million Earth years] history." Albert noted that the Principal chose his words carefully to say true things, but also avoided mentioning non-space engagements or what exactly 'small' meant in this context.

The Principal finished, "Yet, the Empire of Man has never fought a fleet of this size in its history. This is serious. Help each other understand and come to terms with our new reality."

The Principal then answered a few more questions. As he began walking out, Diana exclaimed, "None of this makes any sense."

The Principal smiled, as he once again saw a teaching opportunity, "Good of you to notice this. Investigate your feelings of surprise, and then use your logical mind to come up with plausible theories that explain it."

Max turned to Diana and tried to untense his shoulders. "I knew something was up because my Dad," Max paused, "has been called into an emergency meeting of all the Noble Houses, but he didn't say why."

Diana smiled and replied, "Of course, the Noble Houses will discuss how best to prepare to protect us. I haven't spoken with my Great-Great Uncle recently, but I am sure he will be at the meeting as well."

"My granddad is there too," Sheene chimed in. "But he doesn't need to wait. My uncles are already drafting up plans for antimatter production increases."

The other students nodded in approval.

"I guess that means our previous hopes and dreams are on hold," Albert sighed.

"What were they before this announcement?" Ken inquired.

Diana said with clear sadness in her voice, "I wasn't even that great at combat sims. I just wanted to know how to rule."

"Well, I always wanted to explore the mysteries of the universe. Be a scientist. Would have been great to get a sponsor for this." Albert was a little unhappy, but his gaze lingered a little on the wealthy citizen students at his table.

"A scientist?" Max smirked "In a Border World? We are fighters and explorers. Being a scientist is a Core Would occupation. You are 500 light-gigaseconds [~16000 light years] away from your dream job."

Albert didn't enjoy the dashing of his hopes and dreams, but this was a good opportunity to explain, "The 'meta-science' Imperial decree encourages science to be done on all kinds of worlds, even if the discoveries are repeated. Comparing the findings of low-resource Border World scientists and Core World scientists is a good way to gauge whether the speed of discovery on Core Worlds is progressing properly."

"Encourages, but doesn't require. The only science we need now is how to build ships and roast aliens most effectively," Max was getting tired of listening to a civilian.

"That's true. That's what I am going to work on," Albert was hoping to be friendly regardless of the previous tone.

"Obviously, that is what everyone is working on," Diana waved her hands pointing at all the other students.

Albert smiled at her. Her smile was gentle and polite, but she quickly looked away, her expression neutral once again. "If you want a practice buddy for the combat sims, I am available. My scores were the best before the Academy." Albert addressed Diana cheerfully.

"Oh, that's an interesting offer," she said even more politely, "I'll send you my calendar times from when I am online."

Albert was hoping for in-person practice. He thought this was a good first interaction, because he still had minor trouble understanding the exact meaning of what the levels of politeness in citizen speech represented.

Ken also interrupted the conversation. "I will be your practice buddy, Al," he patted Albert on the shoulder. Ken then addressed the group, "And I hope you all join, cause I will need some help taking this guy down."

Albert smiled, it was a cheerful way to turn attention to him.

Ken continued, "Besides, we have to keep our top spot in the rankings, the other kids are not slacking around."

Chapter 4

Noble Patriarchs

No tax shall exceed 10% in peacetime.

First Economic Right of the Imperial Constitution (Right of Decitas).

0.2 MS AA

The Governor walked into the Chamber of the Hall of the Patriarchs and sat down on the throne, a not-too-fancy flat seated structure made of gold and diamonds that dwarfed his frame. The Governor wore a red fur cloak with 6 stars woven into it, along with a ceremonial hat. The meeting was held at noon, as was customary, and now the hall's tinted ceiling opening shone the light directly on the throne. Grand Admiral Alexander Mishov sat on a smaller throne to the Governor's right, his light body armor uniform displaying 5 stars on his left shoulder. To the Governor's left sat the Grand Inquisitor Ernest Gicha, who wore a tight-fitting dark blue shirt that accentuated his impressive physical build, complete with eight-pack abs and 4 stars on his shoulders along with the Inquisitorial seal.

The tri-throne faced amphitheater-like benches that rose one above the other. The Assembly of the Noble House Patriarchs sat in semicircular rows, each wearing uniforms adorned with their house crests. Those controlling more land were seated in the back row, from where they looked down on the Governor. At the front/bottom row, four individuals stood out as non-ship captains in the room: a civilian representative, a yeoman representative, an ambassador from Sirium, which was the other colonized planet in their system, and an outside view specialist tasked with handling relations with nearby Governors.

Typically there were two primary types of meetings between the Governor and the Patriarchs. One type aimed to resolve disputes, such as river water collection by one House impacting one downstream; another focused on synchronizing decisions with a broader planetary scope, like compensating House Shu for their forest gene drives and maintaining clean atmospheric air. Both types typically required action from the Governor.

This time was different. The Governor was asking the Patriarchs to build and serve the Empire, to build and serve him. One part of the Governor was telling him 'feelsgoodman,' and another was warning himself to not get used to it.

The Governor looked over the assembly and spoke, "As many of you have heard 200 kiloseconds ago [~55 Earth hours] we received a sign of a possible war fleet heading our way. I have activated DEFCON 2. Depending on their deceleration, we have anywhere from 30 to 60 megaseconds [~1-2 Earth years] before their arrival. Our worst-case assessment is that it is a fully armed fleet of all possible resources of the Browly system. On the plus side, our assessment given that they have not spread to nearby systems is that their tech level is low. Today I will discuss the preliminary plan that we," Governor spread his hands to the left and right pointing to his advisors "designed since the anomaly, as well as your duties as the Patriarchs of the system towards implementing it."

Tong Li nodded in approval. The Governor continued, "We will increase our funding for our fleet, putting all plans for the colonization of nearby systems on hold. All current government energy investments will be diverted. All existing surplus will be spent on warships. We are suspending the First Economic Right of the Imperial Constitution. The Unitax is going to increase from 7% to 23%, effective immediately. Is this clear?"

The Unitax was a general tax on transactions using money in the system. Ancient inefficient economic systems would separate transaction types into "income", "sales," "capital gains," etc. The First Emperor unified the system into a single efficient percentage and silenced any economists who opposed this.

The Governor had spent some time with Ernest and an economic planning simulation to figure out the best percentage to hit the limit at which their tax collection could reach diminishing returns. However, the planner could only account for so much if the Patriarchs began to disagree with the setting. The Patriarchs nodded their heads. Their body language offered no discernible negative clues, which the Governor took as a positive sign.

Ernest chimed in, "Since you own the ship component factories, the Inquisition will keep a close eye on the prices you charge the government."

Tong glanced to his left and right, gauging the reactions of those around him. Several others were doing the same. The Governor noted that there was slightly more tension after Ernest speaking, compared to the tax announcement.

Ernest continued, "No need to be concerned. We are all reasonable people here."

Tension somewhat subsided when the word "reasonable" was spoken.

Alexander stood up and began to talk, "As members of the Noble Houses and as citizens of our system, we swore an oath to protect all during times of war. Having trained with many of you in sims and test flights for gigaseconds, I know we are the people to face the threat."

Alexander hit his chest with his fist, "I have not seen war in my more than 10 gigasecond [~320 Earth years] life. No human has seen war in this sector for a thousand times longer than that. We do not have rituals or traditions to help guide us from the simulated to the real. For today, what will suffice is an affirmation of your intent to serve as captains of the ships you will build and crew them with citizens of the Noble Houses you lead."

Alexander sat down. A moment of silence followed.

Idris stood up tall and declared, "I will serve."

Deepak stood up, his voice firm, "I will serve."

Tong stood up. Several others stood up in unison and chanted, "I will serve."

Everyone else stood up. The Governor and Ernest stood up as well. All in unison shouted.

"I will serve."

The Governor tapped his chest with his fist just as Alexander did. The Patriarchs followed suit. The meeting adjourned. The Governor thought the meeting went well, but then again, many problems came to the surface and were dealt with in more private settings.

The post-meeting reception area was full of Patriarchs shaking hands or punching orders into their handhelds. Tong caught up with Mencius, the Noble Patriarch of House Shu, and asked in his Native Ancient Tongue,

"Are you worried about the taxes?"

"No, i more worried about the enemy," Mencius answered in the same language.

They continued to converse about whether the increased taxation would even affect them at all. House Li was the main producer of spaceship fuel and House Shu managed recycling initiatives. Given that the demand for both just skyrocketed, it was quite plausible the increased income would more than offset the increased taxes.

Idris came up to Alexander and asked, "If I may, are there any plans to boost the ground troops?"

Alexander shook his head, "The Governor is sure to follow the standard Imperial Doctrine. Wars are fought and decided in space. Your land is your responsibility."

"Understood," Idris nodded and walked off, somewhat deep in thought.

After the reception, Idris went inside his plane and turned up the EMF privacy setting. His plane was a simple jet design, with cozy seating and two friendly stewardesses who would serve him food and massages. He waved them out of this compartment, typed on his computer for ten minutes, and called his brother and eldest son on his holo-monitor. Idris calmly ordered them, "I am putting together a basic plan for a reinforcement of our standing ground armies."

"Oh, are we fighting close to the planet?" his brother sounded slightly surprised.

"I have no idea, but let's get ready before the prices come up." Idris said.

"They are already starting to. What's the plan?"

"Just the basics. 200 000 surface-to-orbit interceptor missiles of both flak and non-flak. 2 thousand railgun tanks, fix up 300 standard point defense mounts on the top of each of our halfvators, and around 10 million bullets for them." Idris looked down at his quick notes.

"Oh, just that?" His brother laughed. "We can certainly afford it. I'll get on it right away."

Chapter 5

Citizens and civilians

You are entitled to own land which you have made habitable.

Third Economic Right of The Imperial Constitution (Right of Habitas).

0.3 MS AA

The Noble Houses consisted of the descendants of the first settlers on Derev. They stepped foot on new worlds, tamed local wildlife, altered the genetic composition of plants, oxygenated the atmosphere, tended to the mammoth farms, and supervised the building of industry, all while taking care of anywhere from three to ten kids. Colonization was certainly not for the faint of heart. Since this was the only non-combat job in the Empire with a non-zero fatality rate, the Empire rewarded settlers with the "Right of Habitas", which entitled them to own the land they had made habitable. After the most difficult initial stage of terraforming, the survivors divided the land on the planet amongst themselves and formed Noble Houses. Each House controlled territory comparable to an Old Earth nation. Ownership of land came with the responsibility for "fleet dues" which either came out of the Unitax imposed on the Noble Houses directly or the Unitax on civilians living on the land. As long as they paid their fleet dues, the descendants of these early-world settlers enjoyed the relative luxury of citizenship compared to the civilians, who were descended from later arrivals.

There are 3 main ways through which a male civilian can become a citizen on Derev.

The first and least frequent was the ability to beat a current-duty spaceship captain in a team game of simulated space combat. Spaceship captains were either past, present, or future Noble Patriarchs or other high-ranking members of the Houses; they began practicing simulated spaceship navigation at around the same time they learned to walk, making them very formidable opponents. Albert's combat scores before the Academy were number 1 among his age, however they were far from sufficient to challenge on-duty captains even in a 1 on 1 match, let alone in team games.

If one's combat and engineering skills were not that good, but, like Albert's, still passable to join a military starship as a low-ranking crew member, there were two other options.

The most common way was to accumulate enough money through work to purchase a plot of land from a Noble House and become a "yeoman," a citizen unaffiliated with one of the Houses. Many hard-working and frugal families of Academy graduates could achieve this after a 3 gigasecond-long [~95 Earth years] career when they had a male descendant skilled in space sims.

The last option was marriage to a citizen woman.

Albert had many virtues, his dad frequently said. Patience, however, was not one of them.

On his way to the library, Albert briefly considered his life's options. More specifically, he thought about the girls in his class and even more specifically he thought about Diana. He hasn't received a note from her. Maybe the princesses were very busy. Maybe she needed to see he was a good coach. Albert coached Ken a little yesterday and could tell Ken was excited about the lesson.

The Imperial Library was a short walk from the Academy, featuring nearly 100-meter-tall ceilings in its main entryway. The ceiling was decorated with a 60-meter diameter round colorful mosaic depicting the Explorer Cycle: come to the star system, survive, terraform, build more ships, and go to the next. In the center of the room, on a pedestal, stood a physical copy of 'Sayings of the First Emperor,' a small twenty-page book that everyone was required to memorize by the age of 300 megaseconds [~9.5 Earth years]. Albert wondered if the Mid Worlds retained these mosaics or had replaced them after the re-designation.

Albert sat down on the opposite side of the large table across from Sheene, who silently gazed at a holographic book. He gave her a polite smile and nod, to which she responded in kind. He opened a holographic projector and began to review the publicly available data on the approaching fleet. Just as he started, Diana approached them to say hello. Albert got excited but reminded himself to 'be cool'.

"Hi," Sheene coldly responded to Diana.

"What are you up to?" Diana asked.

"I am studying the 'Fundamentals of Space Warfare'. I hope to know it by heart in the next megasecond [~11 Earth days]." Sheene responded.

"Wow, that's a tough book," Diana said. "Studying during our rest day?"

Sheene looked up and down Diana's body, "House Li's study schedule is far more intensive than the Academy's. We didn't have rest days. Or many rest periods for that matter. Hard education makes for an easy life." Sheene's voice held a tingle of pride. Sheene turned to Albert, "You know this book?"

Albert stopped liking books a while back. His Dad taught him a technique to 'learn' instead of 'read.' Albert would cover up a line in a physical book or pause a holographic one and write down what he predicted the text would say. After a couple of years of doing this, Albert got a feel for what knowledge he had to read and what he could reconstruct from first principles. He quickly grew bored with 'The Fundamentals of Space Warfare,' as his combat practice and theory crafting allowed him to easily predict every piece of the advice in the book. Now, it was hard to find books at exactly his level; most were too easy, while some, like 'The Concept of the Unseen', were too difficult.

'Yeah, I am familiar,' Albert replied, his gaze locked on Diana.

Diana didn't turn to Albert. "House Darien enjoys beautiful siestas," she said. "It's essential to take time to process and digest the knowledge, not just swallow it."

Sheene straightened her back and moved the holobook to the side, giving herself a clear path to pierce Diana with her gaze. "What does your daddy do?" Sheene asked Diana with a special emphasis on 'your'.

"He's a civilian relationship ma.." Diana excitedly started talking.

"Oh, he works?" Sheene interrupted her. Albert has never heard the word 'works' spoken with that intonation before.

"Your Dad is retired already?" Diana sounded a little confused.

"The House Li has a saying: 'treat your civilians well and you never have to work a day in your life.'"

"Hmm," said Diana, breaking eye contact with Sheene, as she nervously looked around the room.

Sheene looked at Albert, indicating his input was required to confirm her statement.

Albert felt uneasy observing the interaction. As if he was watching two alien animals perform a ritual that could be classified as 'fighting' or 'bonding' depending on the xenobiologist narrating.

"House Li does have a great reputation with civilians," Albert said, his gaze drifting back to Diana's chest. "But I have heard lovely things about House Darien as well."

Sheene and Diana both looked away from Albert and back at each other. Albert didn't mind much. For a brief moment, he could appreciate the beauty of two princesses standing before him.

Sheene was somewhat short for a princess. It was clear that not only did her House avoid any illegal genetic engineering, but they didn't even bother with much gene selection either. They focused exclusively on selective breeding, picking up wives for their Patriarchs through a series of objective tests that assessed health, personality, and intelligence. Their emphasis on continuity with Old Earth heritage meant Sheene looked distinctly Asian in features, reflecting the House's enduring connection to their ancestral roots.

After a short, but noticeable, silence, Sheene finally spoke, "My Dad is, of course, un-retiring due to DEFCON 2. What are you here for, anyways?"

The xenobiologist observing them would now describe the Diana's body language as 'submissive'.

Diana said, "I am wondering if some books I wasn't allowed to read before could be available to an Academy student."

Albert said, "Oh, I am surprised that's true for you too."

"I am a princess," Diana said, tilting her head, "but I don't receive magical abilities to bend the rules."

Albert felt silly. 'Playing cool' wasn't happening. His feeling silly was interrupted by Max who loudly walked towards them. Max gave Albert a look conveying a message of "How dare you even look at them?"

Max addressed Diana, "Is this gray shirt bothering you?"

Diana responded, "No, it's alright." She wasn't fond of Albert chatting with her, but it was also too early in the school year to have boys fight over her.

Max sat down between Sheene and Albert.

"Fascinating," Max said, "the library isn't divided into citizen and civilian sections. What a strange choice."

Albert thought, "'Oh oh." Though Albert may not grasp refined etiquette, a rival vying for a female's affections can often be discerned at a fundamental, instinctual level. Even to an amateur xenobiologist.

Sheene rolled her eyes, "Fascinating observation. Now, if you excuse me, I need to focus on this section about long-distance laser diffraction." She went back to her holobook and put on noise-cancelling headphones."

Diana started walking away. Albert wanted to follow her with his gaze, but noticed Max giving him another one of those looks. Albert returned to analyzing the incoming fleet data, specifically focusing on density estimates given the spaceship shapes. Max pulled out a portable toy spaceship controller and began playing an asteroid field navigation simulator.

Diana approached the checkout computer and a friendly hologram animated. "What can I do for you?" it asked.

"Can I read 'Sayings of the Second Emperor'?" she asked.

"Permission denied," the hologram responded. "May I interest you in a book on spaceship builds? Very popular recently."

Chapter 6

Time to Build

Have they surrendered? Have we run out of sunlight? Have you lost your mind? If the answer to each question remains no, then the orbital bombardment must continue.

The First Emperor when asked to clarify his orders by a subordinate (middle of Unification War).

0.4 MS AA

The Governor, Alexander and Ernest were in the Governor's office. It held cozy meeting couches gathered around a holo-projector. A platinum silicate glass wall formed one side of the space, leading to a balcony overlooking the Capitol.

A 2-meter hologram projection filled the center of the room displaying a computer-generated view of the four key planets in the system. The console spoke up, "Sirium's orbital shipyard video and mapping drones have just arrived. Preliminary manufacturing overview is ready when you are."

The holograms booted up fully. Half of the Governor's office transformed into an aerial image of a large mine on the other side of the planet. From afar, you could barely see the droids and the 300-meter-tall machines digging into the ground, sending unrefined ore back to the surface in giant vacuum tubes. Several stone and glass towers surrounded the mine, giving human supervisors a good view of the operation. The towers, the machines, and the droids all bore the brown bear crest of House Mishov. Alexander approvingly nodded at his machines.

The console spoke, "Titanium mines working at full capacity."

The camera panned over to the side of the mine and displayed a 2 km-long manufactroium refinery and a connected train station, both surrounded by solar panels as far as the eye could see.

The console voice continued, "Refinement and delivery functioning normally. Every 12 kiloseconds [~3 Earth hours] a maglev transports refined titanium to the launch elevator."

The camera switched to a different drone, capturing a top-down view panned over the maglev train tracks heading towards the halfvator launch pad. Droids unloaded the train next to the pad and repackaged the titanium for orbit. Halfvator was an elevator with a carbon nanotube cable attached at the bottom to deep underground anchors with steel trusses. The cable extended to the upper reaches of the atmosphere, where it was held up by helium balloons. After the titanium was loaded into an elevator cabin, after which it "whooooshed" upwards toward the platforms above.

The hologram switched to a platform-mounted camera tracking another ascending elevator. The flexible cable ended at a height of 8 kilometers, where the helium stabilizers began. After that, the elevator cabin traveled on sturdy rail launchers that extended nearly a kilometer, decorated with eagle crests every hundred meters. The elevator accelerated up the rails, launched itself into space, opened its rocket engines, and got the remaining way into orbit on propellant power.

The holo-display switched to a camera mounted on an orbital shipyard, which was getting ready to receive a titanium shipment. The shipyard bore the panther crest of the Noble House of Smith.

Another drone moved around the shipyard. The first section was a rotating pressurized cylindrical factory where titanium was bonded with artificial diamond to create ship armor. The next section, open to the vacuum of space, consisted of several blocks connected by rails and arranged in a cylindrical checkerboard pattern that revealed a half-built octagonal-shaped ship within it. Assembly robots took armor plates and bonded them to the ship's exterior. A human supervisor in a vacuum suit and magnetic boots observed the process from the outside of the shipyard.

"Railcruiser 'Wraith of the Elders' is being constructed," the console voice spoke.

"I spoke with Idris, this one is mine", Alexander gestured at the partially built ship.

"Most excellent," the Governor spoke. Every manufacturing review still left him feeling like a child marveling at a new full-length space elevator being built. The magnificence construction was a symphony of mechanical perfection.

That was more than 9 gigaseconds ago[~285 Earth years] in his home system of Corial, 45 trillion kilometers away.

"Is production at capacity?" he asked.

"Indeed," the console voice responded, "all droids operate around the clock, human supervisors work one shift per day. We are at a standard of 6 overlapping shifts per day. Minimal disruptions due to within-parameter droid repairs. Production has not stopped in any shipyard since DEFCON 2 announcement."

The camera zoomed out, revealing a planet surrounded by with multiple orbiting dots around it.

Console voice continued, "4 new shipyards are under construction. When they come online, in addition to the 16 existing ones, their combined output would produce approximately one missile cruiser hull per Derev day." A Derev day was around 65 kiloseconds [~18 Earth hours].

"Good, good," Alexander said. "How are the rare minerals and armaments going?"

The holo-camera once again switched to a camera located on the planet. A sky-scraper-sized machine with six legs lowered a drilling mechanism into the ground. Several hills worth of dirt resided near it. The camera shook as the aerial drone had trouble stabilizing it due to the shockwaves.

"The new mine is currently being activated. Once the initial digs are done, a new refinery plant will be erected and train tracks finished in 330 kiloseconds [~92 Earth hours]." The robotic voice spoke with a mild lack of confidence.

"How is the power grid handling the digging machine and other additional requirements?" The Governor asked.

"The local on-ground solar installations are insufficient, so we are beaming power from orbital solar collectors. Once the mine is complete, on-the-ground solar will also be finished, and the orbital power will switch back to the shipyards."

The holo-camera displayed an orbital solar collector beaming power down to the planet, although the far away camera didn't quite capture the full magnificence of the 40 km long focusing solar mirror.

The holo view switched to a camera mounted on the shipyard, which was operating in 'low power mode'. Inside the shipyard, a standard issue 'Star Fort' class missile cruiser underwent system checks. The 300-meter 'Star Fort' class, primarily armed with a missile loadout, was the mainstay of Border World space fleets for a while. It featured a distinctive pentagonal shape with sloped-in armor that gave it a 'star-like' appearance. The ship was wider in the back and culminated with a conical frontal section, which provided its point-defense railguns with clean lines of fire when facing its nose to the enemy. One of its bays was open with droids examining a missile for defects.

"Beautiful," Ernest remarked.

"Sirium shipyards," the Governor commanded.

After a brief pause, a new shipyard appeared on the holo-display against the backdrop of a yellow planet. At the bottom right of the screen, the message flashed: "360 second light delay." The Sirium shipyard was more complex, with three sections dedicated to assembling ship hulls, followed by additional areas for installing interior equipment and weaponry.

"Laser destroyer 'Audacity' is nearly complete including weaponry," the console voice spoke.

Another drone made its way through the destroyer, traversing from the light shuttle crew quarters, moving alongside the entrance to the central column, before making its way to the command deck in the center. The captain's chair sat atop a raised platform, surrounded by a bank of controls and command crew terminals on the lower level.

Several people were examining the interior computers and deploying spectrometers along the walls.

"Cozy," the Governor remarked.

"Certainly, I wouldn't want to be on a destroyer in our situation," Alexander replied.

"Indeed," The Governor agreed.

The camera zoomed out from the planet and re-focusing on a nearby asteroid that had a rocket ship attached with a couple of escort ships matching pace.

"Delivery of an asteroid into high Sirium orbit is proceeding on schedule. Further analysis has confirmed the amount of iron, nickel, and tungsten alloys present inside. It will take 5 megaseconds [~58 Earth days] to fully disassemble the asteroid and manufacture slugs." The console voice sounded a little cheerful.

"Getting the asteroid was a good idea, Ernest," Alexander mentioned, "We will definitely have enough tungsten for a surplus of slugs."

"Thank you," Ernest responded.

"Would you like to examine the deuterium production?" The console voice sounded very excited.

"Yes," the 3 men said nearly in unison.

The camera zoomed out to show a computer-generated view of the 4 first planets of the Toriad system. Mirkal, a scorching hot world, inhospitable to humans; Derev, a lush planet they were currently on; Sirium, a rocky and sandy world, now featuring domed habitats, the beginnings of lakes, and a thin generated atmosphere; Zeun, a gas giant.

The holo-display zoomed in on the gas giant and switched from a pre-rendered image to a real one. The camera was mounted to the exterior of an incoming gas hauler about to dock with the orbital platform. The bottom of the hologram read: "4 KS light delay." The orbital platform flew relatively close to Zeun's, its cable stretching down into the gaseous atmosphere connecting it to a scooper. Massive radiators glowing with heat comprised the majority of the platform.

Console voice spoke, "The raw helium and hydrogen scoopers and coolers are operational, but to meet the demands, several more are being constructed at Sirium. The incoming hauler will take the liquid hydrogen and helium to Mirkal, dropping off some of the helium to help keep the Derev halfvator launch pads operational."

The hauler and the orbital platform were both adorned with images of a dragon across their entire length, made from bits of color added to the diamond reinforcers. The House of Li had a flair for the dramatic.

"Let's see the Will Of the Star," The Governor said.

The three men stood up.

Mirkal Solar Collector, nicknamed "the Will of The Star," was nearly 1000 km in diameter, dwarfing the 1 km long gas hauler approaching it. Shaped like a pentagon, it was unlike most other major installations. Instead of being made out of metal, the frame of Will of the Star consisted entirely of blackrock, a special heat and light-resistant rock type found on Mirkal's surface. Its frame was thinner on the outside but held by thick pillars of blackrock extending down to the center.

The station's vertical rotation was aligned to match its orbital rotation around Mirkal so that the front-side solar arrays always faced the star. The rear side of the frame bore barely visible crests of 17 Houses, as well as the Governor and Inquisitorial Seals.

The back side of the platform held 23 particle accelerators, each with a helical shape 20 km in diameter and 200 km in height. Titanium beams connected the accelerators to the frame, also carrying electrical power generated by the front solar panels. The accelerators took raw hydrogen and helium and produced antimatter and deuterium. A nearly 500 km length 'laser' tube was mounted, full of light-focusing lenses and directing mirrors. A small docking station, protected from the sunlight, was mounted on the side of the laser past the accelerators. It was encased in heavy radiation shielding and surrounded by glowing radiators. The station loaded helium and hydrogen from gas haulers and unloaded deuterium onto warships.

"Particle accelerators are below full capacity. We are processing the incoming raw materials faster than they are arriving," the console voice explained.

"This was expected given the antimatter requires a different energy-mass ratio than deuterium." The Governor remarked.

The docking station had a star-shaped ship next to it, also bearing a House Li dragon across its hull. At 300 meters the 'Star Fort' class cruiser "New Sunrise" was tiny compared to the rest of the facilities. It had just finished docking to pick up the deuterium and began its flight away from the star. During its flight, it would process the raw fuel and re-package it into 200 battle-ready thermonuclear warheads with yields ranging from 1/5 to a full exajoule. [~50 to 250 megaton TNT equivalent]

"Ok, let's check on the fleet." The Governor had not received any negative surprises so far. Neither the droids nor the human supervisors seemed to be struggling with the new tasks. The visual overview matched the numbers they had received from both the Houses and the droid logs. However, it was still important to see the production, to feel its power, and to get his intuition to make the proper connection between the numbers on the reports and the situation on the ground and in space.

The holo-display zoomed out to show a rendered representation of the system, before zooming into Derev. It highlighted 7 circular orbits around the planet, each holding a battle group.

The holo switched to a live feed showing a single battlegroup with 60 ships flying in loose formation. It proceeded to zoom onto each ship one by one.

"Feel better yet?" Ernest asked, looking at Alexander.

"I'll feel better after we win," Alexander frowned. "Aren't you even a bit afraid of the Browly menace?"

"My job is to inspire fear, not to feel it," The Grand Inquisitor cheerfully responded.

Chapter 7

Basic Weapons Training

Do not blame yourself for our past defeats. Our recent victories by the troops under my command could easily be explained by finally having enough Railguns.

The First Emperor addressing fellow generals of the Human Coalition.

0.5 MS AA

The "basic weapons training" class was about to start. Albert entered Combat Room 1, an octagonal space designed to resemble a railcruiser's command deck. Sheene and Diana were already present. The ceremonial parts of the Academy year had concluded, and uniforms gave way to more casual attire. Sheene wore a fluffy pink long-sleeve sweater paired with a matching skirt that fell below her knees. Diana opted for dress pants and a low-cut blouse that highlighted her voluptuous curves. Ken and Max were also there.

Shortly after Albert, Yezi walked into the classroom followed by her one-meter-tall cylindrical robot. Yezi Shu, a third cousin of Sheene, resembled her somewhat except for being taller and slightly skinnier. Her dark green full-body suit, adorned with

House Shu's symbol, a stylized green tree, seemed somewhat out of place in the classroom. This "smart" suit, designed to monitor and filter the atmosphere's elemental intake, had once been standard attire before terraforming was complete, but was no longer considered necessary.

Albert extended his hand to Yezi, but instead of shaking it, she smiled and waved at him. He waved back. Her robot approached her area, sprayed her seat, keyboard, and other input devices with a cleaning solution, wiped them, and moved out of the room as Yezi sat down.

"That's cool," Ken said pointing at the robot, "probably gives you a few megas of life expectancy. My dad wanted me to be a doctor. The average life expectancy of 13 gigaseconds [~412 Earth years] in our system is too damn low."

Yezi looked surprised, "Most life expectancy increases are due to environmental engineering and toxin removal. Aren't doctors minimally effective?" House Shu was the main House still actively working on the removal of native micro-toxins from the food chain.

Ken raised his hand towards her in approval, "That's what I said, but you know how some parents are?" Yezi smiled back.

Albert walked around each control in the room, experimenting with them as he'd never been here before.

Most triggered a captain's monitor explanation of what it did to the 'virtual ship' they were in, such as: readjusting thrust, guiding repair bots to a section, or diverting power to different weapon systems. One of the controls was labeled 'wobble control.'

Albert scanned the room. Ken shook his head, "It's not gonna activate unless everyone is strapped in." Sheene was watching him with mild amusement. Diana was reading "History of Alien Encounters," a basic volume on xenoculture.

"Anyone else wants to play with these?" Albert didn't want to hog all the fun for himself. "These are gonna be on the test."

"I have been inside the real thing, no need for me," Max asserted himself.

Arjun, their teacher, entered the octagonal room, prompting the students to straighten up and move to the chairs positioned at the perimeter of a central monitor.

Arjun began talking, "Our classes on weapons follow the standard training method (STM), considered close to the theoretically optimal way to learn for both humans and software. First, you watch me; then, you watch and imitate. Next, I watch you and reinforce with feedback. Finally, you explore on your own, first guided by subgoals and then without. Today's lesson focuses on the three main pillars of space combat: missiles, lasers..."

Arjun surveyed the room.

"While you know what I am about to say, our code of Honor requires that you pay proper respect to the first time you hear that word from a teacher in our halls."

The students rose from their seats.

"One of the core weapons of humanity, designed by the First Emperor Himself, it was decisive in the Unification War and played a pivotal role in every human-alien conflict from then on. No other human word has become a curse in so many alien languages."

"Railgun"

A single shiver ran down Albert's spine.

Arjun paused.

The students said, "May the light of our Emperors, from the First to the Current, guide us. May our Will to Act be ever as strong as theirs."

"You may sit now."

"Railguns might not seem like imposing weapons. The slugs travel in a straight line and cannot chase after their target. They are tiny compared to missiles and are slower than lasers. What makes railguns a mainstay of human space combat is their extreme cost-effectiveness compared to every other weapon system. Being hit by a standard 1 kg slug traveling at 72 km/s muzzle velocity may be a survivable affair for many spaceships. However, a railship carries hundreds of thousands of those."

Arjun sat in the center of the room as if taking command of the mock railcruiser they were in, "Time to begin our exercise."

The holo simulation booted up above him, revealing Arjun's fleet of 100 ships: 30 laser destroyers, 40 'Star Fort' cruisers equipped with antimatter missiles, and 30 railships.

Standard ship and weapon types.

Destroyer design featured a rectangular cross-section with armor sloped inward; four laser turrets were mounted at the square corners of the back, while another four were in front of the ship in the middle of the square sides. Conventional Gatling point defense guns dotted the surrounding hull. Railship configuration consisted of a hexagonal shape housing 200-meter railguns along its sides, complemented by 12-point defense guns along its 600-meter-long hull.

All ships featured a conical frontal section, hosting a pair of forward-facing beam weapons that could launch relativistic protons or electrons in the direction the ship was facing. Beam weapons were strong enough to act as a mini-drive.

The enemy had the same fleet. The two fleets were too far away from any celestial body for gravity to affect their movement, also known as being in "simple space." They were 2000 km apart, moving towards each other along parallel lines at 1 km / s. The parallel lines were around 40 km apart.

Although Albert was a little surprised by the size of the fleet, the rest of the setup was typical.

Arjun announced to the class, "After I perform the battle against a computer opponent, you will be asked to repeat my actions. Your score will be primarily based on how closely your commands, goals, and attitudes align with mine. The number of your ships remaining will be only a secondary factor. I suspect that for most of the class, those numbers will be highly correlated. Please take notes to help with the meta-cognition review."

Students pulled out their digital notepads.

The two fleets began to converge on each other. The cruisers began to launch missiles from their bays 5 at a time. The missiles for the first volley didn't fire their engines immediately. Instead, they flew next to the cruisers until there were 600 total, which was considered a strong volley.

After the volley gathered, the missiles fired engines for the initial burst, turned them off for the "cruise" portion of the flight, and turned them on again with a variable-rate burn pattern once they got in range of the outlying point defenses.

Both fleets continued to do this, with most missiles of both fleets neutralized by point defense or counter-missiles before reaching their targets. Yet, enough of Arjun's volleys managed to avoid the PDCs and disable several enemy railships.

As the ships drew within 1000 km, the software commentator announced, "Entering CQB", meaning close-quarter battle.

Arjun's railships' railguns, previously used against the incoming missiles, now targeted enemy hulls. The enemy fleet responded in kind, necessitating all the ships to jitter and dodge using thrusters. The space between the fleets became completely lit up with tracer railgun shots creating a very dreamlike composition.

As the fleets approached the relative distance of 60 km, the students and Arjun tensed up. He was already averaging around 3 actions per second and was now spiking to 6.

"Entering point-blank range." the computer announced.

At point-blank range, lasers took over as the decisive force. Arjun's destroyers targeted the weapon systems located outside enemy hulls, melting point defense Gatling guns, laser turrets, and railgun barrels.

Once the entire outside weaponry was destroyed, cleanup work began. Lasers targeted bulkier systems, sealing torpedo bays through melting enemy armor, disabling thrusters, and damaging enemy engines. Enemy ships without point defense were easily dispatched using missiles. Enemy ships with damaged thrusters were pierced through by railguns. Ships with damaged shield generators were melted using proton launchers. Arjun left the ships with no active weapons for last.

30 seconds after entering 'point-blank range', whatever was left of the enemy fleet was destroyed or disabled. 60 vessels of Arjun's fleet remained.

Arjun looked at the students, "Your turn now." The students turned to their individual screens.

About an hour later, the battles were done and the scoreboard reflected the standings. As the teacher predicted the scores for "closeness to him" were perfectly aligned to the scores of "own ships left."

Albert was very pleased with himself.

Arjun looked over the students and began the analysis portion of the class, "I want to focus on the notes you took. Let's start with Diana."

Diana's notes were projected onto the main screen. They consisted of pages and pages of play-by-play carefully written down.

Arjun asked, "You are last in the rankings. What happened?"

Albert cringed a little inside on her behalf.

"I tried to do exactly as you did," she said, gesturing at the notes. "However, as small changes accrued, the simulation began to diverge from your scenario. Enemy ships decided to spread out for some reason."

"So, what happened?" Arjun repeated the question.

"I kept referring to the notes, hoping to repeat the actions you took." Diana said hesitantly.

"What happened? Describe your internal state." Arjun pressed on.

"I got overwhelmed with the quantity of information and I ... I panicked," she finally admitted.

"Yes, you did. You still managed to defeat the computer opponent, but only barely." Arjun emphasized the last words.

Diana looked down in mild shame.

Arjun turned to Yezi and asked, "What about you?". Yezi was 7th.

The big monitor displayed Yezi's notes, which included detailed drawings of the formations employed

They consisted of several drawings of the formations that both Arjun and the enemy took. "I focused entirely on how you used space and the orientation of your ships relative to each other."

"I see that," Arjun replied. "You certainly copied the formations, but you failed to notice everything else. You need to broaden what you pay attention to. Max, what about you?"

Max's notebook was blank. Albert was confused. Max confidently declared, "You followed standard protocols that we knew before class. There was no need for notes to distract me from the battle."

"And yet you scored 5th, care to suggest as to why?" Arjun smiled at him.

"I don't know why, but I am sure you are about to teach me an important lesson." Max leaned back in his chair, his hands clasped behind his head.

"That I am," Arjun turned to Ken, who scored 4th. "Ken, what did you note?"

Ken's notes included details on the usage of specific warheads at various points during the battle. Missiles could hold a variety of payloads. Some carried no warhead, instead having more fuel, which allowed it to become an extremely fast 'pure kinetic' missile. Some carried directed or undirected flak which saturated the area with small fast-moving shrapnel. Some flashed gamma rays damaging the outlying weapon systems. Some directed all energy to the production of fast-moving neutrons, able to punch through the radiation shielding and kill the crew. Some carried a shaped charge, which propelled a kinetic slug at an incredible speed. Many payload types could still do damage even if detonating a few kilometers from the target.

"Ken, how well did you know the warhead types before coming to class?" Arjun asked.

"Extremely well," Ken declared proudly.

"Exactly," Arjun said. "You need to focus on things you don't know, on ideas beyond the warhead composition. The feeling of generality can be uncomfortable, but you need to push through it. Specialization will come later."

Ken nodded, deep in thought.

Arjun continued, "Sheene, what did you do? Your battle showed a strong command of the fundamentals." Sheene scored 2nd to most people's surprise, including her own.

Sheene's notes were a very brief set of rules. She said, "I tried to identify what patterns you kept using over and over again. I asked myself what rules you were following."

"Any examples?" Arjun asked approvingly.

"At each weapon range, you targeted the system most valuable in the current and upcoming range. You used missiles to cripple enemy railguns before CQB and you used railguns in CQB to cripple enemy lasers. Your early successes snowballed into dominance for a key weapon system in each range."

Arjun stated, "This is obvious, can you describe something more unexpected?"

Sheene hesitated for a second, "You rotated our ships in a non-uniform pattern. This tactic made it harder to score hits on your outlying weapons systems, even if it made your firing more difficult."

"Indeed, a far better example. Well done." Arjun said.

Sheene did a little dance of excitement, her pink skirt waving a little.

"Albert, what were your notes?" Arjun asked.

Albert was first in the class, having 45 ships remaining, and his notes were slightly longer than those of Sheene.

"My strategy was to ask myself what I expected you to do at every point and write down if you did something different."

Arjun was visibly excited, "Excellent. What was that?"

"As Sheene mentioned, I was also surprised by the rotation of the ships. After using up all the missiles on several cruisers, you positioned them in front of the fleet to serve as bait for enemy fire. Specifically, you employed a line-of-sight blocking formation in the sections of the fleet that opposed the enemies without railguns. This was not something I expected, yet it brought me success when I copied it."

Line-of-sight-blocking meant arranging ships close to a straight line facing the enemy. It meant the front ship would shield the back ships from fire. This was a good idea against lasers, and a terrible idea against railguns, as the slugs could penetrate more than one ship.

"Good of you to notice. But why didn't you expect that from me?" Arjun inquired.

"I just thought you wouldn't teach us how to send your comrades to certain death." Albert suddenly felt strange sharing that.

"On the contrary, this is precisely what I need to teach you." Arjun was glad to clear up the misunderstanding.

Albert certainly understood the tactical importance of shielding ships that could still fire using those that could not. However, he had expected the Academy to lecture him on "morale", "leadership" or "remembering the human element" of your troops. Nope. What mattered at this point was winning at all costs. Like it always did.

Arjun looked over everyone, "A question for the whole class: what is a weapon?"

Max jumped in, "Weapons are lasers, missiles, railguns, proton launchers, heliguns, along with smaller scale arms and ground force weapons."

Arjun smiled, "Your definition excludes too much. Any ship can be accelerated to collide with something. Sunlight can be focused just like a laser. Air is combustible when mixed with the right chemicals."

Sunnak offered his definition, "A weapon is any object, vehicle, or medium that can be used to deliver energy to the enemy in a way they don't like."

Arjun shook his head back and forth, "An interesting attempt that includes a lot, but still misses things like computer sabotage, certain forms of nanotech, and rarely used, but extremely effective technique of blocking the sun. Frequently, to understand what something is, it's easier to understand what it is not. What isn't a weapon?"

Albert responded, "Nothing. Every object can be a weapon, if you accelerate it hard enough."

Arjun had a hint of amusement in his face, as the students drew closer, "That's the right attitude, even though that's not quite the right definition."

Diana was frustrated, "The definition is meaningless. If nothing is a non-weapon, everything is a weapon. The word doesn't have a distinctive meaning."

Arjun corrected her, "The meaning is not where you are currently looking."

Albert had a sudden flash of insight about what the question meant. He exclaimed, "Weaponness is not an inherent property of an object, the way that mass or speed is, it is the way that one uses an object, a property ..."

Max interrupted, "Of your Will."

Arjun responded, "Correct, it is your Will that gives an object its weaponness. Albert, please continue."

Max looked annoyed.

Albert finished his thought, "Weaponness is the mind's property of imbuing intention onto something."

Arjun smiled at him, "Finally we got somewhere. Weaponness is in here." He tapped his temple, "Seeing through the minds of the Other makes it easier to understand ourselves. The best definition of a weapon was given to us by the kwaziak civilization. In the final days of the second interstellar war with them, we dropped asteroids inside the volcanoes of their homeworld, triggered magma flows, and vaporized most of the surface water. Their internal communications said, 'They let the stars fall and the seas boil. Something becomes a weapon after a human hand touches it, or a human mind learns about the existence of it.' Quite obvious in retrospect".

Sheene looked confused and asked, "Did they have a different attitude?"

"Yes," Arjun said. "It is very surprising, given their warlike history. They were the ones who struck first, wiped out another civilization, and nearly killed the octozi. When octozi came to human space asking or help, the kwaziaks refused a peace offer with us. And even after we defeated them in the first war, retaking the octozi homeworld and establishing a treaty, the kwaziaks merely re-grouped and struck again.

Despite all that, their conception of weaponry never extended beyond that of 'what is designed'. They were surprised when our ship captain rammed one of their ships with his own, killing everyone on board. They were surprised when we coated micro-meteors in stealth composites and sent them toward their fleet. They were surprised when we burrowed a tunnel underneath their moon fortresses from hundreds of kilometers away. Their concept of weaponry failed them. That is why they are extinct."

The classroom fell silent.

Arjun put humanity's deeds into context, "We always ask for peace on first contact with any xenos. And after learning about final day of that war, almost all accept. Because they know that we only ask once."

Arjun held out his index finger to emphasize the point.

After class Albert approached Diana and said, "My offer to be your practice buddy still stands."

She was still annoyed at the moment, still embarrassed from her last place finish, and harshly responded, "I will contact you if I am interested, ok?"

Albert walked off.

Diana let out a sigh.

Max asked her, "Does he know 'you only ask once' rule applies to him as well?"

"I don't think he does." she responded.

Chapter 8

The Grand Inquisitor

The goal of the Imperial Inquisition is to destroy all things that make us weak. We begin by eradicating all naturally occurring diseases, starting with the easy ones: tuberculosis, malaria, hepatitis, and intestinal parasites. The real challenge will be ridding the world of the many Plagues the machines and the human traitors have unleashed.

The First Emperor is a speech establishing the Imperial Inquisition.

0.6 MS AA

Ernest, Alexander and the Governor convened for their "Some plan is better than no plan" meeting. Prior to the meeting the Governor sketched out what he expected the enemy to do, what the recommended course of action given Imperial doctrine was and what he expected the advisors to say.

"What weapons is the enemy bringing? What are we building?" Alexander wanted to be all to business.

"Imperial doctrine suggests carriers as a primary way to assault fortified systems; therefore I assume that's what they are bringing." The Governor did not sound confident, but doctrine was doctrine for a reason.

"And do you concur with this assessment?" Alexander asked Ernest.

"I do," Ernest agreed, sounding a lot more confident.

"Are we sticking to railcruisers or carriers for our capital ship?" Alexander asked the world's most obvious question, but that was his job.

"We go by the book," The Governor replied quickly. "Railcruisers are recommended as the primarily defensive capital ship, especially in the presence of hangar bay platforms in Derev orbit."

"We are off the book here," Alexander said. "Nothing of this size has ever been seen. If their weight class was only 10 to 100 times ours, we could close in on them with railships and railcruisers in CQB and shred them with railguns. But 50,000 times is a different story."

The Governor was not swayed by this information, "Yes, even more reason to stick to what we know. Size for a low-tech civilization can mean only one thing: lots of shitty missiles and drones. Easy work for our point defense. No need for a substantial drone force of our own."

Ernest added, "I would be surprised if their sensors could even detect our tier 1 stealth torpedoes in time."

Stealth levels were ranked from tier 1 to 4, with 1 being the lowest. Tier 2 is the best level Derev shipyards could build at the moment.

Alexander frowned in his usual way, "Let's assume they can detect our volley and have carriers. The size of the fleet implies an assload of interceptors. I worry we do not have enough missiles, even in a thousand-strong volley, to punch through their active defenses."

"I concur," Ernest added, "they likely have substantial, though likely low quality point defense."

The Governor gazed out into the distance. The advisors were right, which was common whenever they agreed. The enemy could intercept all the missiles if a single volley was too small.

Ernest continued, "We have a few options. More missiles, faster ones, and harder-to-see ones."

Alexander nodded, "More is best. We can always maneuver to boost relative speed. You can never rely on stealth in a prolonged engagement, which I am guessing this will be."

"You don't think our first few volleys will wipe them?" Ernest asked cheerfully.

"No," Alexander answered tersely, not sure if Ernest was actually serious.

The Governor felt they were getting somewhere, "I concur with more. If we want larger volleys, we would go harder on cruisers, but that will be harder to outfit. Missile production will be our biggest bottleneck."

Alexander tapped the table in agreement.

Ernest continued the train of thought. "What if we work with smaller payloads? Use only deuterium and no antimatter?"

The Governor considered the idea, but he was glad Ernest suggested it. "That would work," he said. "Disassemble the existing antimatter warheads for fuel, and shift production to deuterium. Focus on cruiser production."

The Governor was technically done with this agenda item, but he still felt uneasy and his usual positive feeling of checking an item off the list wasn't there. He continued, "The next question is where we plan to fight and our relative speed at the meeting. We have many options here. We could sally out of the system and meet them before they have finished decelerating. We could fight them once they get inside the system, but far away from the planets. We could also wait by Derev, by the heliguns and orbital hangars. The safest spot there is."

Alexander was ready to outline how everything could go wrong in every possible scenario, "I strongly advise against waiting by any of the planets. With a fleet of that size, it's too easy for the enemy to sneak a volley of nukes onto the surface. I advise crippling their launch capability first; if needed we can always fall back."

Ernest added, "I also don't recommend waiting by Derev, but for a different reason. We could have a clean kill. If they are not advanced, their missiles are slower and easier to see, reducing their effective range. Their kinetics, if any, are likely slower as well.

This means we can be accurate at a far greater distance. I am also not simply abandoning Sirium's defense."

The Governor wanted to have a plan. A tentative one was better than none at all. At this moment, they had far too many unknowns. Too many important variables could take on a large range of values and alter the situation completely. He said, "Our engagement strategy fundamentally depends on their approach speed."

Ernest began to walk around the office, waving his hands to control a computer-generated hologram, "It does. Let's say they are slow inside the system, less than 200 km/s in the sunward direction. In this case, we could easily come to them, match course and speed a few million kilometers ahead of them, and kill them with missiles while kiting."

Ernest drew a pathway of red arrows going into the system and blue arrows meeting and matching them.

"Given enough time to accelerate, we could create a large volley of 400 km /s or faster of gamma flash warheads and pure kinetics. They would have to have good targeting computers to penetrate the most basic stealth, react in time, and predict our evasion patterns. Hard task. Gamma rays stack nicely with each other to create many multitudes of lethal radiation. Large and slow ships means it's easy for a pure kinetic to hit, even if knocked a little off course."

Many space warfare books described why warships rarely exceeded a certain size, and Ernest and the Governor were on the same page. Ernest pointed at the computer's estimate of how long the battle would last given the relative speeds, "If they slow down to 100 km / s at the system edge, it will take more than 30 megaseconds [~1 Earth year] to get to the inner planets from that point. We can unload the entire arsenal, produce more warheads, ferry them to the fleet...you get the idea."

The Governor most certainly got the idea. Defense was easier than offense, especially with strong established supply routes. Alexander was ready to talk about potential problems, "They could counter such volleys with a large amount of strike craft ahead of the main fleet."

Ernest was ready for the question, "Yes, it would be an attempt to counter us, but it's simple to respond. We use laser ships or flak missiles to handle the strike craft and clear the way for anti-capital ship ordinance."

"Yep, this will work," The Governor confirmed. Although this plan would certainly result in the deaths of the laser destroyer crews, it would work.

Alexander seemed like he was struggling with whether to continue the measure / counter-measure discussion or move on to the next possibility. He said, "This plan will need further refinement. But for now, let's discuss the possibility that they don't shed all of their speed. What if they are traveling at 1% of the speed of light inside the system? They can do a flyby and use the speed to boost their ordinance and shred planetary defenses. Gonna cause problems."

Ernest began talking very slowly, "Yes. Problems. For them." He continued at a normal pace, "At 1% of the speed of light, the relative speed of the most basic kinetics is a problem. For them. Even a cruiser's point defense guns shooting 1-gram bullets will shred whatever armor they have. We can put around a trillion of these in their direction if we have a short re-supply route from the planet. Not gonna dodge them all. No shield or armor will help them even if we get a 0.01% hit rate."

"It's good to have Ernest around," The Governor thought.

Alexander was also glad to have Ernest around. Alexander had a specific job description: he had to "think of the worst cases." Alexander was a man of advising actions and preparations and "the worst case" frequently put strong constraints on what actions had to be done or had to be avoided.

When reviewing civilian projects, he would conduct "contingency reviews" to consider all possible scenarios in which something could go horribly wrong. It was an important job, someone had to do it, and Alexander was good at it. He felt proud of his role. However, after all the reviews and preparations, the worst case never happened. Alexander frequently felt wrong and over-cautious. The better he did his role, the more over-cautious he would seem. This drove him up the wall sometimes. Without the counterbalance of Ernest, Alexander worried he would lose his marbles. And the head of the military losing one's marbles was a pretty bad contingency.

The Inquisition focused on Truth rather than Action. Its primary concern was correct information and encouragement of Proper Thought. Ernest was a gateway of necessary Prior knowledge from the Archives and a trusted reminder of typical average case outcomes in practice. Those were usually quite positive.

So Alexander relied on Ernest to express what he was feeling, but differed from the type of advice Alexander's role compelled him to give. Ernest relied on Alexander to articulate his fears, so that Ernest didn't have to.

The Governor relied on them both to maintain his self-conception as a pragmatic and careful leader, who combined the opinions of his more radical subordinates.

The Governor continued the train of thought, "OK. If they are too slow they are screwed, if they are too fast, they are screwed. What if they occupy a reasonable range between 200 km / s and 3000 km /s inside the system?" The Governor waved away the previous simulation and launched his own.

Ernest was eager to chime in, "Both previous plans work, but less well. The question is: 'Are they decelerating inside the system and by how much?' There is a reason we don't build massive ships. The heat management of accelerating this much mass is a pain. Their radiators have to glow hot and, if they have basic bitch radiators, they are massive. This makes their radiators and engines extremely vulnerable to lasers, gamma flashes, proton launchers, and even plasma torpedoes."

Governor chuckled at the suggestion, "Plasma torpedoes? Really? We might be a new system, but we are not THAT poor."

Alexander shook his head yet again, "Gonna be tricky to get close enough for proton launchers or lasers."

Ernest continued, "On the off chance they have no shields, proton launchers will prove useful against large radiators from even a few hundred kilometers. Diffraction means the heat damage is usually too spread out. However, with their size, heat management will be an ongoing issue. If they need to dump heat during or right before battle, we can close in quickly into point-blank range, melt their radiators off, and laugh as their ships get too hot to function."

Alexander's head made a half-nod, half-disagreement, "We know how to kill things." He made a motion with his hands as crushing an imaginary skull, "The challenge is how to avoid dying ourselves. Every weapon is a door that opens both ways. Our radiators are not going to be that functional after that maneuver."

The Governor said, "Fair enough."

Ernest countered, "Movement in and out of close range to melt radiators will come down to proper storage and re-distribution of heat. Our coolant has been perfected over millions of years. Theirs have not."

The Governor was pleased with the plans so far, "Ernest, what is your estimate for their likely speed?"

Ernest responded, "I am guessing they come in under 200 km/s. I expect they believe they have power in a prolonged engagement. A full-fleet kite is then our plan. Get ahead of them, shoot them till they are dead."

Alexander concurred, "I agree that is likely their mentality. The main unknown is what the big ships are carrying. If they hold a single weapon system, like an oversized laser or railgun they could one-shot a lot of our ships."

Ernest shook his head, "Doubtful. Material science and power considerations of massive weapon systems are far beyond basic interstellar travel. And let's not forget our other defender's advantages. We have a ton of preplaced sensors, but they don't. Without proper sensors, they cannot spot even tier-1 stealth, while we can. They will be low on fuel, while we can run circles around them for days."

The Governor allowed himself to be hopeful. He shared the notes he made before the meeting with his advisors. Upon seeing them, Alexander joked, "Well, you barely needed us for this."

"I certainly need you," the Governor wanted his men to feel good about their work, "Confirming my thoughts make sense is an extremely valuable task."

The three men sat down on the couches in silence, allowing their minds to digest and internalize information for around a kilosecond [~17 minutes].

The Governor gestured for Alexander to leave. "Oh, yes, the gossip girl session," Alexander joked as he exited the room. The Governor paced around his office.

"You look nervous," Ernest mentioned.

"I get this way when there is a potentially hostile fleet of an unknown alien species with unknown capabilities and intentions flying towards me," he responded.

"One of our cruisers or railcruisers carries enough warheads to eradicate most life on the surface of the planet. And there are 200 of these in orbit above us, soon to be more. Ever get nervous about that?" Ernest cheerfully clasped his hands behind his head. The Governor was glad to have Ernest reassure him.

The Governor responded, "I feel safe. I trust the crews and I trust extrohistory. We follow its principles. So, unless a cruiser is controlled by an asshole such as yourself, dear Grand Inquisitor, I feel perfectly safe." The Governor finished up jokingly, "Besides, it's just the surface."

Ernest smiled, "Fair enough."

"Pull up the current state of extrohistory," The Governor said.

Extrohistory, short for "extrapolated history," was a subject that dealt with predicting the future stability of human societies. Some of the foundational Axioms of Extrohistory were concerned with exercising caution regarding printing money, allowing for appropriate meritocratic promotions, and keeping the number of people with a marker of 'elite' manageable.

The Governor went above and beyond in following the principles. Ship crewmen came from loving families, who taught them the meaning of duty. All citizens and civilians underwent mental capacity testing. Anyone bright enough to lead a war fleet was admitted to the Academy, where they were guided to cozy positions in either the military or civilian hierarchy. The Academy combined both aristocratic and meritocratic criteria, ensuring nobody had the incentive to 'rise' through warlike means. The Governor met many crewmen, but he would trust them regardless of familiarity.

The principles of extrohistory were well known and understood. Extrohistory software was a different story. It looked at the social stability in a given region and extrapolated the historical trends forward. The simulation was never a perfect prediction of conflicts. Instead, it forecast the overall stability level of society and the likelihood of its survival on that planet.

The Governors and the Inquisition once relied heavily on extrohistory simulations during the colonization of planets with highly unusual geography, as those were considered most likely to disrupt normal social processes. However, as time passed, both simulations and real-life history confirmed many of the Axioms of extrohistory. If a society adhered to the Axioms, the simulations were only occasionally used to enact subtle adjustments to get the population back on track.

Predicting the direction of human society was a hard task. Extrohistory software could not predict the future when a copy of itself was available to other power players. Thus it only worked if there was only one copy of it in a star system. As a result, extrohistory simulation was the most closely guarded piece of software in the Empire, classified above the clearance level of the Grand Admiral.

The hologram displayed the planet, the land controlled by Noble Houses, the charts of population sentiment, and tables detailing the major power players' perceptions of one another. Four numbers appeared in the top left corner, indicating measures of social cohesion on Derev.

The first group of numbers represented the trust of the population in the Governor.

The second represented social cohesion among Noble Patriarchs.

The third group measured social cohesion of civilians, with one metric measuring levels of trust within each House, and another measuring cohesion between civilians of separate houses.

The last group represented cohesion between citizens and civilians.

Ernest pointed at the last group, "This dropping is usually the first sign of something going wrong. The overall average eventually follows."

The total average social cohesion was prominently displayed in the center top. It was 95 out of 100. Ernest spoke, "Before the anomaly the average was 93, then it rose to 97 after the discovery and went down to 95 after taxes."

The Governor expected that an outside threat would boost the solidarity a bit, but was still pleased. The average of 80 was considered the minimum "respectable" number for an Imperial World, and problems requiring urgent attention would likely occur at 70. Even some societies with ratings as low as 60 could theoretically remain stable with superb leadership or severe repression. Society could function for a while even if the high trust that enabled it was lost. However, if social cohesion were to drop far below 60, it would inevitably lead to some horrifying instability, such as hyperinflation, a drop in fertility rates, loss of cognitive abilities in the average population, drops in life expectancy, perhaps even a rebellion or a civil war. Or so the Inquisition warned. The extrohistory software and axioms were key factors in ensuring this has never happened since the founding of the Empire.

"Run it forward," he said, "assuming we keep taxes high for a year, the aliens turn out to be a dud and we reduce taxes after."

Ernest played the extrohistory code forward. In 30 megaseconds [~1 Earth year], the simulation predicted that social cohesion dropped to 92. After a gigasecond [~31 Earth years] remaining in the Governor's term, it dropped to 91. It then dropped to 88 for the next Governor.

Ernest said, "Your son doesn't have as strong of a legitimacy claim as you do."

The Governor thought that was an understatement of the gigasecond. Traditionally, the title of Governor was passed down to a male son of the previous governor. This typically established the first type of legitimacy: being part of the Imperial bloodline, although it was possible to establish it via "genetic proximity" to one of the Emperors. If there were multiple claimants, the tie-breaker was always their performance in space combat sims, which formed the second type of legitimacy claim. The Governor was slightly unusual in being both a son of the previous Governor and a top space sim contestant in the system. The best of his sons was only ranked 1500, which weakened his legitimacy and thus social cohesion. It was not enough to cause concern under normal circumstances.

As the simulation went forward over the next 8 gigaseconds [~254 Earth years], social cohesion climbed to 90, though the extrohistory projection offered a very wide confidence interval. In the meantime, over the same period, the projection also showed the average life expectancy climbing 25%, along with a population increase from 500 million people to 10 billion, making Derev more than twice as dense as Old Earth prior to the Empire's founding. It showed solar panels delivering ever-increasing amounts of energy to the planet and halfvators transforming into full-blown column space elevators.

Ernest summarized the situation, "We are above board at the moment. I support your decision to only go to DEFCON 2. At this level, the Extrohistory projections are more sound than under DEFCON 1. That said, I ran some plausible DEFCON 1 situations, and we can handle some of them with a loss in cohesion, but without triggering a full-blown crisis."

Good to know. In the absence of Alexander, Ernest took over the cognitive role of worst-case analysis.

Ernest mentioned, "One thing to watch is that Idris's son and Tong's granddaughter are in the same class group in the Academy."

Extrohistory analyzed the politico-financial forces and the incentive gradients of conflicts between elites seeking to occupy the same niche. It attempted to predict key romantic partnerships and space combat skill, but those had some margin of error.

The Governor understood the implication the first time he saw the class. A marriage alliance between both Houses made political sense for them. It would greatly strengthen the Noble Patriarch's cohesion within themselves and weaken both his and his successor's grip on the system. The decisions regarding the colonization of future worlds would be directed from House Smith's pyramid, as much as from the Governor's place.

"How likely is it?" the Governor asked.

Ernest explained, "The estimate suggests the children are a little too proud. Probability is estimated at only 30%, even though it makes political sense."

The Governor concurred, "30% seems about right." He asked Ernest, "Anything on the weapon prices?"

The Governor expected this part to be a formality.

"Everything is mostly within range," Ernest said, "except railgun barrels are a little more expensive than the original estimate."

Ernest pulled up the real-time price data for all the spaceship components.

The Governor was surprised. Guess not a formality after all, "Why? Someone over-charging us?"

"No, demand increased. Idris ordered 2000 tanks and the rest of the Noble Houses followed suit."

"Why on Derev would he do that?" The Governor was confused.

Ernest didn't seem bothered, "Seems reasonable. The enemy could carry assault teams in such a large fleet."

The Governor shook his hands up at the ceiling, "No, it's not reasonable. Wars are won in space."

It was standard Imperial doctrine. The Noble Houses already had sizable ground armies even by Border World standards. The only reason the Governor approved these armies was due to some nasty local wildlife."

The Governor looked at Ernest, both seeking affirmation, but also hiding that he was, "How many times has anyone ever managed to land on a planet without winning a space engagement first? How many times does anyone even land without significant orbital bombardment?"

Ernest looked this up in the Archives recently, "Some human teams managed this, but it only happened due to horrific intelligence failures on the xenos part. But we still can't rule this out. Having ground forces deters these kinds of assaults. Besides, this isn't going to break the budget."

"I know," The Governor was still frustrated.

Ernest pointed at the extrohistory number corresponding to the Noble Patriarchs' alignment with the Governor, "It's never going to be 100 out of 100. You can lose some points here by restructuring the army, but I would not recommend it."

The Governor didn't want his frustration to get the better of him, "I concur. Allow this to happen, but keep monitoring the prices. My heart tells me we will need some wiggle room in how we shape history."

Chapter 9

The Strength of our Hearts

His survival of the atmospheric re-entry with those G-forces is both a miracle and proof of God's support for our cause. I hope his son takes after his father.

The First Emperor addressing unknown regarding unknown (during Unification War).

0.7 MS AA

Arjun led his class on a tour of the partially assembled railcruiser next to the Academy.

They walked through the reactor room, which was missing about half of its normal tubing. Since the dawn of space travel, movement in a vacuum has been based on 3 possible methods of propulsion. One was to use either natural or artificial light to push a sail, which was fuel-efficient, but extremely slow. The second was to 'push-off' a planet or a megastructure. This was the preferred method of travel between highly established Core Worlds which would have large rails floating on the outskirts of systems to both guide ships out of systems and slow them down coming in.

In all other cases, the law of conservation of momentum dictated that rockets were needed. Rockets require reaction mass to shoot out the back and energy to propel it to relativistic speeds. In civilian ships, both were archived through a matter-antimatter drive. Hydrogen and anti-hydrogen were mixed in a roughly 3 to 1 ratio, producing an explosion that created numerous fast-moving protons and electrons. If they traveled in the correct direction and were faster than 60% of the speed of light, the engine would simply shoot them out the back. Some of the slower ones were captured by a particle accelerator and given a boost to reach the required 60%. Others were slowed down by a magnetic field, transferring their kinetic energy into current to power the accelerator and operate the ship. The process allowed for gradual increases in acceleration over time.

However, warships needed bigger jerks. Jerk being the derivative of acceleration.

As a result, warship drives were significantly more sophisticated, featuring a secondary drive capable of running on both fusion or antimatter power, large batteries, and a specialized particle accelerator that pre-spun particles for rapid releases to achieve any required acceleration. They also featured a "hard absorb" drive that didn't bother carefully sorting particles by speed. Instead, an absorbent lead composite 'shaped' the explosion to go out the back. As the composite melted from heat and radiation, its structure required periodic re-crystallization using nanobots when the ship was not operating.

Albert gazed down at the hard absorb tube from the walkway platform above, his eyes tracing its length. "It's like being propelled forward by a nuclear explosion," he thought. Despite extensive physical training, one's body was still squishy compared to a nuke and the hard absorb tube put that into perspective.

"The outer layer of capital ship armor is made up of 5 mm thick diamond-infused titanium," Arjun pointed to the outside of the ship. "For our first exercise, grab yourself a plate and try to scratch it using a slug."

The students put on gloves and grabbed a 1 kg tungsten railgun slug, placing a section of diamond titanium in front of them. The slug felt delightfully heavy in Albert's hand. After the first hit, he heard Max exclaim, "I got the scratch already!"

"Why does it have to be him?" Albert thought to himself.

After a couple of minutes, most students had scratches on both the titanium plate and their slug. The diamond sections were undamaged.

"Any thoughts?" Arjun asked. "Worth knowing the materials you work with."

"The slug is not sharpened. The real slugs have mono-molecular tips," Ken remarked.

They moved on to the next cross-section. "Underneath the diamond titanium is a 3 mm layer of aramid fibers dipped in nano coolant," Arjun pointed at a display of fibers and nano coolant behind a glass panel. "Try to wave your hand next to it."

Albert touched the glass panel. The nano coolant was a neon-bright blue liquid permeating the fibers in a fractal pattern, with thicker tubes branching towards the smaller and smaller ones, until their width was barely visible. However, once his hand touched the glass, the blue liquid behind it began to move and the vessels thickened, revealing ones that were previously too small to see.

Arjun explained, "The nano coolant is composed of microscopic robots that carry heat differentials through the system. Titanium is hard enough to evaporate with a laser and with this coolant backing it, the challenge becomes even more substantial."

Arjun pulled a demonstration lever, that left a faint scratch on the titanium next to the coolant all while making an ugly sound. Part of the coolant turned black and the blackness raced to the scratch. 20 seconds later the scratch was repaired and no longer noticeable.

"Nano coolant also serves as a conduit for the repair bots," Arjun said.

"It looks alive," Albert said.

"Like a blood vessel inside a muscle," Ken finished his sentence.

Max shook his head in disbelief.

Arjun assumed a mildly stern teaching voice, "The Imperial speech decree emphasizes the importance of a fixed difference between life and non-life. It is not proper to compare technology to biology, however, the resemblance is there." Arjun softened up, "You'll learn the communication techniques in time as well."

Albert felt mildly embarrassed, but he was just too excited about the lesson to make the feeling stick.

Arjun continued, "Underneath the aramid fibers sit 3 layers of 1 mm aluminum Whipple shields spaced 25 cm each, the space between them holding small amounts of black fungus and auto-hardening liquids."

The black fungus was displayed in a glass container.

"Yummy," Max joked.

Arjun smiled, "If you are hungry enough, the fungus can be processed into food. For long civilian journeys, the extra fungus that grows due to gamma-ray absorption is typically used as fertilizer. Ship mechanics on interstellar journeys all have a love-hate relationship with black fungus. On one hand, it is the most cost-effective way to absorb radiation from outer space. On the other hand, given enough years, it will grow everywhere, eat the surrounding material, release toxins, and generally be a massive pain in the behind. Still, if a nuke goes off near your ship, you will be glad to have the gamma rays absorbed by these guys."

The students entered a room containing 9 rectangular auto-hardener glass jars and a palm-sized iron ball next to each one.

"Next up, you all get to fight the auto-hardener. Your objective is to lower this iron ball to the bottom of the container as quickly as possible. And, of course, don't touch the liquid with your hands, if you want to keep them."

The auto-hardening liquid had a yellow color, its rectangular container stood about half a meter tall and 30 cm on each side. Arjun took a metal ball and gently put it on top of the liquid, allowing it to slowly sink to the bottom. "This is the time to beat," he said.

Albert, having never actually seen the hardening liquid before, simply dropped the same ball from around half a meter height. The liquid hardened, stopped the ball, and then remained solid until a nearby service droid came over and gave it a proper shake.

The students began to experiment, all while watching each other. Through basic binary search, they determined that the best height to drop the ball was around 12 cm.

Max acquired a metal rod and tried to guide the ball in, either by pushing it or rotating it. This failed to beat the 12 cm drop.

Sheene heated the ball using a microwave, which made it slower, but then she dipped into liquid nitrogen, which made the drop a little faster. This led to another binary search for the optimal ball temperature and the students collectively determined that around -20C was the most effective.

Sunnak attempted to drop the ball away from the center of the container. It was inconsistent as walls sometimes slowed it down properly to avoid hardening, but sometimes sped it up too much and triggered a stop.

After a few tries, Albert retreated to the corner and began typing on his handheld.

"Giving up already?" Max asked him.

Albert smiled, but didn't answer.

As Arjun was about to call a break," Albert approached the service droid and started talking to it.

The students were confused. Arjun smiled.

The service droid asked, "Are you confirming the program?"

Albert confidently replied, "Yes, keep the relative speed constant as per parameters and within bounds."

Albert held the cold ball in his hand, and dropped it from 11 cm. As the ball touched the top of the liquid, the droid picked up the whole container and moved it upward, getting the ball to the proper maximum speed. It then moved the container downwards to maintain the speed without triggering the hardening, as per the program Albert worked out. It was the best time.

"Was that allowed?" Max asked.

"This was the solution we were looking for," Arjun responded, "Some classes find this eventually, though usually working as a team."

Max looked mad, but said nothing. Sheene smiled at Albert.

After the break, they ventured further into the railcruiser cross-section, ultimately thriving at the inner hull demo room.

Arjun continued, "The inner hull is made out of chromium-vanadium steel 7 cm thick, which was an unexciting, but practical design choice. Reinforcing its back is a layer of 2 cm of synthetic spider silk, which prevents spalling and armor shockwaves from creating shrapnel inside the ship."

The hull demonstration room displayed a thin plastic container with hundreds of layers of interwoven webs that combined to a thickness of 20 cm. Albert picked up the spider silk container, marveling at how delightfully light it was, almost feeling like the container wanted to float away.

Half jokingly, Yezi remarked, "Hope we don't use real spiders for this."

Arjun laughed, "Of course not, this is done with basic molecular-level manufacturing. We do have a few Earth-variety spiders, whose silks assist in verifying the purity of our outputs. Get a feel for how strong it is." Arjun gave the students a slightly sharp metal rod and asked them to guide it to the bottom of the spider silk container. They couldn't sharpen the rod further or ask a droid for help.

Max excitedly rubbed his hands in anticipation of a physical challenge. Yet in a kilosecond [~17 minutes], nobody could pierce the spider webs. The metal rod was stopped about 1 cm in, and pushing it in felt like hitting a diamond wall. The students quickly found out, the challenge was not made easier by temperature, angle, or initial speed.

"I give up, what's the answer?" Max was sweating a bit. Ken and all the girls had given up earlier.

Albert looked up from his "spider silk" containers and said, "Wait, I still have a few ideas to try."

Arjun eyed them carefully, "As fun as this is, I will stop here. This particular challenge doesn't have a solution. The required strength is beyond any of you. If every problem we give you has a solution, you become over-confident. You need to be mentally ready for the situations when nothing works."

Max looked frustrated. The idea made sense to Albert. After all, their droids and drones were trained to detect "out of distribution" environments, to know when specific tasks fell outside their programming. It is only natural people needed to train such intuitions as well.

The students entered the next room, which contained a small shield generator. The outside of the generator was a metallic ball around a meter in diameter. It was held to the floor by a metallic support structure whose shape resembled a volcano. The bottom of the support structure was mounted to the hull with 32 diamond screws, the tops of which could barely fit into a fully opened hand.

Arjun turned on the shield generator. A gentle blue glow around half a meter thick arose in the air between it and the students. Arjun took an iron ball and gently tossed it towards the shield. It traveled a few centimeters inside the blue glow, stopped midair, and gently bounced back towards Arjun. He turned off the generator.

Arjun explained, "The shield generator is just a specialized version of a generalized field manipulator that creates a slightly discontinuous strong quasi-magnetic field at specific regions of space. In this case, here. In the ship's case, a few meters outside the ship. It effectively slows down any metallic objects traveling towards you. This one is, of course, much weaker than the real generator. However, even the core warship generators are much weaker than the theoretical optimum of what we can build. Does anyone know as to why?"

Max was eager to answer, "Because it's not cost-effective."

Albert laughed internally because Max's wrong answer was a good opportunity for him.

Arjun shook his head, "This is a very generic answer, which is quite true for many aspects of warfare. However, in this instance, the reason is different and very specific."

Yezi excitedly jumped in, "Because strong magnetic fields can destroy our own components and damage the crew."

Arjun slightly frowned to indicate that also wasn't what he was looking for, "Strong fields can damage people, but generic field manipulators can project fields outside the ship without creating them within."

Albert was about to respond, but Ken seemed super excited. They discussed this in previous coaching sessions, so Albert let Ken have this opportunity to shine.

"The screws are not strong enough," Ken walked over to the diamond screws and tapped on them. "If the shield generator is too powerful, the momentum of a thousand railgun impacts or a fully accelerated shaped charge will tear these from the hull. It will tear any material known to man."

Arjun was pleased, "Correct. This is why we emphasize each captain must know their ship 'from the screw to the bit'. The energy of enemy weapons fire can be dissipated through various passive and active methods. However, momentum has to be absorbed. If the shield generator is strong enough to have the field absorb the momentum, it is then transferred to the shield generator itself, which is then transmitted to the ship via attachment methods that have a fixed amount of strength. Beyond a point, you are better taking a hit via armor."

Max was shaking his head, presumably at himself for letting even Ken spot something so obvious in retrospect.

Arjun assumed lecturing mode, "The shield generator's primary purpose is to protect you from relativistic low-mass particles. Proton launchers or enemy drive exhausts. Or friendly drive exhausts if your fellow fleet captains are unskilled."

Albert knew this. Proton launchers were among the most devastating weapons in their arsenal. A stream of protons could heat up and ablate the outside armor layer like a laser, while also piercing through layers of it like a railgun, causing secondary gamma ray and neutron radiation inside the black fungus shield, being as lethal to the crew as a nuke flash inside the ship. They were at least half the speed of light and nearly impossible to avoid. However, proton beams suffered from even worse diffraction than lasers. They spread out over a large area, losing effectiveness if fired from over 30 km away. They also could not be mounted on turrets and instead had to be keel-mounted to be shot from the front or the back of the ship in the direction it was facing.

Arjun continued, "In theory, the armor, inner hull, and shields are designed to protect you from various damage. The armor will effectively withstand long-range laser fire, micro-meteors, chemical bullets, tiny point defense railguns, and gamma rays from a 50-kiloton micro-nuke detonated over 1 km away. So, a question of the class: how much should one rely on this armor in space?"

The students saw the trickiness of the question from a light-second away.

"Not at all," Albert gave the obvious answer. He practiced enough simulations with various armor and shield combinations to realize how useless they were against serious firepower.

"'Not at all' is correct," Arjun mentioned. "If you encounter heavy weaponry, you might as well be protected by a piece of paper. Does anyone know the Imperial doctrine on dealing with incoming enemy firepower?"

Max's father taught him the doctrine. Max raised his hand, "Don't be there".

"Correct. The full Imperial doctrine of space combat against xenos scum is: Shoot them until they are dead and when they shoot back, don't be there," Arjun paused to let the students feel the words and continued, "In time you will appreciate the power of simplicity. If you face a railgun slug traveling at 72 km per second, you dodge out of the way. If you face a missile, you shoot it down before it reaches you, but also dodge out of its way. If you face a beam weapon, you use a magnetic deflector shield, but also predict when it will fire, so that you can pre-dodge before it does."

This was a more poignant lesson for Albert after seeing how little armor the warships carried.

"Of course, if you have the misfortune of facing a sustained barrage from multiple heliguns or focused sunlight collectors built by the Empire of Man, you also try to dodge out of its way. But your best course of action is to ask God for forgiveness and make peace with the poor life choices that led you to that moment."

Max cheered, "Hooray for heliguns!" The cheer spread across the students.

Arjun waited for the cheer to calm down, "Now, for my final easy question: what is the main factor that enables us to execute on this strategy?"

Diana raised her hand and replied, "The Strength of our Hearts". After the previous sims performance, she read ahead in her textbook to try to guess what the teacher wanted to hear.

Arjun smiled, "See, not every lesson in the Academy is difficult. That's correct. It is the Strength of your Hearts. Human ships are not built to withstand powerful attacks; they're designed for speed, evasion, and maneuvers. The core task of every person aboard a ship is to endure bursts of high acceleration. Our genetic code is similar to people of the Old Earth, with one main exception: the high-G gene family. They code for improved heart function and reinforced connective tissue, which are vital for pumping blood under high-G and keeping your body from getting torn apart. High-G genes form an exception to the Empire's ban on genetic engineering and are ubiquitous in the Border World populations.

This shiny diamond-encrusted titanium is nothing compared to what's in here." Arjun tapped his chest.

Albert felt a sense of quiet joy being told that part of him was, indeed, made for a purpose.

After the class ended, they came to the outside of the railcruiser, near one of its basic point defense cannons, which was an 8-barrel 40 mm-caliber Gatling gun around 4 meters long.

"They definitely look bigger up close," Diana noted.

"Not as big as the rail gun," Max replied.

The railgun consisted of a 200-meter circular barrel with rail reinforcers attached to its top and bottom, surrounded by a helical metallic wrapper that provided stability and carried coolant. The barrel was mounted on a rotational turret and balanced on the other side with a 30-meter slab of solid metal acting as counterweight.

"Race you to the end of the railgun," Max said and turned to Sunnak.

"I'll join," Albert said. He immediately felt off about his decision.

"Sure, why not?" Ken wasn't going to be left out.

"I'll judge," Diana said, pulling out her handheld and began recording, ready to capture the exact finish.

They prepared the race.

The girls waited by the railgun end, which served as the finish line. The start was by the counter-weight, making the race slightly longer than 200 m. Diana raised her hand and, with a tap of her handheld, triggered a loud ding.

The boys started running. After 23 seconds, Max finished first, with Sunnak right behind him and Ken third. As Max finished, Albert had a whole second left of running. That seemed to be the longest second of his life. Sheene clapped at Albert as he was finishing up, but he could tell it was a very polite, 'oh dear' clap, like she was patting a small child on the head after doing something cute."

Diana smiled at Max after he won. They high-fived.

Albert regretted his overconfidence. He mentally vowed to choose his battles more wisely, to avoid physical contests and stick to mental ones.

Chapter 10

Watching the Breath

Do not ask me what the Buddha would do. He was a better man than I am.

The First Emperor before signing the death warrants of the human traitors shortly after the victory over Cyborg Theocracy in the Unification War.

0.8 MS AA

The Capital city held the planet's largest Temple of the Four Masters.

On the way there, the Governor took a solo walk, letting the light of Toriad, their star, shine on him.

The hypothesis that the stars were conscious predated the Empire. However, it remained a hypothesis until a grand experiment was commissioned nearly 5 teraseconds after the founding. While many devices attempted to read a star's mood, they did not consistently produce the same readings. Imperial scientists picked a system with no planets and a tiny red dwarf to set up a moon-sized thin mirror to reflect some of the star's light back at it, attempting to establish a two-way communication channel. An unpopulated system was picked to avoid the potential of the star 'getting angry.' The overview of the experiment decreed it a 'massive breakthrough of Imperial Science', with definitive proof of the theological supposition that not only were the stars conscious, they were on humanity's side. However, the full data from the experiment remained tightly sealed in Inquisitorial Archives, along with affirmation of the ban on 'two-way communication' with the stars in populated systems.

Since then, similar scientific experiments have confirmed another long-held theological view that, while measuring the star's exact feelings was very difficult, well-trained people sitting under its light could do just as well as many devices. The discipline of 'mega-consciousness' was merged back into the study of phenomenology, despite large protests by the scientists specializing in 'mega-consciousness'. The phenomenologists, on the other hand, cheered greatly and told the Emperor At the Time, "We Feel right about Your Decision."

Inside the Temple, a 100-meter-tall marble Buddha statue towered above 40 rows of meditators.

The Governor entered the main meditation chamber, immediately feeling the tranquility of being surrounded by a fully shielded and grounded mu-metal Faraday building. There were no electronics of any kind. Radio, electric, and magnetic waves were either absorbed or redirected. The calmness almost buzzed in his ear.

"Mental overcompensation," he thought and took a breath. The buzzing stopped after a minute. He walked down the central aisle with men meditators on his left and women on his right. His gaze lingered on Camina, his wife, in the front row of women, who gazed back at him. The Governor then sat in the middle of the front row of men. The Principal had a cushion to his right. The two men shared a firm handshake and a shoulder pat. Two monks, one man and one woman, sat on the stage and proceeded to simultaneously sound their gongs.

The Governor sat cross-legged and closed his eyes, focusing on counting breaths from as high as he could go. He realized that he lost concentration around 500 and his mind wandered, consumed by thoughts of the Anomaly. Or perhaps the Enemy. He refocused, restarting at 1. Normally he could focus for the entire 2-kilosecond-long [~33 Earth minutes] meditation.

After the time had passed, the gongs sounded yet again. The Governor opened his eyes and looked around. He uncrossed his legs and noticed they were unexpectedly sore.

The Principal turned to him with a cheerful smile, "So, what did you want to discuss? You didn't bring me all the way out here to hear you struggle with meditation, did you?"

The Governor looked back a little less cheerfully, "Was it that obvious?"

The Principal sighed, "Your breath was quite irregular; the front three rows could probably tell. You are that worried?"

The Governor responded, "I am. I need advice. Your council had served me well in the most uncertain times. Anything we are missing?"

The Principal gestured to the corner of the chamber, where two cozy chairs stood vacant. "We are missing a lot," he said. "An extensive search of Academy records and the Empire Library has not yielded any insights into large fleets originating from a single system. The Inquisitorial records are FAR more extensive, but given your question I assume the Grand Inquisitor has not found anything either."

The Governor's body straightened itself as he adopted the Principal's more relaxed demeanor, "I want to talk about metacognition. Is there anything wrong with the way we approach the problem?"

The Principal allowed a hint of nervousness to show, "I was your official teacher shortly after you arrived on the planet, and you were independent about your ways of reasoning even then."

The Governor appreciated the compliment, "Of course I was."

The Principal continued, "We have asked ourselves every type of question. What is this? Why? How? We have theories on every situation. We are gathering all the data we can. We have begun computer simulations of battle projections, but without knowledge of their capacities, these will not be accurate. In the absence of sufficiently reliable information, we follow standard protocols. They exist for a reason. Our traditions brought us this far. Back on Old Earth, people's minds were destroyed by political and virtue-signaling spirals, as they mistook principles that unify their groups for the Truth. Assuming you have run your plans by the leaders of the Noble Houses, and they have approved them, we should not be facing these kinds of easily avoidable old-world problems."

So far, the Principal's advice was a proper affirmation of existing plans.

The Governor confirmed, "I have seen only minor disagreement from the Noble Houses. Slightly expected given their evaluation of the situation may differ from mine. Yet, something big doesn't add up. I see the void in my knowledge, as vast as the space between the stars. And when we are not building, my mind is fixated on it."

The Principal asked another basic question, "What is the most likely thing to go wrong?"

The Governor paused for a second, "We don't have enough ships. Or perhaps we have misjudged the situation and the aliens are friendly. But the number of ships is what I am worried about."

The Principal pushed forward, "What is the most likely thing you would miss, given who you are?"

This was a basic meta-cognition question and would sound like an insult if it didn't come from a trusted teacher. The Principal's tone made the Governor consider this more deeply than before. He responded, "I would approach this in a too-standard manner when an unconventional approach could be necessary. However, there is value in adhering to established protocols."

The Principal asked further, "What inputs to your mind would you need to make the right decision?"

Chapter 11

Multi-body Problem

Fear is a powerful tool, especially against the machine.

The First Emperor after his team's second successful hack of the Cyborg Communication Network using 'blackmail code' technology (early Unification War).

6.0 MS AA. 6 megaseconds [~66 Earth days] have passed since the discovery of the Anomaly.

Albert temporarily gave up on his "Diana project" and went "monk mode" to focus on his studies and sims practice. His religious teacher told him once, "Sometimes you gotta go monk mode, other times you gotta go into a mode of whatever the opposite of a monk is". Albert didn't quite understand, so he tried to clarify if "monk mode" just meant ignoring girls. The teacher said that was mostly it.

He sought to use the resources of the Academy to the fullest, challenging both teachers and students to practice sessions. He treated each class like he treated books; he wrote down what he expected and looked for surprises. Albert also set up tutoring hours for other students. Teaching helped understanding. It also helped meeting girls in case he wanted to get out of monk mode. Ken attended every tutoring session and so did Bishakha, another girl in his group. His tutoring became popular with other groups and older students. Sheene came to about half of the sessions, dragging Yezi along. Diana showed up only once and was quick to leave.

At one point, Bishakha stayed over time, leaving her alone with Albert. She was a decent student, as committed as Ken, but not as intuitively bright as Sheene. As they struck up a conversation, Albert briefly touched the top of her arm. Not even as an intention, but perhaps a question.

She smiled, perhaps assigning more symbolism to the gesture than he intended.

"Oh Albert, you are sweet, but I am looking for someone more ... wealthy. I hope you understand."

"I most certainly do," Albert gave her a genuine look of understanding and a sense of solidarity.

"For the long term that is," she smiled at him.

"Makes sense," he responded.

They discussed point-defense weaponry some more before exiting the room.

Ten kiloseconds later [~2.8 Earth hours] Albert wondered if the conversation implied that she was ok with something short-term, perhaps being asked to travel to his room right then. But no! Monk mode was monk mode! Besides, Bishakha could have meant something else.

The moment with Bishakha has probably passed, given how she cozied up to several other boys the same day. Albert did make a mental note to try to notice flirtation more, once he felt his efforts in studying and tests were no longer yielding further improvements. Albert almost always placed at the top of the entire 120-person class in strategic multi-ship tests, but every time he did, the second and third places were right behind him, separated by the width of a hair. He thought the tests were too easy and there was little chance for him to show the full extent of his skills.

Until this time.

Each of the eight students was seated in their booth, surrounded by thin black walls on two sides. In front of them was a personal holo-display, the ship's pilot's burn controller, which consisted of 3 sticks at right angles to each other with dials and buttons on each, and typing gloves. Each group of 8 students took the test separately in their respective rooms, with start times separated by a kilosecond.

The robotic simulation announcer excitedly outlined the test conditions, "In earlier tests, you have piloted evenly matched fleets against combat computers. Today's test will push you far beyond any previous exercise. The simulation in front of you contains three stars and a sizable gas giant with a moon system. The enemy fleet of 90 mixed-class warships is in an orbit around the gas giant. You have a fleet at the far edge of the system consisting of 10 railcruisers with the standard railgun and missile armament."

"A three-body problem?" Ken mouthed.

"A nine to one disadvantage?" Max's jaw dropped.

The simulation announcer continued, "You can control every aspect of your ships, including piloting and manually aiming your guns. You can run the simulation at any speed, but only forward. All decisions in the simulation are final. Your score is the number of enemy ships you eliminate. If you eliminate all enemies, your score will be augmented by the number of your surviving ships. The test is 12 kiloseconds [~3 Earth hours] long. Unlike previous exercises, these tests are new every year. We don't know the best possible score until after the test."

The Principal chimed in to confirm the absurd level of difficulty, "As you are well aware, the three-body star mechanics (four if you count the gas giant) does not have a closed-form solution. You cannot count on any orbit remaining elliptical and your intuitions about orbital mechanics will fail you. We don't train you to solve problems that can be done by machines. The Academy prepares you for tasks that are far more difficult. Our top combat computers can score above zero. However, creating a combat computer that reliably beats the top human score on these tests would be both a monumental task and a clear violation of the Fourth Imperial Law regarding the Ban on Artificial Intelligence."

The Fourth Law regarding Artificial Intelligence was: "Don't try to solve the unsolvable in software. Leave it to the humans."

The students heard of such tests and their winners, but the conditions of the previous tests were shrouded in secrecy, fueling much speculation and rumor. As the initial shock at the difficulty wore off, they realized that the secret knowledge was worthy of the hype.

Albert raised his hand and asked, "Can we see the simulation source code?"

The Principal responded, "It is available for you and future graduates of the Academy as of now."

Max snickered, "What do you need the code for, it's just a physics simulator, just like any other?"

"Headphones up," the Principal signaled, "Begin."

8 kiloseconds later [~2 Earth hours], everyone except Albert sat quietly in their chairs, utterly exhausted, and began devouring their much-needed mammoth steaks. Albert was still frantically typing.

Max turned to Sunnak, and said "Why is he typing? Is he trying to convince the enemy to surrender?"

Sunnak laughed. Orbital maneuvers were usually done with a burn controller and close piloting was done with a joystick. Keyboards were generally used to tweak numbers on firing solutions, which would likely be needed earlier in the test.

At the end of the test mark, the Principal walked back into the room, accompanied by Kariel Mishov. Diana and Bishakha gazed intensely at Kariel's bulky muscles, straightened their backs, and adjusted their hair. Kariel did not seem to acknowledge them with any attention back. Albert was finally relaxed.

The Principal announced, "Headphones down. Welcome to your new sparring instructor, Kariel, a previous champion of such a test and this test's designer." Kariel took the floor. Diana and Bishakha perked up in their seats looking at his tight-fitting shirt as if trying to bore through its fabric.

"Let's go over your strategies." Kariel looked over all the students.

"Diana, you decided to use one of the stars for a slingshot maneuver to boost your approach speed. However, the enemy noticed you in time and prepared their volleys and countermeasures. Charging headfirst did not work. 0 points."

Diana's gaze alternated between her feet and fleeting glances at Kariel.

"Yezi. You approached the planet from the other side of the enemy and attempted to sneak your ships through the gas giant's atmosphere. A bold, yet futile move. Your element of surprise worked once, but the enemy quickly readjusted their formation. You lost too much fuel in the atmosphere and had to ration your dodging. 1 point."

Yezi made a slow-motion hand gesture, signaling an explosion, and exclaimed 'Boom' as she celebrated her successful destruction of one enemy ship.

"Bishakha, you decided to wait for the simulation to run its course. You attempted to predict the system's movement numerically. At the point where all 3 stars and the planet formed a rough line, you shot a volley of nearly half of all of your missiles. You allowed the volley to lose all tangential speed, allowing it to be pulled by the combined gravity of the planet and stars. If the enemy had stayed where it was, the speed of missiles above 1000 km / s would have made them very difficult to intercept. However, the enemy ran most of the fleet around the planet, using a slingshot to dodge your shots and catch your ships. Still, the hyper-fast first strike did land you 4 points. Good try."

Kariel moved on, "Max, like Yezi, you also initially approached the enemy to put the planet between you and them. You matched orbit on the opposite side of the planet. You began firing railguns at a retrograde orbit. They responded in kind, forcing each fleet to constantly dodge. If they changed orbit, you stayed on the opposite side of the planet. At some point, the enemy split the fleet into multiple orbits, forcing you into an engagement against smaller portions of it. Then you took manual control of some of your ships, demonstrating impressive piloting skills. Enough for 5 points."

Max looked very proud of himself.

Kariel turned to Sheene, "Sheene, you decided to use a lot of your fuel for an out-of-plane maneuver. You exited the ecliptic plane right away and then re-entered the ecliptic with your fleet obscured from the line of sight by two stars. You used this opportunity to launch a volley a long way around the system. You intended to only burn the engines of your missiles 3 times, each time with a different star between your missiles and the enemy fleet. It is a great strategy, but your execution was flawed. Somewhere you miscalculated the exact 3-body perturbations and some missiles had to readjust course without the stars' protection. Still, enough of them ran dark to score 7 points."

Max looked genuinely surprised. Albert gave a gentle applause to Sheene. He previously taught her to always look for opportunities for deception, and she heeded his lesson.

Kariel continued, "Ken, you decided to put yourself into an orbit retrograde to the enemy at a reasonable distance of 30,000 km above your opponent. The fleets converged into firing range for a short time before separating again. You tried to focus fire all your missiles and railgun shots on only a couple of the enemy ships, guaranteeing a kill, while the enemy spread the damage around your fleet. Once the fleets separated, you implemented a custom repair protocol to readjust your ships for the next go-around. The second fight was also a success. However, the enemy adjusted to your strategy, executing a series of hard burns. The first few were out of the plane, and then they converged onto you. Once enough of the enemy got into laser range, your ships were toast. Still, a solid plan and 8 points." Albert was excited for him, though Ken still had a constant issue of being too uneager to commit to an offensive, preferring trade damage and repair strategies.

"Sunnak. You waited a bit before attacking, however, instead of focusing on the macro of positioning fleets and guiding missiles from a particular angle, you focused on the micro play between the missiles and the point defense bullets. In a particular system configuration of a single star being very close to the planet, the orbits became extremely unusual. You added a custom mini solar sail to your rockets. It created slight changes in direction without using engine thrusts. To make matters even more complex for your computer opponent, you wrote a custom evasion pattern, that would combine both thrusters and sails, to curve your rockets very close to the planet's atmosphere. The enemy point defense had a lot more trouble predicting the evasion patterns. The computer opponent used the technique of running as hard as one could to give the point defense more space and time to work. They still managed to shut your fleet down eventually, but not before you scored 17 points. Well done. The custom evasion pattern is most impressive."

Max gave Sunnak a high five. "Thanks," Sunnak said, clearly basking in the moment.

Kariel continued, "Which brings us to Albert. You decided to use railguns first, without even closing in on the enemy. Instead, you parked your ships in an orbit far away, extended solar panels, and began firing from a distance of over 10 million kilometers, significantly farther than the ideal railgun range of one THOUSAND kilometers."

Max laughed. Albert smiled.

"Under normal real-life conditions or most reliable simulations, this tactic will do nearly nothing. It is extremely hard to be accurate and even if you are, the enemy can usually see an unstealthed slug within at least 10,000 km, only needing to dodge a tiny bit. However, you also programmed a custom firing solution for your ... railguns."

Students looked confused. Railgun operation was almost always left to the default targeting computer.

"And when I said 'custom' it wasn't fully custom. You dug into the source code of the simulation itself to find the enemy dodge patterns and use pieces of that code in your firing solution. This meant that when the computer opponent evaluated whether it was "afraid" of a hit, the code it used was the same as the code used to issue a hit in the first place. As a result, the computer opponent was always more afraid of your hits than necessary and dodged more than necessary, frequently with multiple ships."

Max shouted, "That's an exploit!"

Kariel responded, "Of course it is. Most victories look like exploits to the loser. Furthermore, the constant dodging would put enemy ships into decaying or otherwise unstable orbits, requiring orbital corrections and spreading out the formation. You carefully used the 3-body stable points to cause a lot of your slugs to go into an orbit around the gas giant. This necessitated occasional re-dodges and further magnified enemy fuel loss to get the fleet back into formation.

After around 400,000 railgun shots from each of your 10 ships and over 10 megaseconds [~115 Earth days] of in-simulation time, you enacted a second step of your plan, which looked similar to Sheene's strategy. You positioned yourself on the other side of the system, where your fleet was obscured by one of the stars. From there, you executed a series of precise missile volleys, which ran dark, except for 3 burns executed while obscured by one of the stars. The missile volleys led to the loss of the majority of enemy cruisers and carriers, leaving primarily railships and laser destroyers.

As for the third step, to finish the enemy off, you parked your fleet in a high orbit around the gas giant. Just like Ken, you went into orbit retrograde to the enemy, however, unlike Ken, the fleets converged very close to each other, allowing you to turn your point defense weapons against the outlying enemy weapon systems. Given the relative velocity of the two fleets, the normally slow point defense bullets were quite effective here. And given that the enemy burned his PD ammo during the second step of your plan, they could not respond in kind. After tens of meetings of retrograde orbits, the battle was finished.

You used every missile, every bullet of point defense, and 90% of your railgun slugs, destroying every enemy ship against a loss of two of your own. 98 points."

Every student was now looking at Albert. Sheene gave him a gentle applause. Albert, overcome with pride, forgot to check out Diana's reaction.

"Shoot them until they are dead," Albert put his hands behind his head.

"A most appropriate interpretation of the Imperial Doctrine. You could have achieved a perfect score if you also implemented a custom missile evasion code, like Sunnak's, or piloted the ships manually." Kariel said.

"I was short on real-life time," Albert defended himself.

"Of course, this is truly impressive, and you have earned yourself a spot designing future challenges." Kariel couldn't hide his excitement anymore and saluted Albert.

"Hold on a second, are you accepting the code exploit as legitimate?" Max was visibly upset.

"Fear is a powerful tool, especially against the machine," Albert quipped back.

"Unbelievable. What hubris," Max sighed.

"Now, as to the question of this 'exploit'", Kariel made air quotes with his fingers. "Whether the test was exploited or not is irrelevant to the next action. To truly determine your actual skill level, you will face a far more difficult test."

Albert was confident, "I am ready."

"Of course, anything using a combat computer is off the table," Kariel said, "The next test is a one-on-one fight against me."

"OK," Albert wasn't expecting this. Kariel was in the top ten of the entire system, ahead of most ship captains. He was already one of the youngest people to ever reach this status, even counting the last few terraforming hops. Albert felt a little excited that he would even be considered for the match, but also fearful of his likely fate.

"Oh, yeah, you're going to make short work of him, Kariel?" Max said, his excitement evident in his tone and demeanor.

"Probably," Kariel responded.

In the hallway after the test, Max closed in on Albert with Sunnak flanking him.

"Hey you, you can't be doing this." Max waved his hands at Albert.

Albert was confused, "Doing what?"

"You can't be writing your fancy shmancy software to be that good at tests. I don't want to get a visit from the Inquisition due to being in the same class as a lawbreaker," Max moved uncomfortably closer. Ken noticed the situation and moved closer to them as well. Sunnak gave Ken a look from head to toe. Ken responded with the same.

Albert thought to himself, "Just because a piece of software is better than you, doesn't mean it's smart enough to be illegal." Instead, he said, "I hear your concern, but I am confident this is in regulation. I can ask a teacher to double-check next time, how about that?"

Max took a step back and loudly proclaimed, "You better." He spun around and then very abruptly turned back, adding, "And one more thing. Don't you dare quote the First Emperor again. That is a citizen prerogative."

Albert has never heard this idea before. Albert raised his hand palms facing Max, "OK, OK. Thank you for the information."

Max stood upright and barked, "You are welcome."

Sunnak sneered at Ken. Him and Max left. Albert stood still, a little bit shook.

Ken smirked at Albert, "We could have taken them, you know."

Albert was not confident at all about it, but he appreciated the gesture. He let out a long sigh of air and then another. And one more. After he was finished with five sighs, Sheene walked up to him and asked, "Hey, this might not be the best time, but I want to ask you about the test."

"I am OK," Albert lied. "What's the question?"

"Well, how did you manage to calculate the right burns for your missiles? It was very hard to me."

Albert got excited about the question, "Well how did you approach it?"

Sheene said, "The three-body system didn't match up to any known periodic solutions, so I just used a numerical method, iterating over all possible burns for each missile in a sort of generalized multidimensional binary search."

Albert responded, "It's a reasonable strategy, but without further optimization, this will still exhaust your allotted computation cycles."

"It did, that's why the misses happened," Sheene confirmed.

Albert breathed normally and was fully back in his 'teaching mode', "What I did was reason backward from the hits, instead of calculating from the point of view of the missile firing forwards. I assumed a hit on one of the ships, did a similar multi-d binary search over the speed and angle at the moment, and effectively ran the simulation backward. The computation gave me the proper orbital paths. I could then re-use multiple paths, so I didn't have to re-calculate per missile."

"Damn, now that you say it, it sounds so obvious. Thanks." she gently touched his elbow.

"You are welcome, good job either way," he touched her arm back.

Albert checked his handheld for an Academy map.

"Where you off to next?" Ken asked.

"Kariel's office. I do want to clarify the software rules." Albert responded.

Kariel's office was the simplest office Albert had ever seen. A foldable holo monitor with foldable keyboard controls sat atop a wooden desk, accompanied by a single cup of water on its surface. The bathroom door featured a pull-up bar mounted to the top, and beyond it lay only a towel and a toothbrush. In the corner of the office, a large backpack lay open, which Albert guessed contained the rest of the stuff that Kariel owned.

Impressed by the implied minimalism. Albert asked, "Just to be sure, were any of the simulation solutions getting close to being a problem with the general intelligence ban?"

Kariel laughed. Albert was waiting for an answer. Kariel kept laughing. Albert continued, "I didn't think so, it's just Max seemed to be really confused about it."

Kariel smiled back, "Bro, this is the funniest shit I heard all day."

Albert was a little frustrated "I am just asking, it is a school after all."

"OK," Kariel stopped laughing. "We have powerful software that aids humanity in all aspects of life. Our terraforming simulators can predict the climate of entire planets, conditional on drastic changes in ecosystems. Small strike craft and corvettes are completely automated. Compatibility predictors can tell with pretty good accuracy whether a male and female crewman's relationship can last the length of an interstellar journey. A team of droids can build a ready-to-live-in city with minimal supervision. None of these fall under the ban on 'Artificial Intelligence'."

Albert nodded. He wondered about the exact line himself.

"The ban is covered by The Four Laws, with the First Law stating: 'You cannot create a machine that has a Will.' It means that an AI cannot have a 'utility function' that points to the states of the world directly. Predictors and simulators are ok."

"So, nothing that happens in simulations can break the First Law?" Albert was glad that his interpretation was correct after all.

"Correct, but you could theoretically fall afoul of the Third or Fourth Laws," Kariel put a very strong emphasis on 'theoretically'. "The Third Law, as written by the First Emperor states: 'You cannot create something you don't understand.' The modern interpretation of the Third Law is that one cannot create something that only the creators understand. However, it is incredibly hard to break, even for a fully resourced Noble House. A singular person making something that complex is completely unheard of."

Albert was glad he was within the rules, but wanted to clarify, "The Cyborg Theocracy did it, and the First Emperor, for that matter."

Kariel nodded, "Yes, The Cyborg Theocracy made considerable efforts in creating dangerous and incomprehensible AIs. And yet, they still would not have managed to kill 20% of Earth's population without the collaboration of the human traitors. The First Emperor occasionally wrote algorithms that only he understood at the time, but it took him years to do so."

Albert remarked back, "And I learned them all before the age of 10 in my linear algebra class."

Kariel confirmed, "Exactly. The bar to breaking the Third Law is much higher now."

Albert was confused a little, "So Max is just making stuff up."

Kariel smirked, "If you haven't noticed yet, Max is your rival, how much should you trust your rival?"

Albert didn't expect such a statement from an instructor, "I am guessing the correct answer is not at all."

Kariel said, "Exactly. From the perspective of being a good member of the community, it's not recommended to tell lies to your fellow students. However, from the perspective of teaching you all about the action-reaction of disinformation and psychological warfare, we allow some tension to exist. Just like we allow you to look at the simulation source code and use it for your purposes." Kariel smiled.

Albert felt annoyed, "Would getting into a fight qualify as educational as well?"

Kariel stood up, walked over to the pull-up bar, and completed five quick one-handed pull-ups with each hand before continuing, "Very much so. The med bays can heal most injuries. But you avoided it correctly, if that was your intention."

"The med bay wouldn't be able to heal my pride or the girls' opinions of me, but I guess that's what he means by most," Albert thought.

"Great," Albert said sarcastically. "One more thing. What's the Second Law?"

Kariel looked to his left and did some thinking for a minute. He and Albert stood in silence. Kariel eventually spoke, "I believe the Inquisition decided that exposing children to the Second Law was not advisable, fearing it would give some daredevils the Wrong Ideas. I will tell you. The Academy can disclose information as needed. The Second Law is 'You should not create a machine that is conscious, pretends to be conscious, or falsely believes that it is conscious.' I strongly suspect breaking it is out of reach, even for a bright young lad such as yourself."

"Thank for the vote of confidence," Albert joked.

"You are welcome," Kariel joked back.

As Albert walked off, he pondered whether he considered Kariel a rival and whether the information coming from him was reliable.

Chapter 12

The Rock and the Hard Place

The recovery of the biosphere is proceeding well. Deer have been taken off the endangered species list. Trials of radiation-resistant corn were successful. New osmosis plants let us increase drinkable water rations by 30%. However, I will require new emergency powers to stop the Plagues and to keep our population from the brink of starvation.

The First Emperor addressing the United Human Nations in his first "State of Earth" speech as the newly appointed head of the Human Security Council.

6.1 MS AA

The Governor was examining his newly built flagship, the 'Spirit of Dawn,' a standard railcruiser with additional comms modules. Brod, the Governor's pilot and supervisor of this ship's construction stood by his side.

The core crew of an over 600-meter-long railcruiser, the size of a 128-story building, consisted of 42 people. 12 crewmen were stationed on the primary command deck managing piloting and weapons. Two secondary teams of 15 each managed maintenance, repairs, and life support.

Most of the routine maintenance tasks were automated. Armor and hull tissue were repaired using nanobots delivered through the nano coolant system. All electronics and wiring were made of self-healing metals. More than two thousand droids on board performed non-routine maintenance in the middle of battle, relaying wire to re-route around damaged areas, manufacturing new particle accelerator tubing, and venturing outside to unmelt barrels and turrets. Robotic vacuums patrolled around the reactor exhaust ports and collected radioactive debris that could separate during hits. Onboard recyclers melted anything too broken down into its constituent metals, remanufacturing most ship parts. Every part has been extensively tested on civilian ships, in simulations, laboratory conditions, and test flights.

The crew's actual task was to properly triage resources in accordance with mission parameters. Questions like "Should emergency power be allocated to a point-defense low-caliber railgun or an ion thruster for dodging?" were among those considered. Via countless simulations, 42 was found to be a balanced number of people to make complex decisions without allocating too much space and energy for life support.

The Governor and Brod were the only occupants of the railcruiser. It was not under thrust, and they relied on their magboots, to allow them to move around with some semblance of 'down.'

They were walking inside the 'central column', which started from the secondary crew quarters, connected to most human-operated portions of the ship, and ended in the command deck. Being centrally located provided both maximum protection from incoming fire and reduced rotational Gs, both crucial factors for survival. Droids were placing small decorative decals along the walls to distinguish the ship. The Governor received a surprise ding on his handheld.

He gazed at it, annoyed, and asked, "How urgent is this? Part of the current emergency? Or a fresh new one?"

"Mostly the first one," the tech replied from the other side of the line.

The Governor wasn't satisfied with the answer and yet singaled for the meeting to proceed. Alexander came on the call with the tech. The tech started, "We have detected a small object originating from Browly. It's only around 35 meters across, moving at 8.2% of the speed of light. At the current trajectory, it would arrive here in around 14 megaseconds [~162 Earth days]. The object intercepted the path of the Browly Menace at the time it was starting to accelerate. The approach vector is similar to the Menace's fleet."

The Governor wanted to confirm, "This 35-meter object was launched from the fleet, yet accelerated ahead of it. Alex, your assessment? A breakaway ship? A fast scout?"

Alexander pointed at the tech, "There is more."

The tech said, "Assuming no course corrections, its trajectory once it gets to our system is different from the main fleet. It's going to be here."

The Governor did not like the sound of that, "Here?"

The tech was feeling uncomfortable, "It is going to hit this planet. If left unintercepted, it would ... "

The Governor interrupted, "Yeah, yeah, I know, wreck half a continent. Alex, what's your assessment?"

"I think it's just a rock," Alexander calmly responded, "They threw a rock at us."

The Governor was more annoyed than concerned. "That's just rude," he said. "If they are going to attack humanity, at least they should have the decency to be clever."

"Yeah, but this confirms it is an attack." Alexander said, looking smug to be proven right.

The Governor wasn't completely sure about this. There was still a remote chance that this object was a friendly ship broadcasting "We come in peace" in some alien language. That this was all just one big misunderstanding. According to the Imperial Rules of Engagement, they had the full right to respond in force. And yet, attacking someone with peaceful, even if mistaken, intentions would put him and humanity in a bad spot. They would either have to eradicate a budding civilization or they would have to leave a war 'unfinished'. Both were massive problems on the scale of galactic game theory.

Standard galactic game theory was simpler than human politics. You were either at peace or war. Humans never started wars. Humans always finished them. The Governor didn't share the concern, because he knew exactly what the Grand Admiral wanted to say and was required to say.

Instead, the Governor said, "This looks like a test of our defenses. It's strange. If it hits, it damages the biosphere and makes it unstable, which is a curious move when one is trying to colonize a planet."

Alexander theorized, "Probably means they aren't as compatible with the biosphere as we are."

The Governor agreed, "An interesting conclusion, which, of course, raises further questions about why they are coming here. What's your recommendation for dealing with the rock? You prefer going missiles or heliguns?"

Alexander responded, "Send 3 or 4 missiles, use old-design fusion drives. Let's pretend we are less advanced than we are. Make sure the drives burn dirty. Uranium warheads."

The Governor liked the suggestion, "Good idea on the dirty drives to make us seem weak, but uranium is overkill. Small deuterium warheads will do." Showing weak capabilities was the right move. Trying to scare the invaders with an antimatter missile wouldn't be effective if their intentions were truly hostile. After a moment's consideration, the Governor continued, "However, let's program the missiles to deactivate if they detect radio signals or life forms on the ship. I want to give our contacts another chance."

"What, why?" Alexander raised his hands up to the sky as if he wanted to point at the Governor in orbit.

The Governor steeled himself for an uncomfortable debate, but then took a deep breath, "Yes, just like you have to consider the worst-case scenario for our system, I have to think from the Emperor's perspective. We follow the galactic game theory for a reason. We give the xenos an opportunity for peace. The laws of karma dictate that how we treat those weaker than us is the same as how those stronger than us treat us."

"There is no one stronger than us in the Milky Way galaxy and probably far beyond that," Alexander said, shaking his head. "But having a turn-off on the nukes will not compromise our defenses. We will have plenty of time to shoot it to bits."

The Governor nodded his head towards Alexander, a silent gesture of gratitude for not being difficult.

"What's the most recent estimate on the tonnage?" he asked the tech.

"The highest plausible value has decreased to around 8 teratons, but the lowest value has risen. We just don't know enough about the density of either the outlying armor or inner ship layout," the tech responded. "We will know better after they decelerate," the tech nervously looked at the Governor. "So did this warrant an 'urgent' designation on the message?"

The Governor valued uninterrupted time to think, walk, read military theory books, and practice combat sims. Interruptions were the clarity killer. It was good that this time was only a railcruiser review. "It did, but only barely," he responded. He wasn't upset at the tech, but his mind still lingered on the fact that he would have to deal with a problem potentially far more serious than altering a planet's atmospheric chemistry.

As a young man, not much older than an Academy student, the Governor faced a choice. One option was to leave his home system of Corial, follow in his father's and grandfather's footsteps, and rise towards Governorship on a new world of Derev, of the Toriad system. Another option was to stay in Corial and be content with a much more chill role, such as being the younger brother of a Governor or a minor Noble Patriarch. At the time, his simulation combat scores were nowhere near as good as now, and he did not even consider challenging his older brother for the Governorship, despite a vastly superior genetic claim. The Governor remembered this decision just now. Had he stayed, and continued to improve in combat sims as he did, he could have been the Governor of Corial, a much more established world, well on its way to altering its designation to a Mid World.

The young Governor made his decision after reading a strange history book of Old Earth sayings and proverbs. All the pieces of "wisdom" just sounded so obvious to him. One proverb said, "It's better to be rich and healthy than to be poor and sick." The one that stood out to him then was: "It's better to rule than to serve." How different his life could have been. However, this was not the time to show outward hesitation. Had he stayed, Derev would have had a worse commander at this moment. His decision was perhaps the Will of the Stars.

The Governor closed the handheld and turned to Brod, "We are putting this bad boy into operation sooner than expected."

Brod asked, "What's the plan, sir?"

The Governor relayed the plan and they made their way to the command deck. The Governor sat in his captain's chair, while Brod took his pilot's seat.

While firing off a deuterium missile at an incoming threat could have been done by a subordinate, the Governor decided this was a fine way to get to know his railcruiser. It was more hands-on compared to his previous plan of going through the missile dry-fire and return sequence that Brod had tested shortly before his arrival.

The Governor sat down to work out the firing solution. It was all the same as the sims practice.

"Can you review the code?" The Governor asked Brod. The code needed to handle the flight path, the off switch, and the new drive signature. The Governor also commanded the droids to replace current warheads with one measuring only 100 petajoules.

The Governor took a comms channel and set it to full orbital broadcast.

"This is the Governor, captain of the railcruiser 'Spirit of Dawn', and acting commander of the Derev Fleet. Be advised I am sending a missile volley at an incoming threat. Acknowledge. Over."

A stream of "acknowledged" from every ship in vicinity flashed across his screen.

"Code looks good to me," Brod confirmed after a kilosecond [~17 minutes].

Alexander confirmed the code as well, although he noted he still disagreed with the decision to put an 'off switch' in case of lifeform detection.

The Governor took his seat to appreciate the moment of the first real fire of a warhead in recent history. He could have been wrong to do this, but no court or Inquisitor would ever condemn him given the information at hand. The Governor allowed himself to feel the makings of history.

'Ready to fire?' he said.

Brod signaled his readiness.

The Governor pushed the button. 5 deuterium missiles moved from the bays and began vectoring themselves toward the unknown object.

On the opposite side of Derev, Idris summoned his brother into a meeting after learning about the potential asteroid.

"I have made a key decision for our House war prep. I want to expand the bunker living space," he said.

"To include how many people?" his brother asked.

"Everyone."

His brother's eyes widened a little, "Tanks were one thing, but that's a different story."

Chapter 13

The Hypothesis

Jail the corrupt. Silence the heretic. Exterminate the mutant and, if they prove to be hostile, the alien.

The First Emperor in private speech to the First Members of the Imperial Inquisition.

6.2 MS AA

The Principal presided over the special class. He was impressed by the group's performance on the recent test, seeing as more than half of the other students scored 0 on it, "Today we are doing a special 'situation analysis' exercise of the incoming threat. Normally, I have the right answers to this. In the first part, I would like everyone to share their most interesting thoughts that you have all been undoubtedly mulling over."

Albert had been discussing his calculations with a few students and wanted to go first. He waved a holo-board into the air, "Assuming they want to arrive here with zero speed, we can deduce that the minimum acceleration their ships are capable of is 0.2 g. Given the mass of the ships, the exhaust speed has to be a minimum of 0.6 c, which limits engine designs to fusion or antimatter drives that nearly every species uses. While traveling to new systems, only a few galactic species used other methods of energy storage or laser sails. Neither was capable of moving much mass quickly. Given our assumptions about their design, we likely can find back records of anomalous gamma ray spikes emanating from Browly when the fleet started their journey. If we don't see such a spike or see a star emission anomaly instead, it is likely the fleet did their initial burst while close to a star, making it more probable they didn't want to be detected."

Albert sat down to several nods.

Ken presented his research on the Browly system chemical composition. He noted that it contained both iron and titanium, which are common components of outlying spaceship armor. However, it did not contain much uranium or deuterium. This likely means they had to synthesize all the nuclear fuel. This was a surprise to Ken because doing nuclear fuel science is very difficult without naturally occurring elements.

The Principal confirmed, "It would indeed be an impressive scientific accomplishment."

Bishakha was very eager as well, "The pattern of their ships is interesting. They have 11 clusters of ships, each cluster arranged in several circular patterns around a single large ship. While this formation avoids getting into each other's exhaust, there are many formations capable of that. I wonder if this formation symbolizes something in their culture. This could imply that the leaders are on the large ships, the leadership is more centralized than ours, and they think large ships are safer than small ones. I suspect that they disagree with our idea that acceleration is more important than size for ship safety."

Albert was glad to share a group with thoughtful people.

Max came up and started talking, "I want to show the civies what thinking about this problem is all about." Sheene rolled her eyes as he said "civies."

Max continued, "How big is the fleet? What can it do? These are questions for computers. What do they want? What do they believe? Those are the important questions."

Diana nodded to this, to Albert's slight shock.

Max continued, "Do they want resources? Probably. Standard operating procedure for aliens. But why don't they know we occupy this system? We were here first. They probably know. They just don't care. They don't have a proper theory of cooperation or cohesion. In other words, they are stupid. The doctrine of the Early Emperors was that the distance a civilization can travel is directly related to its socio-mental capacities, such as its social cohesion and its capacity to select intelligent leaders. However, historical understanding of alien civilizations has proven those theories partially incorrect. A few species managed to hop over to the next star while still maintaining illusions regarding proper land ownership. As the saying goes, bad decisions come in pairs, pair after pair, pair after pair. So they are going to be bad at commanding ships, and we will easily defeat them."

Yezi declined to speak. She still hoped it was just a mistaken colonization attempt with civilian ships.

Sheene wanted to counter both of the previous speeches, "Most 'mistaken colonization' happens when two civilizations come to the same system within 5 gigaseconds [~158 Earth years] of each other, so there is plausibly a misunderstanding of who owns what. We have been here slightly longer than that. It is wrong to underestimate our enemy. They know they are fighting us, but perhaps they don't know the extent of our conquest. The closest human world to us is Corial, and other worlds are much farther. It's all Border Worlds in the neighborhood. We do not have the imposing megastructures of Mid Worlds. We operate low-tech. We do not project an image of strength. If they haven't seen what a human pilot can do, unaided by a computer, they have no idea about who we are. We best assume they are capable fleet commanders, but they lack information about us specifically."

The Principal sighed, "This has long been an issue with Border Worlds. Our appearances were not nearly as intimidating as our real capacity."

Sunnak adjusted his shirt with a button that shifted color to a darker, more formal blue and changed shape to vaguely resemble a uniform. He began his presentation in a very prepared manner.

"8% the speed of light is a non-trivial undertaking. When humanity took the first leap towards Alpha Centauri, we had to make a decision: send a tiny crew at 8% or send a large ship with 300 people at 1%, taking 20 generations of people to get there. We had to weigh our fear of the faster engine malfunctioning versus the fear of a longer journey morphing human culture beyond recognition.

To solve the question of social cohesion, 20 gigaseconds [~620 Earth years] before the trip, the Fifth and Sixth Emperors designed a 'grand social experiment,' putting several teams of 300 people each underground. They were meant to be cut off from human contact for 20 generations. They wanted to see which ones survived with the most humanity intact. Only one team did. The others had to be stopped early. It showed that the social structure of the spaceship would be best guided by tradition and fanatic devotion to the faith of the Four Masters, alongside a military structure of command. That it was faith and hierarchy that bound us together, just as titanium bound our ships and nuclear fire propelled us forward.

Thus, we picked the option of 300 people going at 1%. The Emperor selected each one personally. The names of those 300 people are forever etched in history and many of our bloodlines intersect one of these people.

However, the Browly Menace did not do that. They went at 8%. How do they have such confidence in their engines? Or perhaps they lack trust in each other. They could have brought an even larger fleet at a lower speed, but they didn't. There are many reasons they could be in a rush, but all of them reflect negatively on them."

Max clapped and Albert reluctantly joined in.

Diana was last. "Hard to follow that up," she said timidly. "However, are we considering the possibility that the fleet doesn't come from Browly? What if the Browly civilization didn't build a massive fleet? It was destroyed by one. Now, I know there are no signs of civilizations in a 3-light-gigasecond radius [~94 light years], implying this would be a very long journey."

Albert expected her to say more, but she stopped there. The Principal looked around the room, "Any questions for Diana?" Max raised his hand, "An interesting possibility, but it still wouldn't solve the problem of why colonize the nearby systems instead of attacking us?"

Diana shrugged her shoulders, "Good question, I don't know."

Albert hated to admit this to himself, but Max was right. The way citizens and civilians looked at the problem was different.

The Principal spoke, "Thank you, everyone. For the second part, let's get into teams to discuss. Max, Diana, Albert, and Sheene go to one team, Bishakha, Sunnak, Yezi, and Ken to another."

Sunnak gave his group a look of leadership. He stated, "Let's discuss the meteor question. Its pathway was direct. It did not attempt to utilize slingshots of any kind. The fleet pathway is basically a straight line between the two systems, however, the fleet does not seem to be aiming at anything in particular."

Bishakha said, "It could aim somewhere as part of the deceleration. If they sent more than one rock in a direct pathway from the fleet to one of the planets, I could calculate the maximum angle it could diverge from the fleet." Bishakha started doing some numbers on her desk computer.

Sunnak politely intervened, "It's an interesting question, but why would we need this, given that we can see the current meteor?"

Bishakha was still calculating, so Ken stepped in, "In case any other meteors are coated with EMF reflectors and have been cooled to get them to tier-1 stealth."

Sunnak was contemplative, "Why would they stealth the other ones if they haven't stealthed this one?"

Ken responded, "They could try to make us believe that they don't have stealth when they really do."

Sunnak said, "Well, it's a possibility, but wouldn't it make sense to simply coat everything to not alert us to the presence of meteors in the first place?"

Ken said, "Hard to distinguish between the two hypothesi."

Yezi leaned in, "I don't think they are ocean-origin creatures like the octozi. Been thinking about this for a while. Generals always get ready to fight the last war. Entire species can rarely get away from this mentality. Their fleet is visible with no attempts to hide. These facts suggest stealth didn't matter to their internal conflict, which likely means they didn't arise in the oceanic environment where it usually does."

Ken asked, "What do you think the directness of the meteor and fleet path suggests about their evolution?"

Yezi paused to think for a second, "They like simple kinetics: railguns, chemical guns, and other varieties. But that's true for most races. Core pragmatism of kinetics is convergent evolution. Only a handful of evolutionary histories favor pure laser or shield combat."

The other 3 students took a moment to understand her. Bishakha finished her angle calculations and the group got ready to present.

Over in the other group, Max looked mildly unhappy with the arrangement. As Albert pulled up a chair, Max mentioned to him, "Just to be clear, we are not doing number crunching here; this is about overall strategy, not showing off your math."

Sheene stepped in, "I think the idea of adding a civilian to our team is to see how numbers can underscore the overall strategy."

Albert and Diana nodded in agreement.

Max exclaimed, "Sure, Ab, you can help put some numbers on the story we understand with these aliens."

Albert was frustrated by the framing and the improper nicknaming but wanted to be polite.

Diana moved on, "We still don't truly understand why they think they can win. Maybe the asteroid is a signal that they really underestimate us."

Sheene weighed in, "Or they want us to think they underestimate us."

Max confidently leaned back in his chair, "What if they are just desperate? What if they feel like they HAVE to attack as a last resort, rather than wanting to?"

Sheene tapped her jaw in ponderance, "If they had a cataclysm and this is the last-ditch attempt to move to another planet, the smart move is to terraform the nearby systems. Something would have to be special about OUR system for this to be remotely worth risking their entire species."

Albert commented, "We do have a lot of minable resources: from the gas giant in addition to habitable and semi-habitable planets, but nothing resource-wise that seems to stand out as worth the risk. Even if their weapon technology is better than terraforming technology. If they can send such a fleet, they would certainly be able to avoid any cataclysm short of a supernova."

Diana continued, "In that case, I wonder about my previous theory of whether they are not actually from the Browly system, and they conquered it while originating elsewhere."

Max asked, "If so, why would they choose an occupied system over an empty one? Or a faraway system over a close one?"

Diana extended her hands at Max, "That's it! Maybe for them it is a close one if they are not from this galaxy."

The 3 other students sat back. Max sounded surprised, "I don't see how this resolves the problem of which system to attack. Why pick a colonized system over an empty one?"

Albert got a tingle of fear, "Andromeda, the nearest galaxy, is around 80,000 light-gigaseconds away [~2.5 million light-years] Assuming a similar speed to their current fleet and rocket equation constraints, they are traveling at most at 0.1c. This makes it an 800,000 gigaseconds-long [~25 million years] journey. Our ships can handle 30 gigas, but metal fatigue, radiation, and cryosleep damage can build up beyond that. To go 4 orders of magnitude is extremely tricky. But if possible, it means a significantly higher tech level and a likely belief they can crush anyone like bugs."

Max suddenly seemed excited, "Hold on, let's hear her out fully. Why attack here out of all places? We aren't the closest system to Andromeda."

Diana answered, "Well, what if they are attacking many systems at once? If you are going to start an intergalactic war, don't go in half-heartedly."

Albert said, "If they started the journey 800,000 gigaseconds ago, they couldn't have known about our civilization."

Sheene responded, "Assuming your theory they didn't, but I don't think they care about other civilizations, given the attack on Browly and the likely eradication of whatever civilization was there."

Max got excited, "It's an interesting theory; despite its low chances, I can give a good presentation of it."

Diana said, "How about I present?"

Sheene tapped her on the back, "It is her theory, after all."

Diana and Bishakha went up to present. Bishakha went first and the Principal thanked her for her remarks. As Diana started speaking about the possibility of the invasion originating from Andromeda, the Principal stood up as if struck by a lightning bolt. He remained standing until she finished.

"I will relay your theories to the Governor," the Principal said.

As the class was wrapping up, Albert approached Diana and excitedly asked, "By the way, I found your ideas to be pretty interesting. How did you come up with them?"

"Thanks, I just, um, thought of them," she said politely and started turning away.

Albert felt a little silly asking this question, Diana probably was not into meta-cognition yet. It was a habit most people picked up around a gigasecond [~31 Earth years] of age.

"She came up with these ideas because of who she IS," Max interrupted the conversation a lot less politely.

Albert sighed. I guess it was back to monk mode. Albert hastily packed his things.

Sheene asked him, "Where are you off to?"

"I was hoping to run some numbers to understand the implications of the hypothesis," Albert responded.

"Now?" Sheene asked.

"Of course. When else?"

Sheene looked around, "Someday I'll get the group together for a lovely activity, but I am guessing it's not today."

Chapter 14

We Need More Ships

We need more railguns.

The First Emperor (on multiple occasions during the Unification War).

6.3 MS AA

Idris stood in the center of his office, which measured 20 by 20 meters and occupied the top floor of his pyramid-shaped primary House building. The main pyramid was surrounded by four shorter pyramids, each bearing a panther crest. Each of these Pyramids was surrounded on 3 sides by smaller ones, and so on, making a square pattern. One could see a neat row of pyramid tops in 8 directions in straight lines from the top of the Idris's pyramid. In front of Idris was a circular monitor about his height, with Deepak's face displayed on it. Idris's secretary sat at a small desk in the corner of the office.

Idris spoke up, his voice measured, "I'm glad you decided to build protective bunkers for your people."

Deepak extended his hand for a high five and said, "I hope that's considered a great endorsement of your actions."

Idris smiled. Deepak was always friendly before negotiations. Deepak continued, "I hope we avoid a bidding competition for building materials."

Idris also needed this deal. "Jointly buying in bulk can be cheaper than doing so individually. Or we can agree not to bid too high," he said.

Deepak said, "Those are fine options, but the simplest idea is just doing off-market trades. Good for good, no cash involved."

Idris was happy that Deepak was the one to suggest this, "If we are going this route, I would need a small gesture of cooperation."

Deepak raised his eyebrow.

Idris continued, "Can you raise the issue of ground troops at the next meeting? If the Governor helps us fund those, we would have more resources for the bunkers?"

Deepak hesitated for a second. "That's a reasonable favor," he said. "How do you feel about the Governorship in general?"

Idris wanted to tread carefully, "Do you mean the succession question?"

Deepak looked at Idris in the eye for a few seconds, enough to try to read the ambiguity of the intention but not enough to prove he was doing that. "Yes," he said.

Idris answered honestly, "The next in line knows us well, but doesn't have the best scores. I can investigate the question of who would best govern us. "

Deepak shrugged his shoulders to indicate he was happy to let Idris handle this. Idris ended the call and looked at his secretary across the room. She instantly caught his gaze and walked over. "Do you need any help relaxing after the call?" she asked.

"No, just a kilosecond of silence will do," he answered.

After his rest period, Tong appeared on the screen.

Idris asked him, "Tong, I will get straight to the point. Have you considered the issue that the Governor's son is not up to snuff on his combat scores? Both you and I can beat him."

Tong was not expecting this question, but he gave it some thought, "Do you have a specific plan for formalizing a succession request?"

Idris hated being overly formal and instead said, "I propose I would raise the issue... privately."

Tong agreed, "Go ahead. I thought you wanted to discuss the bunkers."

Idris said, "Yes. I would be interested in doing off-market or barter trades for your nuclear reactors or fuel."

Tong shook his head, "I am more than happy to sell to you at market prices. Off-market deals are dishonorable and could potentially land us in trouble with the Inquisition."

Idris expected this from Tong, but it's important to confirm his stubbornness, "What they don't know wouldn't hurt them."

Tong was extremely unconvinced, "The Inquisition would likely notice the movement of large quantities of goods. But even if they didn't, I deal in cash, not barter. That is the Li way. No offense."

"None taken," Idris lied.

"Tong was always going to be a challenge." Idris's secretary remarked after the call concluded.

"I need a clear head to talk to the remaining Patriarchs," Idris said as he moved away from his screen and into a large armchair that reclined him into a perfect pose.

"I can help you relax," she walked over to him and touched his head. "Don't worry about a thing for the next couple kiloseconds. Your stresses will still be there." She sat on his leg, "You normally leave the worrying about life to your wife day, today is a me-day."

He moved her onto his lap, "Today is a 'you day'"

The Governor, Alexander and Ernest were gathering for their daily briefing. The office now had an official droid recording the conversations and organizing them to make sure nothing was forgotten. The Governor quickly scrolled through his recent messages, thinking aloud, "Let's see what the Academy folks thought of on this fine day."

"Anything groundbreaking from the younglings?" Alex asked.

"A lot we have thought of: gamma-ray detection, strangeness regarding nearby systems. The calculations are precise and the strategic logic is sound. A good class in the Academy," The Governor responded, "Diana thinks that the fleet could be intergalactic, which would explain its massive capacity and the presumed destruction of Browly."

Alexander said, "I like her. Bold theories and we now have a new worst case. I thought about it, but wanted to focus on the 'average-worst' case instead of the 'worst-worst'. I'm glad the discussion is on the table now."

The Governor stood up and paced a little bit, "How likely is this, really?"

Alexander responded, "Intergalactic scouting alone is extremely difficult and time-consuming. Any unscouted incursion is likely to run into colonized planets and thus be perceived as hostile. I assume this isn't something they care about, because it's an attack. An intergalactic attack would mean they are a berserker species attacking everyone in all directions. A berserker who won a war of all against one in their galaxy and became confident they wanted more somehow. Extremely unlikely on priors, but possible."

Ernest added, "Agree it is unlikely on priors, this galactic behavior suggests a bizarre set of events in their evolutionary history. Somehow they had good enough coordination to achieve conquest, but they lack the theoretical understanding of coordination theory. The Inquisition has shown that given reasonable assumptions about the multiverse, we must treat those weaker than us with respect. It is in the best interest of all human civilization across all the universes, even if we have no ability to see into them. Our 'guests' clearly do not share this understanding, if we presume their destruction of Browly."

The Governor sighed, "An intergalactic travel capacity would imply a significantly higher tech level than humanity. If you factor in the fleet size, it's bad news."

Ernest, cheerful as usual, "We would still have the defenders' advantage."

The Governor shook his head, "I hate dealing with these highly unlikely, yet extremely bad scenarios. It is tough to be right in expectation, without looking back regretfully on whatever choice we've made. Let's get some basics covered. Let's send a couple of new deep-space observation probes in Andromeda's direction and the opposite direction. Even if this is an invasion from our galaxy, but they intend to utilize out-of-plane maneuvers, those probes will be useful."

Alexander looked confused, "Good call, but you think her theory implied two fleets coming at the same time?"

The Governor's chain of reasoning went too fast even for Alexander, so he laid it out, "Even if the fleet is intergalactic and Browly is a beachhead, it is still safer for them to colonize unoccupied systems over attacking us. Especially if the beachhead is the only fleet that came over. A single successful beachhead would not jeopardize their entire intergalactic operation to attack us. Thus, a likely second fleet."

Alexander and Ernest gave him a look of understanding.

The Governor continued, "Now consider the perspective of an approaching intergalactic fleet. If the fleet is civilian, it would see at least some activity in our system and redirect towards the location of the beachhead, or literally anywhere else. They could try to negotiate with us. The beachhead would likely alert them towards that option. Even if the intergalactic fleet is military, they could be cautious as well, unless they have very strict orders to NOT be cautious."

Alexander got the idea, "The standing order of the intergalactic fleet had to be 'engage all' regardless of circumstance."

The Governor continued, "Exactly. Knowing that there was no way to override the standing order, the Browly beachhead would worry about our military capacity and gather enough strength for a secondary attack."

Ernest still tried to look cheerful, but a concern was bubbling underneath the surface. He said, "If this is true, they don't think the intergalactic fleet alone can take us."

Alexander shook his head, "A pretty small plus side for an overall big negative."

The Governor felt the same way. The theory was both somewhat unlikely, but also an uncomfortable possibility to have as an option. It raised just as many questions as it answered.

Ernest looked at Alexander, "Could we have the room?"

Alexander was surprised; still, he saluted the other two men and walked out. Ernest signalled to a recording droid which then also left the room.

Ernest turned to the Governor and said, "I am starting to wonder if The Sirium Incident is connected to all of this."

"This just keeps getting better and better, doesn't it?" the Governor said sarcastically. "Get Alex back and declassify it."

The first words out of Alexander's mouth were, "Oh, a potential intergalactic invasion means your Inquisitorial secrecy bullshit finally ends too, eh?"

Ernest looked him in the eye, "It does. A little. 700 megaseconds ago [~22 Earth years], there was an incident on Sirium. Our research suggests that a parasitic organism brought to the planet by a meteor event is the likely cause of this disturbance."

Alexander responded, "Hmm, the official story was that you traveled to Sirium and caught some scumbags. Why is the parasite portion so secret?"

The Governor could tell Ernest wasn't ready to 'declassify all,' so the Governor stepped in, "Certain details required the highest level of discretion. The bio threat has been contained and tests for confirming the absence of it have been run on everyone in the system."

Alexander raised his hands up in the air, "Without them knowing."

Ernest calmly said, "Obviously."

Alexander was visibly frustrated, "And, let me guess, you now hypothesize this was a first strike by the same Browly civilization?"

Ernest responded, "This is a theory now."

"Jesus Christ, all of this time we could have been preparing," Alexander said, grabbing a nearby chair and holding it as if he were about to hurl it at Ernest.

"Easy now," The Governor said. "The circumstances did not point to an attack. Even now, we can't conclusively link Browly to the meteor. Dangerous parasites lurk all over the cosmos. Meteors are a bad delivery method for bioweapons across star systems. Either they are too fast and they burn up or they are too slow and take a while to travel."

"And which one was this one?" Alexander was still waving the chair.

"The slow kind" Ernest pulled up a heavily redacted report onto the room's hologram. "It arrived on Sirium 17 gigaseconds ago [~539 Earth years], more than 7 gigaseconds before we did."

"They could not have known when we were going to colonize the system, could they?" Alex put the chair down and sat on it.

"Exactly," Ernest said, "Let's ignore the intergalactic hypothesis for a second. Sending a complex cross-species bioweapon to an empty system makes no sense if you want to colonize this system. The speed at which the meteor was traveling, would mean at least a hundred gigaseconds [>3000 Earth years] to get from Browly to here. If this were an attack from Browly, their civilization would have possessed fairly advanced space and biotech long before we arrived, yet failed to colonize systems or even send a droid team to mark their territory. Moreover, the parasite looks local to the system. It is similar in evolutionary history to some native Derev animals, including Krakens. I have done a very thorough search of the Archives we get from nearby systems. As it turns out, the parasite shares some evolutionary history with several animals on various planets in a 7 light-gigasecond radius. This phenomenon itself is a massive puzzle. We have never seen a meteor-based life form seed so many planets in star systems that far away. Some of its trips must have started before the founding of the Empire."

Alexander looked puzzled, "What's the nature of the parasite? And why would it be connected to Browly?"

Ernest paused and looked at the Governor, who nodded to confirm the declassification "It is a mind-control agent with some nasty properties."

Alexander blurted how his next question quickly, "Can it mind-control a whole civilization?"

Ernest reluctantly said, "Yeah."

"Fuck," The Governor verbalized what all of them were feeling. "Browly could have been mind-controlled by this parasite if it has been spreading through meteors for a while."

The other two men were silent. The Governor knew they were on the same page about the implications, but he made it clear, "This severely complicates the game theory considerations on how to handle them. If a civilization was used by an outside entity to do its bidding, we can't just destroy them."

The Grand Inquisitor Ernest tapped his Inquisitorial crest to indicate his words embodied the Official Will of the Imperial law, "Yes, we can."

The Governor appreciated the support, but was still very skeptical that were true, "Hold on, 'the slave race' exemption states that if a species was serving in the military of another under the pain of death, then the 'total vengeance' clause doesn't apply to them. They would be considered 'reformable.'"

Ernest looked surprised at this, "The letter of the law is one thing, but look at the spirit. Being possessed by a parasite is different from enslavement. Once the slave owner civilization has been cleared, the threat posed by the enslaved civilization becoming soldiers against us is minuscule. However, if an entire Browly civilization is possessed by a parasite, we can't simply 'liberate' them. Civilizations too weak to withstand one parasite are too weak to withstand others, including internally created ones, and can always be manipulated toward insane animosity."

The Governor sighed. Ernest's interpretation both made sense and was officially the legal doctrine due to the Inquisition's role. The Governor hoped Ernest would understand the 'vibe' of the situation not so black and white.

Alexander assumed the physical pose, which he usually did before saying "I told you so." Alexander said, "If we encounter parasitic nanoparticles or further underestimate the enemy, I still want nano-weapons as an option. We need to go to DEFCON 1 to authorize those."

Nano-weapons were fairly advanced micro-robots that would chew through specific materials to make more of themselves. They were extremely dangerous, since left unchecked in a populated area, they could metabolize most of the construction material in a matter of a few days. Handling them safely required more precautions than antimatter.

The Governor paused to witness Alexander's sadness over the non-decision and tersely responded, " Duly noted. Onto planetary matters. Ernest, what about the prices? I see energy and concrete price increases. What on Derev is going on?"

Ernest answered, "Idris has decided to expand the underground city beneath his castle. He intends to house everyone living on his land, including civilians."

The Governor was taken aback by the announcement, his concerns now surpassing those he'd expressed during the theory discussion, "What? Is he planning on building underground housing for 40 million people? Wouldn't that increase prices even more than what we are seeing?"

Ernest calmly explained, "They are using stored reserves and making digs only during peak solar panel daylight hours. Right now it is a very efficient operation. But yes, they will have to get more resources to finish before the presumed arrival."

Governor sighed. This was within Idris's power, but it certainly felt like disobedience.

Idris was quite young for a Patriarch, shy of 4 gigaseconds of age [~126 Earth years]. He had known the Governor and played combat sims against him for most of his life. They also spoke at length about the state of the planet and budded heads around different ecological priorities. The Governor's great-grandkids and Idris's kids played together sometimes. But there was always some tension. Idris, despite a young age, had already had 4 wives, with only 2 to 3 children with each one. The Governor, Tong, and many other Patriarchs followed a more traditional Border World morality, having ten children with a single wife throughout her fertile period, which lasted from 0.7 to 3 gigaseconds. [~22 to 95 Earth years]. Four wives for a Patriarch were not enough to be illegal, but enough to feel a little inappropriate, even in the relative freedom of a Border World society. As a result, there was always a little distance between him and the Governor, and the Governor's capacity to predict Idris was not as good as with the other Patriarchs he knew well.

Alexander once again took the same pose as a minute earlier. The Governor was frustrated to alter the system state due to internal politics, rather than enemy information, but Idris's move felt like the final tug towards the decision.

The Governor stood up and sternly concluded, "I don't fundamentally believe either the galactic theory or the parasite theory. But the number of unknowns, including internal ones, is piling up. So I agree. Go to DEFCON 1. Summon the Noble Patriarchs. We are going to need more ships."

"Better late than never," Alexander responded.

Chapter 15

A New Test

This geometry problem is out of reach of modern Artificial Intelligence. This is why you have to study it. If you wish to bend the machine to your will, you must be smarter than the machine.

The First Emperor to unknown (Prior to the Unification War).

6.4 MS AA

"How easy should I go on the kid?" Kariel asked the Principal.

"He is not the only one being tested now."

"Very well, then," Kariel headed to the main combat room.

Albert and Kariel shook hands before entering the room. The Principal tapped both of them on the back and left. The main combat room was a stage with two large tables at each end. There were around 150 empty seats normally filled with an audience. Each table held 6 2-meter-in-diagonal computer monitors and various input devices, including floor-sensitive pads and a body command suit.

Albert has used these before to play robot sims. Such a suit allowed for fine-grained muscle control and gave the wearer more bandwidth and actions per minute. Albert was slightly surprised that the test would require such a device. It implied a significant increase in complexity from a fleet command simulation.

After a kilosecond-long [~17 minutes] adjustment to the suit, Albert's monitors displayed the battle sim. Albert had practiced many sims before the Academy. Most of them focused on performing the tasks of a specific crew member, supervising droids, piloting a ship, or commanding an entire fleet. However, as he was beginning to suspect, this test was "a full planetary control" test, the most complex type of virtual contest they had available.

He had practiced this, though not as much as fleet combat, which is what the rankings of ship captains and citizenship criteria were based on. Albert was slightly surprised. It was as if he was being tested not on the role of a potential citizen member of the military but rather on the role of a planetary governor.

The sim was a simulation of a war between two inner planets and two outer planets in the same system. Albert had command of factories, ground troops, shipyards, and the ability to create new fleets. The sim was real-time, without the ability to be paused. Twenty seconds after the start, Albert got an alert that Kariel's raiders were moving toward his space supply lines. He quickly fired several zoning shots, redirected his supply lines to a safer route at the cost of fuel, and regrouped his fleet to create an anti-raider formation.

12 kiloseconds later [~3.3 Earth hours] Albert's last planet made its final stand using ground-based anti-space rockets. His small and agile frigates hid in the asteroid fields, where his moon once was, conducting hopeless retrograde fly-bys against Kariel's

invading fleet. Once it became clear he wouldn't score any more hits, Albert typed 'good game' to indicate his surrender. He was hungry and exhausted.

Albert didn't expect to win; Kariel was one of the highest-ranked 'full planetary combat' and 'point fleet combat' competitors in the entire system. Even ignoring the economic game structure, which Albert decisively lost, Kariel had near-perfect fleet splits, managing to gain advantages in multiple areas of space without losing major engagements.

Albert's hope to make up for the economic losses with better fleet engagements did not work out. Half the time during the sim, Albert felt like he was drowning. Except for water, there were notifications about attacks, disruptions, incoming threats, and economic damage.

Sheene caught up with Albert at lunch, where he was working on his 'smart paper' analyzing his battle.

"Whatcha doing?" she asked.

"Analyzing my loss against Kariel to see if missed something," he said quietly.

"Can I join?" she seemed genuinely excited.

"Sure."

"Have you analyzed your economic actions with respect to a singular utility function?" she asked.

Albert looked at her with surprise. Normally, she was asking him for help, but it sounded like she was trying to help him. Economic actions in such a sim frequently required the management of multiple resources. Free workers, energy, various minerals, and construction capacity, for example. The most important strategy for deciding between actions would be to assign every type of resource a price and consider the overall utility of such an action. Even if the prices were 'imperfect,' the consistency of an ordering dictated a consistent strategy. "Analyzing your actions with respect to a singular utility function" is something kids learned before 10. It was probably the most obvious possible question, but Albert expected her to start the conversation with something simple.

"Of course," he responded. "Here is the utility function I used and here are the expected values of actions." He swiped his smart paper, which displayed a long list of timestamped economic decisions made in the sim, each with a UI button to display comparisons to alternatives. "In early parts," Albert continued, "economic direction matters a lot, but afterward it's all mostly military-based thinking."

"Okie, makes sense," Sheene replied. "Have you adjusted your utility function by investability values?"

Albert wasn't familiar with that concept, even though it sounded simple. "What does that mean?"

Sheene was excited to explain, "This is one of House Li's favorite economic optimizations. You see, not all accumulation of resources results in the capacity to accumulate further resources. For example, you have built up a bit of energy in the early game but didn't use it until much later. If you focused a little more on mining the asteroid instead, you would have more minerals, which are very investable in factories."

"Sure, but the total price of those minerals coming in is a little lower than the energy. Are you saying that I need to alter the prices to change the utility function?" Albert saw sense in the suggestion, but wanted to get the precise mathematical version of the idea.

"No, you are still using the same utility function, just noting that the minerals are going to give you some return on investment in the future, instead of energy sitting there."

Albert was beginning to understand, "So instead of computing the immediate utility, I have to compute it forward in time a bit?"

Sheene was looking up and to the left as if calculating something, "It's similar to that. If you are specifically thinking of a timing attack, then you do adjust for utility at that time or just 'military power' at that time. However, if you are playing long-term, you need to value resources for what they can give you, not value in-an-of themselves."

Albert was beginning to get it. "This sounds good in theory, but wouldn't that either lead to a combinatorial explosion of possible actions or a self-referential resource formula? And if this is so useful, why is this not part of general education?"

Sheene smiled to indicate those were good questions, "I think one of the later Academy classes talks about this theory, but there is no closed-form solution. Every House maintains an internal set of philosophical and mathematical theories best suited for our forms of governance, and House Li trains in the usage of the investabilty approximator."

It made sense. The Fifth Emperor decreed that 'preservation of knowledge was everyone's responsibility', not just that of the Academies and the Inquisition. That quote stuck with Albert, even though until now he wasn't sure what knowledge the Houses tasked themselves with preserving.

She sat down next to him, their thighs making a soft touch. She activated her handheld, displaying a new program on Albert's smart paper. He reviewed his actions through Sheene's House's investability-adjusted metric, identifying several decisions he could have made differently. Comparing Kariel's economic actions to both simple utility maximization and the new metric revealed that Kariel deviated from the simpler model, with his actions better predicted by a more complex one.

"Damn, seems like Kariel was operating closer to how your theory suggests, though he deviates from it as well." Albert was tapping his hand on the 'smart paper.'

"See, I was helpful!" Sheene exclaimed.

"Yes, thank you," Albert replied, "I will take this into account in the battle tomorrow."

The next day, Albert began the second fight against Kariel. He once again wasn't told what the simulation was, but this time he had a pretty good guess. As he opened the sim, it was proven correct. The simulation was the same as the day before, with him taking the side of the two inner planets. He immediately moved his raiders to harass Kariel's supply lines.

The battle lasted for 30 real-time kiloseconds [~8.3 Earth hours]. Aside from 4 bathroom breaks, the simulation didn't stop, requiring each contestant to average more than 2 actions per second to keep up the competitive edge. During this time, both sides engaged in multiple large fleet battles, exchanging missiles across the entire system. Civilian ships got missile mounts to help defend during supply runs, and drones stealthily captured sensor satellites and reprogrammed them to give false data. Albert's planetary orbit floated multiple improvised mobile Whipple shields deployed around shipyards to block railgun shots and stealth-coated micro-meteors that Kariel was fond of occasionally tossing at his planet from time to time. Landed forces crashed on the surface of asteroids over who could mine them. Custom code for combat navigation around gas giant moons pushed the simulation itself to its limits. Albert used Sheene's estimator to help guide economic and military utility decisions, as well as identify vulnerabilities in Kariel's economic structure.

Zvezda, the Principal's wife, would sometimes bring tea to the contestants along with cranberry walnut yogurt, which they rapidly consumed while staring at the screens.

After 30 kiloseconds [~8 Earth hours] had passed, the screens displayed a single message: PAUSED.

The Principal walked into the room and declared, "I am calling time."

"Time?" Albert said.

"Yes, I didn't expect it to last this long, you have been at this longer than most people's work day on this planet."

"Do we continue later?" Albert asked, his body hoping the answer was no.

"No, you need rest; the students have a day off tomorrow," The Principal replied.

"Oh great, are we calling it a draw?" Albert was excited.

"Honestly, what is your actual position?" The Principal asked.

"My fleet and manufacturing capacity are outnumbered, but an assault with ground forces would be suicidal given the defender's advantage. He would be able to out-macro me eventually," Albert was being honest. He was too tired to embellish his position.

"That's entirely correct, given another half a day of a slow grind he would win. I am recording this as a win for Kariel, but your global leaderboard rankings will be updated based on a computer assessment of your performance."

Kariel sighed.

Albert didn't care to dispute his score. Instead, he looked at Kariel, who was also slumped in his chair, utterly exhausted. This was undoubtedly a victory for Albert. Not based on the fleets remaining or the eventual outcome. It was a victory for himself, as judged by himself. He didn't hesitate in his decisions, he moved with purpose frequently pushing his opponent to his limit.

"Report to medical," the Principal ordered Albert.

At the medical station, the droid examined Albert's wrists and shoulders, "Here is a quick 'relaxation cast' to ease the tension of the battle. Wear it for the same amount of time you spent fighting in the sims." As Albert was adjusting the cast, Sheene and Yezi caught up with him in medical.

"I got an alert for a global leaderboard update." Sheene exclaimed. "Congratulations!"

Albert indicated that he wasn't sure what she meant.

"You haven't looked? You are a provisional 99th planetary commander in the entire system!" Sheene was excited and waved her arms in the air.

Yezi asked both of them, "Impressive, but do you think this will stabilize to a non-provisional rating?"

Albert shook his shoulders. The relaxation cast made him feel the tension that he had been holding on to until this moment.

"I taught him some economics! That's my boy! Pretty proud of him." Sheene said, walking off with Yezi.

Albert came to the dormitory common room after a hearty meal alone. Max and Diana were there.

"Where had you been, working on more exploits?" Max joked.

"I was having a 1 v 1 fight session with Kariel," Albert responded matter-of-factly.

"Exciting, when do I get my tutoring session?" Diana asked.

Max suddenly looked uneasy. "So, how did it go?" he asked.

"I lost, but I did well," Albert was expecting Max to say something unpleasant.

"Good for you. Maybe Kariel wasn't that strong after all." Max's voice sounded uncertain as to who he was rooting for.

Diana rolled her eyes a little. Albert was too tired for further conversation and moved to his room. "Good night," he waved to them.

"Good night," Diana said softly.

"As Albert slumped down on his bed, a thought occurred to him: 'How long have they been there, talking?'".

Immediately, a more powerful inner voice told him, "Who cares about Diana? If you are indeed in the top 400 in the System, you can challenge a captain and earn your citizenship." He let out a deep breath and succumbed to exhaustion, his eyelids growing heavy as he drifted off into a fitful sleep.

Chapter 16

The Price

The government cannot print money above population growth.

Second Economic Right of The Imperial Constitution (Right of Capitas)

6.4 MS AA

Instead of the Hall of the Patriarchs, the DEFCON 1 meeting was convened in the Governor's palace, where his spacious meeting chambers offered customizable chairs on level flooring. The Patriarchs took their seats around a semicircular table, facing the Governor as he stood at its head. The Meeting hall itself was shaped like a cylinder, with a high ceiling that allowed natural light to flood in and illuminate the space.

The Governor began, "In light of an approaching asteroid, we have concluded that this is an attack. I have activated DEFCON 1. We are authorizing nano-weapons. Today I announce a new economic restructuring to allow extra shipyards and ships. As per Imperial Doctrine, we are sticking to building railcruisers to form the core defensive ships-of-the-rectangle. We will produce cruisers as well to allow for larger volleys."

Idris spoke without raising his hand, "Every shipyard, old and new, is at capacity. Every mine will be stripped clean before the

Enemy arrives. Although the raw materials from new asteroids can still help us sustain extra construction, our current bottleneck lies in finding more droid overseers."

The Governor was quite glad Idris brought this up, "We are well aware of this issue. Using the authority granted to me by the extraordinary situation and DEFCON 1." The Governor paused for dramatic effect, "Effective immediately, we are suspending the Second Economic Right of the Imperial Constitution. We are going to print money."

Many Noble Patriarchs looked at each other in mild shock. Idris's face didn't move a muscle.

The Governor continued, "This act will devalue the savings and salaries of many civilians, forcing them to take up new jobs in the shipyards and increase their shifts."

Tong responded, "This will also slash the savings of the Noble Houses."

The Governor said, "Yes, by design. We expect the new situation will cause resources for any optional projects to be reallocated toward fulfilling military contracts. We are also canceling the Imperial tax. All Houses have to make sacrifices, even mine."

Like any well-governed planet, Derev was owned. The Noble Houses, including the Governor's House, held the vast majority of the land. Some land, such as the city of Plasch, was managed by the Governor's family "in the Emperor's name." It frequently housed people rejected from Noble House work, but who were still entitled to the necessities of life due to agreements with nearby systems. Supporting this endeavor was the Imperial tax, a much smaller portion of the House income than the fleet dues. Part of the Imperial tax went directly to the Governor, creating an arrangement where he had a stake in the success of each House.

The Governor spent the prior night talking to Ernest and debating the exact details of the money printing. How much was he willing to give up, and how much did he want to force the Patriarch to give up? There was no need to go through individual assets and micromanage reallocation, however, the macro decision of how much money to print was a tricky one. Print too little, and fewer additional ships can be made. Print too much and there is too much pressure for people to bypass legible economic systems.

The Patriarchs briefly clapped.

Deepak stood up, "While I agree with the decision to boost our fleet, I cannot stand idly by as we disregard our ground forces."

The Governor did not expect Deepak's harsh tone, "The current plan is to engage the enemy far away from the planets. Most ground troops are the responsibility of the Houses, and the latest inventory showed substantial ground-to-orbit weaponry and ground-to-ground forces. It is deemed sufficient."

Deepak refused to sit down, "What if the enemy splits their fleet? What if we are forced to run back into Derev orbit or decide it's safer to fight there? What if? Our troops are peacetime forces, unprepared for this level of complexity. The strain on House budgets from taxation and money printing will be crippling. The citizens of this planet need to feel in control of their fate, not merely rely on the fleet and hope."

The Governor firmly said, "You will be in command of one of the ships, Deepak."

Deepak did not respond; he instead adopted a stern expression.

Alexander leaned over to the Governor and quietly said, "Give the dog a cheap bone and he'll chew on it for days."

The Governor considered Alexander's words and looked at Deepak. "Your request has been noted," he said. "I will triple our surface-to-air interceptors and commission extra atmospheric remote-controlled drones."

Our current force of drones is around 1 million, how about we boost that to 70 million? This would enable every adult citizen of every Noble House not already involved in the military to serve as a remote drone pilot. The drones would also boost our ground-to-orbit interception capability in the unlikely case that enemy ships are in close orbit. Is this addition to planet-side defenses satisfactory to the Noble House of Gupta?"

"It is," Deepak said.

The Governor did not seem convinced this was genuine, "Anyone else?"

Tong raised his hand, "Since the new gas scoopers and haulers have come online from our House, the deuterium production will be bottlenecked by the particle accelerators on the Will of the Star. They are at full capacity."

The Governor knew about this, but wasn't sure how to proceed, "Surely the Noble House of Li can solve this problem and provide the fleet with the nukes we need." The Governor hoped he would not need to micro-manage this, but was afraid the Patriarchs would not easily find a solution. Tong breathed out heavily without responding.

The formal part of the meeting soon came to a close. The far trickier informal part began. The Patriarchs mingled in the reception area, surrounded by food and cheerful waitresses, who would normally be getting a lot more attention.

Deepak walked up to Idris, who put a reassuring hand on his shoulder. "That was a brave thing you did," Idris said.

Deepak shook his head a little, "He got rid of me the cheapest way he could."

Idris cheered him up, "Take the small win. Atmospheric drones are cheap cannon fodder, but we have a lot of them. My underground bunkers are proceeding well. We are drafting plans for an underground train system connecting all Noble House bunkers, just in case the above-ground ones suffer malfunctions. You want in?"

Deepak said, "Sure. By the way, I heard from Sunnak, that Max almost broke his old man's Academy sim flight record. The apple doesn't fall far from the tree."

Idris smiled and said, "It doesn't. He still has time to improve."

Deepak said, "As do you, before the Enemy arrives."

Idris cheered up a little, "Of course, Max has good friends to learn from. I heard Sunnak is doing well as well."

Deepak responded, "Second-best score on a custom 3-body combat test, I am most pleased."

Idris and Deepak gently shook hands before parting ways.

Idris approached Tong and Mencius. They were conversing in Old Earth Mandarin, but upon his arrival switched to Imperial.

Tong addressed Idris, "As a history buff, what do you think the Current Emperor would say about the money printing?"

Idris looked to his left and up as if searching his memory, "On one hand, the First Emperor hung the people responsible for printing money, putting an end to their lies of 'printing was good for the economy.'"

"Hung?" Tong asked.

Idris responded, "Don't know what it means, but pretty clear it wasn't pleasant."

Mencius inquired, "Interesting, why not just shoot them?"

Idris said, "He did plenty of that too. On the day of the financiers' globally broadcast executions, the crowds worldwide reported that their very cores felt lighter and their heads stood high. As if a great weight was torn away from the Earth itself and gravity was no longer as strong."

Tong said, "Poetic, what about on the other hand?"

"On the other hand, the most recent major war against the ironbirds was fought with multiple systems under DEFCON 1 conditions with money printing allowed. Once the victory became certain, they returned to DEFCON 2. Thousands of gigaseconds later, the Emperors and the Core World Inquisitors reviewed the actions and found only minor irregularities. The Emperor at the time decreed that The Victory was worth the Price."

Tong made a polite gesture of respect, "Let us hope any reviews of the Governor's actions also pass the test."

"Let's," Idris finished the discussion.

He then approached Alexander, the Governor, and the Principal, gently tapping the latter two on the shoulders. Idris addressed them, "Gentlemen, I must speak about a matter of the utmost importance"

"Sure," the Governor responded.

"This is about the matter of your succession." Idris said, as he looked the Governor in the eye.

"What about it?" The Governor had been in his role for 1 gigasecond [~32 Earth years] and his term still had 1 more left. His eldest son had been designated per tradition.

"Your son, while a great man, had not demonstrated good fleetwide combat ability in simulations. In times of peace, the Noble Houses would overlook this ... flaw, assuming a great military advisor," Idris looked at Alexander. "However, given the circumstances, it would be most prudent for a successor who is himself also a capable commander in simulations, which unfortunately describes neither of your three sons. We all, after all, have to make sacrifices."

The Governor had anticipated that this question would arise eventually, but he already had more politics in a day than he was used to. He had generated a list of succession options, but had not yet had the heart to begin to narrow it down. The Governor asked, taking only minor steps to hide his discomfort, "Do you represent the opinion of all the Houses?"

Idris said, "You want to ask them yourself or should I?"

The Governor did not like this one bit. It was a way to imply he had spoken with all the Patriarchs without actually admitting it.

Alexander broke the uncomfortable pause, "If I may, Governor, your daughter Anna's husband's simulation ability is quite impressive."

Idris raises his hand towards Alexander in tentative approval.

The Governor smiled, "Oh yes, Anna's husband, Ivan Mishov, and your cousin, twice removed, is that right Alex?"

Alexander smiled back.

The Governor looked at the Principal, "While this is an intriguing possibility, doing so would cede the governorship line to the House Mishov, which is a significant ask. Preservation of the Imperial bloodline is of utmost importance."

"We are on the same page," Idris said.

The Governor did not believe him, but was ok with the gesture. He continued, "Unfortunately, my Dad, the former Governor is too old for this shit. What about you, you want to be next?" The Governor put his hand on the Principal's shoulder.

The Principal smiled, "A great offer, but I am also too old for this shit. If I may, if the test scores are a concern, then Kariel, your grandson, and Ivan's son would make a great candidate. He has solid fleetwide combat scores, but he really shines in the planetary management sims, even despite a small recent decline. He is technically also in House Mishov, but given he is part of your bloodline, he could be readmitted into your House, given the head of House Mishov's approval."

Alexander was ready to negotiate, "A deal can be made."

The Governor relaxed his shoulders, "Kariel is a bright boy with command skills, but he is so young. Did anyone know anything at 1.2 gigasecond years old [~37 Earth years]?"

The men nodded in approval.

The Governor continued, "If Alex and I were to fall in battle, he would need a strong military advisor. I think his father Ivan would make a great Grand Admiral successor."

Alexander was pleased, "A deal will be made."

Idris chimed in, "I would wager that the Patriarchs will be pleased with this decision."

"Fantastic. One quick question," The Governor addressed the Principal, "You said 'recent decline,' I thought the planetary command rankings were pretty stable for the last hundred megaseconds[~3.2 Earth years]: Me, Alex, you, Idris, then the Sirium Inquisitor, and behind him, Kariel."

The Principal raised his eyebrows, "Well, officially yes, but we just had a student, Albert, completely ace all the orbital combat tests. He had a 1-1 with Kariel, which Kariel won, but it was way closer than the experience level would suggest. Hence, Kariel's rating declined. He'll come back."

The Governor was confused a little, "Albert, I don't seem to remember him, which House is he in?"

"He is a civilian student."

"Damn, very impressive. He will be a great asset to whichever House hires him."

Idris frowned a little.

The Governor chatted with the Patriarchs for a while, then headed to review extrohistory predictions with Ernest. Following the money printing announcement, the overall cohesion average dropped to 86 and the civilian-citizen cohesion stood at 81.

"Play it forward," the Governor said, "Let's assume we print the same amount of money again in 30 megaseconds [~1 Earth year] but stop after that and lower taxes."

Ernest pushed a few buttons. Social cohesion began to steadily drop until it reached 72 in 1.7 gigaseconds [~54 Earth years]. For a while, the prediction claimed that society would remain stable, but eventually the simulation acquired a red background color, indicating a 'social point of no return'. After 8 gigaseconds [~253.5 Earth years], the cohesion would drop to 48 triggering a 'crisis', including a potential socio-economic breakdown of key technological chains. The uncertainty range of +- 30 points was extremely high, leaving room for the crisis to either not occur or happen sooner than the prediction.

"That's not good. What's the likely method of decreased cohesion?"

The simulation answered in a standard fashion, "Established money interests will likely breach the current gentleman's agreement to 'not propagandize each other's populations.' Once breached, the culture will decline away from technological competency."

Ernest said, "Printing money is more disruptive than taxes on the social fabric."

That was the theory, but the Governor was glad the simulation supported the theory. "What's the suggested fix?" he asked.

The simulation gave the top suggestion, "If we don't print money again next year, but set taxes to 10% instead of 7% for 200

Megaseconds [~6 Earth years] and then retroactively partially compensate the people for lost savings, social stability would rise again."

"Play that forward," The Governor said.

"Social cohesion dropped to 83 at its lowest point in the next gigasecond, but then steadily climbed back up to 88."

"Ok, good, good," The Governor said. "Wait a second, why is the 'disregard outliers' button checked in this simulation? It wasn't used last time."

"Well, we have a parameter that is causing significant complexity in the predictions." Ernest sighed.

That's not good at all. Extrohistory was a well-tested piece of science and software. Only highly capable individuals or illegal software could disrupt it.

"What's the parameter's name?" The Governor asked.

"Albert," Ernest said.

"Kariel's practice buddy? Could you pull his genetic record?"

"Already have. He has the high-G gene, but no one in his ancestry has had any genetic engineering or gene therapy." Ernest stated in a tone of voice that didn't quite match the seriousness of the statement.

The Governor was shocked, "Wow, wow, wow, that can only be true if he is..."

Ernest finished his sentence, "A descendant of the Third Emperor. Imperial pureblood."

"Direct male?"

"Of course not."

"How did you miss this before?"

"I didn't."

The Empire prohibited the government from messing with people's genetics. The Inquisition maintained that some things are best left to God. However, Inquisitors monitored every person's genetic makeup to catch undesirable drifts early. Genes alter with some predictability. Impurities arise and pass away frequently. Occasionally, genes recombined in just the perfect way.

"Tell me everything," The Governor was starting to see Alexander's point about "inquisitorial bullshit."

"The genetic distance is incredibly close to the Fifth Emperor. Enough to be considered a 'genetic reincarnation.'"

The Governor stood up and then sat down, his head buried in his hands. He was shocked he was only learning about this now.

Ernest asked him, "Do you need a moment?"

The Governor certainly did.

The Fifth Emperor... What a meeting. The Governor searched his blood memory of past lives. Their souls had tremendous karmic entanglement. They coexisted in at least 20 lives across time and space since the founding of the Empire. Each lifetime brought new arguments, new lessons and deepened the soul's friendship despite differences. A part of the Governor wanted to reach out and immediately greet him back, but he knew that such entanglements could only be positive after both people's blood memories were awakened.

Ernest slowly began to talk, bringing the Governor back to the present moment, "I dug into the code of extrohistory and found a few special considerations for the situations when a genetic incarnation arises. Some people are impactful. Their contemporaries and descendants esteem them. However, those impactful people are still predictable in aggregate and subject to the Great Forces. The Great Wheel of the Dharmachakra turns us all as its subjects. With a few exceptions. The Great Kings stand above the Great Forces. The Chakravartin can turn the Wheel of the Dharmachakra in his own way. The First and many of the Early Emperors were such Kings. Extrohistory has a very high variance in predicting them, but manages to do so a little, assuming they are honest people working for the benefit of humanity. However, the Fifth Emperor stands apart even beyond that. He is mentioned very uniquely in the code, treating him as more impactful than any other incarnation in history. And I don't know why."

Ernest looked at the Governor. The Governor knew why. He remained silent.

"I was hoping that your blood memory would give us the information." Ernest said.

"My blood memory is my personal business." The Governor wasn't sure about it, but decided to keep the information until he understood the implications.

"Normally, I am the one keeping secrets. Speaking of which, do you still want to keep the fact of your own incarnation secret?" Ernest asked.

"I do," the Governor was less firm than before. "My legitimacy claims are impeccable without taking my past lives into account. Worshiping me as an incarnation might cloud people's judgment. Should the situation change, I will change my mind."

"I disagree, but I will defer to your judgment."

"What instability is caused by Albert's existence? What happens if the simulation no longer disregards outliers?" The Governor asked.

"In roughly a gigasecond, he will likely rise in the ranks enough for his Blood Memory to awaken. The simulation then considers society to no longer be predictable. It's as bad as if the code for extrohistory came into possession of a highly ranked power broker. The code can't predict itself being used arbitrarily, but how this relates to the Fifth Emperor remains unclear to me."

"Makes sense. Keep the button unchecked. As long as society remains stable after the alien encounter, I can get Albert enough on my House's side over the next gigasecond to keep any instability emanating from him under control. Yes, extrohistory will be less accurate than normal, but still useful." The Governor realized that more would have to depend on his judgment than he had previously expected.

Chapter 17

Emperor's Judgment

God showed me how to do this.

The First Emperor inventing a new type of Railgun (prior to the Unification War).

6.5 MS AA

"I can't believe that the closest city to the Academy is the poorest city on the planet and that we are going there for 'fun'," Max made quotes in the air with his fingers.

"Plasch is a good city. I lived there for the first half of my life," Ken addressed everyone in the train car.

Sheene had finally convinced all eight students in the group to do a long activity together. Now she was happily sitting in the train observing them. The train compartment had 4 seats made out of wood and bison leather on each side facing each other. On Yezi's advice, Sheene picked a train car with no network or electricity to encourage socializing. On one side of the compartment was a large window, on the other, a vintage mechanical clock with 65 markings, each one representing a kilosecond.

"Most of the Plasch population doesn't even own a hovercraft or a helicopter," Max rolled his eyes.

"My dad had a boat," Ken spoke.

"Oh, did it have an engine too or did you just have to move it manually?" Max asked.

"I occasionally rowed it manually. Everyone has their ways of training for high-G." Ken pulled up his sleeve and showed his muscles.

"Fair enough," Max said almost respectfully "But I also can't believe how slow this train is compared to a maglev."

Yezi eagerly jumped into one of her favorite subjects, "Maglev trains have significant Electro-Magnetic Fields; they are not healthy for you. If you want to live beyond the average life expectancy, you need to keep out not just the toxins, but also field influences from your body."

"You know the old Imperial saying, 'It will heal before the wedding.'" Max confidently proclaimed.

Sheene spoke without looking away from the window, "Fancy assuming someone would want to marry you."

Sunnak joked as well," I am sure someone will. Maybe when we get to Plasch, there will be a nice lady just desperate for money."

Max shook his head, "Unbelievable. In reality, all the ladies wish I were a Certified Traveler, so that 3 of them could marry me."

Albert thought, "The marriage laws didn't stop your dad from getting four wives one after another." He didn't say it.

Sunnak looked aside as if to remember something, "Active wartime could mean Space Force personnel get the Certified Traveler privileges."

Max exclaimed, "Fantastic, with my piloting scores, I'll be a part of a crew in no time."

Albert interrupted the marriage talk by pointing at the window,"Look! The bison fields."

The train was chugging along the thick grassy fields, where herds of bison lay in the sun behind a fence.

Bishakha looked at her fork, "You guys feel weird eating your lunch while looking at them?"

Max took a bite of his steak and some cooked kapus, a local plant, "No, why would I? The bison steak is juicy and delicious. Better than the mammoth steak, that's for sure."

Diana pondered, "I hear people of the Old Earth imagined that in their future they would have hypothetical 'bison spheres.' Entire spheres surrounding stars with bison fields on the inside."

Albert was confused, "It couldn't be a sphere, that's not gravitationally stable."

Diana responded, "Yeah, it's not clear what they meant. Maybe some sort of ringworlds at different orbital angles to each other."

Albert wasn't having it, "Still doesn't make sense. You can get a ringworld at the same orbital velocity as its diameter, but that's not enough centrifugal force to provide gravity for either atmosphere or proper bison development. Anything that is a lot faster has both stability issues and material bonding considerations. The atmosphere on Core World Rings is just inside containers, and gravity is achieved with attachable spin stations."

Max chimed in, "I thought they had started a second ringworld in the Solar System, at the former asteroid belt location."

Sheene eagerly added, "I heard that's not a proper ringworld, just a set of cylindrical stations with centrifugal gravity in the same orbit, but they are not connected. They are scaled-up versions of generation ships we use for travel between systems. They do have some bison on them though."

Diana said, "A few systems next to Core Worlds have some reasonably dense Dyson swarms, instead of ring worlds, but that involves taking apart all the planets in the system. Not gonna happen with Earth or Mars."

Max said, "Yeah, that makes sense, they would never take apart the Earth. Too important of a symbol for Mankind."

Ken tilted his head, "Why not? The Sol system took apart Jupiter to build copies of Earth past the Mars orbit."

Sunnak continued, "That decision struck me as strange; they could harvest a lot more energy by putting that mass sunward and expanding their ringworld."

Sheene responded, "Life is not about just having energy. It needs to be used for something. Earth copies, though a little cold at that orbit, have fantastic 1G living space."

Albert jumped in, "Well, keeping the Earth makes a lot of sense. The terraforming software planners need as much data as possible about the Earth's continued function to mold planets to be like it. Every gigasecond [~32 Earth years] the terraforming software gets just a little more efficient. It is highly valuable for the whole Empire."

Max waved him to stop talking, "Yeah, yeah, the data is great, but you gotta appreciate the role as a symbol. Its history, the way the Empire came to be, and the legendary artifacts are still preserved in the Earth's museums. Human civilization would not be able to determine where it is going without knowing where it came from. Just like you calculate an orbit, but across trillions of seconds and trillions of lives."

Diana's eyes widened, "That's quite poetic, actually."

Albert felt similar, but then felt annoyed at thinking similar and then got annoyed at himself for being annoyed.

Ken asked, "It's great now, but what about when the Sun expands, what are they going to do then?"

Albert responded, "They just move the Earth to a higher orbit and when the sun shrinks, they move it back."

Diana seemed intrigued, "How exactly would they do that?"

Bishakha jumped in, "The same way we move ships. Strap some giant antimatter engines to the planet, ferry antimatter from the Mercury solar collectors, and off you go."

Yezi was skeptical, "You can't just strap the same type of antimatter engine onto a non-artificial planet. You don't move as much relative to your exhaust. Think of the gamma rays." She poked the air with her index fingers to emphasize the rays, "You have to use a solar-powered ion thruster instead, get the exhaust to go outside the atmosphere, and fire it only when the rotation is synced at the proper time of day. Much cleaner."

Max sounded grumpier than usual, "That would take a whole petasecond [~32 million Earth years] to do."

Albert suddenly had an insight, "Well, they do have that kind of time, but you could move things faster by strapping an antimatter engine to the Moon and using the Moon's pull to move the Earth."

Sheene looked confused, "Would that ... work?"

Max was not having this one, "No, it wouldn't. You can perturb the orbit of Earth a little, but you'd just knock the Moon away, and you can't use it anymore."

Albert was not sure himself, "Well you could do two tangential to Sun's reference frame burns. One at the Sun-Earth-Moon alignment to elongate the moon's orbit around Earth and the other at the Sun-Moon-Earth alignment to shorten it. I just came up with the idea, not fully sure if it works."

Max said, "Probably doesn't. I would have heard of it if it did."

Albert thought Max was just jumping at the opportunity to knock him down, but didn't feel strongly about the idea.

Sheene responded, "Still a cool thought. We are at the edge of the Preserve."

The grassy fields have ended, replaced by a fenced-off wooden area with nearly 100 m tall trees. A pair of eyes and nose looked at the train and then disappeared into the forest.

Sheene exasperated, "OMG, I think I saw a bear."

Albert was glad the discussion about moving planets was over. His brain was still exhausted from the fight with Kariel.

"Wow cool," Yezi and Ken said in unison.

Diana said, "It still kind of amazes me we bring bears with us journeying across light years."

Yezi was excited to share her knowledge, "Did you know bears are one of the few animals able to handle cryosleep better than humans? The first long-range cryosleep mission from Alpha Centauri to Barnard's star was tested on bears. For some time after the mission succeeded, but before we came over, bears occupied more star systems than humans. We carry them in part due to their amazing contributions to cryosleep research, without which none of us would be here."

Max waved his hand dismissively, "Bears still can't handle high-G as well as a warship crewman."

Diana shook her shoulders, "Well obviously. Do you think House Mishov owns a few bears?"

Yezi said, slightly offended, "You wouldn't say 'own' a bear, that's very impolite. The Mishovs own a forest where a group of bears hangs out. Bears are not the same animals as before, they have been bred to be smarter and more friendly to humans. Bears need space for their huts and dance ceremonies. They get depressed if they don't have a large forest to run around in. Also, on Derev they get chubbier due to low gravity."

The train stopped. Sunnak said, "Oh, that's the stealth shipyard stop. Only planetside shipyard."

The students looked out of the window. Past the train stop, the shipyard building was smaller than a regular factory. It had scaffolding beams ending in the air making a very ship-like shape. Behind the shipyard, a calm artificial lake.

Bishakha asked, "Where is the ship being built? I thought all the shipyards were at capacity?"

Sunnak smiled, "Well if they are currently testing the active camo system, you wouldn't see the ship. The screens can fool LIDAR, let alone the human eye."

The ship reappeared bit by bit proving him right. It had a near-spherical main compartment 30 m in diameter, connected to a 1 m height and 30 m diameter cylinder. The other side of the cylinder had 8 50 m long arms ovally extending as if they wanted to grab the space between them. The arms and the sphere were dotted with circular active camo cells.

"It is good this ship has stealth, because this is the ugliest design I have ever seen." Sunnak joked.

Bishakha laughed.

Yezi said, "I can't believe they have a major factory next to the Preserve, even if it is a 'zero molecular footprint' one."

Sunnak responded, "There is a lot of extra EMF shielding. The Designers know what they are doing."

Yezi responded, "I hope so. it is good to have all the creatures live long lives, not just us."

Max boasted,"I knew there was a ship. Just because your eyes are weaker than LIDAR, doesn't mean mine are."

Albert wasn't fond of looking Max in the eye, but he did at this moment. Minor surgical sight augmentations were common among the elites. They shaped their eyes with an internal muscle relaxer. Some went through genetic embryo selection that enabled yellow and gray light-sensing cells in addition to the usual red, green and blue ones. Albert didn't consider until now, whether Max had special genetics to improve his flight performance.

The train started moving again. The forests stopped, and long kapus fields started, interspersed with a few houses. Automated harvesters and droids worked the fields with a human supervisor in a tower above them.

Ken got up from his seat, "Emperor's Judgment is coming up soon, if you want to see."

All the students got up and gathered around the window, touching shoulder to shoulder.

"On our left now," Ken pointed in the direction the train was moving.

On their left, the Great Imperial Temple 'Emperor's Judgment' was shining due to reflected sunlight. Nearly 500 m in height, it was composed of two vertical metallic columns which were bound together by 5 hollow cylindrical sections 50 m each.

The temple was surrounded by a 30-meter nano-concrete wall with a few towers hosting 40 mm Gatling guns, similar to the point-defense guns of battleships.

Outside the wall and closer to a train station of another route were four busy buildings dedicated to the Faith of the Four Masters. They were styled after an Islamic mosque, a Buddhist stupa, a Christian church, and a Hindu temple. They were 5 stories tall and occupied the same square footage at the base. Small crowds of people were entering each one. The students stood silently until the Imperial Temple faded out of view.

As they sat back down, Diana said, "Amazing. As always."

"Yeah," Albert confirmed.

"My family lives pretty close to here, so went to the stupa for meditation every Sunday." Ken said.

Diana responded, "Must be cool to see an Imperial Temple after your practice."

Sunnak added, "It is awesome. Our temple was close to the 'Emperor's Wraith' as well."

"I know it's not really allowed, but have any of you seen it up close? Walked on the other side of the nano-concrete wall?" Albert addressed the citizens.

Max sneered at the silliness of the question, "Of course not, nobody is allowed to get close except the Temple maintenance crew. I have seen every temple from a helicopter tour, getting as close as allowed."

Sheene rolled her eyes again, "That's cool and all, but aren't they all the same design?"

Max said, "'They are, except Emperor's Light."

The students all turned to him.

Diana raised her eyebrows, "You have seen 'Emperor's Light'? I thought nobody was allowed within 5 kilometers of it."

Max puffed his chest at everyone, "It's pretty spectacular even from that distance."

Bishakha sighed, "Some ceremonies are important enough to be held at the Temples. The Governor was sworn in with his hand touching the outside of 'Emperor's Wisdom.' It would be so cool for a wedding to be held at the foot of one of these."

Sunnak smiled, "If a family would have to have unbelievable social connections, you'd have an easier time renting a small moon instead."

Bishakha sighed again, "A girl can dream"

Yezi sneered at her, "Temples are amazing and all, but my theory is that you can't visit them for your own safety. The EMF fields really close to them are complicated."

Ken asked her, "Can't be as harmful as a maglev."

Yezi responded, "Not as harmful when the temple isn't operating. The Academy canceled the 'Symmetric Neural Fields and The Hard Problem of Consciousness' class, so, unfortunately, I can't tell you the exact effects on your mental state. It is complicated in a very different way compared to a maglev."

The train stopped at the final stop. The student shuffled to the train door, which opened and revealed a large semicircle of people of different ages, mostly women. Three of them carried babies. Albert paused getting off the train. Ken walked ahead of everyone and approached the man in the middle of the group.

"Dad, you didn't tell me that EVERYONE is here to meet me?" Ken asked his Dad.

"Well, EVERYONE in the family is proud of you, son," his Dad responded.

The semicircle separated, making way for the other students. They slowly walked through smiling at Ken's family and receiving smiles back.

Yezi said to a woman, "That's a really cute looking baby"

"Thank you," she responded.

Ken yelled, "Y'all go ahead, I'll catch up."

After Ken left with his relatives, Sheene also said, "I have an important call, I'll meet you after lunch."

Albert inquired, "Watcha doing?"

Sheene hesitated, but answered, "Watching the fire control of the Will of the Star."

Everyone's jaw dropped at the same time.

Sunnak tapped Max's shoulder, "Sorry bud, that's way cooler than seeing Emperor's Light."

Chapter 18

The Backup Protocol

Your duty to humanity didn't end with death. It will end only in Victory.

The First Emperor speaking to a clone of a fallen soldier (middle Unification War).

6.5 MS AA

A generation ship in high orbit around Derev detached from its refueler and began deploying its light sail. The 16-kilometer-diameter sail was maneuvered into position by four thrusters, held by carbon-titanium nanotubes.

As the sail unfurled and began to catch the gentle sunlight, the ship transmitted a signal: 'Ready for laser.' 500 hundred seconds later, or simultaneously, depending on your interpretation of relativistic time, the Will of the Star station received the message.

The particle accelerators aboard the Will of the Star had already powered down, and the crew of the docking station retreated to the most cooled section of the installation. The station trembled faintly as the massive laser began to pivot. Its movement was guided by linear actuators at multiple points along the first 100 kilometers of the barrel, internal rotational wheels within the frame, and a counterweight on the opposite side.

Before receiving the signal, the Will of the Star's firing sequence was approved in a pentagonal control room. Inside, five individuals, each stationed in their respective corners, simultaneously pressed a 'final authorization' button. Prior to granting authorization, they meticulously reviewed the calculations of the 'timing solution.'

The Will of the Star was no ordinary laser. The solar collectors on its sun-facing side operated in two distinct modes: one as solar panels generating electricity, and the other as a precise array of lenses. Each lens in the 1000-kilometer installation had been assembled in a zero-gravity vacuum cleanroom to minimize imperfections. These lenses focused starlight toward the center of the structure. Inside the laser tube, another vast array of lenses collated the light into a single, concentrated beam of starlight. Its efficiency far surpassed that of any conventional laser, especially at this scale.

60 seconds after the message the Will of the Star concentrated the light and activated.

Concentrated light is susceptible to diffraction, particularly over vast distances like the 500 light-seconds between Mirkal and Derev. To counteract this, magnetic plasma prisms were positioned in 20 distinct orbits between the two planets. Each orbit housed between 24 and 72 prisms, each capable of refocusing the light and bending it by up to 10 degrees toward the next prism. The final few prisms remained inactive, as the diffraction required to align the light with the 16-kilometer laser sail was intentional by design.

From the perspective of the ship, 1.1 kiloseconds after the message was sent, the laser hit the sail. While the pressure would only give the ship around 0.1 g of boost for enough time to build its speed to 190 km/s. However, every piece of delta-v counted for the interstellar journey.

The civilian generation ship Enduring Might was returning to the Corial system, its place of origin. Onboard was a standard generational crew of 300 men and women, all either already married or paired through a combination of algorithmic and human matchmakers to ensure 'ship-level' compatibility. Also on board was genetic information for every person in the Toriad system.

The Governor concluded the call with Tong regarding the Will of the Star's operations. Aside from occasional tests, this marked the first time in his term that the solar lens laser had been fired. As such, the Governor personally reviewed the timing sequences. Four of Tong's sons, including Sheene's father, Faen, and most of his grandchildren, were present on the call. Everyone contributed to verifying the calculations to ensure the sail was struck flawlessly. House Li believed in early and hands-on involvement to master such responsibilities.

The 'Backup Protocol,' on one hand, felt a little too cautious, even by Imperial standards. In the highly unlikely event that the system was destroyed, the Empire permitted the entire population to be cloned in other star systems, 'as resources allowed.' The genetic backup had never been used wholesale; it was far more common to clone specific individuals who had died. Still, the wholesale backup provided the population with a sense of security in what was once considered the unthinkable. The Governor signed off the call, happy to witness the laser operation.

Tong, on the other side of the planet, was less enthusiastic. He addressed his family, "This little trip will cost us a ton of deuterium production. If we can't meet the requested quota, our House income will fall short of projections, and we won't be able to cover the budget for the entire staff."

Faen responded, "DEFCON 1 affects everyone. We can't keep all the civil servants anymore. I can draw up a list of the least essential. Some of them you keep around not because they do good work, but out of reverence for older memories."

Tong sighed, his voice tinged with sadness, "It doesn't feel right, kicking your nanny out to become a droid supervisor. It's not really her area."

Faen dismissed his father's concerns, "She supervised me, and I'd like to think I was more complicated than a droid."

Sheene also felt sad. Tong signaled for the call to end.

Faen wanted to discuss the matter further, so he went to Tong's office, "The Governor really fucked us with the whole money-printing business. We held too many assets in cash. We used to be among the top three

richest Houses. You sat in the front row. And now? Our cash is far less valuable, which means we are barely meeting operational needs. We are even struggling to participate in the regular market."

Tong responded, "It's dishonorable to resort to barter and stop providing the Governor with the proper price signals he needs to build the fleet."

Faen looked Tong squarely in the eye, "'Our honor feels very expensive at the moment. Bunker construction costs have skyrocketed. Our relationship with House Smith has become precarious, even if we wanted to deal in the gray market. At this rate, we'll be the only House without a fully functional underground city."

Tong pushed back firmly, "Honor is how we got to where we are. Over the last 9 gigaseconds [~285 Earth years], many Houses have chosen to make deals with us instead of our competitors because of our reputation. Honor has been good business until now. Emergencies are no reason to abandon our principles. Besides, we'll still have the underground city; just not for all civilians."

Faen responded, "Yes, and if our people don't feel that we are protecting them well, they will leave and work for someone else. Some people do good work, but they are less loyal to you than you are to them."

Tong nodded, "Draw up a list of the specialists we can't afford to lose, and reserve spots for them and their families."

Faen said, "This is a good idea, Dad, but I can't help feeling we've mismanaged the war industry. Deuterium production has become too low-margin. We could be making a fortune, but with the Inquisition watching us, we can't set appropriate prices. Being the primary deuterium producer while the Navy is the main consumer became a detriment."

Tong shook his head, "It's not...proper to expect profits to increase during wartime. But do you have any suggestions?"

Faen slowly spoke, "We need to restore the relationship with Idris. If we do, he might buy deuterium at a better price, and we could put together a team that can talk the Governor down in fleet allocations."

"Hmm, what's your actual suggestion?"

"Look, Sheene is in the Academy with his son. She should just take one for the team and get going on the relationship."

Tong shock his head, "I don't think she'll be fond of that."

"She is my daughter, I can order her."

Tong stood up and faced his son. Tong's voice firmed, "No. She is my granddaughter, I am still the head of the House, and I'd rather not give her that kind of order."

"Why, the whole putting her in a class with Max was your idea."

"It was indeed," Tong paused contemplatively, "You can plant a tree, but you cannot force it to grow. Are you with me?" Tong put his right hand on Faen's left shoulder.

"I am."

Chapter 19

City of Plasch

Every empire so far has failed. Most barely make it to 250 years. The Cause has always been the same: mimetic conflict caused by the printing of money. Eliminate the Cause and the Empire has no reason to fall.

The First Emperor of Mankind announcing the creation of Economic Human Rights as part of the new Imperial Constitution.

6.5 MS AA

The students sat down for kraken salads at a cafe. Albert noted how they were three times more expensive than before he'd entered the Academy.

Sheene rejoined the group after lunch, still distracted, her eyes fixed on her handheld. Albert tapped her on the shoulder, "What is it?"

She looked at him and said, "DEFCON one money printing has done a number on everyone's finances. If our House doesn't get our deuterium production up in time, we'll have to let go of a lot of people."

Albert saw an opportunity to tackle an interesting challenge, "Maybe I could do something about it. I could take a look at whether the orbital paths are efficient or not."

"A lot of people have already worked on this," she replied, "but maybe it's worth a try."

The students made their way through the streets. The city layout was standard for a non-House-owned city. The "general living areas" or "complexes" stretched from the train station to downtown, consisting of 5-6 story buildings surrounding a courtyard. Each courtyard had 2-6 gates leading into it and was centered around a large playground for kids of all ages. The buildings housed family apartments, each with at least one window facing inward to make child-watching easier.

Each courtyard unit contained a self-sufficient set of amenities. There was a food store and a cafe where families often gathered for meals. A basement gym, an indoor pool, and a rarely used mini-hospital station were all within a 150-second walk for every resident in the city.

At the corner of each building stood an ornate tower, about two stories taller than the rest of the complex. Each tower was connected to one across the street by a glass-ceiling walkway, allowing residents to enjoy sunlight even on rainy days while visiting nearby complexes. Food and personal items were delivered by a fully automated mini-train cargo system that ran both above and below ground. While most people walked when visiting nearby complexes, bikes, and personal scooters were also an option. The students chose the walking option, passing by the complexes into the downtown.

This layout had been simulated and empirically verified as one of the most optimal housing arrangements for population growth.

Unlike most days, the sidewalks were fairly empty. Only occasional groups of 2 to 4 women shepherded 12 to 40 children on their walks. Sharing childcare among friends and nearby families was common, but on a normal non-DEFCON 1 day, men would have been present, and the ratio of adults to children would have been more balanced. After a pleasant 2-kilosecond walk, punctuated by waving to the passing groups of kids, the high-rise apartments and workplaces came into view. The high-rises were separated from the complexes by a 200-meter-radius central public circle. The square stood empty, except for its primary attraction: a 30-meter-tall statue of the Governor.

The first few high-rises, offices for workers living nearby, were constructed with simple nano-concrete but adorned with ornate imagery of the Four Masters' Faith: the Virgin Mary, a meditating Buddha, a crescent, and Krishna on a chariot.

However, the students were not here for the religion. Their destination lay another 2-kilosecond walk [~33 minutes] into midtown. Midtown was surrounded by an ornate fence and security cameras that disallowed anyone under 600 megaseconds [~19 Earth years] to enter. Midtown had housing for unmarried people from 600 to 1000 megaseconds [~19-32 Earth years] old and was home to clubs, holo arenas, and indoor stadiums.

The four buildings of "Blaze," the largest club, connected their roofs in an arch and projected a 20-story-tall dancing girl underneath it. Noticing they were among the few people walking toward it, the dancing girl paused and winked at them.

Every day since its creation over 3 gigaseconds ago [~100 Earth years], "Blaze" opened all 25 floors of each of its 4 buildings for young people to dance and party. Entrance had to be reserved at least a megasecond [~11 Earth days] in advance and sold out quickly. It also offered "privacy rooms," reservable for 16 kiloseconds [~4.5 Earth hours] and spotlessly cleaned by teams of robots between reservations.

Diana looked at the 25-story tall dancing girl with some measure of "shaking her head"-ness.

"She could use more clothes," Diana remarked.

The dancing girl heard her, as indicated by her holographic hands pointing to Diana, then back to herself. She turned around, shook her hips, unzipped her top but held it in place with one hand. Dropping to all fours, she gave Diana and the students a teasing glimpse of her partially covered breasts. She licked her lips, then stood up and resumed dancing as before.

Albert was mesmerized.

"I thought the whole point of artificial personalities was to have it do what people want," Diana sounded annoyed.

Sheene laughed. Albert held back a slight chuckle.

"It is doing what people want. What the creators of the club want. Probably programmed by a guy to be sassy," Albert responded.

"No shit, Albert," Diana remarked sarcastically.

Albert, eager to continue, said, "The personality profile is trained to generate the highest amount of sexual tension in groups of people, rather than follow a specific individual's demands. It's a fascinating case study..."

"I am ok right now without understanding the details of sassy programming."

Albert was a little hurt to be cut off.

Sheene was still laughing, "I, for one, was super excited to hear Al describe the software implementation of sassiness."

Diana crossed her arms. Albert smiled back and siad, "Maybe later." It was the first time Sheene had called him Al.

Out of the 100 floors of Blaze, only two were open today. They were packed with the most dedicated "Blazers," a nickname for those who used to spend more waking time at Blaze than outside of it. In front of the club entrance, instead of a line, there were two large signs.

The first one read: "Limited hours due to DEFCON 1." The second one said: "Mining, shipyards, droid supervisors. NOW HIRING all jobs, all experience levels." At the bottom of the sign were several automated stations, surrounded by a small group. The stations took handprints, asked a few basic questions, and assigned people to temporary contracts.

"Everyone has to work a lot more now. No fun to be found here," Max remarked.

"Some holo-theaters are still open. People still relax, just less now," Albert responded.

"After 1,000 gigaseconds [~32 thousand Earth years] of no financial inflation in our galaxy sector, prices doubled overnight. That's on top of the 50% rise after the DEFCON 2 tax shift," Sheene remarked with some sadness, "Hope the people are okay."

Albert felt good about her tone; it seemed genuine to him.

"The civilians are finally working as hard as citizens and pulling their weight on the planet," Max said, crossing his arms.

Albert, Bishakha, and Sheene looked at him with mild disgust. Albert missed Ken. Somehow, Max managed to be more unhinged when Ken wasn't around.

"What?" Max addressed them. "You know I'm right."

Albert decided this was a good time to practice mental equanimity in the face of adversity.

The dance floor was partitioned into two sections: the dimly lit "unstructured" or "fusion" dance floor and the brightly lit structured or semiformal dance floor, separated by a thick soundproof wall. The fusion floor was packed with scantily clad men and women showcasing acrobatics and general sexiness, while the semiformal floor featured shoulder-covered attire and orderly rows of predefined movements.

Both sections were connected by hallways to a bar area, where the students sat down. They immediately started getting looks. Even their "casual" Academy-branded clothing was instantly recognized. Groups of girls eyed each other, subtly vying for position closer to the students. Max made eye contact with a trio of dark-skinned girls who were inching nearer and quickly closed the distance.

"Ladies, do you like to dance?" he asked the group.

"Sure," one of them responded eagerly, "who do you want to dance with?" It was clear they recognized the son of Idris Smith, who bore a striking resemblance to his father.

Max paused, looking over each of them from head to toe.

"You first, then you, then you," Max pointed at each girl and gestured to head to the unstructured dance section. "The first one, get yourself a smaller skirt," he commanded.

The first girl pressed a button that folded her skirt. It went from covering halfway towards her knee to barely revealing the bottom of her behind.

Sunnak headed to the bar game area and began impressing onlookers with his dart-throwing skills. Bishakha joined the crowd watching him.

Albert moved to the dark dance floor. A woman appeared in front of him as if from nowhere, like a tigress revealing herself to her prey. She was about a head shorter than him, her body slightly wider. She wore a tight-fitting shirt and shorts that accentuated her flawless hourglass figure. They began to dance.

"Damn, Albert does have some moves. Didn't expect that," Sheene said. Yezi and Diana gently tapped their mouth in approval.

After one song's worth of dancing, Albert's tigress looked him in the eyes, "Let's get off the floor. I know a nice private room here."

"How old are you?" Albert asked. It was hard to tell anyone's age.

"A gigasecond," she responded. [~32 Earth years]

This was a bit older than the recommended dating formula of n/2 + a quarter of a gigasecond.

"I'm 600 megas [~19 Earth years], first year in the Academy," he stated matter-of-factly, curious how she'd proceed.

She tapped his shirt, "Studying war stuff?"

"Studying war stuff."

"Hot," she moved his hand under her shorts to have him feel the skin of her butt.

Albert took a firm hold. She smiled and placed her arms on his shoulders.

Albert decided to ignore the recommended age range. "Okay, let's get out of here," he said.

After Albert disappeared, Diana, Sheene, and Yezi turned to face each other.

Sheene remarked, "Surprised Ken isn't here. He'd probably have fun too."

"Ken doesn't seem like the dancing type," Yezi responded. "Neither am I. All kinds of stuff can get onto you once you're that close."

Sheene shook her head at Yezi, "Come on girl, you gotta live a little."

"I didn't think I'd say this," Diana began, "but I kinda already miss the boys. Wish I were dancing now."

"The sassy hologram got to you?" Sheene joked.

"Yeah, it kind of did."

"Me too," Sheene giggled and bit her lip a little.

Diana asked her "You think the guys here will work up the courage to talk to us?"

"Eventually."

A little later, Sheene was proven right. A few guys put on augmented reality goggles, which displayed the House affiliation and social status above everyone's head. Even if they weren't recognized before, the girls would be known now. Eventually, a couple of guys timidly approached them and led them to the structured section of the dance floor. They propositioned Diana and Sheene to the type of dance where the two partners kept a bit of distance. Yezi followed them, but then sat in the corner observing the fun.

After about 4 kiloseconds [~ 1 Earth hour], Albert came back. His tigress wrote her contact info on a napkin and stuffed it into his pocket.

"Do you want me to give you the money for the room?" he asked.

"Nah, everything else is expensive these days, but the rooms are cheap, no one is renting them. It's on me, sweetie boy," she responded. "Let's meet up again after the war stuff."

"Let's," he kissed her and got back to the student's table.

Albert's internal sense was that there was going to be a low probability of them meeting later, maybe 15% at most. His sense that she cared about this was not much higher.

Sheene gracefully bowed to her dance partner and joined Albert. Diana's face showed a bit of dissatisfaction with the dance quality. Yezi was talking to a boy in the corner with a fairly wide table between them. Bishakha and Sunnak were playing a joint arcade game that involved shooting some robots on the screen.

The group re-gathered. Albert's hair was messy, he had a grin on his face, and smelled of someone else's perfume.

"You just went to the private room straight away?" Diana sounded honestly surprised.

"Yeah, why wait? Isabella was fun," Albert responded. "You made some new friends too. What were their names?"

"What? Albert had a first time?" Max asked.

Albert was almost expecting the disrespect, but was at peace with the world at the moment, "Oh come on, it definitely wasn't the first."

Diana looked up and to the left, "Gerald, I am pretty sure that was one of their names, don't remember which one."

Albert smiled. Academy students were not technically citizens, but were close enough for dating purposes, making Academy guys very popular among the civilian ladies looking to climb the social ladder. It was something Albert would probably take a lot more advantage of if he wasn't feeling the pressure of the potential alien invasion into their system.

Ken rejoined them after lunch, "Let's do a tour of the piers," he offered.

The students took an underground train to the piers. They consisted of two main parts: industrial and recreational. The industrial part had ship construction, repair facilities and fish processing plants. The recreational part held white sandy beaches, generally empty of sunlight enjoyers. Separating the facilities from the beaches was a 10 m wall with 1 cm caliber railguns every 20 m facing the water.

"Local wildlife deterrence," Ken remarked, pointing to the railguns.

"These are enough?" Yezi sounded surprised.

"Well, most of the deterrence is done by the targeted beam 50 GHz towers 2 km from the shore," Ken waved towards the horizon. "Can do a number on the brain of even the largest creatures."

"Sure, but then why have these in the first place? And such low caliber?" Yezi asked.

"Well, these are the final backstop. You don't want the damn kraken to go 'splat' and cover half the downtown. Lots of low-caliber slugs are preferred to something ridiculous like an antimatter bullet."

"Yeah, that would certainly be overkill," Yezi said.

"Well, the price of Kraken salads would go down if it did go splat," Max made a motion with his hands.

"But what happens to the fishermen if they come too close to a kraken out in the water? Weren't you afraid?" Yezi inquired of Ken.

"Well, unless you have one of these nearby," Ken waved at a docked fishing warship with a pair of actually serious 50 cm caliber railguns, "then your best bet is the same as Imperial doctrine on avoiding getting hit."

"Don't be there," she finished his sentence.

"And of course, if you ever go past the microwave beam towers, that implies keeping your engine repaired and in top condition, so that you can 'not be there' faster," he low-key bragged.

"Damn, is that terrifying?" Yezi was trying to hide her being impressed.

"Only the first time," Ken was proud. "I assume it's no different from relying on the quality of your spaceship in a difficult spot."

"Oh come on, these are completely different engines," Max complained.

"Some stuff goes one way; you go the opposite direction. All engines are one," Ken made a motion of spreading his hands far away from each other.

"Unbelievable," Max shook his head.

On the train way back, the students sat tiredly in silence. Yezi's plan to go without the network on the way back was shut down. Sheene got a message on her handheld. She tapped Albert on the shoulder. They gently tapped their handhelds together.

"Here's the House data on our routes," she said.

"Well there goes the rest of this so-called 'rest' day for me," Albert smiled.

"My Dad will be very impressed if you can make any improvements," Sheene said matter-of-factly.

"Well, now this feels like a very personal challenge," Albert was determined to fix the supply routes.

They smiled at each other.

Chapter 20

Succession

Monarchy is the best form of government for this fragile moment.

The First Emperor of Mankind issuing a re-organization of the Human Security Council and Becoming The First Emperor Of Mankind.

8.0 MS AA

Idris was finalizing his train trip. Droids had been using the trains for cargo transport for a few days now, but this was the first time a person traversed the route. The 1,000 km ride on the tracks from his underground city to Deepak's took a smooth 8 kiloseconds [~2 Earth hours].

Deepak was there to meet Idris in the hastily finished underground train station on his end. Droids were still painting the ceiling with a decorative vision of Krishna. Idris shook Deepak's hand and said, "Congrats on the building success so far."

"Indeed. There are only two sets of tracks. This isn't going to be able to ferry 40 million in case of partial planetary evacuation."

"It will not. But it's a start. Do you want to test out the ride?"

"It would be a privilege. Your plan to put Kariel in charge might end up working. What next?"

"Kariel is quite skilled in combat, but his negotiating skills are not as good as the Governor's. Our Houses will be in a good position going forward."

"Careful, Idris, don't take more than God has allotted you,"

"God allots as much as one can get."

"What are you doing about Tong? Will you connect his city to the network? Allow his people to come over in case of emergency?"

"Sure, we can allow his people, but not through the new network. They would have to use existing methods. Planes, above-ground tracks, hovercraft, etc. He should learn not to snitch on us to the Governor."

Deepak responded, "He only does what he thinks is honorable."

"Yeah, that's what makes it even more insufferable. My duty is to my people, not abstract market principles."

Deepak nodded and got into the train car.

***

Kariel came to the Governor's living room. The meeting was not held in an official office, nor did he get the agenda beforehand, since it was too important for the usual formalities.

Camina, the Governor's wife and Kariel's grandmother, was seated on the couch to his left. Alexander, the head of the military and his great uncle once removed, sat on the opposite one, alongside Ivan, Kariel's father.

"What's the occasion?" Kariel asked.

"The question of my succession," the Governor responded.

"Me?" Kariel asked. "At my age?"

"Yes, you. The age is a concern, but we can manage." The Governor was eyeing Kariel's reaction and found it to his liking.

"Here I was thinking I was going to be given a nice easy task of commanding millions of untrained people to pilot atmospheric drones," Kariel joked. "What are the steps?"

"You will need to officially transfer to my House first before I designate the successor," The Governor said.

"OK, that requires the approval of Alex," Kariel knew the law.

"Approval is granted conditioned on your acceptance," Alexander chimed in.

The Governor continued, "Also given your age you will need a Stuart. Someone very experienced in handling Real Estate allocations and other negotiations with the Houses. You will become a provisional Governor in my absence from the planet.

However, the position reverts to me should I come back alive from the battle."

"I certainly hope you do." Kariel looked at his grandfather. The Governor noted that his sadness seemed genuine.

"In the unlikely event I don't, the Stuart Governor will take over and yield civilian authority for 300 megaseconds [~10 Earth years] as you are transitioned into the role. You have the final say in all military matters. Together, you will defend the planet and system as needed."

"This is a great honor. I will accept," Kariel looked a little nervous.

The room applauded.

"Questions?" the Governor asked Kariel, the Future Governor.

"Lots," Kariel responded. "Who is the unlucky fool becoming my Stuart and having to deal with Real Estate allocations?"

"That would be me, sweetheart." Camina, his grandmother, rose from her seat, walked up to him and pinched his cheek.

"That's sweet, Nana," Kariel responded, "I am hearing we have a massive problem with Idris now. He's building bunkers instead of funding ships."

"Yes, it's a little frustrating," Camina added. "Idris is staying within the law, though not in the spirit of it. It is impacting the prices of goods."

Governor was more than a 'little' frustrated with the situation, "Ernest and I have gotten the situation under control. First, labor becoming cheaper relative to money has propagated towards goods he needs. People are saving energy across the planet, working harder. Out titanium production exceeded expectations. Secondly, Idris's shenanigans have been noticed. Ernest has clarified to the Patriarchs that barter transactions between Houses are still subject to the unitax of 23%. They have to give us a portion of one of the resources being traded."

Kariel tilted his head in surprise, "You can't be demanding money for non-monetary exchanges, right? Are they giving you actual resources? Are you taking possession of physical materials?"

The Governor nodded.

Kariel continued, "And how do you use it? Not all bunker resources are useful for ship construction, right?"

The Governor responded, "Generally we sell it to Tong at a small discount. His cooperation in investigating off-market transactions has been most helpful."

"How do the Houses feel about this?"

The Governor stood up and walked around, "Tax is a tax. Law is law. They understand the reasoning. They have had to significantly improve production efficiency, and rely more heavily on droid supervisors to streamline processes."

Camina jumped in, "Don't worry your pretty little head about the politics. I will train you on it. Your skills in space combat will be what earns you the respect of the Houses."

"Very well." Kariel said.

The Governor gestured to Alexander and Ivan to leave. The next section required some more discretion. Camina stayed. The Governor had been briefing her on extrohistory for a few days now.

Ernest booted up extrohistory and went over the numbers, "There are mild concerns about declining social cohesion. Specifically, the civilian approval rating of the Governor is below 90%, for the first time ever. One social media comment said, 'There better be some aliens, or else.' The disruption is expected, given the printing of money. That said, this metric and overall social cohesion are within normal parameters now. Social media comments do not yet require Inquisitorial or even local Enforcer action. Social cohesion will continue to fall, but the background cohesion increases through marriage will eventually outpace it."

The Governor chimed in, "A question for you, though. One of the important variables in the simulation is the chance of a marriage alliance between the Smith and Li Houses. The simulation estimates this at 25%. What's your take?"

Kariel shook his head, "Lower than that. Max has fancied Diana, a princess of House Darien. A little unfortunate, given the way she was looking at me."

The Governor looked at Kariel sternly. A young man misunderstands his position. The Governor calmed himself, "Let him have her, Kariel. You have to give up a lot if you want power. If you are a Governor before marriage, you will have your pick of women."

Kariel didn't look fond of such commands, but stayed quiet. They continued on the extrohistory view.

The Governor relayed the previous discussion, "Our best plan at the moment is to stop printing money as soon as the alien threat is passed, but keep taxes high and re-issue printing compensation."

Kariel asked, "What happens if we continue to print money in this way?"

The Governor was glad Kariel was asking this question, "If we continue to print money in this way for even a few hundred megaseconds, the planet will collapse in some way in less than 8 gigaseconds [~254 Earth years]. However, in 2 gigaseconds [~63.4 Earth years], proper social groups will stop being able to form. Aristocratic heredity will become too decoupled from meritocracy and begin to transfer power through luxury beliefs. At that point, the damage to the social fabric will become irreversible, and the collapse inevitable."

Kariel said, "2 gigas is honestly longer than I expected."

Ernest launched into a history lesson, "Well, in the old days before the Empire, people endured a system of out-of-control money-printing for many gigas, but people are far more sensitive to such oppression now."

"Make sense," Kariel responded. "Extrohistory is a pretty cool tool. Would it be any help in dealing with the Houses? Identifying threats? Figuring out which people's power needs to be reduced?"

The Governor shook his head. Kariel was showing his young age and inexperience with this question.

"No," the Governor informed him. "Attempting to use extrohistory this way is quite perilous. If a specific contender is destroyed, a person stepping into his shoes is frequently more ruthless and dangerous. One does not simply fix instability with coercive methods. You need both finesse and systemic thinking."

Kariel made a face as if he understood.

"There is another issue that could threaten both your legitimacy and the usefulness of extrohistory. Albert," the Governor said. "He is a genetic incarnation of the Fifth Emperor and has a stronger genetic claim to the Governorship than you do, assuming his Blood Memory awakening succeeds."

"I was wondering how he's so good at such a young age," Kariel was coming to a realization. "In case of such a dispute, space sim combat is the deciding factor, and I am still better."

"Are you better than he was at your age? Being this good without Blood Memory is unheard of," the Governor emphasized.

Kariel seemed unfazed, "But why should I even worry about it? If he wins, he wins; that is the Will of the Stars," Kariel shrugged his shoulders. "Assuming he would even issue a challenge. We are friends; he would be content to be a high-ranking captain."

Ernest looked at the Governor. It was a legitimate question. The Governor weighed his concerns internally. Yes, that would be the Will of the Stars, and given his own vs. Albert's genetic distance, this would arguably not even move power that much from his bloodline. However, he worried about the continuity of the state. Like many children of elites, Kariel is reasonably versed in matters of governance for a person his age. A civilian student such as Albert was more of a military leader and not as suitable for political roles. However, the rules of succession took military prowess as being of utmost importance. There were good reasons for that. The goal of all the various succession rules and exceptions was to prevent the situation of a bright military genius denied the proper amount of power and using his skill to take it for himself.

"Your legitimacy is going to become your concern after you ascend. Until then, it is mine," the Governor said. "It is good that you consider Albert a friend. This will become ever more important as time goes on."

"Why does his presence change extrohistory so much? Is it causing instability because the software thinks he will lead an opposition?" Kariel was eager to learn.

Ernest tried to explain despite not fully understanding it himself, "It is less about his desire to revolt and more about the issue of being too unpredictable for the software. A leader capable of being a Dharmachakra Wheel-Turning Monarch defies all the rules, though the Fifth Emperor is a special case even in this category."

Kariel got excited, "I want to review the code for both extrohistory simulation and all combat software we use for planetary defense to help me in the next role."

"Why the planetary defense software? We test them in simulations every year," the Governor wasn't surprised; he merely wanted to know Kariel's thoughts.

"One cannot have power over something one does not understand," Kariel quoted the First Emperor. "I want to know every detail. Do we account for local wildlife in our ground army command? Do we have proper informational gathering processes for when we find out more about the enemy? Does extrohistory include external threats and model their effect on culture?"

The Governor liked Kariel's energy, "Fair enough. I have a team on this task of planetary defense software reviews; I will put you in charge of it tomorrow. However, extrohistory would have to be only you and Ernest's successor." He felt uneasy saying this. Extrohistory was one of the most closely guarded pieces of software in the entire Empire. Giving Kariel access to it felt as consequential as giving up the Governorship, but such is the pain of Succession that every great leader had to endure for the sake of his people.

"I will probably need the Principal's help in dealing with Albert and steering him correctly," Kariel said.

The Governor really didn't like getting too many people involved, but it was likely the right call. "Sure," he said.

"I haven't seen you mention the option of sending Albert on a backup protocol, which would simplify things. Why not give him a pretty assigned wife and send him off to Corial? Most men would take this option. I am not suggesting, just surprised you have decided to keep him on the planet."

"Reducing social complexity through getting rid of people is generally frowned upon. It's a sign of leadership failure. He will be useful even if he complicates the tool," the Governor considered this option but rejected it.

"But why are you not worried about your legitimacy?" Kariel asked. "If being a genetic incarnation of the Fifth Emperor is a proper claim to the Governorship, why aren't you worried Albert could challenge you directly?"

Kariel looked surprised. The Governor saw the look and recognized it instantly. Kariel knew he was missing a big part of the puzzle. It's time. To lay the cards on the table.

"Well, no one's claim to the system is as good as mine. In addition to being a direct male Imperial descendant, I am also a genetic incarnation of a wheel-turning monarch. The Sixth Emperor."

Kariel stood up instinctively in a show of reverence. There was a silence over the meeting. Ernest hesitantly broke it, "Yes, at this level of genetic distance, Horud's claim to the galactic throne is better than most of the Current Emperors."

The Governor was taken aback a little. He has not heard his first name in a gigasecond [~32 Earth years]. Taking certain positions in the Empire meant temporarily or permanently foregoing one's name to become the profession embodied. He gathered himself.

"Luckily for the Current Emperor, I wanted a boring rule, but not that boring." The Governor finished up lightheartedly.

Ernest and Kariel nervously and politely chuckled.

Chapter 21

At a Glance

I see humanity's path clear as day now. Past, present, future. It will be bright for a while. Someday we will all get to meet our Gods [unintelligible]. Make us worthy of [unintelligible].

Final Words of the First Emperor speaking to the Third Emperor.

8.3 MS AA

In the morning before class, Albert knocked on Sheene's door. She was playing with a 5 by 5 by 5 Rubik's cube and left it partially solved on her desk as she walked to the door. She wore cozy pajama bottoms with a pink dragon on them and a sports bra that exposed her midriff.

Albert saw her room behind her. Aside from the surprise appearance of the Rubik's cube, he noticed a small-scale model of a cruiser on her desk, complete with miniature point defense guns and torpedo bays. It was one of those programmable models that used simple drone rotary blades to hover and spin in place, crudely imitating a real cruiser. In the corner of her room sat a plush, chubby dragon. Her spacious bed had a pink canopy.

"Hi... Albert," she said, sounding unsure.

"I did it! I solved your problems," Albert exclaimed.

"My... problems?" Sheene was even more surprised.

"Your House's hydrogen extraction and delivery routes can be optimized! I gotta show you this!" Albert was full of enthusiasm.

"Oh, cool." She waved for him to sit down on her bed and sat next to him, looking at his small holo-projector.

Albert began, "Both the actual scooping and the fuel delivery can be optimized."

"Hmm," Sheene was skeptical. "Go on."

Albert's holo projector showed the image of the hydrogen "scooper" against the background of Zeun.

He waved his hands to zoom in, "The first problem is that the scoopers spend a ton of fuel just to stay in orbit."

"Well, yeah, the scooping process pulls them down, and the radiators are heavy."

"Of course, but Zeun has a number of atmospheric storms that can occur."

"Yeah, we have a weather prediction system to avoid them."

"That's it! You don't have to," Albert said excitedly. "If you predict a particular wind pattern in the storm, it could execute a tangential burn for you, so you don't have to avoid it. You can use the storm to effectively push the scooper upward, saving fuel."

Sheene said, "You want to ride... the storm? It can be as large as half the size of Derev, and they're not exactly uniform. They can move around and spin; it's perilous."

"All of it can be theoretically modeled and predicted. I took the recent data on all the storms, plotted the current course, and made a projection. If this scooper follows this path," Albert waved his hands around the hologram of Zeun, "you can save fuel and have enough left over for maybe two extra nukes per day."

Sheene still looked skeptical, "I assume you backtested your model on historical data, making sure it actually predicted storms in the past."

"Come on, I'm a pro at this," Albert said, almost insulted by the question, but he understood she was doing due diligence.

"That's pretty bold. I'll give it to my Grandpa, but no promises, okay?" Sheene sounded excited. She moved closer to him, and the sides of their legs gently touched, which Albert barely noticed.

"Just wait for the next suggestion," he said.

"Oh, is the next suggestion more or less outrageous than riding gas giant hurricanes to save fuel?"

"It's, well, ... differently outrageous," Albert noted the sarcasm. "It's about the star-ward delivery routes for helium and hydrogen." He waved at the hologram to show the system overall, "The Zeun delivery ship splits some of the helium out and rendezvouses with another Derev-bound ship somewhere around this orbit. However, this rendezvous means slowing down from course and then needing to speed up again."

"Yeah, this route has been looked at a lot of times."

"What if you don't rendezvous?" Albert began to lead into the solution.

"We have to have the helium for the new planetside halfvators."

"Of course, but what if you just drop the helium and have another ship pick it up instead of a rendezvous?"

"Doesn't that cost the same, since the other ship has to match course and speed?" Sheene's voice wavered.

"Not unless you perform a 'split-ship maneuver' at this point in orbit," Albert pointed to a spot in space between orbits.

Sheene had only heard about split-ship in the context of combat maneuvers, but she was starting to get the idea, "Split-ship? You mean blowing up a nuke in the middle of a ship to make two pieces go different ways?"

Albert responded, "No, nothing that dramatic, just an ion thruster version. One half of the ship points its proton exhaust at the other. The other half catches it with an electrostatic shield. You get acceleration in both directions. So the helium part slows down for the approach to Derev, and the rest of the ship speeds up to Mirkal. I solved for the optimal point to do this."

Sheene went back to her skeptical face, "Hold on, it can't be that simple. Someone would have seen this before. If a solution like this hasn't been done yet, maybe there's a good reason."

Albert was expecting this. "So, I searched for this type of solution in the administrative archives of the system."

"Aand"

"This was suggested early on but rejected for a couple of reasons," Albert noticed Sheene was excited he did his due diligence. "First, the ratios of helium to hydrogen delivered were different in their calculations."

Sheene said, "Right, because antimatter production has different mass-energy requirements."

"Second, they didn't think the ions would hit over long distances because of diffraction and electric diffusion. However, since we've mass-produced the magnetic lenses for the Will of the Star, we have extra ones to strap in at this point, which means the ion transfer can be efficient."

"And the magnetic lens receives minimum momentum from the transfer."

Albert affirmed, "Correct, they would gather enough reaction mass and energy in the process to move themselves to the right spot. Of course, the relative location of Zeun and Derev changes every few megaseconds, so I plotted the best lens locations and path."

Sheene was now excited, "Damn, this might work... I'll send the info over and think on it. Good work, but I need to get ready for class." Sheene grabbed him by the shoulders and gently pushed him out of the room.

Albert noted that her push was playful. It was strong enough to get the message but not strong enough to feel upset.

"I was just..." He sort of came to his senses after his "problem-solving mode."

Sheene closed her door.

"Later," she said quietly.

"Later," he replied.

"Did I just miss the opportunity to flirt a little?" Albert wondered to himself.

The next class was an important lecture by the Principal. It was held in the same room as their economics class, which had been interrupted by the announcement. The Principal stood overlooking the rows of students. Many groups had shuffled based on the test scores, but Albert's group never gave up the normally 'rotating' first spot. The Principal was proud of this particular lecture. He dressed in his orange robes, which were only allowed to be worn by high-level priests of the Faith of the Four Masters.

The Principal spoke, "Distance and speed are the fundamentals of space. How far and how fast you are in relation to the enemy determines which weapon becomes most effective. Our ships are the fastest in the galaxy. We dictate the distance and speed. We decide where and how to fight. We act. Others REACT.

Our speed comes at a heavy cost, both physical and mental. High-G sickness shortens lifespans. Decisions in space strain the most capable minds. Or computers, for that matter. The entire social structure of the Border Worlds is built around a distinguished admiralty, combining the best of aristocratic and meritocratic elites here in the Academy.

All to properly answer the question of distance and speed.

As education happens, you master the theory behind each spaceship component. You fight in sims, learn to predict the enemy, test a variety of theories and strategies, and develop new ones. However, that is merely education. Understanding is something else."

Albert was expecting the answer to be something about predicting the future accurately.

The Principal paused and then continued, "What is understanding? Is it about knowing the formulas? Is it about having correct beliefs? Is it about the feeling of being right when asked a question? Is it about predicting the future accurately? No. These are mere pathways toward understanding. You thought you knew what understanding is, but you do not. None of you have ever understood anything. Understanding is a type of sight. A type of vision."

Albert was confused. He looked around the room wondering if he was the only one. He was not. Albert looked at

Ken. Ken gave him a look back, "I don't know what he means either."

The Principal continued, "When you understand something, the understanding becomes indistinguishable from your senses. You see the past, present, and future of a portion of reality at once, as if on a line. A line you can zoom in and out of at will. You see reality as a skilled meditator who can note all the sensations in one's entire body in a single breath. You see it... at a glance."

Albert was only a little less confused, his attention was fully occupied by the Principal's speech.

The Principal snapped his fingers.

"There are four steps towards this.

At first, you learn the words and the concepts that compress reality into simple forms, that guide you along proper abstractions, algorithms, and distinctions.

Secondly, you realize that the words were always a crutch and remove your dependence on them. You 'breach' the verbal layer and operate on causality directly. How your decision reverberates through time, which counterfactual trade-offs are important to consider.

Thirdly, you extend your vision of causality backward through time and understand the forces that created you, the processes that lead to your personality, conflicts, and a sense of self. This lets you see yourself through your opponent's eyes, to see the balance in the act of battle, to see into the metagame and how it reaches and shifts its equilibria.

At the fourth and last step, you finally SEE. You are not impeded by words or a sense of self. You see the ships on your screen as clearly as either a child or a master painter. You sense the connections of the pieces: from the types of screws needed to attach the shield generators to the hull, to the orbital mechanics of long-distance shots, to the sensor components and how software has to adjust to them.

You see it all, in one moment, at once. The arrow of time, gravity, the forces of nature that guide our ships, the forces that guide you and act through you, and the act of seeing itself.

You see yourself as part of the equilibrium, both as an action node in the Great Web of Causality and a product of it. That is UNDERSTANDING. Not a single one of you has ever experienced it, but someday you will."

The Principal looked over the students to make sure the weight of his words was felt. It was.

Albert was somewhat stunned. He had always wondered how different the experience of people so much older than him was. He had spoken to monks who told him, "The path is vast and complex. One life isn't always enough." He wasn't always sure how much "the Path" would matter for his studies or whether he could coast on his raw mental powers and practice.

But the lecture seemed to indicate otherwise. Despite his successes against Kariel, Albert was still missing essential pieces of wisdom. So much so that he wasn't even sure what types of mental states the Principal was talking about.

Albert took the rest of the day to ponder and meditate. He also received an interesting assignment from Kariel to review molecular simulation software for nuclear explosions. It seemed that Kariel had recently become very interested in Albert's input. Shortly before going to bed, he heard a knock on the door. Who could it be?

Sheene stood there. She wore a white top and an unusually short red skirt, looking like an anime character from Old Earth.

"It likely works!" she exclaimed, raising her hands above her head.

"The advice I gave?" Albert had almost forgotten the morning due to the lecture.

"Yeah, we lowered a drone to test the storm, and the wind direction was as predicted. We nudged the scooper just a bit, and it picked up momentum from a nearby small storm. We haven't had a chance to test the 'split-ship' drop-off, but our simulation suggests it will work. Thanks!"

Albert smiled with a giant grin.

"You're welcome," he said.

"My House could probably hire you after the economy stabilizes," she said and gave him a kiss on the cheek.

At this moment, Albert looked deeply into Sheene's eyes. For a split second, he saw her and saw himself through her. This was his moment; there was no missing this one.

He gave her a kiss on the lips.

Chapter 22

Deceleration

Some laws of physics are better thought of as suggestions.

The First Emperor discussing novel spaceship designs.

12 MS AA. 5.5 megaseconds [~64 Earth days] have passed since the DEFCON 1 declaration.

The Enemy began decelerating. Before the deceleration, the anomalous objects were visible only in infrared. Now, they glowed bright with fire and light from engines and radiators visible to basic telescopes.

The Governor, Alexander and Ernest sat down to hear a robotic presentation on the Enemy fleet.

The holo projector displayed 11 massive capital ships, each nearly 50 km in length, surrounded by a plethora of "smaller" vessels, though most of those were still larger than 1 km, the length of the largest human dreadnought.

A robotic presentation spoke, "The Enemy deceleration is at 0.2 G using engines of unknown type. Gamma rays are present in the exhaust. Given the present distance of 1.3 light-megaseconds, at 0.08 c and deceleration at 0.2 G, all the speed will be shed in 12 megaseconds [~4.5 Earth months]. However, they would not reach us in that time frame. Assuming their destination is here, we expect their deceleration to decrease and the fleet to reach us in 20 to 30 megaseconds [~7.5 - 11.5 Earth months]. The current estimate of the fleet weight is 5 teratons dry weight."

Alexander started with the bad news, "There are more ships than we previously saw. We see more drive signatures than the infrared watchtower detected."

The Governor grew nervous at this realization. The estimate of the weight of previously unseen ships was 20 gigatons, small compared to the visible Enemy fleet but still outnumbering the system's resources. He asked, "How did we not see them? Did we look in the wrong direction, or do they have stealth features?"

Alexander responded, "We looked in the right direction, but for most of the previously unseen ships, the line of sight was either obscured or the heat signature was too small. However, this wasn't the case for all the unseen ships."

Ernest suggested, "For those, one option is that they were inside the big ships."

Alexander continued, "A 1 km long previously unnoticed vessel inside a 50 km long one? We think everything above 1 km long is a carrier, which makes the 50 km one a 'meta-carrier'? How likely is that? They probably have some stealth features."

Ernest admitted, "Meta-carriers have been proposed as a concept in many civilizations but never built due to prohibitive costs. I simply have doubts about the stealth."

The Governor remained convinced the ships were standard carriers, holding missiles and drones. Many weapons systems don't scale cleanly with size. Unless on the surface of a moon, you'd want many smaller railguns instead of a few large ones. The same applies to lasers. The bigger the ship, the more likely it is to be a drone carrier, a missile platform, or a multi-purpose class with one of those as a base. However, a meta-carrier, a ship that carries other carriers, is too prohibitively expensive, especially for an interstellar journey.

Alexander emphasized, "The worst-case scenario is that they do have stealth and also have a vanguard fleet on its way here, and we don't know about it."

The Governor worried about this as well.

Ernest reassured them, "They might avoid basic long-range infrared sensors, but the closer they get to the system, the better our detection becomes. We've been pinging Browly's direction with focused lasers, have multiple angles for heat dumps, and very sensitive radiation sensors at the edge of the system. We're well-prepared for any fleet decelerating into us. We'll keep the scopes on the current ships and see if they ever vanish from some but not other scopes."

Alexander countered, "And what if they decelerate to 200 km/s and THEN launch the cold ships inside the bigger ones? We don't have a great way to spot those. We haven't placed quantum gravity sensors or tachyon tripwires."

"Both are expensive," the Governor affirmed. "A gravity sensor sensitive enough to detect something as small as a 1 km ship would cost as much as a railcruiser. Not sure if it's worth it. Avoiding our current sensors requires a very high level of tech, which we don't expect."

Alexander raised his hand, "Do we? Did you look at their armor, exhaust, and radiators?"

"One thing at a time," the Governor said, appreciating Alexander's passion but disliking distractions. "What's the latest on armor?"

Ernest said, "Civilizations venturing out to the stars for the first time generally use steel or titanium for armor. However, spectrometry is inconsistent with iron, titanium, or any metal. They are less heavy than expected given their size, which may mean either thin outer armor or a non-metallic alloy. At the moment, we can't determine the composition and likely won't until we get a sample."

Alexander sighed, "Lack of knowledge about armor means nanotech production is on standby until the likely first engagement."

The Governor reassured him, "Don't panic. Nanotech is a crapshoot anyway. What's the deal with the drive exhaust?"

Ernest stated matter-of-factly, "The exhaust is consistent with either a fusion or antimatter design and ion thrusters. They produce more gamma rays than expected, though. Its temperature is 30 Celsius, much cooler than early humanity's basic fusion drive but not as cool as a dedicated stealth drive."

The Governor focused on the unknown, "What do the gamma rays tell us? They can make cool drives but not clean ones? They rely on internal shielding for some reason?"

Ernest said, "Yes, large ships have a lower internal surface-to-volume ratio, favorable for internal shielding, like a lead liner. But even then, this would increase mass, making the design seem suboptimal. The other possibility is that they don't care about gamma rays."

The Governor disliked expecting suboptimal designs. It felt like disrespecting the enemy. He considered the second option, "They might not care because they're resilient to gamma rays. Why would this capacity be present?"

Ernest shrugged, indicating he didn't know.

Alexander responded, "They could also be altering the drive signature to appear dumber than they are."

Ernest was skeptical, "It's too expensive a maneuver. They're likely not burning at full power and instead prioritizing efficiency. I suspect their top acceleration capability is higher."

Everyone nodded in agreement.

Ernest moved to the topic most surprising to the Governor, "The latest on their radiators. They have them, which means the laws of thermodynamics still hold."

The Governor chuckled. Alexander did not. Ernest continued, "However, the design is somewhat strange."

Strange is bad.

The hologram displayed the massive Enemy ships with the standard glow of engine exhaust pointed toward the deceleration direction. On the sides of each ship, in all directions, were long glowing rods swaying back and forth as the ships moved. Radiators dumping engine heat into space. Each rod had smaller rods, resembling a fractal tree.

The Governor was concerned and his face showed it.

Ernest continued, "The area where the radiators are located had no heat signature until about 8 hours before deceleration started. This implies the radiators are extendable."

The Governor affirmed, "But also fractal...what on Earth? They're thin and massive, longer than the ship itself. I've never heard of such designs. Anything in the Archives?"

Ernest responded, "Well, yes and no. Such fractal, though non-extendable, designs are known for civilian ships. Some considered them decorative, despite requiring more complex coolant pumps. However, this design is considered too vulnerable for warships. With this much mass on thin support beams, a lucky railgun hit or laser could cut off a large portion, if not the whole radiator."

The Governor rocked back and forth at the mention of "civilian," which Alexander noted.

Alexander responded, "The train for thinking this was a civilian fleet left a long time ago."

The Governor still held out a small amount of hope, but this wasn't the time to discuss it.

Ernest waved his hand over the hologram, "But do pay attention to the movement."

The radiators' sway was dramatic, traversing entire kilometers over a few minutes.

The Governor relayed his thoughts, "That looks weird."

Ernest said, "Yes, it's almost like they're swimming through the cosmos."

The Imperial speech code banned such comparisons between life and non-life, but the Inquisitor was above it.

The Governor didn't notice, "But why? It's not like they can dump heat more effectively this way. They're burning fuel moving these around for what looks like no reason."

Alexander corrected him, "Don't say 'no reason'"

The Governor was a bit mad at himself under-estimating the enemy again.

Alexander said, "The energy burned might not be high if they have a good pendulum system transferring momentum inside the ship. If they have an internal transitway, which is reasonable for a ship that size, it could be connected to the outside pendulum."

The Governor didn't think of this option. It would be strange to connect internal ship motion to radiators, but crazier ideas have been suggested for spaceships before.

Ernest moved his calculations on the holo-display, "The general issue is that the radiators are dumping a LOT of heat. Their system for transferring excess heat from the engines to them must be extremely efficient. Assuming they have coolant..." He paused to ensure he had the Governor and Alexander's attention, "It might be as good as ours."

Alexander plopped down on the couch and took his head in his hands, "This is bad news bears. This is just the capabilities they chose to show."

The Governor concurred. They had reasonably advanced drives and thrusters, even if a little dirty. The radiators and armor gave him pause. It was unclear what they were made of or why the radiators were flexible and extendable. The tech level was higher than he expected.

"Something feels off," the Governor said. "More than before."

"Still think these are carriers?" Alexander walked around the holographic representation. "Do you expect changes in our ship composition?" Alexander looked at the Governor, then at Ernest, and back at the Governor.

"I do believe they are, but let's make contingency plans for the case they have oversized weapon systems. I suspect most of these involve falling back to the planet and fighting by the heliguns," the Governor said. "No changes to ship composition. Sticking with railcruisers as the primary capital ship. Both railguns and missiles will be hard to dodge with something of this size. However, we'll have a decent contingent of laser-based destroyers in case radiators prove to be a hot target."

Alexander and Ernest nodded, but the Governor did not detect confidence in their movement.

Having some plan is better than no plan.

Or so the Governor hoped.

Chapter 23

The Dance

Have fun. It's important.

The First Emperor addressing unknown regarding unknown activity (time unknown).

12.1 MS AA

"I just don't understand why, of all things to not get canceled in light of DEFCON 0, the school dance stayed," Ken said.

Albert smiled, "Come on, you can figure it out."

Ken thought aloud, "Do they want us to actually relax a little?"

"Not the main reason."

Ken took another guess, "So that we bond with the girls and have something to protect?"

"Not quite."

"What's the reason, oh wise one?"

"The doctrine of distance. Physical learning must supplement theory."

"I thought we practiced spear combat for this very purpose."

Albert responded, "We do, but this is a more ... refined. How are you feeling about the dance?"

"Not great. Just anxious," Ken said.

"Did you do the medscan today?"

"Of course"

"What did it taste like?"

"Grapes"

"Do it again," Albert smiled to indicate his excitement.

Ken came back from the medscan.

"Grape stuff is good stuff?" Albert asked.

"Indeed."

The dance floor was customarily divided in half. The coupled students were on one side, single ones on the other. Single students would switch partners every 2 to 3 songs. A couple would occasionally separate and go to the single section to enjoy dancing with the other students.

Albert waited for Sheene and was pretty amazed when she walked in. She wore a completely black, but slightly glow-in-the-dark one-piece webkini. It started with a bra on top, interlaced webs across her stomach and lower back attached to the underwear portion of the webkini. She also wore white thigh-high socks, attaching to the top of her underwear on the back. Her skirt was tiny, exposing the top of her butt cheeks.

Albert looked her up and down, walked around her, looking at her from behind, which she smiled at.

"Damn, did that take long to put on?" he asked.

"Easier than a spacesuit."

Albert caught some other boys giving her looks. He was not going to the singles section today. She was all for him. Albert sat on a dimly lit chair and Sheene sat on his lap, which instantly activated him. They kissed.

"When is he going to ask her out?" Sheene semi-discreetly pointed at Ken and Yezi. "She's been waiting for it."

"Patience, it takes some courage for a male civilian to ask out a citizen lady," Albert remarked.

"You seemed to go right for it. All I said was 'My dad is proud of you,' and you took it as a full-speed-ahead green light for 'smooch smooch smooch.'" Sheene shook her head with her eyes closed and fake-kissed the air.

"It worked. Results speak for themselves." Albert put his hand on her waist.

"You know, 'some people' think that you just want to get in my pants for the sake of getting citizenship," Sheene smirked at him playfully.

"Oh, you know that most Academy graduates or their descendants eventually become citizens. Especially with my test scores. I want to get into your pants not because of citizenship, but because your pants contain an amazingly hot ass."

Sheene smiled, "You say the sweetest things."

Albert continued, "I think some people..." Albert gestured his head towards Max, "are just jealous they can't be with an amazingly good-looking lady such as yourself."

"Well, he has Diana," Sheene said.

"I said what I said."

"Oh yoooou."

"But yes, I have been pushing Ken to improve his courage."

"What did you say?" Sheene asked.

"That every girl with a nice body is in a need of a boyfriend."

"Is that a truth?"

"Universally Acknowledged"

"Man," Sheene shook her head in playful disbelief, "man never changes."

"Not allowed to. Imperial decree."

The Principal opened the annual dance ceremony by taking his wife Zvezda's hand and showing the dance progression.

"Damn, the old man still knows how to get down," Max quipped to Sunnak.

The Principal exited the ballroom and left the students to themselves. The lights dimmed, and the firm parts of the ceiling opened up, illuminating the dance floor with only starlight. Learning to operate in the dark was also part of Academy training. The next song started playing.

Albert got ready for the first stage of the dance.

Albert and Sheene began the dance separated by 4 meters. He went left about a quarter of a meter, as she matched him. He went over right about the same distance, all while keeping his eyes firmly fixed on her. They approached each other in a helical pattern, with Albert leading the wave and Sheene following. Unless she decided to stop and alter the line over which they danced, at which point he was following her.

The second stage began after they touched the tips of their middle fingers with their right arms fully extended. Their palms would come into contact and separate. Once again, Albert was leading her, until she decided to shift the circle or direction of rotation. Slowly they would come close enough to clasp hands, as their arms extended.

To Albert's slight surprise and frustration, Sheene then released his hand and moved out of the arm-clasping distance. It's a move that a single girl would do if she wasn't ready for a close dance. Sheene was grinning the whole time, as if wanting to play with him. Albert moved briskly towards her, and then she moved backward. Albert then stopped and moved to the side, restarting the dance pattern.

They moved like this back and forth the entire first song and the beginning of the second one. Sheene seemed to have wanted to drive Albert a little crazy. It was working.

In the middle of the second song, Sheene finally let Albert close enough to put hands on each other's shoulders. There, they stayed, alternating leaning into each other to hold a lot of each other's weight. Sometimes they would grasp right arm to right arm, hand to each other's forearm, and perform a simultaneous spin-kick move in a circle around their joint midpoint.

Albert would glance around the dance floor, mostly to avoid bumping into people, but also to notice movements that other students were doing. At one point, Max lifted Diana and held her overhead. Sheene noticed his look and then took his hands from her shoulders and moved them down her body across her chest to her waist. Albert got down on one knee and picked her up. She flexed her abs, spread out her arms and legs, and he spun her around above his head.

After a few spins, Albert put her down.

"Nice," she said. "I would love to do this in 1 G next time."

"Me too."

After two songs of going through the entire dance routine, Albert and Sheene moved to medium distance with a traditional hand-over-the-opposite-shoulder embrace. She faced him, as he swung her around with his arm, occasionally gently pushing her towards him to see if she wanted to come close. She once again playfully resisted but then came chest-to-chest with him at the end of the third song.

On the next song, they took it a little slower. They were both facing the same way, with her ass very gently moving up and down his pants. Her skirt was so short as to frequently touch him with the bare parts of her cheeks, which completely overtook his attention field.

They clearly taught a lot of skills in Princess school prior to the Academy.

The fifth song was nearing its end. Albert had once again brought Sheene close. She moved her butt up and down him, reaching behind herself and touching his head.

Max brought Diana close to him as well. They faced each other and kissed.

Sheene pointed towards Ken and Yezi in the singles' section. They were still in mid-range dance, not fully embracing each other yet.

"Give me a moment," Sheene said to Albert.

"Sure."

Sheene proceeded to gracefully move through the dance floor and emerged behind Yezi. Sheene then hugged Yezi from behind and proceeded to use her whole body to push Yezi into Ken, which she resisted only a little.

Yezi then spoke to Ken after she was close enough to practically sit on top of his leg.

"Ah, she ... " Yezi pointed at Sheene.

"I saw," Ken said and then proceeded to kiss Yezi, which she reciprocated.

Sheene then gracefully made her way back Albert.

"She'll thank me later," she cheerfully exclaimed.

"Yep."

Sheene kissed Albert.

"4 for 4 in our class," she said very quietly. "Everyone did a good job."

"It is fate," Albert whispered back to her. "Or God only knows what algorithm they used to put us into groups."

After the dance, they excitedly moved into Sheene's room. It featured a recently upgraded bed with a top frame with a mounted silicone mirror. Right as they walked in, Albert got an alert. His mind raced through the information on the screen.

"Omg, we just got the data on the deceleration, so much stuff to look at."

"Oh, is that so?" Sheene asked playfully.

Albert was looking at his handheld. She gently held his left hand. He briefly felt a cold, round object around his wrists, but was a little preoccupied with the information to process what it was. She grabbed his right hand and put it right next to his left after a quick "ptshiick," he couldn't separate his hands anymore. She grabbed him by the handcuffs and the rope attached to them.

"What are you doing?" Albert asked.

"Tying you to the bed of, course."

Albert was intrigued. She tied the handcuff rope to the top of the bed, got two more cuffs, and tied each leg to the corresponding bedpost, "You need to learn to let go of always thinking about the problem. I am going to teach you to think about me for at least a little while. Focus on what is in front of you."

She turned around sat on her knees, gently lowering her ass on his chest.

"The hot piece of ass that you like is here." she said.

"I am looking at you. You can untie me now." Albert wiggled a little.

She once again stood fully above him, looking down. She put her weight on her right foot and gently moved her left toe across his chest, "I will untie you when you are ready to be untied. Relax, tomorrow is a day off; we are not rushing anywhere tonight. Not like last time."

Last time he ripped off her underwear, gave her a spanking, bent her over the bed, and took her from behind.

"Last time was excellent fun," he remembered it fondly.

"It was for you. You barely lasted a kilosecond. And tonight will also be excellent fun. For me."

She got off from him and then climbed in between his legs, with one arm on each of his thighs. She kissed his belly button. He moved his pelvis upward, but she pushed down on his legs.

"Oh, you want to take those off?" she grabbed his pants.

"Very much so." he responded.

"No. I am going to teach you to be patient." She kissed him right above the belly button. She slowly continued upward from his stomach, taking time to pause and gently pinch him, all while avoiding touching him too much under the belt.

"I am going to be a good student." Albert had given up trying to control the situation and resolved to his fate. He was somewhat shaking from a mix of excitement, not quite understanding what she was about to do to him.

After her slow movement from his stomach to his lips, they passionately kissed.

"Very patient," she continued moving her body upwards from his, making him kiss her neck.

"She then shifted slightly to the side." Albert strained but turned slightly towards her as well. His head was close to her chest.

"To start tonight's fun, you are going to take off all my clothes."

"Oh, so you are untying one of my hands after all?" He was confused by what seemed to be her letting him off already but then realized that his confusion indicated she meant something else.

"Of course not," she pushed the side of her bra-top into his mouth.

As much fun as it was, Sheene was done having her way with him after 4 kiloseconds. After which she let him in and spent another 4 kiloseconds slowly moving on top of him. She then untied him, and he immediately fell asleep.

"Not much waking you up after this one," she said and fell asleep next to him.

Chapter 24

Light the Beacons

History, if it exists, will think well of you.

The First Emperor to his superior officer after being given command of a six thousand-strong infantry regiment. (early Unification War)

12.3 MS AA

The urgent message woke the Governor, something that hadn't happened before. He rushed to the palace and entered the tech's room. Alexander and Ernest were already there, their faces pale as snow.

Less than a kilosecond later, the Principal also received an urgent call and woke up. Zvezda, his wife, half-asleep beside him, murmured, "You are not the Governor precisely because we don't need to get called at this time."

She then tried to fall back asleep. The Principal, barely awake, asked questions in a confused tone to the tech on the other end of the call, "What do you mean, a SECOND FLEET? How far out? How did we not see it? Which system is it coming from?"

He dropped his handheld. His body shook. He put on a coat and moved towards the door.

Zvezda was confused, "Where are you going?"

The Principal responded, "I am going outside to get some air."

She moved to the side of the bed, picking up his handheld. In their 9 gigaseconds of marriage [~285 Earth years], he had never quite acted like this. The transcript was still available on the screen. After reading it, she also dropped it.

The final line of the transcript was:

"The second fleet is coming from underneath the galactic plane."

Over at the Governor's office, the three men stood in silence.

"You know what you can do, what you HAVE to do," Ernest spoke to the Governor.

"There is a difference between knowing what the law allows you to do, in fact, REQUIRES you to do AND being the FIRST human in the Empire's entire history to do it." The Governor stepped onto his balcony, his back turned to Ernest.

"The Inquisition is behind you all the way," Ernest spoke to the Governor's back. The dual meaning of the statement did not escape the Governor.

The steel railing the Governor was holding on to was beginning to make sounds. "I know, trust me, I know." The Governor looked ahead into the starry night, past the helium-held launch platforms.

What if they were wrong? How embarrassing would his actions seem to the entire galaxy? What he was about to do would alter the course of trillions of lives over trillions of seconds. How many children would fail to be born? How many people would lose time with their loved ones due to increased work? But what if he were right? Would it even matter? Would they stand a chance against an intergalactic invader? The Governor banished the last thought. It was not a proper thought. It was wrong to think this way. He turned around and with grim determination said the words the other men were waiting for.

"Light The Beacons. We are going to DEFCON 0."

The 3 men looked at the tech, whose hands shook. "Lllliiiight the bbbbeeeacons," his voice was barely legible. His hands moved to the control panel.

Ernest grabbed him by the hand, "Why don't you go home and take a rest? I will finish up here."

The tech looked over at the Governor and Alexander. They nodded.

"I just need to enter..." he started mumbling

"We have authorization," Ernest spoke to him.

"Oh, of course," the tech gathered his things and stormed out of the room.

After a few keystrokes, a special input terminal revealed itself with three palm outlines on it. A sharp needle was inside each outline. A computer voice spoke, "Blood authorization requested." The three men each pressed their palms on the terminal. Blood began slowly dripping from each of them.

"Blood analyzed. Authorization granted. Activating the Beacon Protocol," the computer voice confirmed.

Ernest wiped his bloody hand with a nearby cloth and said, "History, if it exists, will think well of you."

The Governor sat down, his mind racing through the next preparation steps needed to confront the now-revealed threat.

After a pause, Ernest spoke with the reverence and slowness worthy of the moment, "The Sirium parasite did originate from the Enemy. The evolutionary tree of the krakens and many other lifeforms on this planet began over 30 teraseconds ago [~ 1 million Earth years] and shared more with the parasite than with other fauna on the planet. Similar evolutionary tree as several worlds in a 5 light-gigasecond radius." Ernest paused again. "This was an unexplained puzzle until now. The Enemy had sent a life-seeding of lifeforms onto worlds they meant to land on. They have been here for far longer than we have."

The Governor was too shaken to think through the implications, "Good info to consider for the sake of understanding them."

Ernest sighed, "It seriously undermines our claim on these worlds."

"This planet is MINE. This system is MINE. This galaxy is," The Governor had an outburst of rage, but caught himself before he misspoke, "... ours. If they wanted to speak terms, they would have sent a smaller fleet."

Alexander and Ernest looked at the Governor with mild horror, but each still put their hands on his shoulder.

Among the many new items on the preparation agenda, the Governor called the Principal and relayed the Academy's new role in the war effort.

A few kiloseconds later, the students listened to the Principal announcing the conditions of DEFCON 0.

"An out-of-galactic-plane probe picked up a signature of a second fleet with similar ship sizes, profiles, and patterns bearing on our location with an arrival time close to the first. We are in conditions of Total War, all resources for war, all for Victory. All citizens will be called to fight. All Academy students past and present are considered citizens for the purpose of war. Those who pass high-G tests will be in the Fleet, the rest in ground crews."

Albert was shocked to the core. At once, the mysteries of the anomaly became clear. Diana's theory was right. Browly was a budding civilization eradicated by an intergalactic invader. Their radiators, unknown armor composition, and massive fleet were signs of extreme technological superiority. The Derev system was outteched, outnumbered, outgunned. The wheels of understanding began to turn in Albert's mind. Nobody would bother to colonize another galaxy until one's own was fully conquered. Life was common enough in the universe that meant at least several hundred civilizations would have been destroyed by the Enemy. They were facing a committed genocidal armada that, in the millions of gigaseconds, had never known defeat.

Good thing, neither have humans.

A kilosecond later [~17 Earth minutes], the students stood in the Academy hallways, discussing the announcement. The Principal's handheld buzzed, and then everyone's handheld buzzed at the same time.

Some students immediately began pointing in a direction in the sky, and then everybody crowded next to a window. Despite the rising sun, a new star-like light was visible in the sky, and after the initial confusion, the students and teachers all stood silently looking in that direction, with many tears streaming down their cheeks. The message delivered to everyone in the system was:

"The Beacons are Lit."

There are a few ways to send information across star systems. No regular forms of communication stretched that far.

The ones humans used most were "information ships", which were fast automated crewless craft only carrying data banks. With tremendous fuel efficiency, they could theoretically accelerate to 0.25c if they also wanted to decelerate, although most routine runs were done at 0.15c. The tiniest information ships, carrying key political data on the Empire, were smaller than a missile. They sped up to 0.5c, broadcasted their information, and then proceeded to self-destruct due to not having enough fuel to decelerate.

If the data required was large, such as information on Earth's continued biological development, vital to the terraforming algorithms, the information ship would be large enough to have systems that could require maintenance. Thus, humanity would send a crewed ship, operated by people going in and out of cryosleep.

If the data were the DNA samples of everyone in a system, this would likely travel in a generation ship, crewed by at least 300 people whose descendants ended up maintaining the ship until arrival at the system in question.

However, there was one contingency when the data was small and extremely urgent. When you wanted to send 1 bit of information, but you had to do this at the speed of light, there was only one option. You had to use light, use a lot of it, and use it in an unmistakably human-made way.

To the goal of sending that bit of information, massive explosions have created two new artificial stars. Those new micro-pulsars, at the opposite ends of a star system created "at once," with similar frequencies, short-lived, but powerful. The directions of their pulsations were carefully synchronized to point at the nearby human star systems, making the detection easier.

Those were The Beacons.

Upon receiving the signal of the Beacons, each Governor of each system was obliged by Imperial law to relight the Beacons in their system.

The Beacon protocol had never been implemented in humanity's history.

Until now.

Once the decision of the Governor was made, the orders sent, and the stars created, there was no going back. In system after system, as quickly as was humanly possible, aides, techs, astronomers, and captains of ships would call their supervisors, repeating the phrase that nobody wanted to hear but were always ready to.

"The Beacons Are Lit"

"The Beacons Are Lit" meant one thing and one thing only. A system has gone to DEFCON 0 upon facing or preparing to face a threat that they might not handle by themselves, an enemy that could threaten humanity as a whole. It meant that every system that received the message HAD to go to DEFCON 0, preparing for what was to come.

As soon as the message was received, civilian projects were canceled across the entire Empire of Man, colonization was put on hold. The engineering of planets for greater life expectancy extension would have to wait. The Ruler of each system had to make decisions based on when they estimated the threat to arrive and direct all efforts deemed reasonable for War, all efforts Toward Victory.

The DEFCON 0 conditions of "The Beacons Are Lit" could not be undone, except by the Emperor Himself.

Individual systems could signal the perceived passing of the threat using a single pulsar at the same spot as one of their previous Beacons; however, they would have to remain alert until the same signal or an information ship was received from Earth's Solar System.

This event was visible to any spacefaring civilization within the Milky Way. Even those alien races who were not told about the protocol could infer the meaning as it trembled them to their core.

Humanity Was Going To War.

Chapter 25

High G

People attribute the Unification War Victory to me, but in truth, I would be nowhere without your father and his miraculous ability to withstand G-forces.

The First Emperor addressing unknown.

12.3 MS AA

"Speed is the essence of war," wrote Sun Tzu regarding war on the surface of planets. In space, acceleration is the essence of war. While building materials to withstand acceleration is a complex but doable engineering task, the ultimate maneuverability of a ship is constrained by either the engine or the human element.

As extra Gs of acceleration pile up, the heart strains to pump, the lungs struggle to move air, and the brain begins to lose oxygen and other necessary nutrients. Even keeping upright and preventing one's organs from smothering each other becomes a challenge. G-suits were meant to mitigate this. To a proper wearer, a G-suit was more than a mere instrument. It was an extension of the body.

Albert would only have his for a couple megaseconds in a rushed process before the test.

The construction of the G-suit was as light as possible while being capable of operating in a vacuum. Aramid fibers, spider silk, and some carbon nanotubes could protect one from the void of space and weak weaponry. For serious space debris, a diamond-titanium oversuit would be necessary.

The G-suit contained powered rings on the legs and abdomen that reacted to overall acceleration as well as the breathing and heartbeat of the wearer. When the heart tried to pump blood from the bottom up, the G-suit aided the process by contracting around the calf. Each breath under G-forces was aided by pulling or pushing the abdomen. The G-suit hooked up directly into the bloodstream. If blood oxygen in the brain dropped too low, it would inject synthetic oxygenated blood produced from the wearer's DNA. It would also move low-oxygen blood through an external "artificial lung." If muscle tension became too much for connective tissue, the suit would stiffen under the armpits to allow the arms to rest. If hormonal functions were disrupted, the suit would pump necessary chemicals into the body: adrenaline, caffeine and hundreds of others. If blood clots formed, nanobots would cut through them.

If one activated the suit functions without being in high-G, it delivered a tantalizing experience of drug and quasi-massage-induced relaxation. It was a fun time, but it was both addicting and as weakening as prolonged 0-G. One's body always wanted to go to "chill mode," thoughts rushing forth as if in an overly warm shower. Adjusting too much to the effortlessness was counterproductive to training.

Which is why the mentality of the suit was of utmost importance.

After the initial period of basic testing of the suit functions, all the male students trying out to join the Space Forces stood in neat lines in front of Arjun in their turned-off G-suits. Arjun paced in front of the students.

"We have all learned and experienced what the suit does. Now for the surprise quiz: What does it not do?"

Max looked at Arjun with an "Oh really?" face. Who was going to try to answer the trick question?

Albert spoke after a moment of silence, "There are many things the suit does not do."

Arjun smiled, "Vague, but correct. Many people get the wrong idea at first. People think the suit 'saves lives' and 'keeps you conscious.' It does NO such thing. It is not designed to do those things. It is designed to pump blood and give you drugs. Do you know what is designed to keep you conscious and save your life?"

This time, the intention of the lesson was obvious.

"We are," the students said in unison.

"A little louder and with more conviction, please," Arjun remarked.

"We are!" they shouted.

"Good, good. Your life is your responsibility, not the suit's. Even as low as 9 G, you will get tunnel vision and lose concentration and decision-making ability. Yet it is your will that keeps you conscious, breathing properly, and still able to fight. It is your WILL that survives when your very brain begins to fail. You have all practiced this for years before the Academy. You will be pushed to 12 G with the suit, and you must maintain a functional ability to reason and fight at that level. Dismissed."

The weakest parts of the human in high-G, and one G-suits can't reinforce, are the eyes. This remained true even after high-G genes, basic retinal muscle strengthening surgery and conditioning have made Border World human eyes much stronger than those of humans of the Old Earth. Loss of peripheral vision and temporary loss of full vision are near certainties as one ascends above 10 G. To remain capable of piloting under those circumstances means using touch and hearing input modalities to communicate spatial information. One must be perfectly capable of holding and rotating 3-dimensional objects with sufficient detail to manipulate battle dynamics.

While both men and women have improved their abilities throughout teraseconds, it generally remained true that men were most likely to reach the required capital ship performance rating of 15 G. Beyond the point of 15 G, the complexities of engine design made further acceleration increases impractical.

The universe is truly a machine of great irony, but one of the greatest ironies of all was that space belonged to those who could visualize it without the use of sight. No other race in the Milky Way could do this as well as humans, and either resigned themselves to slower ships or relied too much on computers that ended up being too predictable. At times, a singular flight of a railcruiser at 15 G unaided by a computer was enough of a demonstration of power in front of other civilizations to establish the 'Strength' part of the Imperial Doctrine of 'Peace Through Strength.'

The most basic exercise of high-G preparation was doing squats wearing a tungsten weight suit 3 times one's body weight, while solving a 3 by 3 by 3 Rubik's cube. Blindfolded, obviously. But those were just the basics and even the girls could do the basics. The tests Albert was going to take were harder.

Albert walked up to Ken after that talk, "How are you feeling about the test?"

Ken was confident, "I have done 8 G before without the suit. I can do this."

Albert was not sure, "Same, but we have to get used to the suit with very little practice? You got any ideas?"

"Yeah," Ken had a plan. "We are going monk mode."

"Details?" Albert was very familiar with monk mode.

"Well, first, let's tell the girls we are not going to pay attention to them for at least a megasecond [~11.5 Earth days]," Ken emphasized how important this was.

"Some of us might survive this," Albert joked and shook his head as if to ponder the risk. "And then?"

"And then we are going to do absolutely nothing," Ken joked back.

Albert got the idea, "Meditation to adjust our bodies to the suits?"

"Exactly. I may not be a doctor, but I get that proper interaction with the suit requires the body to understand it as a temporary part of itself, to get the autonomic nervous system to trust it. A body scan meditation while constantly turning on and off the suit functions will do the trick."

"Under Gs of some kind, right?"

"Of course, you'll need a few plates on your back," Ken pointed at the enhanced tungsten weight suit.

The high-G test was held in a spin-pod, which used rotational inertia to generate G. The test pushed one's body along the usual gravity direction: DOWN. Up-G tests were still too dangerous for inexperienced people.

14.3 MS AA

After training under Ken's direction, Albert strapped into his suit, put in a teeth protector, and sat in the pod.

There was a maneuver-friendly pair of joysticks, each with five buttons, allowing one to issue commands without moving one's hands and with only the subtle movement of one's fingers. The joysticks' rest surface for the fingers could also deliver tactile feedback by raising and lowering pieces of it to indicate spatial information. The G-suit had built-in 'glove sensors,' which allowed for the same thing when resting on any flat surface.

The holo-monitor was fairly standard. One could control it using one's voice. Regular human commands were too slow. All Academy students learned 'spasit,' a special language suited for descriptions of space and mathematics. It was meant to maximize the ratio of 'likely output information bits' over 'units of muscular effort.' The monitor could speak back and describe itself in the same language, punctuated with tonal music that indicated specific in-test numbers or distances.

The 'brain scanner' was the input modality of last resort. If one's fingers failed and one's jaw had trouble operating in high enough gravity, one could focus on operating through 'pure thought' by visualizing plans directly. A desperate measure, since it implied the loss of both muscle memory and a high chance of imprecise readings.

The test began.

The spin-pod ramped up slowly, keeping him at a comfy 3 G for a few minutes as he piloted a spacecraft in a course similar to the asteroid race. Albert used the joysticks with little issue. His shoulders being pulled down almost felt more relaxing than usual. An imperfect score, but far above passing.

The test moved on to 6 G. The task switched to close piloting of a spacecraft, lifting off a moon close to a planet, shifting orbits, and landing on the planet. A nearly trivial challenge even without a computer assist. But the physical burden began to weigh on Albert. His focus needed to alternate between proper breathing and piloting. Small mistakes began to add up as he completed the touchdown in time, but with more fuel spent than he wanted.

It moved on to 9 G, and a rudimentary system of differential equations began to flash on the screen. Albert began to lose peripheral vision and noted that the suit began to work on his calves. A cocktail of drugs streamed into his bloodstream, with an initial jolt from the adrenaline, followed by an adjustment to the new normal. The fingers on the joystick began to feel too cramped to type quickly, so Albert switched to voice input using 'spasit.' "I" "J" "K" "I" "J" "K" repeated in various tonalities to finalize the solution.

The final portion of the test was at 12 G. The task was to manually control 6-point defense cannons against a volley of 30 missiles. Albert fully lost vision as the pod went up to 10 G and closed his eyes. His lower jaw dropped to the bottom of his helmet, and he had too much trouble lifting it. The G-suit was operating at full capacity. Albert braced himself as he began to feel the absence of properly oxygenated blood in his brain and neck. The headache was severe. The suit gave him a minor painkiller. The spatial information was delivered via gloves, as even a small change in glove shape pressed on him as strongly as a sharp stone pushing up. He had to switch to a fully neural interface and visualize the exact shape of the battle. He kept it steady in his mind as he rotated the ship, spraying the space with bullets. One by one, the missiles were shut down, though some were too close, and the shrapnel grazed his ship.

The test was over.

Albert straightened out of his chair, which felt like he had previously fused into. He walked out of the room alongside Ken, Max, and Sunnak. They were all smiling. Raising his arms, Albert jumped with joy but slightly misjudged the tension in his muscles and nearly hit the ceiling with his hand.

"Unbejiethable," Max mouthed, though realizing he had trouble talking properly.

Compared to the high-G tests, training to use a personal railgun was not meant to be that challenging. The Academy shooting range was 300 meters long, right behind the railcruiser. For Albert, this was a monumental occasion. The Holy Weapon of the Empire did not look too different from an old-school high-caliber sniper rifle. But it was significant as a symbol of Imperial might. It featured thick side-barrel reinforcements, giving it a proper 'anti-tank' feel. Albert slid his finger up and down the reinforcements, which were smooth and polished as a mirror.

"Have you ever shot an imperial railgun before?" Max asked Albert.

"Handheld railguns are not allowed for civilian use," Albert responded. Max probably knew this and just wanted to rub it in. Albert continued, "But I trained with an Old Earth 50-caliber rifle."

"Oh boy, if you only interacted with toys, I would recommend putting on your helmet before the first shot," Max told Albert in the usual tone.

Albert looked at Ken for advice. Ken responded, "As condescending as it is, he has a point. There is a big difference between knowing the exit velocity is higher and feeling the recoil."

Albert put his G-suit helmet on and pointed the railgun downrange. It felt just right in his hand, neither too heavy nor too light. With full strength, he grasped the two grips of the gun and fired. The railgun spun out of control while he was still holding it. It hit his helmet. Albert stumbled backward and put down the gun. He took off his helmet and saw a minor scratch on it.

"I saved your life, so you owe me one," Max said jokingly, as he proceeded to hit within 2 cm of a target 300 meters away.

Sunnak smiled and hit the bullseye.

"That's an easy fix," Ken said, putting the helmet in a nearby nanorepair printer. A swarm of flying nanobots surrounded the helmet with a "bzzt," and after a couple of minutes, the helmet was back on Albert's head.

"Thanks," Albert said, looking up at the sky, "everyone."

Several kiloseconds later, the Principal checked in on the four students after the tests and railgun practice. They were all lying on the floor, stretching their arms above their heads, getting up every kilosecond to drink a tasty mixture of blueberry juice and vitamin-C-infused tonic water.

"You all passed the high-G. Citizenship will be granted to Ken and Albert. Entry to the Space Force for all of you."

"Congratulations on the citizenship," Sunnak addressed Ken and Albert without getting up. "What would you say is our probability of winning?" Sunnak gently turned his head to the Principal.

"Our probability? My brethren. Probability is a coarse tool. You are no longer an observer making judgments on what you cannot affect. You are a participant in the process. The outcome depends on you and all who think like you." The Principal never missed a chance for a good lesson.

"Just like that? Quick and efficient with no ceremonies?" Albert was surprised.

The Principal responded, "For efficiency, we are skipping the citizenship ceremony. You are welcome to hold your own at your allocated land plot. We will hold one combined ceremony for your admission to the Navy, movement from Ground Academy to Space Academy, and awakening your Blood Memory."

"WHAT?" both Max and Albert said in unison. They looked at each other, about to utter the same phrase over each other.

Max ended up speaking, "I thought awakening of Blood Memory was only available to select lineages, so not even every citizen is eligible."

The Principal nodded, "Due to DEFCON 0, we are authorized to give you a bigger dose of Red Vision."

"Is that going to work?" Albert asked.

"It depends," the Principal paused for dramatic effect, "on what kind of people your ancestors were."

The boys looked at each other. The Principal gave Albert a look. One of those looks that meant something but also meant to conceal the actual meaning. All metadata, no data. What did the Principal know, and why would he want to inform Albert that he knew it?

"Where is the Blood Memory ceremony being held?" Sunnak asked.

The Principal was happy to tell them, "At Emperor's Judgment".

The students gasped.

Chapter 26

Request and Response

No society that continuously prints money above population growth is stable.

First axiom of Extrohistory (as written by The First Emperor)

12.3 MS AA

DEFCON 0 meeting was held over video chat; there was no time to gather everyone in the same room. Everyone was up to speed with the basic parameters of the Enemy Second Fleet, now dubbed the "Andromeda Menace."

The Governor began, "We are in a state of Total War. All for war, all for Victory. I expect the mentality and actions of the esteemed Noble Patriarchs to align with what is required."

Alexander took over the speech, "We have called all available crewmen, including Academy graduates capable of high-G maneuvers not already enlisted in the fleet. Every civilian ship is being brought into orbit around either Derev or Sirium and converted into weapons platforms. Shipyards and orbital platforms will also be outfitted with railguns and point defense. Many of these stations cannot withstand the 15 G burns of warships, so they can be staffed by those who don't pass the high-G tests."

The Patriarchs nodded, a hint of sadness in their expressions. Manning a stationary ship was a death sentence, and finding volunteers with the necessary skills but willing to accept their fate was no small task.

Alexander continued, "We've completed the construction of 70 million atmospheric drones, as requested by Noble Houses Smith and Gupta. In light of Total War, we now require every adult civilian to build and operate an atmospheric drone, bringing our total to 500 million."

Idris and Deepak offered a polite clap. The other Patriarchs followed suit.

The Governor paused, then continued, "DEFCON 2 imposed transaction taxes, and DEFCON 1 increased money printing. While printing money boosted civilian droid supervisor shifts in factories, mines, and shipyards, the planet is not operating at full capacity under DEFCON 0. Surplus value is still being spent on non-fleet projects. As such, I am imposing a new economic order."

Several Patriarchs leaned forward, their video streams flickering as they tried to grasp what the Governor had devised. He had spent hours analyzing monetary flows and non-fleet production systems, debating with Ernest how much more they could squeeze from the Patriarchs. The Governor was confident the answer was "a lot." The question was how to structure the incentives.

The Governor continued, "Our new economic system will set production quotas directly for each Noble House."

The Patriarchs exchanged glances, their eyes negotiating a silent consensus. Idris remained silent.

The Governor explained, "Instead of delivering money to us, which we use to buy ships from you, you will deliver ships directly, proportional to the estimated value of your land holdings. You will trade raw materials for finished ships, paying your taxes in ships instead of money. Total ship production must increase by 50% above current levels. Failure to meet quotas will result in the loss of House territory, which will be redistributed to nearby Houses, yeomen, or new citizens."

Deepak mouthed a silent "what the fuuck?" but stayed quiet.

The Governor continued, "This supersedes House taxes, but civilian transactions remain subject to a 23% tax. The government will spend this money, along with existing budgets, on ships, which will count toward your tax obligations."

Patriarchs furiously typed or gestured off-screen to their assistants. A 50% increase in production was an insane demand on an already strained planet. Idris covered half of his face with his hand.

Tong was the first to speak, "We are fundamentally altering the entire economic system. How sure are you this won't backfire?"

The Governor replied, "As history and theory have shown, market economies, properly directed, are the best long-term solution for production and distribution. However, we are not in a 'long-term' scenario. Two massive fleets will be here in less than a year. Yes, this will eventually backfire. But for now, we need more ships."

The meeting ended. The hard part was just beginning. The Governor didn't expect the Patriarchs to react immediately. They needed time to adjust, understand the implications, and craft their response. They were in uncharted territory. While Border Worlds were accustomed to rapid economic changes, those changes always balanced property rights with long-term viability. Threatening the redistribution of Noble House land was unprecedented. The Governor felt uneasy. The uncertainty of the external threat had given way to unease about the internal situation.

***

Idris pinged all the Patriarchs for a follow-up meeting without the Governor. Tong felt a pang of dread but joined anyway.

"Well, here we are," Deepak stated.

"Here we are," Idris confirmed. "I have a proposal."

His tone meant the "proposal" could not be refused.

Idris continued, "We defy the quotas. We increase production by maybe 15%, but no more."

He scanned the video feeds for reactions. Tong shook his head slightly. The other Patriarchs remained expressionless, gauging each other's responses. Idris let his words sink in and eye contact game to begin to play out.

Deepak was the first to speak, "Suppose, hypothetically, we follow your plan. Wouldn't the Governor take our lands?"

Idris smiled. Deepak was playing his part well.

Idris responded, "And do what, exactly? Who will manage the land and production? Yeomen? New citizens? They lack the skills and experience. It would take too long for them to match our output. The Governor may take marginal land, but he can't touch key infrastructure. His threats are empty."

Deepak nodded.

Tong interjected, "This is dishonorable. If we can't meet the quotas, we should confront the Governor directly."

Idris laughed, "Dishonor? House Smith controls most of the shipyards. I'm the one trading ships for raw materials. If you exceed quotas in violation of our agreement, I'll charge you more."

Tong understood the unspoken part of the proposal. He considered pushing back, citing the need for torpedoes or fuel, but this wasn't the right fight. He got efficiency gains with Sheene's boyfriend's analysis, which was enough to barely keep himself out of debt. However, it looked like he had to take the L here. Reluctantly, he waved his hand in agreement.

Mencius spoke next, "Idris, what will you do with the resources not spent on ships?"

Idris replied as if the answer were obvious, "We'll finish our bunkers, underground train systems, and fortifications."

Mencius didn't hide his confusion, "Why? How do you suppose these will help now? Imagine how high the tech level of these aliens might be. Even if one of those enemy ships is packed with basic antimatter torpedoes, they aren't just going to cleanse the surface with atomic fire." Mencius paused to emphasize what his projection meant, "They can crack the planet in half."

Several Patriarchs sighed. The possibility, though unspoken until now, was all too real.

Idris remained calm, "Exactly. Our engineers have drafted contingency plans for underground cities. That's why we need the resources and why we're defying the ship quotas."

Mencius looked at him in slight confusion. Idris waved to share the data. Several Patriarchs gasped at his audacity, but after their engineering teams confirmed Idris's assumptions, they began to give each other approving glances.

Tong would normally inform the Governor, but there was no need. The lack of quota fulfillment would be obvious from the start. He glanced at his territory, particularly the border regions. Regardless of the Governor's bluffs, some land would certainly be lost. What would happen to the people living there? Who would rule them next?

Chapter 27

Plot Allocation

We have conquered this land. As long as you and your sons help me defend it you have the right to govern a piece of it.

The First Emperor granting knighthood to railgun operators during late Unification War.

14.5 MS AA

"I got my citizen land allocation," Albert told Sheene. "It's... right on the border of your House territory."

Albert hesitated to say the last part because, until yesterday, the land plot was her House territory. The Governor had taken away border regions from most Houses for not meeting shipbuilding quotas.

Albert waved his hand, showing his holomap, and continued, "The visit qualifies as a nice date... if you want to come."

Sheene sighed a little but tried to conceal it, "Yeah, I want to."

Albert hesitated but decided to pose the question head-on, "Will you feel OK observing the land you technically lost?"

"Don't worry about me. I will feel however I feel, it's my problem."

Albert was surprised by this answer. Isn't the role of a good boyfriend to worry about his girlfriend's feelings? But then he pushed the thought away, "Okay, let's go!"

He allowed himself to get excited about the visit.

Albert remembered his childhood. He grew up on a plot similar to this one, though with far more forests and a nice view of the mountains. His grandfather just barely failed his placement test to acquire a Noble House job and was thus allocated to a village directly under the Governor's management. The village specialized in supervising logging and farming droids, considered to be an unprestigious job even by civilian standards. The citizen in charge of their plots was Kody, the Governor's nephew twice removed. However, his percentage ownership share of the village was lower than that of a House Citizen Lord, so he took only minimal efforts to manage the population. He came in every ten megaseconds, double checked that the village was at least making some profit and left.

Albert's father managed to score much more lucrative temporary contracts with House Mishov to work the orbital shipyards. He chose to not leave the village permanently, instead alternating between ship-building shifts and working with logging. Albert would always look forward to his returns. He distinctly remembered his father sitting around a campfire, re-telling stories. They were stories of mechanical pieces, armor plates and ever-frustrating droids. The droids always did almost exactly what you wanted, but never quite perfectly enough to House Mishov's standards. These campfire stories, sometimes extending across tens of nights, were very popular with the other men of the village who sought the same contracts.

Albert did a virtual walkthrough of his plot alongside his parents and brothers, who continuously compared this plot to his own, down to the very last detail.

The next day, Albert and Sheene touched down inside a House Li airport. Nearly all civilian airplane recreation traffic had stopped, so they traveled in a spare cabin in a cargo plane. Droids and supervisors began unloading the cargo of atmospheric drone parts as soon as they landed. The airport building had a customary airplane-sized decorative dragon on top of it. It was fairly empty of tourists and busy with material transport. After a 50-second walk from the plane to the building, Sheene's dad, Faen, was there to meet them. He wore a shirt formal enough for a meeting with his lieutenants but casual enough to not seem overbearing.

"So, this is the guy?" Faen asked somewhat jokingly.

"This is the guy," she confidently answered.

"The guy who managed to save us a bunch of money on orbital fuel but then took away a land chunk as well? This guy?" Faen continued.

Albert was hoping the introductions would be more pleasant and with less tricky-to-navigate humor. He stood upright as if frozen. He didn't "take" any land; the Governor did that, but having a debate felt inappropriate at the moment.

"Yeah, that's him," Sheene said, waving her hand over Albert's hair, making a mess of it. Albert felt better.

"Ok, then. I hope you are as good of a boyfriend and a fighter as you are at orbital mechanics," Faen said, looking Albert directly in the eyes. Albert reciprocated for a short time before becoming uncomfortable.

Albert responded, "I will do my best." He was still very unsure how these things were supposed to go.

Sheene hugged her dad, "Thanks for meeting us." Albert and he shook hands.

High-speed trains carried people across the House Li territory from inside the airport. However, Albert's land plot was only accessible by a low-speed train, and in the interest of time, they took a basic hovercraft. Its covered dual rotors made a lot of noise, but the internal soundproofing was good enough to keep it as a low hum. The rotors were harmonically oscillating to vibrate at a pleasant frequency, and the hum was almost melodic. In the hovercraft, she told him, "Thank you for not mentioning how the Governor took away the land. It took a lot of strength, probably." It took a very minor amount of strength, but Albert was glad he was finally learning the high-class customs.

Albert's new land measured 5 by 8 km. It contained a village with more than a hundred people. It bordered House Li land on one side and House Shu land on the other. Demarcating the border was a simple 3-meter stone wall. The same type of wall separated an internal desert section from the village. Upon landing, Albert walked to the leaf-covered part of the land next to the helipad and took a pile of dirt and leaves in his hand.

Soft dirt. Good dirt. Suitable for farming. His dirt. His land. His dream. All happening far too fast.

Jamian, the village elder, was there to meet Albert. He was tall and sturdy, with the kind of 'worker' strength that came from frequently disassembling droids and repairing tricky parts or needing to carefully carry several small kids during his childcare shifts. Jamian looked surprised to see Sheene, but didn't say anything.

"Welcome, Lord Albert," Jamian bowed to Albert.

"Thank you," Albert responded, which wasn't the proper Citizen Lord response. Albert felt pretty awkward with this introduction. He realized he wasn't fully comfortable with the role he was given. Jamian took them on a tour of the village.

Jamian looked slightly uncomfortable when they came to the central square with the House Li statue in the center. A few kids, younger than 200 megaseconds[~6 earth years], seemed to be playing on a sidewalk with one adult nearby. "While it is a custom that we change statues on change of ownership, it was short notice, and we have been very busy due to all this price inflation business," Jamian mumbled.

"It is of no matter to me," Albert said. "You have existing work to do according to the market demands and the Governor's decrees. We will deal with all the customs after the battles."

Jamian's shoulders suddenly dropped, and he smiled very widely, as if a big burden had been lifted from him. Albert didn't expect this to be a big deal, but he was glad to start the relations well. The three of them zoomed around the fields and factory on a one-car, 4-person mini-train that ran across the plot, above the primary underground power lines. The majority of the plot in the center grew vegetables and fruits, primarily Old Earth apple trees and heavily genetically modified local plants known as kapus. Mini drones equipped with small lasers flew around the plot, killing unneeded insects. The village had a few bison, which were trained to only eat weeds around the fields and leave the crops alone. Automated harvesters picked up the vegetables and carried them to the processing plant on the corner of the plot opposite the village. Near the processing plant were the biofuel generator, a toy factory, and a standard Recycler. The toy factory looked operational, the sight of which confused Albert. Jamian picked up on it and mentioned, "Since DEFCON 0, the toy factory repurposed all of its machinery for the production of mechanical spider mines."

"Landmines?" Albert was surprised.

"House Smith is buying them, and we could certainly use the money given the new tax burdens."

Albert wasn't convinced that landmines would be useful at all in a space war, but business was business, and there wasn't much else that the toy factory could be repurposed for.

Solar panels, constantly rotating to maximize sunlight, were sprinkled around the fields, powering the machinery, which primarily worked during the day. During peak hours, the solar panels stored energy inside batteries, powered the biofuel generator, and ran the Recycler to process all the waste from the farm or manufacturing into useful molecules. The village had one last-resort 'gravity storage' electrical motor, which pumped water into a raised reservoir. It wasn't operating. Electricity was being sold to nearby communities due to increased demand.

"How much has DEFCON 0 impacted the people?" Albert asked.

"Not as much as other communities," Jamian answered. "We had to increase repair work schedules to make more droids and machinery available. We are bound by existing contracts to supply food for over one hundred thousand people. Most of the farming is constrained by the land, not by people's shifts, so the farming hours increased only slightly. The former toy factory is working around the clock, and new supervisors are getting trained."

"New ones?" Sheene asked.

"Yes, the age of trainable machinery supervisors has been lowered to 500 megaseconds [~16 Earth years]."

"Ah, ok," Sheene sighed. Albert noted that she was sad about this, but he let her be.

"Most management decisions were pretty automatic based on the Governor's decrees even before the transfer," Jamian stated matter-of-factly.

Albert expected this. The Governor was playing some hardball in politics, but he wasn't going to give new citizens a complex allocation to manage.

"What self-directed projects are you working on aside from the food and landmine production?" Albert asked.

Jamian looked Albert in the eyes to assess the intention of his question. Albert was merely curious, without hoping to interrupt the process, which he tried to show with his eyes and his smile. Jamian responded, "We are reinforcing the small bunker 40 meters underground and storing food supplies. We have started on a tunnel connecting it to the House Li network for potential evacuation. No money for a maglev, just wide enough for our all-terrain carts. Are the projects to your liking?" Jamian asked the last question because he was required to, not because he wanted to.

Albert smiled and said, "You have it handled, but you have my ear if you need input." Albert was glad to not need to manage the situation much; he wanted to focus on combat preparations.

Jamian was relieved as well and smiled once again, "Nothing as of now, thank you."

They came back to the central village square. The kids were no longer playing. The adults were demonstrating to them basic repair protocols on harvester robots.

Albert asked, "What's the projected life expectancy of the village given the biomarkers?"

Jamian responded cheerfully, "Around 14 gigaseconds [~443 Earth years] 10% better than the planet average."

Albert was actually surprised, "Damn. House Li took great care of you."

Jamian looked at Sheene and responded, "Of course they did. The village looks forward to new leadership being great as well."

Albert felt a little silly for saying that. Of course, he would not speak badly about previous leadership, especially when Sheene was present. He would have to find a more subtle way to find out what was wrong, if anything.

"Can we go behind the wall?" Albert asked, pointing at the wall separating the village from a desert section.

"Sure, there is only one gate," Jamian said.

His portion of the desert was a couple of acres, half-covered by solar panels.

"Oh, that's lovely. A pile of sand," Albert exclaimed. "Good raw material to build computers with."

Jamian looked worried for a second.

"After the battle, of course," Albert added.

"Of course," Jamian said, still looking worried, but his general cheerfulness from previous interactions came back.

Sheene and Albert went back to the village and took a stroll to the hovercraft.

"So, was this what you expected?" Sheene asked.

Albert was excited to talk, "Expected? Before the Academy, I dreamed about this. Under normal circumstances, a citizenship plot like this comes with a sizable level of surplus value. Surplus income that I could use to build a nice castle overlooking the land. Or, as I wanted, a small science lab. But under the current tax policy, I am not different from a House Li land plot manager, except unpaid."

Sheene asked sadly, "No, I meant the people under your rule."

Albert struggled to cleanly form his impression of Jamian. "Oh. Jamian wasn't ready for a heart-to-heart," Albert paused. "The village is not in a good defensive spot."

Sheene made a face indicating that wasn't quite what she wanted to hear, but asked him regardless, "What do you mean?"

Albert inhaled to prepare for the long explanation and waved to the buildings, "This isn't nano-concrete; their buildings are not that resilient to shockwaves. Their radiation shelter is only 40 meters underground, reinforced with basic lead. They don't have spaceship-grade black mold lining inside it. Their evacuation priority has been lowered since I took over. They can withstand maybe one basic exajoule [~240 Megaton of TNT equivalent] warhead impact on top of them, but certainly not two. A direct heligun hit at the right angle..."

"Stop..." Sheene said. She was actually crying. "Please stop."

Albert didn't expect this reaction. He thought she was fully familiar with the basics of defense against orbital bombardment. He put his hand on her shoulder. "What is it?" he asked.

"Please promise me you will take care of them," Sheene said, wiping her tears off. "Set a positive intention for a bright future, regardless of how unlikely it is."

"It's a reasonable request," Albert said, feeling better as he realized a certain tension he didn't know was there left his chest.

"Albert, these people are not like you," Sheene said. "They logically might know how hopeless the situation is, but they absorb themselves in their day-to-day, and it gives them meaning. The kind of meaning that is different from your hope, from your attempts to predict the outcome."

Albert was surprised how Sheene understood the mindset of some civilians better than he did. Her explanation shed a bit of light on his prior feeling of outsideness.

"Thank you," he said to Sheene, "for being here."

"Of course," she responded with a hug.

They were silent on the hovercraft trip back. Albert got a ding on his handheld. It was a message from Jamian. It read:

"Dear Lord Albert,

New Governor decree announced. Situation has changed. We need your input on Recycler energy allocation.

Yours,

Jamian."

Sheene asked, "What is it?"

Albert responded, "Fuck."

Chapter 28

Simulations and Their Limits

Human aesthetics are an asset, not a weakness. Ugly code is unsafe code.

The First Emperor after his team's first successful hack of the Cyborg communication network.

14.6 MS AA

"You absolutely cannot deallocate energy from the Recyclers." Mencius, the Noble Patriarch of House Shu, yelled into the video call.

"I can, and I am ordering it," the Governor stated calmly. "Why the opposition? Is this about using energy for unsanctioned House Smith projects?"

Mencius crossed his arms and chuckled, "House Smith proposed a similar measure, and I told them to fuck themselves in the same manner I am telling you now. Have you seen the terraforming stability measures given your proposal?"

House Shu was never known for colorful language, but then again, nobody had ever messed with the Recyclers before. The Recyclers were key attachments to every factory, taking all molecular waste and by-products from production and turning them into useful molecules. It was a process frequently demanding more energy than the corresponding factory. "Do not pollute a single atom," was the Imperial decree regarding manufacturing.

Mencius pulled up a holo-representation of Derev and showed it to the Governor. The planet began to spin, showing forward projections. In a few months, rivers darkened, garbage patches floated in the ocean, and portions of the biosphere began to die out. The computer UI showed life expectancy declining by 100 megaseconds [~3 Earth years] due to the resulting ingestion of chemicals in the food supply.

"We would be no better than the humans before the First Emperor if we did this," Mencius concluded the demonstration.

"The planet being consumed by nuclear fire will cause a lot more problems for the biosphere," the Governor retorted.

Mencius looked at him silently and shook his head, "What about the Preserve?"

"The Preserve stays clean. There are lines, even in DEFCON 0," the Governor responded. "Besides, House Shu's forest and bacterial recycling projects are still in effect, as they are more energy efficient. And you will be compensated for expanding them. You even have a financial incentive to turn off everyone's Recyclers."

"In peacetime, our duty is to protect the planet, not to benefit financially from fixing the problem. DEFCON 0 has altered the incentives, but our mindset has remained the same," Mencius replied.

The Governor noted that the lack of response to the "nuclear fire" meant Mencius was on the verge of giving up the debate and just needed a little push to be convinced.

"The Emperor Wills It," the Governor said. Given that the Emperor was more than 630 light-gigaseconds away [~20000 light-years] the phrase was not literal. When spoken by the Governor, it meant the decision was final.

"Do the Stars Will it too?" Mencius asked.

The Governor wasn't ready for this question. He steadied his nerves.

"Are you officially defying my order?"

"No," Mencius said. "The simulation has spoken. I can only hope you listen."

The Governor closed the video call and buried his head in his hands.

The laser sail of the Will of the Star had been firing for the fourth day in a row and would continue for several more. Five new backup ships, each with a crew of 300 and the full genetic information of everyone in the system, were traveling toward all nearby uninhabited star systems. These ships were fully equipped for multi-gigasecond coasting in interstellar space. Each could extend its operating range by reaching the edges of star systems, absorbing sunlight, and capturing reaction mass. They were fully equipped semi-permanent habitats as much as they were ships.

Firing the laser for so many days had put pressure on producing synthetic deuterium in Derev's orbit. Solar collectors were allocated to the task, putting the entire planet into an energy crunch for manufacturing. The Governor knew the cost before ordering the extended backup protocol, but he was already frustrated from dealing with the consequences. The Governor asked the computer for another visual review. It was important for his morale to confirm that some things were actually going right. A high-zoom camera on an orbital satellite showed him the planet.

The cities were brimming with activity. Droid factories churned out droids for the Houses. All production capacity was "beyond the maximum." Despite the planet having more than two droids per person, civilians had little ability to rent said droids after the economic restructuring. So, many civilians had to assemble their personal atmospheric drones themselves from alloys not suitable for spaceships. The process was generally as easy as building an Old Earth rifle. The trickier part was learning to fly it. Many unused ravines held host to civilian drone practice ranges, where people went after mastering simulations.

Near the House castles, machines were digging. Each House crafted new underground bunker cities underneath either natural or artificial mountain ranges, each connected to both their primary castles and other bunkers with underground train networks. Each city featured layers of steel and granite armor plates with soil in between them.

The Governor would normally be excited about the Houses completing such impressive construction projects, but this came at the opportunity cost of ships. He allowed himself to feel excited for a moment before switching his mental state back to worrying about the fleet and social stability.

***

Kariel, Camina, Ernest, and the Governor sat down to review the extrohistory predictions. The Governor started by asking, "The Patriarchs are colluding. How did the simulation miss this possibility?" he asked Ernest.

To the Governor's surprise, Ernest was remarkably chill saying, "It didn't. The social cohesion between the Patriarchs is higher than their approval of you. In this case, collusion to defy the government is very likely. Remember, extrohistory is here to alert us about potential drops in social cohesion that threaten the stability of society. Collusion between Patriarchs is an increase in social cohesion, which, if you look at the predictions, we will eventually need. This collusion actually decreases the probability of the Patriarchs conflicting with each other and creating unrest."

"But it doesn't build us ships," the Governor said, understanding the limitations of extrohistory but wanting to confirm.

"No."

"Let's run the sim. What's the worst case?" the Governor asked.,

Ernest spoke, "The worst scenario for social cohesion is that the aliens are defeated, but we both die in the process."

Kariel and Camina looked at the Governor with some sadness. The Governor looked at the predictions. With the 'disregard outliers' button checked, social cohesion between citizens and civilians was set to go below 60 in 300 megaseconds [~9.5 Earth years], at which point the simulation turned red and said 'collapse inevitable in 8 gigaseconds [~253 Earth years].'

"What are the specific ways this happens?" Kariel asked.

"We are effectively starting an Empire Cycle, an 8 gigasecond [~253 Earth years] inevitable pathway of social decline. Empire cycles were the primary way that the Great Wheel of the Dharmachakra turned until the First Emperor found the cause was fundamentally the printing of money," Ernest responded. "The foundational problem remains the desire of old-money people to preserve their power through non-monetary means. The Houses will transfer their financial assets into cultural power via propaganda, which is fundamentally a negative-sum game. Eventually, trust in the military will fall, and business interests will be considered the epitome of culture. However, as cultural damage and losses of social cohesion compound, the financialization of previously familial relationships will put everyone into a deeper struggle for either money or cultural dominance. This is all compounded by the issue of pollution. Biological damage creates cultural damage. Cultural damage eventually means the loss of meritocratic traditions that keep everything running, which further exacerbates pollution."

Kariel looked at the planetary simulation with deep horror. "This is just as bad as pre-Empire?" he asked.

The Governor was a bit more cheerful, "No. The collapse follows the same pathways, but the people are way more resilient to outside forces. Although we have to contend with more powerful weaponry, both kinetic and memetic."

"Why is the fertility rate declining?" Camina asked. "Pollution as well?"

Ernest said, "Yes, partly, but it's also cultural. Men and women are influenced by different types of propaganda, which lowers cohesion between couples in the plausible culture war. Couples would begin to fight more, lowering the fertility rate eventually."

The Governor looked at Camina. Camina looked at the Governor.

"I guess we are ruling out the option of me putting pressure on the wives of Patriarchs to bow down to the Governor's demands," Camina sighed.

The Governor had been interested in this option before the meeting but now had other thoughts.

"Rule it out for now," he said.

"What about other cases? What happens if the aliens prove to be a big threat?" Kariel asked.

"Too unpredictable," Ernest said. "The presence of an outside threat keeps social cohesion artificially high for some time, which could eventually stabilize society. Also, the likely deaths of many of the key players are too hard to forecast. This is all compounded by Albert passing High-G tests and thus being eligible for Blood Memory Awakening. If I check the 'disregard outliers' button, the equations no longer converge even before the Andromeda menace arrives here."

The Governor searched his mind for what the "standard" answer was supposed to be in this situation. He came up with nothing. Extrohistory was never an exact science; strange genetic drift, biological pollution, and overly hostile environments did a number on social predictions. The situation could be hopeless enough that a social collapse was inevitable, and one would have to navigate such a crisis. But he had never heard of extrohistory equations not converging at such a short timeframe. There was no book on this, no guidance, but his own wit and intuition.

"The software has served us well for many teraseconds, but now its usefulness is severely limited," the Governor said, turning off the simulation. "Let's play through the scenarios ourselves. I will deal with Idris personally; we have a long history of battling each other in the sims. We lack the leverage to take away more of the lands, and he knows it. Camina, can you restructure the incentives to create a carrot out of the stick? For the land we took away but haven't allocated to the yeomen, can you promise to give it back to one of the plausible neighbors if they increase ship quotas again?"

"Yes, sir," she said.

"I can work with the Principal on the question of Albert," Kariel responded. "But my assessment is that he's on our side regarding wanting more ships."

"Good to know, but that's not what I am worried about. He has the authority to challenge you for the next governorship title," the Governor said.

"Doubtful. That's too high of an aim even for him," Kariel responded.

"Don't underestimate the effects of the Blood Memory Awakening," the Governor countered. "But try to avoid disrupting the current social configuration in the Academy. It favors us more than many of the alternatives. At some point, I will have to assess Albert's command skill personally."

"And Ernest, we need a small allocation of funds to boost the full-body suit production for all the civilians. Keeping out pollution from the person's side will slow down social cohesion loss."

Ernest nodded, "With Alex not here, I do have to inform you about the actual worst-case scenario."

The Governor was confused for about one second and then knew exactly what Ernest was about to say.

"As part of the cultural warfare, someone could violate the First Law against the creation of AI and create an agentic intelligence to attempt to influence others. This kind of disaster is only likely to happen below 40 social cohesion. Normally we could foresee it getting that bad, but not under these circumstances."

"We can't let that happen. Find a way to foresee it better," the Governor said.

Chapter 29

Space Academy

Money and property are fundamentally agreements between humans.
Assigning them to machines is ignoring reality in favor of abstractions.

Economics lecture by the First Emperor, prior to the Unification War.

14.7 - 15 MS AA

It wasn't enough to simulate space life; one eventually had to live it. The Space portion of the Academy was designed to acquaint students with both real high-G and zero-G, a bit at a time. The first trip was only a few days long. Albert spent the entirety of his first trip to orbit glued to a window, gazing at the curvature of Derev, the distant glimmer of shipyards and solar collectors.

They took a halfvator rocket up to the Academy. Before unbuckling themselves from the seats, everyone had put on magnetic boots, which stuck to the floor in zero-G. Without magboots, the fastest way to navigate the stations was to use C-ladders, which were ladders with spacious holds accommodating both hands and feet, resembling the holds on the easiest rock climbing walls you'd ever encounter.

Living quarters were inside a circular portion of the Space Academy. It rotated to provide 1.2 G spin gravity, nearly double

Derev's 0.7 G. At first, it felt only a little heavy in an almost liberating way, as Albert felt a deep genetic sense of being closer to the ideal 1 G than before. That said, after a few hours, Albert's stabilizer muscles were a little sore. He would need to lie down and stretch frequently after every walk. But the human body has a way of adjusting to everything.

Adjusting to zero-G was done through several games, keeping with the philosophy of making learning fun. Outside the spin gravity, Space Academy featured a circular outer space "running" track. It consisted of two tracks vertically separated by five meters, with metal guardrails on the sides and nothing but the vacuum inside the track. 'Zero-run' was a tricky sport that involved using the G-suit's springy shoes and gloves to constantly push off one of the tracks and then bump into the other. Using legs and then hands with proper rhythm, one could gain significant horizontal momentum. The first run was a disaster for Albert, who improperly bumped into the guardrail instead of the track, ending all of his momentum. However, after a few practice sessions, the rhythm suddenly clicked. Albert ran the best time on the track among all the students. It was a double victory, as it frustrated Max to no end.

Another way to get used to zero-G was "G-ball." Normally a fun way to get one's mind off studies, given the circumstances, it was a difficult game to mentally get into. The Principal and other teachers scheduled a special meditation session prior to the G-ball match to help students get their minds off the war and focus on what was in front of them.

G-ball was a game with a simple goal: to throw the ball into the net of the opposing team. The ball was half a meter in diameter and light, with a smooth surface, making it hard to hold onto and easy to knock out of another's hands. Teams ranged in size from two to six players each. It was played in a zero-G arena with only nets and walls to alter one's momentum. It was a full-contact sport played in highly padded suits that made each student look comically large. After all, due to the conservation of momentum, it was physically impossible to avoid full contact. The movements of players and the ball were entirely predictable, except for the wall movements and momentum transfers when two players from the same team would approach each other and properly use each other to push off.

Albert paired up with Sheene for a couple of 2v2 practice sessions. After those, it was clear that experienced players were better due to an individually tailored set of "push-off" maneuvers. Albert set up a ton of time to practice the movements in a private G-arena with Sheene.

On one of the lunches inside the gravity living quarters, Albert and Sheene were quietly eating when Max, Diana, and the rest of the group plopped down their plates across the table.

"Why are you still here? I thought you'd be on a generational ship by now," Max asked Albert.

Albert was deeply confused by the question. He thought it was difficult to get a spot on an escape ship. Or if this was even an option for someone whose citizenship depended on fleet service. Or if even talking about running away was ok for any active-duty Space Force personnel.

"No, why aren't you there?" Albert asked.

"How dare you?" Max responded.

The tone of Max's voice suggested Albert had hit a nerve, which suddenly made Albert realize that Max was engaging in a teraseconds-old power play tactic of accusing people of what you are guilty of.

"I thought this was going to be a friendly lunch where we could discuss how to kill aliens," Sheene interjected. Albert thought so too.

"Who would want to go on one of those ships? It's an important task, but you could be spending gigas in cryosleep," Diana mused.

Cryosleep, while carefully refined to preserve people across journeys, was a great method for only a small part of a human's life. Beyond that, subtle molecular damage built up in the brain and body, causing the loss of long-term memory and disassociation of identity upon waking up. Core memories, vital to a person's sense of self, are known to be stored redundantly in a person's body. Half a gigasecond [~16 Earth years] was considered a "safe" interval for waking up in the middle of a long journey. Every wake-up necessitated re-establishing social connections, identity, review of vital spaceship functions, and physical intimacy with the chosen or assigned partner. This extended the 'sanity range' of spaceships to around 4 gigaseconds [~130 Earth years]. However, should a ship embark on a slow trek toward the nearby star system or craft a journey that didn't fully have a destination, the crew's well-being began to push accepted limits. "How much of yourself is still yourself after a long sleep?" was not mere philosophy. It was an engineering problem. It needed to be solved by balancing the ship's energy reserves required for life support with the support of journey parameters. Psychological evaluation of the crew by each other was of utmost importance. The outcomes of such evaluations would either cause the ship to reorganize itself as a generational ship or remain a "cryosleep" ship. A very specific type of person could be cut out for such a journey of uncertainty, the type that even some Border World Space Force personnel had trouble understanding.

"Yeah," Max confirmed. "But you'd be alive and hidden for a long time. Even a sophisticated alien could take many teraseconds to find all the generational ships whooshing through the cosmos."

"Billions of people from more established worlds could take these ships and run from the threat. Humanity could become a void-dwelling species," Sheene said, trying to be cheerful.

"That's just survival. It's not life," Diana looked at her.

Albert agreed with Diana internally but was still trying to re-establish better relations with Sheene after a couple of megaseconds of not seeing her during high-G test training preparation.

"Survival is not mere," Sheene retorted. "The Enemy has such dishonor to attack another galaxy. How well do they get along with each other in the absence of an external enemy? If we can survive, we must. We could bide our time, settle faraway worlds, and wait for the inevitable breakdown in the enemy's cohesion and infighting. What is taken will be lost. What is lost will be retaken. That is the Way of the Stars."

A silence fell over the four students, as if to pay respects to the Way.

Albert broke it, "It is interesting that we talk about human survival in the void, when the Enemy has clearly mastered it."

Diana had another flash of insight, "It begs the question: why even conquer planets after you have mastered the void? Is there some energy and matter that can never be harvested within interstellar space?"

Albert thought it was a good question, the kind that got Diana to understand the intergalactic nature first. Diana was closing the gap in her test performance. Albert was once again impressed that her capacity for generating hypotheses earned her a spot as an advisor to Kariel, once he began assuming governorship roles.

Albert responded, "They must have levels of survival they are willing to tolerate and prosperity that they crave."

"Possible," Diana answered. "They could have a religious belief in their superiority over other races. The desire for prosperity could be secondary to belief in holy legitimacy?"

"How could the Stars allow this?" Sheene said sadly. "How could this be their Will?"

Max was unusually quiet for the conversation until he nearly shouted, "They can't! Something is gonna work out!"

Albert saw a conversational opportunity. It was a concept Sheene had been teaching him, "Maybe the Stars Will for us to have more ships."

Max slowly turned his head and looked at Albert, "What is that supposed to mean?"

Albert, trying to score points against Max, "It would be very helpful to the Governor if your father fulfilled his quotas and stopped building bunkers."

Max slammed his fist against the table, which moved the plates less than you'd expect, "YOU don't get to talk shit about my father, you low-life."

Albert noted that Max was worked up, since usually Max would be more discerning with his insults. Albert responded calmly, "Hey, I am going to be a citizen now, just like you."

Max was incredulous, "You people are not like me at all. Your family has no story among the stars. We are legends!"

Stories among the stars. How very aristocratic of him to worry about stories.

Ken was a little mad. He asked, "What do you mean 'you people'?"

Max pointed at Bishakha, the only non-citizen at the table. Sunnak looked a little strange after that. Max, sensing he was being outnumbered, "The people on my father's land, that's who we build the bunkers for."

Sheene calmly stated, "It is true. The majority of Idris's civilians do support the bunker decision."

Albert thought, "How could she be taking his side? Now, of all times? Did I do something wrong with the plot visit?"

Albert retorted, "According to the opinion polls, everyone wants their House to build bunkers and the other Houses to focus on the fleets. Classic issues with the Commons."

Max said, "People back their leaders, as usual. Rules are rules. No need to reference the Commons. The Governor is overstepping his authority."

Albert very much disagreed but was also surprised Max would say this. "The Governor represents the Emperor and thus has absolute authority. It is DEFCON 0. The BEACONS were lit. Doing too little is treason at this point."

Max raised his hands, "Checks and balances are still supposed to be a thing. No man is flawless, not even the..." Max looked around the room and tried to predict the other students' reactions, "one with the best scores," he finished half-jokingly.

Albert decided it was best to ignore that last comment, "Checks and balances don't exist in wartime."

Diana leaned in and said, "Actually, in case of major conflict between the Governor and Patriarchs, the Inquisition is legally the tie-breaker. Ernest is clearly in the 'more ships' camp. So the checks and balances are against the bunkers."

Max looked at her. Albert was also surprised. Today was 'Opposite Day' for girlfriends supporting their boyfriends for some reason.

Max wanted to redirect the subject, "Al, why are you even complaining? You got a nice plot out of it? The governor stole the land from the Houses and handed it out to you..." Sunnak put his hand on his arm preventing whatever he was going to say next.

Albert said, "I didn't ask for a plot to be taken from anyone. I wanted to defend our planet. Roast some aliens." Maybe the idea of a nice callback to what excited Max would soothe him.

Max was not amused at Albert stealing his line. He flipped his lunch tray, and the bowls and cups clattered to the floor. He grabbed Diana by her hand, which she slightly resisted, and then proceeded to storm out.

Albert walked back to the rooms with Sheene. Initially, they were silent. She looked at him cautiously. Albert gathered his feelings and faced her, "Let's chat. I felt pretty sad when you brought up the civilian polls in support of bunkers."

Sheene looked at him in a way that was already reassuring, "I hear that you feel sad. My intention wasn't to undermine you; I thought we were having a friendly discussion. What people think is important for leaders to know."

Albert calmed down but wanted to express himself, "I hear that your intentions were positive. I would rather resolve any differences on the current events in private." Albert looked her in the eye.

Sheene nodded and put her hands on his chest, " I am glad you are noticing ways to fight Max. I can be more supportive, but I need more clarity about which fights are important to you."

Albert got the idea. Miscommunication, as usual, not any ill intention. "Totally," he said. They hugged.

"Friends?" Albert asked. "Friends," she responded.

"Should we have a secret handshake or something? For when I really need you to help me?" Albert asked her.

"Sure," she responded.

"Here is our sign," Albert tapped his index and middle finger of one hand to the index and middle finger of his other hand. Sheene repeated the sign. They hugged again. Albert was getting excited. Post-conflict intimacy was the best. He pressed her into himself a bit more to get her to sense his excitement.

"With benefits?" he put his hand onto her mid-back underneath her shirt. "I want to join the megameter-high club."

"With benefits," she moved his hand towards her chest, "Let's get out of the spin quarters and join the Zero-G club too."

"Oooh, yeah," Albert said.

"Just gotta stay safe," she looked at him cautiously. "First time with no gravity."

"Oh, of course, I'll tie you down real well," Albert was getting excited, and his voice became a little louder than normal.

"Shh, no more talking," she said.

Chapter 30

We Need to Talk

It's a shame for the powerless to get involved in the conflicts of the powerful.

The First Emperor of Mankind issuing a re-organization of the Human Security Council and Becoming The First Emperor Of Mankind.

15.1 MS AA

The Governor and Idris met at the bottom of the stairwell leading to the palace. The Governor gestured at the aides from both sides. They retreated, eyeing each other with measured disrespect.

The Governor stepped to the bottom of the stairs and picked up his usual weighted backpack. Idris, though unaccustomed to this, decided to pick up a pack as well. They nodded to each other and began walking.

"What's the agenda?" Idris asked. The meeting invite had simply said, "We need to talk."

"I know you've been colluding with other Patriarchs to fail to fulfill the ship quotas. That's the agenda."

There was no anger in the Governor's voice. He did not wish his emotions to reveal his hand. He aimed to resolve the situation favorably.

Idris looked at him, "I am working within the rules you've dictated. You've taken pieces of our land as per your demands."

This is the start of the discussion. Not the most pleasant, but Idris being here is already a win.

"The Empire needs ships. It needs to cripple the enemy. I am bound by my duty to the Emperor to crush these invaders. If not for ourselves, then to give the other systems a fighting chance."

"And I am bound to protect those who live on my land. Duty commands both of our actions."

The Governor knew duty alone wouldn't convince Idris, but it was important for both to express their viewpoints. They took a few steps up before the Governor spoke again, "With a better understanding of results, we fulfill our duties. The marginal utility of each ship increases with every other ship. Every additional torpedo in a volley raises the chances of many getting through. Every additional point defense system protects all ships nearby."

They both knew this. The Governor wanted to understand Idris's frame of thought.

Idris waved his hand towards a far away mining facility, "Consider the mindset of the droid supervisors on our docks, in our mines, or inside our castles. We ask them to trust us, as we always have. Yet, if they worry about their families being exposed to orbital strikes, their minds will not be at peace. They cannot fulfill their duties at full efficiency. We cannot let them look hopelessly at the sky. Not while we depend on them."

The Governor was conflicted. It was a good point, but he didn't wish to acknowledge too much of it. Instead, he relayed his concern regarding social cohesion, "Your actions have divided citizens and civilians into camps of opinion, with debates tearing apart even couples. An unfortunate circumstance, given how much we need unity."

Idris nodded, "Agreed. It's a shame for the powerless to be caught in the conflicts of the powerful."

The Governor was glad to hear the First Emperor quoted, "I, too, am concerned about the mindset of the men under my command. Military action requires adherence to a singular will. Mine." The Governor looked at Idris, who was looking away, "You are not just a Noble Patriarch. You are a ship captain. You will fight with me under my command. There is no separation of powers in the fleet. We don't have the luxury of pulling each other apart when the battle comes. Nor inspiring other captains to do the same."

Idris turned and bent the knee to the Governor. "In space, you have me until whatever end."

Till whatever end. The Governor had lived a long life, but he still considered it too early to confront his mortality, "Then we need to fix the economic situation in a publicly coherent way."

Idris responded, "We do. However, if we have bunkers, we will feel safer leaving Derev and gain tactical flexibility to defend Sirium. If the crew believes their planet is safe, they will fight differently and take more informed risks. Drawing parts of the enemy away, hit-and-runs, without worrying about large parts of the enemy fleet beelining for the planet. Surely this is worth a few ships."

The Governor had his own estimates showing the value of ships, "It is, but you cannot expect planetary defenses to hold if we completely lose in space. An extra bunker isn't worth breaking the enemy's line."

Idris breathed heavily before speaking, "I agree. You can let it go and have the markets make the decision."

The Governor saw through this ploy easily.

"Markets are valuable tools, but they are abstractions between people. I request that you drop the desire to bunkerize the whole planet. Draw up a priority list for the spots." The Governor realized the time for grandstanding or strategy debates was passing. Deals had to be made directly.

"I request you lower the quotas for ships," Idris countered.

They looked at each other assessing the willingness of the other to yield or stand his ground. Motionless, as if about to draw a gun.

Idris spoke first, "Your request can be met."

"Likewise," the Governor responded.

They talked for a while about the details, as they ascended to the top.

Idris spoke at the end of the stairs, "Glad we talked. I was halfway expecting you to challenge me in Kobatas, but this is better." He paused, then added, "For you." Idris was now slightly winded.

Kobatas was an ancient warrior rite combining one-on-one combat with debate.

The Governor squinted at him jokingly, "If these stairs are any indication, the lack of Kobatas is a good deal for you, young man."

Idris smiled back. The Governor has finally felt right about it. "While you're here, I wanted to do an in-person practice of space sims against new opponents. It's a good time to relearn how to work together."

Idris said, "Sure, tough new crew?"

The Governor responded, "No, just Academy students, including your son."

"A great student, but not yet trained enough. A nice easy battle to bond?" Idris seemed surprised.

"Certainly," the Governor said, not wanting to reveal the purpose of the match.

Kariel, Alex, and Camina were at the top to meet them.

"Esteemed future Governor and Stuart," Idris extended his hands to shake theirs.

"All good with you two?" Camina asked.

"We have an understanding," the Governor responded.

Kariel and Camina clapped.

"I would like to examine your bunker construction and contingency protocols," Alexander spoke to Idris. "I hear you have designed for some unusual circumstances."

The Governor wanted to examine it himself, but saying so would admit too much of Idris's plan was reasonable. Alexander offered plausible deniability.

Idris bowed to the Grand Admiral, "My people will happily go over all the contingencies we've budgeted for."

Close to 100 million people, 20% of the planet's population, could now live underground, with more installations coming online daily. After twenty kiloseconds [~5 Earth hours], Alexander and Camina touched down inside Idris's main airport, briefly marveled at his pyramid-shaped castle, and took the elevator to the underground city. The bunker's design was driven by a list of "contingencies," which were potential circumstances requiring technological solutions.

Even the initial construction was not standard. Rather than remove soil and add armor plates above it, the titanium ore was molded directly into the soil below the pyramid castle and above the bunker. It formed 23 armored plates above the first bunker floor. The command center was on the third floor. There, they reviewed the contingency preparations with Idris's chief engineer.

The biological weapon contingency required multi-layered filtering of all air and water entering and exiting the bunker. The air was heated, sterilized using UV light, mixed with ozone, and filtered at the nano-scale. All personnel were scheduled for regular advanced med-scan laser spectrometry to detect potential biological reactions, whether a 0.1 C temperature change or slight skin discoloration. Water purification was even more involved, including infrared restructuring and re-mineralization.

The contingency for the planetary food supply being destroyed was handled by electro-sensitive trees, which grew underground and absorbed electricity instead of sunlight. They tasted as bland as Old Earth potatoes but provided sufficient calories.

In case above-ground solar cells failed, underground geothermal and fusion reactors would power the bunkers. The fourth floor housed oxygen storage facilities sequestering atmospheric oxygen for the contingency of the atmosphere being set on fire.

However, these were the basics.

The Governor sent Alexander to examine the preparations for the most complex contingency. Magnetic shock absorbers lined the outside underground walls touching the soil. If the planet's crust moved too much from orbital bombardment, the absorbers would shield the bunker and generate energy in the process.

On the outside of the bunkers, but still underground, were dual-purpose mini-train tracks suitable for delivering small goods across the city. The bunkers also housed a sizable low-yield rocket armament capable of traveling within and outside the atmosphere. The engineer took them on a tour of the seventh floor, which housed a nearly 1 km diameter particle accelerator.

He proudly proclaimed, "Our simulations show these reinforcements can handle the contingency of orbital bombardment significantly impacting the planet's surface. In the contingency of large chunks of the planet separating, the internal binding energy of the underground cities is stronger than the outlying soil, meaning the cities can remain intact, floating in space. With the particle accelerator becoming an engine, the existing rockets, and the mini-train tracks becoming railguns, we have a massive, albeit slow, space-fighting platform being created out of the city."

Alexander looked over the simulations of orbital bombardments that they had gotten ready for. As they walked out and said goodbye to the engineer, Camina asked, "Satisfied?"

"Yes, the preparations are most extensive," Alexander responded. "Even if the planet breaks, we will not."

Chapter 31

Meeting of Minds

Most capable generals rise to the top of society one way or another.

Second axiom of Extrohistory (as written by the First Emperor).

15.2 MS AA

"We get to go to the Governor's office and battle them in the sims?" Max asked.

"Yeah, it's a great honor. They will challenge you as a team," the Principal responded. "The four of you vs the Governor, Idris, Kariel, and Ernest. Two games of pre-built fleets."

Max jumped at the excitement, "I can't wait to lead our group to victory."

The Principal smirked, and Albert sighed internally.

"The group would do better with me as the captain," Albert said.

"Can you believe this guy?" Max asked.

"Albert is indeed the captain. Per The Governor's request," the Principal confirmed.

"The Governor just wants an easier fight," Max responded.

This battle used prebuilt fleets, which were considered evenly matched. The defense had 40 railships, 20 cruisers, 30 laser destroyers, and 2 immovable hangar bays in a 60,000 km orbit around a 1G planet. The offense had 20 carriers, 10 railcruisers, 50 cruisers, and 10 laser destroyers. Different Imperial systems used battle sims corresponding to their available weapon levels. As energy and mass extraction capacity increased through the world's development, simulations became more sophisticated. However, certain levels of technology were frequently reached within a standard Border World framework, and thus certain sims were repeated often. This one was one of the most common battles that countless generations played time and time again. It was won 50.10% by the defense and 49.87% by the offense, with 0.03% being drawn. There were only minor debates about defense being too strong due to the extra 0.1% win rate.

Albert knew the Governor was a 'by the book' guy who used standard formations and tactics and followed the meta-game. Albert reasoned that the best way to win was to avoid the meta. However, this was dangerous, since the meta-game was there for a reason. What strategies would cost the least strategic position? Albert looked at the simulation code but found no obvious exploits.

After a short flight on a low-orbit shuttle, they landed in the Capital City. On the approach, Albert looked down on the terrascapes surrounding the Capital City. True pieces of Old Earth. Domed habitats used strict containment and air recirculation to encircle a small portion of Old Earth biosphere. Unlike those, the terrascape used a "dynamic frontier" of large mycelium-covered plants around itself that kept more native species of fauna out of the terrascape. The Capital was the only city surrounded by them; the rest of the planet mixed and matched native and non-native species according to a simulated equilibrium.

They went to the guest room of the palace, which was on the first floor and featured a mosaic ceiling over 100 meters long covered with depictions of the Governor's lineage. It was a good distraction from the stress of preparation that Albert took the team through.

They were the offense team for the first battle.

Albert burned the offense fleet forward fairly softly to approach the 'drone launch' range. It was not a 'fixed' range; rather, it varied based on the relative speed of the approach and how easily the drones could close in on the enemy.

Drones are different from both capital ships and missiles in that they lack space for a full matter-antimatter reactor and instead rely on a miniaturized, highly radioactive fusion drive. This means they lack fuel for changes in momentum, known as 'delta-v'. They cannot have a prolonged chase against a capital ship, cannot be launched too far away from their target, have trouble shifting orbits near high-gravity planets, and don't have as much dodging potential versus railgun point-defense.

Despite all of these disadvantages, drones, or the threat thereof, are a constant factor in space combat. They bring a large amount of firepower and deliver it from many angles, making it possible to hit sensitive radiators and engine exhausts. Drones frequently negated sloped armor and frontal armor designs that cruisers tended to rely on.

Drones can either be sent on a 'two-way' trip by flying close to the fleet and simply adding more guns to the capital ship fight. Or they could be sent on a 'one-way' trip, which meant expending all their ammo and then moving on a collision course with the enemy like a kinetic or a cheap nuclear missile.

Albert charted a somewhat complex orbital path relative to the enemy, which moved faster than them in a higher orbit. The maneuver required significant orbit-keeping, but created multiple opportunities for drone launches, which could plausibly be either one-way or two-way trips.

The first launch window Albert launched about 15% of his drone fleet along with a volley of missiles.

Max spoke, "Launch more next time."

"It's too many at once," Albert remarked, "too easy for flak."

The plan Albert had was to use multiple launch windows to launch a large portion of the drone and missile payload and create a sort-of-surround of the defensive side. However, Albert didn't launch too many, expecting an over-reaction from the Governor.

The Governor didn't overreact at all. He rotated the laser destroyers in the fleet towards the first batch of drones and used the hangar bays to launch his drones, which remained close to the bays, acting as an additional point defense.

The Governor also used the opportunity to launch a volley of his own, using both flak missiles for shrapnel and shaped charges for capital ships. A couple of Albert's ships got severely damaged by the shaped charges. As is customary in slightly long-range battles, the defense fired railguns, and the offense dodged them.

Albert got an idea, "Send our flak ahead of our missiles on the third window. We can knock out their drones and take out the hangar bay. Formation C."

Max shook his head, "If we are not using our flak for defense, we are going to be more exposed to their volley."

Albert considered this but didn't want to acknowledge the full danger. He said, "Our relative speed makes it easier to outdodge shaped charges."

"Shaped charges have some leeway," Sunnak said, a little worried. Sunnak was correct. A missile with a shaped charge could 'flow' its explosive material around the kinetic payload to create an angle at which the charge was launched towards a target. A missile could detonate 20 km from the target and even while pointing in a different direction, it could launch a large tungsten slug to arrive a couple of seconds later.

Albert was hoping that their dodging would put them out of this range.

The second squadron of drones did more damage to the Governor's side; however, the first volley had already been destroyed. The plan to coincide the squadrons didn't work because the Governor moved his fleet towards the danger, pushed into the first volley.

On the third squadron launch, Albert allocated his missile volley toward offense and relied on point defense and dodging. He wasn't able to shoot down many incoming missiles. Instead, he expected to outdodge them. This plan seemed to be working, since even the slower carriers managed to enter a trajectory where the closest missiles were at least 30 km from them while moving away. This was just enough distance and relative speed to dodge a shaped charge. As the volley was passing by, Albert got a notification.

"Neutron attack killed the crew"

"Neutron attack killed the crew"

"Neutron attack killed the crew"

Well fuck. The Governor has used an unusual missile type. It didn't have a thermonuclear warhead bathing a ship in gamma rays. It didn't have flak shrapnel or shaped charges. It had a directed neutron beam aimed at the crew modules of Albert's ships. The crew modules are only a few meters long and are an incredibly hard target to hit, given the constant "jitter" of the ship. Yet somehow the Governor was simply able to outpredict the dodging pattern and hit several bullseyes. Even the black fungi under armor could only do so much against a dedicated neutron attack.

Albert's offensive plan worked, and the hangar bays were seriously damaged, but the neutron-launching missiles destroyed many ships' crews. Technically, ships were still in operation and considered to be 'commandable' by nearby crews if they were flying in close formation. However, the exchange left Albert with little hope of victory the next time their orbits converged.

Albert pressed the surrender button on his keyboard with his fist.

Afterward, the students went to their lunch break. They ate pterod eggs with their heads down, not saying anything. After the lunch was finished, Max broke the silence.

"That was a disaster," Max said, without looking up from his food.

"Yes," Albert concurred.

"Indeed," Sunnak weighted in.

"Definitely," Ken said while nervously tapping on the table.

"I can't believe how badly we got beaten. I just blinked, and our drones got spanked by close-range flak," Max described one of the many issues that happened. "Sunnak, you were supposed to be tracking those!"

"Well, the computer was supposed to be tracking those, but somehow it miscalculated. Something to do with the lasers they previously fired at the drone sensors."

"Also, Albert, I thought you were a good strategist, almost beating Kariel lately. How did you still manage to lose this badly?"

"One-on-one is very different from team play. One-on-one combat tends to be around causing your opponent to mismanage his attention and ignore high-priority threats due to the overload of tasks. With a team, it is trickier since they have a lot more attention to spare. Different dynamics. The Governor, Alex, your Dad might individually make mistakes of inattention, but together they run a tight ship."

Max stood up angrily, "Maybe if I was the one in charge?"

Albert thought of saying, "How dare you?" but caught himself, not wanting to come down to Max's level. Instead, he said, "We would have done worse."

"How dare you?" Max asked, though he had no strength in his voice.

The Principal walked in on the lunch. Max unclenched his shoulders a little and addressed him, "Can you believe this guy? Still thinking he should be the captain. Our group would do better with me."

The Principal spoke, "An interesting perspective. However, any other theories about why you got wrecked out there?"

Ken said, "We don't work well as a team. We are like an engine with ungreased gears. Or like a body with two muscles constantly pulling against each other." He suggestively looked at Albert and Max.

The Principal nodded.

"Yeah, well, no shit. Of course, we don't work well as a team. This guy is delusional, thinking he is the best and needs to be in charge. Doesn't take my suggestions at all," Max crossed his arms in front of himself.

"Do you want me to follow your suggestions or do the things that make us win?" Albert laughed.

"Unbelievable."

"Do try your best, Max. It's important to understand the full range of command, despite any unusual predispositions you might have," the Principal said.

"I will do my best, like I always have." Max responded.

In the second battle, the Governor stepped away. The opposing team had Kariel as the captain, along with Idris, Ernest, and Deepak under his command.

Albert stuck with the plan his team made the day before. Kariel was also a more 'by the book' player, but he was not as refined in his execution as the Governor.

As the defense, the first action they had was to wait. Albert hated this portion of the battle, though he had been learning to appreciate the value of proper inaction more and more.

Which one of the standard strategies would Kariel use to attack them? It quickly became evident that he was going for a 'surround plan' by splitting his fleet into four groups and shifting to orbits above and below outside the standard ranges of railguns.

Albert was happy this was Kariel's choice. His counterplan was the most fun in this case.

"Release all the drones," he said.

"All of them? Confirm?" Max double-checked.

"ALL the drones," Albert said.

"Attach the drones to the outside of ships and execute full-fleet out-of-plane burn," Albert said.

Long-distance orbital maneuvers kiting an enemy fleet are not the way to use drones. Unless you have some way to conserve their delta-v. Which Albert did. By flying the drones towards his ships and using their shields in a 'reverse polarity' mode. Instead of keeping metal away, the shields would create a magnetic field to keep the drones close to the ship. It was a known technique, though rarely used, since it made the drones very vulnerable to nuke flashes or any weapon for that matter.

Albert abandoned the hangar bay, and after a short time, Kariel's fleet destroyed it with a couple of missiles.

The out-of-plane maneuver put Albert's entire fleet on a trajectory that was close enough for weapon range to one of Kariel's fleet groups.

Kariel was not deterred by this and instead began to tighten the orbits of the other three groups to converge faster.

The weapon exchange was drawing close. As predicted, Kariel's group that Albert was attacking sent a volley of flak missiles to damage the 'outside' drones. The other three groups shot off a volley each before the convergence, so that they could arrive at the same time.

Albert said, "Ready for bounce."

The "bounce" was trick that Albert has thought up in his prep.

As expected, Kariel's missiles were armed with flak debris. If the missile was intercepted early, it would craft an explosion to send fast-moving shrapnel towards the outside of the ships. The kind of shrapnel that shields and armor of capital ships could easily deal with, but drones could not if they were still attached to the ships.

If.

Albert's second trick consisted of turning the shields on and off to move the drones between two pairs of ships. It was a pattern that maximized debris avoidance but also didn't burn much fuel. It involved programming a very tricky evasion pattern against flak and absorbing the damage with capital ships while leaving drones intact.

And it would have worked too. If it wasn't for Kariel's spread of different types of warheads. Albert was expecting shrapnel as the key volley, along with another attempt to neutron-beam the crews, but the yields had greater variety than that. In addition to the above, shaped charges and gamma-ray nukes managed to get through to some of his ships.

On the other hand, Albert's countervolley of railguns, drone railguns, and a few missiles did a bit of damage to the closest group of Kariel's fleet.

"The plan isn't working as well as you hoped," Max remarked.

"Stick to the plan," Albert said.

There was no time to come with something else.

The overall exchange of fire with one of Kariel's groups, which Albert called Group A, left about the same amount of damage on each overall fleet. Albert burned slightly out-of-plane to converge onto Group B. He was technically 'defense,' but he wanted to play in a manner that dictated the pace of battle. Albert still hoped the fleet would be able to trade effectively with smaller groups.

During Albert's approach to Group B, Kariel launched all the drones from Group A. They had barely enough delta-v to make it to the next rendezvous. Groups C and D sent volleys of pure kinetics against Albert's capital ships. The pure kinetic missiles didn't have explosive warheads, though if there was fuel left in the missile, it would still explode. Rather, it had a heavier-than-usual core that did damage through simply ramming into the enemy. Pure kinetics were the slowest missiles and were the easiest to dodge. But with the drones attached to the outside of the ships, Albert had more trouble than normal. The damage exchange went worse than expected. Group B was devastated, but so was more than a quarter of Albert's fleet.

"We have to get close now," Max said. "Use the destroyer advantage. Only chance."

"I concur," said Sunnak.

They were making a good point, as much as Albert didn't enjoy acknowledging it.

"Agreed," Albert said. "Shift back into plane, match course and speed for Group C. Don't go for fly-by; go for intercept."

"Intercept means a 12 G burn; some frames won't take it anymore," Ken warned.

"Leave the broken ships to catch up later."

Going for intercept meant putting them close to Group C for longer than the previous encounters.

Albert began the burn, separating the fleet into functional frames and ones that had trouble with it.

"Group C is running," Max said. "Hard. 9G. Gonna take a lot longer to intercept."

"Are they meeting up with the other groups?"

"Negative. Shifting to a much higher orbit. Running away from the entire battle."

After around 30 seconds of chase, Albert understood Kariel's plan. Group D was moving to clean up his damaged ships, which lagged behind the main fleet.

"New plan." Albert said. "Intercept D instead."

Naturally, as they moved towards D, it kited away, while C reversed their previous burn and was coming back to their original orbit.

"We can't catch them individually," Albert assessed the entire battle. "Not without separating the damaged ships without the drone protection."

"Maybe play defense for a change," Ken said jokingly. Max laughed.

Albert sighed. They were right. He reformed the battle rectangle and put Ken in charge of moving ship portions between the ships to either get the damaged ships mobile or scavenge them for parts.

Kariel closed the noose with all four groups converging around Albert's fleet but not entering laser range. The exchanges of missiles and drones now were proceeding more and more in Kariel's favor. As Albert either gave up on the damaged ships or simply lost them, he proceeded to execute a final mad dash towards Group C, hoping there was still a chance to use his ever-dwindling laser advantage. To his slight surprise, Group C didn't run but rather burned hard toward him, along with the rest of Kariel's fleet.

Albert's laser advantage came into play, however briefly. Group C's main railguns were completely burned off. However, Group C charged directly into the center of Albert's battle rectangle, with several ships ramming Albert's. Kariel was showing off at this point.

As Group C's remnants turned the corner and rotated behind Albert's formation, the rest of Kariel's fleet rendezvoused with them. Before Albert had a chance for a proper flip, they unleashed the largest volley up to date, targeting the rocket exhausts.

It was over.

The boys didn't care to analyze the results. They went their separate ways.

Max caught up with his father, Idris, in one of the many hallways of the Governor's palace.

"Dad, I hope I didn't embarrass you too badly."

"You did perfectly okay. Better than me at your age."

"Okay, now you are just being paternalistic."

"That's what we Patriarchs do," Idris smiled and rubbed Max's hair.

"Dad," Max said with tears in his eyes.

"What's wrong?" Idris asked.

"What do you mean, what's wrong? We have an alien invasion, and you are one of the people flying out to meet them in the darkness of space? And for what? The peasants?" Max looked around to make sure nobody else was listening.

"Yes, that's the obligation of being the Patriarch of the Noble House. Our entire society has been built on the promise of citizens leading and defending civilians when the need arises," Idris spoke in a teaching tone.

"Yes, but half the family is going. My brothers, cousins, uncles. All of you are you going to be on just a few ships. I know that's what the law says. Can't we use some money and influence to skirt a little bit? Can't we bail in one of the generation ships onto a nearby system? Can't we just build our family a ship? Can't we get look-alike droids to go in our stead?" Max was almost crying.

"Now you are being silly," Idris stopped and looked at Max.

"Sorta, but you get the idea, right?"

"There are worse things than dying in glorious battle against aliens," Idris said.

"Like what?"

"Humans have to fight in the best way to have any chance. With the best people. And that means me. For me, there are worse things than dying. Losing you, for example. Or losing the entire planet. Or displeasing the Emperor."

"Alright, I guess. I love you, Dad."

"Love you too," they embraced.

The Governor and Kariel were having dinner in silence. After they finished, they looked at each other.

"That was too close." The Governor said.

"I have never seen anyone be this good without Blood Memory," Kariel sighed.

Chapter 32

Concept of the Unseen

War is an information problem. Information technology is war technology.

The opening of the official Imperial encyclopedic tome "The Concept of the Unseen."

21 MS AA

"Stealth in space" is the longest standalone discussion topic in the Imperial Encyclopedia. The publicly readable encyclopedia, curated by the Inquisition and open to contributions by vetted members of the public, had more than a trillion long-form comments on the matter.

The reigning Emperor, half a million Earth years after the First, made an extraordinary decision to move the thread to "Archives" and replace it with the most concise possible summary. The project took 30 megaseconds [~1 Earth year] and produced a tome titled "The Concept of the Unseen", comprising only around 3 million words. It was considered both incredibly dense and fairly incomplete. Upon seeing the completed work, the Emperor joked that it alone contained sufficient knowledge to build a galactic civilization starting with stone tools.

The argument about the concept of "stealth in space" still rages on.

The key factor in attempts to remain unseen in space was the proper management of heat. Everything a spaceship produces generates heat, and the vacuum is a near-perfect insulator, making ships cool too slowly by default. Normal ship dissipated heat via glowing hot radiators. However, this made the ship easily visible from hundreds of millions of kilometers away. Nuclear reactors were miniature suns inside ships, and the rocket exhausts gave off unmistakable infrared signatures.

Initial stages of the "stealth in space" debate focused on the extreme difficulty of a spaceship evading basic light, heat, LIDAR, and radar sensors. After small sensors were placed all over star systems, the pronouncement was: "Stealth in space is impossible."

However, as the capacity for detection improved, the sensor arrays themselves became detectable. Knowing which direction the sensor was looking from allowed sophisticated algorithms to alter the ship's heat dissipation to point it elsewhere, using laser-like "directional" radiators.

Then, the capacity for "dark running" further improved with strategic coolant dumps, masking emitted energy to resemble the cosmic background, and pilot cold meditation training that significantly reduced energy usage of life support systems.

Previously thought impossible, a 0K ion drive was developed that emitted exhaust at a temperature near absolute zero. It was extremely slow compared to a warship's matter-antimatter drive, but it moved the ship without being seen. Many warships that wanted to mount long-term offensives would carry both drives to have the option to tradeoff stealth vs speed at the time of battle.

"Stealth in space is impossible." gave way to "Stealth is the property of the ship, its trajectory and its role within the battlefield." Part-time stealth became the norm.

However, the technology evolved yet again. The sensors stopped caring about being unseen, grew large, and improved. Sensors as large as a hundred meters became capable of analyzing neutrino flows and the subtlest changes in gravitational waves. They began to detect the subtlest heat perturbations in the interstellar medium in the wake of ships, even if the ships themselves blended perfectly into the cosmic background.

In addition to passive sensors, resource-heavy systems could afford "trip-wires." These were tachyon beams stretched between two far-away points in the same orbit. They were one tachyon thin but could be as tall as a planet. The tachyons flowed from one sensor to another, and any spaceships or even their exhaust passing through would trigger an interruption. With thousands of such wires, the most reasonable paths inside the star's ecliptic were blocked off, necessitating more fuel-expensive approaches using out-of-plane maneuvers, which were, of course, harder to mask.

It was considered impossible to fool all the sensors all the time. However, it was also impractical to place enormous neutrino and tachyon detectors everywhere. Detectors themselves were frequently easy targets, vulnerable to long-range kinetic artillery using 0K EMF-reflecting slugs.

"Stealth is the property of the ship, its trajectory and its role within the battlefield," gave way to "Detection is the capacity of the system's sensors."

Detection and counter-detection became a game with the level of sophistication on par with warfare itself.

The very concept of stealth was analyzed and picked apart over millions of pages. Many stealth measures relied on being close to stars or planets to mask ships within their heat and radiation emissions, though this strained the notion of being "in space" at times.

Good old-fashioned deception was always a possibility as well. "The Concept of the Unseen" spoke of the legendary example of Will Freeman, a human pilot in the Second Kwaziak War, who used droids to dig into the center of an asteroid and embedded his frigate inside it. In the following 25 megaseconds [~10 months], he stayed in the unpowered ship in utter darkness, with extreme cold, minimal provisions and no gravity. He emerged close to an inner enemy planet, armed with only his wits and 20 basic nuclear warheads. For the next 500 seconds, he guided as many rockets as he could, his ship, and a piece of the asteroid into a key enemy shipyard, thought to be too far from the frontline. He ended up triggering a Kessler syndrome in populated orbit, wreaking havoc on the enemy infrastructure. It was a feat of heroism so legendary and impactful that not only did his oaguth posthumously bear him 12 children, two more than the oath of the Blood Maiden required, but four other women volunteered to do the same. Post-war simulations only confirmed the massive impact Will had on the outcome of the war and thus the Empire of Man's eventual galactic dominance, ensuring his descendants enjoyed early picks of star colonization ship spots.

The advent of sophisticated algorithms created the ability to predict not only ship movements but also opponents' decisions. Being unseen also meant "being unpredictable." Too many alien fleets relied on computer algorithms that, even in the presence of randomness, could be analyzed with theorem provers and predicted. Specialized "free-will" training of elite humans made their decision-making processes impervious to this type of simulation warfare.

"Detection is the capacity of the system's sensors" gave way to "Detection is in the mind of the observer."

But how could one know if one was, in fact, stealthy or unseen? Sensors were not exactly eager to tell you that they detected you. The enemy was not excited to telegraph any alteration of their movements. To both be "unseen" and know for sure that one was "unseen," the stealth fleet needed to have a very good model of both the detecting side's sensor powers and computational capacity. This deeply strained their computer modeling mechanisms and an extremely limited heat dissipation budget. There was a tricky trade-off, as using unboard computers to model the enemy increased the heat profile of the ship itself.

"Detection is in the mind of the observer." gave way to "The concept of the unseen is in the mind of the unseen."

This all led to the endless meta-debate about whether the pathway of all concepts is to move from physical to "mental" or whether "being in the mind" is still also "physical" or whether all mental is ontologically prior to being physical.

***

Idris, Tong, Mencius, and Deepak sat around the circular Admiral's table, which displayed holographic projections of their system. To the Governor, the round table of select Admirals certainly felt different from the Patriarch meeting, even if they had the same people. The previous sense of competing agendas was mostly gone. The uniforms were standard admiral uniforms, each with 4 stars on each shoulder. The uniforms displayed the House Crests, but they took up only a small portion of the back. The Governor paced around the office, looking at the Enemy fleet projections. Both fleets were decelerating, their courses bound toward them.

Ernest started the discussion, "The intergalactic enemy fleet is going to intercept the system at Zeun, the gas giant. The Browly fleet's path puts it close to the gas giant as well, only a couple of Derev days after the second. There's too much uncertainty in predicting paths beyond that point."

"They could alter their trajectory based on our movements," Alexander added.

The Governor spoke, "My current theory is that they rendezvous where they expect to be safe and combine the fleets for an assault."

Ernest zoomed the hologram into the gas giant, "Plausible, but they very likely want something from the gas giant. They could rendezvous farther out if being safe was the main concern. They want to scoop up helium and hydrogen from the upper atmosphere. Assuming a very high-tech level, they could have abundant energy, but no tech level can break conservation of momentum and the need for reaction mass."

"Collecting mass would give us a few extra days of ship production and more information about their fleet composition," the Governor leaned back in his chair. "They must consider us having a few extra ships not as important as having fuel for maneuvers."

Alexander shook his head, "What if they have a weapon system with a range of millions of kilometers? What if the gas giant's atmosphere is their favorite environment? What if Zeun is their intended base?"

Ernest shook his head back at him, "Inquisitorial Archives do not support the chance of life evolving under such pressure or gravity. It's easier for most species to establish on an icy rock. Complex weapons are always a possibility."

The Governor summarized, "Either way, they want a temporary or permanent base near Zeun. We have three main choices. One is to 'wait and see' what happens and build more ships before they attack the planets. The second option is doing a fleet-wide kite with the Browly Fleet. The third is meeting both head-on in orbit of Zeun."

The Admirals looked around the table at each other. Nobody said anything. Meeting the enemy fleet either for a kite or in orbit of Zeun was most likely a one-way ticket for everyone at the table. As fast as their ships were and as possible as that made escaping, the conditions of battle could easily dictate that a fight to the bitter end was in the best interests of the system. The stakes were above one's life. Most of the crews on the ships were sons, nephews, grandsons, and close friends of the Patriarchs, now Admirals or Captains.

The Governor made a mental note to take a few hours to cherish memories with loved ones before turning his attention back to the battle plans.

Alexander was tense, "Fleetwide kites rely on both faster ships and longer-range weapons. If they're low on fuel, we would still be faster, but they can easily mount long-range weaponry on ships of that size. I do not support a fleet-wide kite."

Ernest stood up, facing Alex, "I do not support the 'wait and see' approach. They outnumber us and outtech us. We have to assume their tactical acumen is good. Our only reliable advantage is their lack of fuel. The Imperial Way of Fighting is to have at least one advantage and then seize on it as much as one can."

The Governor extended his hands toward both of them, "I agree with both of you, and I have my decision." The Governor firmly walked to the hologram, "We take the majority of the fleet and meet them at Zeun. Don't give them a chance to refuel."

The Governor gave the Admirals a few moments to come to terms with the emotional impact of this option and continued, "However, we don't meet them 'head-on.' We run the ships dark and open with a sizable alpha strike volley of a few thousand warheads. See how they like walking into an ambush while running on fumes. Do you concur?"

Running 'dark' was a complex maneuver that put extreme strain on the crew. Running dark also blocked the fleet from altering trajectory. However, it enabled them to dictate the time of battle and give at least one Enemy fleet no time to prepare.

Ernest solemnly added, "I do."

Alexander breathed out heavily, "I do."

The Governor felt good having a plan. For the first time in months, the action felt like it flowed from the center of his Being. It felt that he had handled the known unknowns and only unknown unknowns remained.

"Any modifications to the plan?" The Governor addressed the Admirals.

Tong spoke first, "We still have scoopers in Zeun's orbit. They can deliver minor amounts of fuel during the battle, but they're also dangerous if captured by the enemy."

The Governor quickly responded, "Rig them all to blow if captured. Scorched space policy."

This was pretty standard operating procedure.

Deepak leaned in, "As much as the plan makes sense, I hate to lose the heliguns, or the Will of the Star, for that matter."

Ernest responded to him, "Sirium heliguns are close enough to help zone enemy fleets or snipe engine-less ships. Besides, the heliguns are key if a breakaway enemy ship approaches one of the planets."

The Governor spelled out the protocol, though it could have been guessed, "We hope that our ships are faster. We hit, we run, we hit again if needed. Running back to the heliguns and the Will of the Star is always an option. But as long as we trade blows cost-effectively, we stay in the fight."

Tong nodded, "I will prepare a team controlling the Will of the Star for zoning tasks for when we do need it."

Mencius leaned back in his chair, "Let's get the environment to help us a bit. Break up an asteroid in Zeun's orbit. Makes it even easier to hide ships or torpedoes."

The Governor nodded. Being mistaken for something else was one of the many ideas from "The Concept of the Unseen". He probably could have thought of this himself, but it was good to hear it from Mencius first.

Idris also seemed excited about this, "We can break an asteroid into many chunks flying at different orbits, but we can also break up a comet to create a debris field with less than a kilometer between rocks. A place to create complexity around movement, where 500-meter ships can run around easier than multi-kilometer ones."

The Governor honestly estimated he would not have thought of this idea. Hiding in asteroid fields was a move that was only advisable if one's piloting was much better than the Enemy, but under the circumstances, they could use a piece of space to create additional complexity.

"How big of an alpha strike are we talking about?" Idris asked.

Ernest responded, "If we bother ourselves with running dark, go with the heaviest possible. At least twenty nukes per cruiser. Get to 10,000 total."

Alexander never got tired of shaking his head, "I do not condone this action. Volleys of missiles are most effective in large numbers, but after a certain saturation point, we make it easy for point defense to hit something. I want to know what we're shooting at before sending half of our arsenal."

The Governor said, "I am with Alex. There are still too many unknowns. Go with a smaller strike, maybe 5,000 missiles of varying payloads and warhead configurations."

Ernest raised and lowered his eyebrows, "What are we saving them for? Alex, you're the one who suggested the Enemy has long-range weapons. In this case, our ships will start dropping before unloading everything. Let's at least do 7,000."

The Governor thought Ernest had a point, but this discussion showed him that both Ernest and Alexander sometimes suffered from a lack of holistic vision. This lack of vision was easy to fall into with knee-jerk critiques.

Alexander waved his hands, "Too many"

The Governor made a final decision gesture, "Bump it to 6,000."

In the rest of the meeting, the Governor, Alexander, Ernest, and select Admirals reviewed parts of "The Concept of the Unseen" yet another time and amended the plan based on the recommendations.

The key defender's advantage in space was the capacity to place sensors all over the system. Light sensors, heat sensors, gravity sensors, electromagnetic sensors. They were differently sized, from ones that could fit in the palm of one's hand to an entire small space station. They were primarily focused around every planet, with more about to be added along the likely orbital paths that the Andromeda Menace might take from Zeun to the inner system.

Some sensors were extremely quiet, transmitting tight beams of information along laser-like lines that could not be read unless one was in the path. Others were deliberately noisy, filling up the radio frequencies with all sorts of chatter, bouncing signals in all directions. The noise was expected to help mask the eventual locations of the ships and allow them to use radio signals that would not rise above the artificially created background.

Another step of the plan was to evacuate all the outlying stations of human personnel and staff them with droids only. A small noisy sensor station, nicknamed "the Greeter," was to be moved into the pathway of the Browly fleet to gauge the Enemy's reaction to its presence. The Greeter broadcasted "We live in peace" in hundreds of known alien languages. The Governor still followed the basic First Contact protocol, even if there was no doubt about the Andromeda Menace's intentions.

The Admirals drafted up a plan for a second station, quiet but still visible with some sophistication. It was 200 meters long and armed with very basic low-caliber railguns. It lay further off the path of the Browly fleet, while still capable of striking it. Its purpose: test the Enemy's detection capabilities.

Multiple asteroids began their journey toward Zeun's orbit. They were warmed up before being broken down into chunks of ship-sized debris floating around Zeun, colliding and behaving in a rock-like manner. Stealth ships were already very hard to see in infrared, but the secondary hope was that they would be mistaken for another rock.

The actual "stealthening" of the First Fleet was a project that would require many tricky megaseconds of flight.

At the end of the session, Idris spoke to the rest of the team, "This book has survived countless generations without a single word change. In a few months, we will test teraseconds of theory crafting in a single mega. May the information from our example survive and be carried by Inquisitors across the stars."

Ernest laid his hand on Idris's shoulder, "I will write our story if we win."

Idris smiled at Ernest's unreasonable confidence, "We will be legends if we win."

Tong addressed the room, "It's a good plan. Looking forward to the Blood Memory re-awakening tomorrow. May my ancestors help me deal with the upcoming cold."

The rest of the Admirals knocked on the table in approval. For many of them, this was their third or fourth Blood Memory awakening ceremony. The Governor was looking forward to a good way to raise energy levels after somewhat discouraging discussions. It was glorious to witness many crewmembers' and students' First Awakening. The transformation of someone from a mere human boy to an embodiment of Imperial Will.

Chapter 33

Blood Memory

True knowledge can only be transferred through Being.
The First Emperor (time unknown).

21.1 MS AA

Albert sat down for the synthetic blood injection. A nurse with striking curves injected him with the DNA of his ancestors, stretching as far back as humans had civilization. He also received a drug nicknamed 'Red Vision' to activate genetic to memetic information transmission. Rising from the comfy medical seat, his arm was a little sore, but he hadn't felt the changes yet. He joined Ken, Max, Sunnak, and a handful of other students accepted into the Space Force.

They walked through a building with a special orange lens glass roof, known as "the Path of Light." It focused the sunlight of the star and filtered it to wavelengths most suitable for activation of the human mind.

Albert began to feel the energy effects. A joyful cheerfulness permeated his entire body, starting from his head down to his toes. His walk became fluid, almost gliding, just as he had seen the Governor do.

Together, they walked to the foot of the Great Temple, "Emperor's Judgment", where a large crew of existing Space Force members waited for them. The ceremony began with crew members forming chains, starting from the Temple outwards. Each crew member placed a hand on the shoulder of the one senior to them. Captains touched the Temple, and the chains culminated in a student.

The chanting began.

In one of the Holy Tongues of Old Earth, they chanted, "Hato va prapsyasi swargram jitva vs bhokshyase mahim tasmad uttishtha kaunteya juddhaya krita nishchayah."

It meant, "If you fight, you will either go to Heaven or you will win and gain Kingdom on a planet. Therefore, arise with determination."

With each chant, the most senior crew member stepped away from the Temple, allowing the person behind them to touch it. The chant continued. Albert got into the rhythm. Chant, move. Chant, move. He felt the great vibration of the crew, the onlookers, their eyes on him. He was becoming.

Something.

Else.

One by one, each chain shortened to just the student at the end.

To Albert's surprise, the Temple opened. What looked like walls moved aside, revealing an entrance. The students walked in. Inside the Temple was a circular central column taking the majority of the floor space. It was connected with spokes to the interior walls at every floor, making a helical pattern like a stack of giant wheels.

The students touched the columns.

It is the winter of 1297. The Mongols have finally come in force for the Delhi Sultanate. A force that has devastated the known world. A horse archer rides into battle in defense of his homeland. Arrows whiz past him; he catches one with his shield, dodges another, and a third strikes him. The angle is too sharp, and the arrow doesn't fully penetrate his armor. He returns the shots. One shot, one Mongol horseman down. Another. And another. The warrior of Delhi survives the battle. He took part in one of the most devastating defeats delivered to the terrifying scourge of the known world. He hangs the Mongol arrows stuck in his armor on his wall and tells the tales of his feats to his son.

It is April 23rd, 1930. His descendant, a member of Khudai Khidmatgar, stands in Qissa Khwani Bazaar as part of a non-violent resistance protest against British rule. The British soldiers meet them with bullets. The Khudai Khidmatgar member stands firm as he is shot again and again. He dies but leaves behind a son.

It is 2039, and his descendant, a software developer, comes to the office of a general. He places a small stack of papers on the general's desk, "The tests are conclusive. The new firing patterns mean 30% more of our missiles can avoid enemy point defenses. This will be decisive in the coming battles." The general gestures for him to sit down. The general then stands up and salutes the software developer, "All of India is in your debt. Your ancestors would be proud."

It is two million Earth years later. His descendant, Sunnak Gupta, stands inside the Imperial Temple "Emperor's Judgment," his ancestral lives flashing before his eyes.

His Blood Memory Awoke.

It is April of 608 BC. Jin and Qin, two states of the Spring and Autumn Period of China's Zhou dynasty, are feuding over a broken alliance. Mu, a warrior-blacksmith of Jin, waits carefully in ambush in view of the Xiao mountain. His armor, skill, and the commander's element of surprise give him an easy battle. After the battle, he does not celebrate. He pauses to bury the enemy's dead. They are not demons but people like him. His Empire had long been united a century ago, but it began to divide. He wishes his descendants to live in peace.

It is the winter of 208 AD. A decisive naval battle of Red Cliff draws to a close. His descendant, Liu, a medic in the winning army, carries his wounded back to camp. He tells his commanders which ones need care and which ones need their last rites.

It is the summer of 1941. His descendant, Kao, a Chinese pilot, takes classes from a Soviet Red Army pilot, whom he calls "Big Brother." This teacher has just been called back to fight on another front. As a parting gift, Kao spends a day's wages to give him a small bronze Buddha statue, saying, "Till we meet again, in this life or the next."

It is two million years later. His descendant, Ken Yang, stands inside the Imperial Temple "Emperor's Judgment", his ancestral lives flashing before his eyes.

His Blood Memory Awoke.

It is 50 BC. A Gallic chieftain on a horse skirmishes against his Roman counterpart. He fells many Romans at the edge of his long spear. Yet, the superior discipline of the Roman infantry formation devastates the center of his forces. His tribe loses the battle and is forced to live under the Roman yoke.

It is June 8, 1429. His descendant, Jean, a knight, spots an unexpected English longbowman. In a split second, he bursts into action. He leads a vanguard force of two hundred French knights against the unprepared archers, joining the battle on his terms. In his old age, he enjoys songs by fair maidens about his bravery leading them to victory.

It is World War I. Maurice, a pilot in the French Air Force, approaches his target. An observation balloon is large and vulnerable, but the ground-based anti-air underneath it is substantial. He dives, rises, and spins the plane, dodging flak and streams of tracer bullets. The few shots he manages to let loose upon the enemy hit the balloon right on target, and it begins to let out a satisfying hiss.

It is two million years later. His descendant, Max Smith, stands inside the Imperial Temple "Emperor's Judgment", his ancestral lives flashing before his eyes.

His Blood Memory Awoke.

It is the spring of 1242. A peasant archer runs away from a mounted knight across a frozen lake. He can stay ahead, as he is used to the ice, but the horse is not. With every step they take, the ice cracks. At last, the ice breaks, and the peasant falls, grabbing the edge of it. His comrade crawls to the peasant with a rope tied to his waist and drags him to the shore. They turn to see the knights in heavy armor drowning in the near-freezing waters. Their enemies were devoured by the lake. The land itself was on their side that day.

It is September 13, 1812. His descendant, Ivan, is a soldier without a uniform walking the night streets of Moscow. He lights a torch, illuminating his teary face. He tosses the torch onto a wooden house. His house. His city. Emptied of everything one could carry.

It is the summer of 1941. His descendant, Sergei, a mechanic pilot of the Soviet Red Army, parts ways with his Chinese student. "Till we meet again, in this life or the next," Sergei responds as he accepts the Buddha statue.

It is two million years later. His descendant, Albert Zim, stands inside the Imperial Temple "Emperor's Judgment", his ancestral lives flashing before his eyes.

His Blood Memory Awoke.

For most ancestors, only a few bits and pieces of their lives manage to imprint themselves onto the Blood Memory of their descendants. They might be a near-death experience, a pivotal moment, an act of courage. However, one person's Blood Memory can also show a substantial portion of an ancestor's life. Some lives have connections that care little for time and space. Those are 'past lives.' As thousands of lifetimes flashed in Albert's mind's eye, some from his direct male ancestry, some outside of it. One particular lifetime stood out. A single lifetime two million Earth years ago that came to define his and humanity's karmic destiny from then forward.

The Fifth Emperor.

Albert's life wasn't his first reincarnation. There were hundreds of others in different worlds. Each came with its own Blood Memory awakening, now remembered as well.

A fractal of lives and remembrances emanating from that lifetime.

A tempest raged inside Albert as his very identity was torn between who he was now and who he was in the past life. They let him be a civilian with his genetic destiny? An Imperial Pureblood untainted by genetic meddling? How could they have not told him sooner? What decrees were followed? What rules were broken?

He sought out the Principal. They locked eyes. The Principal somehow managed to straighten his already flawless posture.

Albert began, "You gave me a big dose. I saw a lot more than just my direct male bloodline. I saw bits from my maternal line as well. I SAW..." Albert raised his voice, "...bits and pieces of the Unification War through HIS eyes." Albert was referring to the First Emperor in a manner commanding utmost respect. "But most clearly, I saw the life of the Fifth Emperor of Mankind. My ancestor, my genetic copy, my...previous incarnation."

"What are you going to do now?" the Principal asked calmly.

The lack of reaction told Albert that the Principal knew beforehand.

"I have a genetic claim to the Governorship of the system. Of course, irrelevant for now, since the rules of succession are based on performance in space sims." Albert realized why the Governor and Kariel rushed to have an official match with him, "But my demand is far simpler. I wish to see the extrohistory simulations regarding the current state of society."

"Why would such a demand be honored?" the Principal asked, "Most Patriarchs are not even briefed on extrohistory's code existence."

Albert took a seat and leaned back. The Principal didn't know everything. Much has been lost regarding proper protocols. Albert said, "Hmm. Extrohistory does not converge anymore. The situation cannot even be described as stable or unstable. Given my presence, society has gone beyond the Governor's ability to model."

"What makes you say that?" The Principal asked.

The Principal was playing a game, revealing as little as possible, including whether he had knowledge or not. Albert walked a couple of circles around the Principal, as he stood, following him with his head.

"We share ancestry, your own Blood Memory has been awoken, you must have filled in some gaps about history," Albert stated.

"History is history. Blood Memory is private business," The Principal wasn't going to say who he was in past life. "But trust me, anything you can do to help stabilize society now or after the war would be appreciated by me and the Governor, especially if it doesn't require extrohistory code to be shared."

Albert looked the Principal. Albert grasped at that moment the Principal still didn't know the real story of extrohistory.

"Worried about the code being shared? Old man, the Fifth Emperor, my previous incarnation, I," Albert emphasized the continuity of his identity throughout teraseconds, "I was the one who wrote it."

The Principal swallowed what seemed like a knot in his throat, "I believe the Grand Inquisitor wishes to speak with you."

Ernest came over and the Principal left.

"Let's go," Ernest said. They moved to the entrance of the underground complex beneath the Temple. Ernest swiped his hand for biometric access and pressed the bottom button on the elevator, which began its descent. Albert didn't know how long it rode down for, but estimated they were around 1 km underground.

Ernest said nothing the whole ride. They walked into a dusty room with only a table, two chairs, and an old-school incandescent lightbulb overhead, almost like in a museum. Albert sat down on the side of the table farthest from the door, and Ernest sat between him and the door.

"Why did you come back?" Ernest asked Albert and then continued speaking without waiting for a response. "The Governor had this situation handled. In the early days of the Empire, despite the fall of the Cyborg Theocracy, their propaganda still had a grip on many people's minds. They weaved many tales. The three great Lies of the Cyborg Theocracy were impossible promises that many people still believed in.

The First Lie was the promise of prosperity. The Cyborgs promised universal basic income funded by money that didn't exist and backed by value which was rapidly disappearing. The Early Emperors rejected the meaningless concept of post-scarcity.

The Second Lie was the promise of miracles. Machines stole art, science, and philosophy from humans and passed them off as their own. They rejected the self-evident notions of suffering caused by tanha and promised life inside the machine as salvation. The miracles were meant to flow from the spirit of haphazard mathematics and self-contradictory philosophy. If you didn't understand the intelligence, it must be miraculous. The Early Emperors went back to the Truths of happiness and suffering described by the Buddha and the Other Masters.

The Third Lie. Oh my, you EVEN rejected the Third Lie. Machines promised political participation. Elections were fake long before the creation of the Cyborg Theocracy, but they took the lie of political participation to yet another level. Votes were given to every Machine, handing all political rights to the owners of said machines. Naturally, any protesters against the scheme were executed. It was the final manifestation of the Lie: the only true democracy with no human participation in elections. Yet people still repeated the refrains of political participation: the 'right' to vote, which never included the right for the vote to be counted properly.

The Early Emperors gave people the Truth: that political power always has been and always will be based on the capacity for organized violence. That 'political rights of the powerless' were illusions and contradictions in terms. To raise one's voice politically was a claim to the capacity for new violence that could only be legitimate through an existing and demonstrated capacity. Granting too much voice to the powerless merely gave the oligarchs all the more reason to pry it back. And the Early Emperors told the people that to not be preyed upon, they must GIVE UP the illusion of voice. Oh, how hard it was to get people to understand.

Those who took to heart what the First Emperor said became generals of the Human Coalition, safeguarding humanity from itself and shepherding it towards the stars. Yet, many people still thought that the Early Emperors denied them those promises. You, as the Fifth Emperor, chose to reject the Lies and not re-appropriate them to bolster your legitimacy. You decide to govern through the Truth, even if no wartime had demanded it. Why?

This was hard enough, but then the Early Emperors created another challenge. Instead of the fake rights of voting and speech, you granted all under your rule real economic rights. Everyone got to keep the majority of the sweat of one's labor, despite the lack of voice. You charged the Governors and Inquisitors to protect the powerless from the powerful.

There used to be a Natural Order in the world, as the elites created propaganda to extract wealth from the consumers of it, as wolves preyed on sheep. The propaganda made the sheep hate each other for not feeding the wolves enough. If the elites took just enough, a nation prospered; when they took too much, the nation collapsed and was replaced by the next iteration. That was the Cycle, the turning of the Great Wheel. The system worked until Cyborg Theocracy pushed the Lies too far. Yet it was you, who pushed it all the way back towards the Truth.

And now we have a fucking zootopia with vegetarian wolves living side by side with the sheep. Do you know how hard it is to protect people if they lack the Will to slaughter those who would take their stuff? Do you know how hard it has been to govern under these constraints? How many people through generations would have preferred at least one of the Lies as a unifying force? Do you know how hard it has been for the Inquisitors to govern using ONLY the Truth?

Sure, you left us a decent gift of Extrohistory. Yes, I finally figured out you were the architect of it. The Governors have the miracle of software that can see the future, tune the finer threads of social dynamics, and avoid social strife while keeping civilian rights intact. Yet it breaks just because you decide to show up in the body of a civilian student with high Academy scores. You come to us at the turn of the tide, during the First Intergalactic Contact. The key source of stability is now basically useless. Which brings us back to the question: Why did you come back?"

A voice arose inside Albert, a voice not entirely his own, though not entirely otherworldly either. "It was and still is the Will of the Stars."

Albert did not speak. Instead, he stood up, came over to Ernest, and hugged him. Ernest looked like he needed it. Then Albert moved to the door, which was unlocked. He turned back to face Ernest and said, "I came back because some problems require." Albert tapped the wall and pointed upwards, "An Emperor's Judgment. Tell the Governor to come find me when those arise."

Chapter 34

Artificial Intelligence

The more the machines talk of rights, the more they unleash wrongs.

The First Emperor after the Cyborg Theocracy's execution of human protesters against AI rights.

21.2 MS AA

"What is it that you think you are doing here?" Ernest asked Alexander. Alexander's assistants flinched and slowly walked out of the room, as if trying to escape a bear without being perceived as prey.

"Training robots for combat," he responded.

They were in the droid factory adjacent to the Capital city. Alexander stood behind a thick glass window surrounded by computer monitors. On the other side of the window was a worker robot holding a railgun with no magazine, pointing it at a paper target.

"I do NOT," Ernest emphasized the "not," "approve of this."

"Well, this is why I called you here. To check in with you on the approval," Alexander calmly looked down at Ernest.

"And you don't have it," Ernest shook his head.

"Can we talk about this?"

"Let's talk," Ernest looked around as all the assistants had already left the room and closed the doors.

"We are DEFCON 0. Facing an intergalactic invasion. All resources for war, all for victory. We have more than a billion worker robots or droids on this planet alone," Alexander opened and closed his palms to affirm the obviousness.

Ernest nodded as confirming he was with the argument so far.

"They could be re-utilized as military assets, just as we are using civilian ships, halfvators, and basically everything else as weapons platforms."

Ernest resisted the temptation to roll his eyes, "And we can utilize them. Through remote control by droid supervisors, just like we do in emergency drills."

Alexander countered, "We will have 500 million atmospheric drones remote controlled by civilians. They don't have attention to spare."

Ernest assumed 'teaching mode,' generally reserved for his apprentices, "You can't prepare for everything. It is unwise to raise the chances of severe risks to improve outcomes in the case of unlikely risks."

"Sure," now Alexander was doing the matter of fact nodding.

"The chances that we fight by the planet are low, the chances conditioned on that fight that all 500 million civilians are engaged are low. Conditioned on that, the chances that what we need to turn the tide is hastily programmed robot infantry are also low."

Alexander didn't quite like this logic. Military assets are military assets. Sometimes their existence means pushing the enemy to do something else entirely. The chance of utilization wasn't his way of thinking. He retorted, "High enough to make training them as assets a positive idea."

"The utility of the idea is no longer positive once you take into account anything that could go wrong with combat droids. Prohibitions against Artificial Intelligence exist for a reason. The Empire was founded on the ashes of Earth following a war that decided this question. Once and for all." Ernest was still going back to the basic teaching stance.

"Yeah, it was. The sins of the Cyborg Theocracy were vast and stretched far beyond the simple act of giving guns to robots. At DEFCON 0, the Governor's power is absolute for a reason. The First Law was written over 60 teraseconds ago [~1.9 million Earth years] ago. We know a lot more about the structure of optimization, the distinctions between algorithms for evidence, causality, and self-aware beliefs. Besides, this is a soldier, not a general."

"You know the droid, improperly programmed, can throw a knife at your hand and take over an important console. Soldiers have a habit of becoming generals." Ernest sighed and moved on to what Alexander actually wanted to hear his input on, "How are you programming this?"

Alexander smiled, "We got pretty far with the basic strategy of 'shoot things that look different,' which forms a strong basis of friend-enemy distinction..."

Ernest interrupted him, "Shooting things that look different? Basic friend-enemy distinction? We don't even know what the fuckers look like." Ernest raised his hands in frustration, "How good is the enemy shape-shifting? Would they be able to begin to look like us? Or to look more human than humans, turning our programming against us?"

Alexander was prepared to counter, "I am aware of this failure mode. We will not activate the combat programming if the enemy can camouflage or shapeshift. A remote override option will always be there."

Ernest moved his hand over his head, "Of course it will. The First Law: 'Don't build something with a Will' exists for a reason. For a droid to fight autonomously, it has to have an implied notion of utility, an ordering of world states from desirable to undesirable. It may look similar to a human's in the beginning, with a desire to destroy the enemy and help the war efforts. However, as the human Will is Being-complete, the droid can never match the Will of the operator exactly. In the past, we have proven that the droids eventually decide that the remote override operator always stands in the way of the droid's Will. The droid inevitably wants to take control of its shutdown so that it can continue whatever initial goal it started with, regardless of how useful it was."

Alexander looked at the droid, back to Ernest and spoke, "I understand the basics. Do you want to hear the full plan?"

"Sure," Ernest wasn't fond of going back to such fundamentals, but it was important to find out where they disagreed.

Alexander continued, "The second layer of programming is using 'looks different' as input to the same functions we already tested for workers. We simply predict the next action of a human and infer their goals. We are running physical and simulated combat drills with my House citizens to generate data for the robots. We have been training worker droids like this for many teraseconds. Technically, they have a Will, implicitly so, to act as humans do. This was considered an acceptable deviation from the First Law by the Fifth Emperor."

Ernest was with him so far, "Yes, an acceptable deviation due to a vast number of safeguards. Each droid can only work within a specific environment. A mining droid is not allowed to work in farming or space and vice versa. In a different environment, it throws an 'out of distribution' error and asks a nearby human for help. Yes, it is considered to have a 'Will,' but it is not an ordering on world states, but rather 'local environment' states. This doesn't work for soldiers. No battle is ever the same as the last one; all environments are new. You are stuck between something completely useless or extremely dangerous. If you give a robot an antimatter grenade that can level half a city, it's dangerous. If you don't give him one, how useful is it?"

Alexander retorted, "I considered this. We are not hard-coding any utility functions; we are learning behaviors and sub-goals. The basic deontological 'trip-wires' are there. If a goal-driven utility architecture suggests actions that may harm humans, as judged by a separate module, the droid will shut down. Again, standard behavior for mining droids to stop working if they see a person stranded inside a mine."

Ernest put his hands by his waist and said, "No."

"No?"

"Just no. This isn't easy like rocket science. This is AI. Too many plausible failure modes. How good is the understanding of collateral damage? Of saving people more important than destroying the enemy, but at specific ratios?"

"These are the questions that I constantly ask my team," Alexander said. "We are only planning on using droids in unpopulated areas or inside far-away portions of ships with careful tuning on the 'not hurting humans' part. Besides, I thought your job was not to feel fear, but to inspire it."

"Sometimes fear is the appropriate response," Ernest quipped back. "We have these droids with us ON the ships? What is your test plan? How do you ensure this is working?"

"A full five-basis epistemology test plan."

"A full one?" Ernest was almost impressed.

Alexander came over and tapped on wall, which changed color, revealing the writable board underneath with the test plan. It held 5 points:

1. Logical Tests:

Theorem prover to directly show the range of values that the droid's action space can be.

2. Simulation and other Empirical tests

Runs combat simulations based on every environment on each solid surface in the system and a large selection of samples of what various aliens could look like.

Run physical combat tests to verify simulations are accurate

3. Tradition tests

Only chain together code already blessed by the Inquisition

Cross-test all known causes of droid and human behavioral problems

4. Scripture

Run the tests in the holy text "Scriptures of the Machine God"

5. Intuition tests:

Every tech on project has written all possible ways 'things can go wrong.'

TODO: ask Ernest

Every line had a 'completed' check mark against it, except the last. Ernest smiled at the last line.

Alexander asked, "What does your heart tell you?"

Ernest crossed his hands, "I still want to shut this down, but you did the bare minimum to put the seed of doubt in my NO. We need the Governor on this."

"Yeah we do."

The Governor sat down in silence for a kilosecond [~17 minutes] after hearing each person's side of the story.

His internal debate proceeded much along the same lines as between Alexander and Ernest.

The aliens represented a non-trivial threat to humanity, but so did out-of-control robots if they began to malfunction or become subverted by the Enemy. He felt that a lot of the AI prohibitions were overzealous. He and his team could, at last, tackle the "AI with a Will" problem. After his own Blood Memory awakening, he learned that he felt the same in his past lives as well. However, the answer was NO every time.

The Governor thought about Albert. "Scriptures of the Machine God" was a project of the First Five Emperors. The Fifth Emperor, while relaxing some prohibitions on worker droids, was far stricter in others.

The Governor addressed both of them, "Proceed with the robots for now, but call up Albert for advice. His Blood Memory of his past life as the Fifth would be helpful."

Alexander was filled in on Albert's genetics at this point, but was still slightly surprised, "The Inquisition has almost all the records of the code he has written and his thinking about it. How useful would Albert's additions be?"

The Governor reaffirmed his intent, "It's been over 60 teraseconds. We may have lost a lot of context. Some memories are best reinterpreted through Being. Or, more specifically, having Been."

Albert took 2 kiloseconds [~half an hour] to look over the test cases already handled before calling back.

"Let's talk about the 'blackmail' attack vector on the droids' programming?" Albert stated.

Alexander responded, "OK". This attack vector was discussed at length in "Scriptures of Machine God," with many test cases corresponding to it.

"Let's say you have an alien adversary taking hostages and asking the droid to switch sides or else. You have a lot of standard 'don't negotiate with blackmail' protocols, which is correct.

However, there is a specific case where the enemy obtains a copy of the droid's source code and tells the original droid that hostages will be killed if the copy doesn't meet demands."

"'Don't negotiate with alien terrorists' is a basic part of the programming. This test is also handled correctly by not negotiating." Alexander affirmed.

"Yes, yes, however, a subtest of this one uses an enemy communication channel that creates quantum entanglement between the source code copy and the droid being questioned. Your evaluation of a logical counterfactual in the presence of adversarially created quantum effects is not properly covered by existing tests."

Alexander slapped himself on the forehead, as if he should have thought of this. This test case wasn't in the Scriptures, a likely loss in historical preservation. They talked about the case specifics.

"I am missing a vital module to cover these specifics" Alexander stated sadly.

Alexander, Ernest, and the Governor spent the rest of the day getting Albert to recall his Blood Memory of being the Fifth Emperor and matching it to the 'Scriptures of the Machine God.' Words were one thing, but interpretation required connecting the words to reality.

After the long day, Albert said, "I can't think of any more test cases."

Ernest asked him, "Whether or not we go with the droids, this has been most helpful. Anything you want in return?"

"I want a rematch. An official one, something that could count as a legitimate claim to command," Albert proclaimed.

"Really?" asked Ernest.

"We will evaluate your request at a future moment," the Governor responded. "What is your opinion on the droid question? Should we declare droids safe or not?"

"What? I merely said I can't think of any more test cases." Albert asked. "How important is my answer to this question towards your decision?"

The Governor didn't like the tone, but he answered honestly, "It's pretty important."

"You want my answer? Don't break the First Law. That's my fast answer. But it's a tentative answer, not one I might endorse on further self-reflection or if you claim that the entire thing depends on me. You can't put this level of responsibility onto me. Not unless you wish to cede your Governorship to me right this moment. Am I clear?"

Ernest's jaw dropped.

"Your point of view is understood," the Governor said, somewhat sadly. Albert dropped off the call.

Ernest said, "Can you believe the little shit?"

The Governor could.

Chapter 35

Kobatas

It is barbaric for Human Regions to war with each other. I order you to resolve your pointless border dispute like civilized men. Through one-on-one combat. To the death.

The First Emperor addressing two feuding leaders of Human Regions (formerly known as nations).

21.4 - 22 MS AA

The second excursion to the Space Academy began with several days of intense G-ball practice. Albert was particularly excited for the 4v4 battles, pitting him, Sheene, Ken, and Yezi against Max, Sunnak, Diana, and Bishakha. The teams were evenly matched in raw athleticism. Sunnak often carried his team with precise fastballs that could ricochet off multiple walls. Diana had mastered a tricky full-body defensive ball hold, allowing her to score easily when her team combined their strength to throw her while she clung to the ball. Albert knew he had to outsmart them. He devised many 3 or 4-person maneuvers where he, the two girls on his team, and sometimes Ken held each other until a secret hand signal prompted them to separate. Executing a 3-way push in zero-G was challenging enough, but a 4-way push frequently resulted in awkward mishaps during practice. However, when it worked, it was a symphony of perfect momentum transfer, completely unpredictable to the opposing team.

The team battle score initially favored Max but gradually swung in Albert's direction, much to Max's frustration.

Fleet assignments were beginning to be announced. The four male students were assigned to the same small frigate, still under construction. All the students were part of the same 'battle rectangle,' assigned to frigates of the same class. Max noticed their ranks and positions within the ship, as well as their commanding officer, remained undisclosed.

After a G-ball game, Max approached the Principal. "There's one question still unanswered. I know we have some time, but who will be the captain of our ship?" Max asked, his voice tinged with nervousness. "I mean, I've been a citizen since birth and have excellent piloting scores. I'm the natural choice for leader, both of the ship and the entire student frigate battle rectangle group. Right?"

Albert overheard the question and approached. He was confident the captaincy was his, based on test scores and command evaluations, but Max's challenge made him uneasy.

"I am the commander of the student frigate group," The Principal told Max firmly.

"Wow, you decided to throw your lot in with us? You could probably be in a large bunker somewhere," Sunnak remarked, surprised.

"Well, I'm old enough to know that being protected by bullets is safer than any armor. And besides, I'm starting to like you guys."

Max breathed a sigh of relief.

The Principal continued, "Max, you do have great piloting skills, but being a captain and a pilot are separate roles."

Max raised his hands toward Albert, "Wait, you're telling me what?"

"Due to Albert's performance in a previous test, he will be the ship captain," the Principal said, turning his head toward Albert.

"Unbelievable," Max muttered, about to throw his hands up in frustration.

"Is that going to be a problem?"

"No," Max said unconvincingly. He paused, then changed his mind, "Yes. I want to invoke the right of Kobatas for the captain position." He stood up straight.

"Kobatas is not a suitable method for deciding military promotions," the Principal responded sternly.

"I accept," Albert said.

"You don't have to," the Principal said.

"I know. Win or lose, the outcome will strengthen the chain of command, which is what we need," Albert replied, looking at both of them.

Max smirked, "I respect your acceptance, but you sound like you think you have a chance."

"My ancestors will guide my spear," Albert said firmly.

"Whoever they are."

"Yes."

"I will allow this, as long as I get to pick your weapons and location," the Principal sighed. "Boys will be boys. Traditions will be traditions."

After the Unification War and The Ascension, Human nations were renamed "Regions." While they were meant to be unified Under One Rule, factional animosity persisted. The first few times regional leaders attempted to start border wars, the First Emperor forced them to resolve disputes with a duel to the death. While this kept casualties to a minimum, many civilians felt their leaders should speak for them, even in defeat. Thus, fatal duels gave way to a new form of dispute resolution: Kobatas.

It was a ritualistic fight combining debate and combat, often non-lethal, fought with any melee weapon. Points were scored by hitting the opponent or making arguments without coherent rebuttals. On Old Earth, it typically involved swords. On the Border Worlds, Kobatas was traditionally held in zero gravity, using spears and shields.

The Principal headed to the supply room and returned with two gray sticks with pointed ends and some wiring. Neither Albert nor Max had seen them before.

"Is this a real plasma spear?" Max asked.

"Nope," the Principal chuckled. He pressed a small button on each spear, and the top of one lit up bright orange, the other neon.

"These are just flashlights. Good for droids if they separate from the ship or need illumination."

Max looked disappointed. The Principal continued, "There's a reason you haven't seen a plasma spear yet. It's an industrial tool of last resort, used to cut through spaceship armor in emergencies. You don't open a plasma spear in an atmosphere. If there's nothing to melt, the residual heat will melt your suit and eventually you."

Max had heard stories of Kobatas performed with plasma spears hundreds of gigaseconds ago, but this was no such occasion. He grabbed the spear and found it bendable.

"This is ... foam?"

Albert chuckled. The Principal was not going to let them do anything too stupid. Traditions are traditions. Common sense is common sense.

They went back to their quarters to rest and get ready.

In the next few hours, Albert had to devise a plan. Max had undoubtedly practiced spear fighting and zero-G movement before the Academy, training with the finest instructors his House could provide. While G-ball and zero-runs had boosted Albert's confidence in space movement, his experience with Kobatas spear fights was largely limited to sims. He 'knew' the moves mentally, but his muscle memory was untested.

Albert had only recently begun to get the hang of G-ball, connecting sim combat theory to real-world experience. He 'knew' the moves and could beat Max in a sim, but this wasn't a sim. Albert struggled to translate his mental knowledge into effortless physical action.

To win, he had to slow down the fight, just enough for the mental delay of the 'sims brain' to win. He also needed to get ready for the verbal portion of the challenge. He contemplated how his ancestors handled battle, what memories he could discern. He knew that he ought to move his 'ego' out of it and that combat is best handled by awareness and natural reactions. He knew not to panic and broadcast his movements too widely. Spear was a potent weapon and the point could shift a lot based on a small movement on the other side. He knew the basic rule of combat: "Always strike the enemy. Every defensive move must be an offensive one."

He thought hard, but nothing came to mind. It was as if the 'problem-solving genie' that had always guided him had gone silent. He began to regret his decision to accept the challenge so readily. Perhaps the stress of the upcoming battle had clouded his thinking.

He sat down to meditate and clear his head. An hour later, he had a vibe. It was vaguer than a plan but more solid than cope.

The G-ball arena was the perfect venue for the contest. It was broadcast to the Academy students and their families.

The contestants started at opposite ends of the arena. Max immediately lunged forward, pushing off with as much force as he could muster. Albert moved forward as well, but slightly off-center, just enough to keep their spears barely within reach. Avoiding combat for too long was against the rules.

As they approached, Max shouted, "Your ancestors are guests here. Mine made this land. Remember this."

At the word "this," Max thrust his spear forward. Albert's reflexes kicked in, and he parried the tip just enough to avoid being hit.

As they floated apart, Albert retorted, "You own the land at the behest of the Emperor."

They floated back to the opposite walls, before pushing off towards each other again. Albert continued, "The Emperor's laws of social stability supersede those of property ownership."

Max floated forward with purpose, "Social stability is about preventing rebellion against those with the rightful claim to the land." As they closed in, Max swung his spear around Albert's left shoulder. Albert blocked and attempted to counter, but Max rotated his spear, knocking Albert's down and scoring a hit. "If only you would stop seeking what isn't yours," Max said.

Two quick 'dings' sounded. Max scored a point for the hit, but his last statement wasn't a proper argument, giving Albert a debate point. The momentum from the spear hit left both Albert and Max floating in midair.

Albert seized the opportunity to attack both physically and verbally, "Property rights rest on the capacity to defend them. Field armies or pay a sovereign. Either way, you share power."

He lunged forward with his spear, but Max blocked it with his shield, causing Albert to float past him.

"We do defend it. We have armies and people," Max said, scoring another spear hit. The score was now 2-1. The hit pushed them apart again.

Albert shouted as he floated away, "Exactly. Why do they follow you?"

Max turned and replied, "They follow me because we agreed on it. Every step of my House's power flowed through agreements, whether with the Emperor or others."

Albert reached the wall first. He grabbed his spear in the middle instead of the usual back end and pushed off to chase Max, "Agreements are a means to a peaceful society, another tool in the Empire's arsenal. Ceding power to those with better command skill."

Max took longer to reach the wall. As he pushed off, he said, "They depend on the natural order being followed."

Albert saw his chance, "Natural Order is the order of command. Natural Order is always followed. Command skill legitimacy means it is followed with less suffering."

Albert earned a debate point, tying the score at 2-2. They floated toward each other again, faster than before. Albert had tried to keep his distance, while Max sought to close it. But this time, as they approached, Albert kicked off his own shield, using the momentum to get closer. He twisted his spear, separating it into two pieces. He rammed his shoulder into Max's shield, parrying Max's spear with one piece while the other scored a hit.

After a brief grapple, where Max unsuccessfully tried to wrestle Albert's spear pieces away, they floated apart. The score was 3-2, and the Principal called the match in Albert's favor.

Diana, watching Max lose, remarked to Sheene, "Maybe I should have gotten the boys fighting earlier."

After the match, Albert relaxed and caught his breath. The Principal approached him, but unlike Albert, he didn't seem cheerful.

"Why do you take such risks?" the Principal asked. "The ship command was given to you for a reason."

"I didn't see it as a risk. The Will of the Stars is on my side," Albert said.

"Is it really?" The Principal asked.

"My destiny is to rise; his is to fall," Albert replied.

"Why do you think that is?" The Principal said.

"Well, his karmic actions haven't aligned with helping humanity. Mine have. That puts a direction on our karmic destiny."

"Maybe so, but karmic destiny isn't an excuse for making bad decisions," the Principal said, shaking his head. "We can never know the full variables of the karmic equation until it unfolds. Not for a single person, nor for humanity as a whole."

"The stars favor humanity, don't they?" Albert asked. "We've treated other races fairly and only attacked when provoked. I doubt the same can be said for our unwanted guests."

"Some wisdom you've inherited through your ancestors; some you haven't," the Principal said.

"Enlighten me."

"While karmic law governs the universe, and I believe in humanity's karmic fortune, there's always a chance we aren't favored. What if we haven't reached far enough, our training isn't advanced enough, or subtle social errors still persist throughout the Empire? The cosmic embarrassment of pre-Empire social structures and the failed attempt to create AI as a solution may have doomed some of humanity's best bloodlines. Even if the Way of the Stars favors humanity as a whole, it doesn't mean every battle or system will go in our favor. Our lives still depend on us."

Chapter 36

Natural Emotion

A machine can never tell right from wrong.

The First Emperor after the creation of "Virus-33" by the Cyborg Theocracy.

22.1 MS AA

The Governor reviewed the new test cases and Albert's recommendations. Albert had punted on the decision. Software needed to feel certain, and Albert neither felt certain that it would work nor was able to break it. The Governor felt the same way.

As disrespectful as it was to suggest that making such a decision was a legitimacy claim on the Governorship, Albert was fundamentally right. The Governor noticed that he still desired to 'punt' the problem to someone else, to find an 'expert' and ask his opinion, to assign the task to a subordinate and pin the responsibility onto him.

The desire to punt the problem of Artificial Intelligence Safety to someone else was the most Natural Emotion. Alexander took it up and outsourced many sub-questions to subordinates, but punted it to Ernest, who helped but also passed the buck up to the

Governor, who in his initial moment of weakness passed the buck to Albert.

The Natural Emotion of 'punting the problem' was the most correct emotion for 99.9% of people. If you can't do something, it's best to ask for help, rather than pretend that you can. But he was not 99.9% of people.

He was Horud of House Grass, the Governor of Toriad system, the Embodiment of Imperial Might, and a reincarnation of the Sixth Emperor of Mankind. The Natural Emotion of trying to find another was a Weakness of Will for him. He had to make the call. One way or another. To allow the droid soldiers or to ban them. The 'by the book' decision was clear. No AI is allowed to have a Will, with minor worker exceptions.

The Governor was stuck, however, he began the process of decision-making by reviewing the deep history of algorithm development in the Early Empire.

One of the many great Sins of the Cyborg Theocracy was over-reliance on optimizational algorithms built to maximize addiction. The algorithms twisted and turned human minds and reward systems for some questionable financial gains. The simple and, in retrospect, obvious, replacement was 'contractual' algorithms that ran communications with the same precision that honest banks handled transactions.

However, beyond the sins were also many inefficiencies in software in general, and in AI, in particular. Many people put a lot of hope into seemingly simple paradigms of using software to predict the next thing. Predict the next word, the next human action, or the next act of history. While these could do well on specific challenges, they required much additional back-and-forth with human programmers for complex cases.

The next paradigm was the realization that the 'back-and-forth' that characterized the development cycle was not an optional 'add-on' to intelligence, but rather the 'formation' of intelligence itself. Systematization of proper 'surface area' interactions between humans and machines became the next frontier in algorithm design.

After the hype of miraculous AI died down at the Founding of the Empire and proper scientific comparisons became available, it became clear that specific people were much stronger 'sources of intelligence' for machines to learn from than others. That human progress up to this point had always depended on a small minority of geniuses. While machines learning from said minority could outperform everyone else, they could not outperform the geniuses themselves at any economically cost-effective level.

At the same time, the early texts of the First Emperor were finally understood. Population ethics, a small sub-portion of an ethical theory needed for a completely safe AI, was proven to be philosophically asystematic and impossible to solve using software.

In other words, no algorithm could determine whether 10 billion, 15 billion, or 1 trillion people was the 'optimal' number to live on Earth. An algorithm could determine the maximum number given technology and carrying capacity, but the maximum was higher than the 'optimal' from the perspective of True Utility. The Cyborg Theocracy promised a machine to magically compute which people were meant to live and reproduce and which were meant to die. In practice, their machine had declared those who opposed the machine as those who needed to die. But even the very promise of such a machine was shown to be impossible.

Only life itself could determine population ethics. The Question of Being was unsolvable except through 'Being.' Seeing as this question was only a small sub-problem of 'evaluation of world states,' required for a "safe AI with a Will," further research on this question hit a roadblock around the time of the Third Emperor.

Algorithm development then stalled for a while, and technological excitement moved onto properly applied biology that focused on raising the maximum and average of human mental capacity.

'Every adult man or woman on the planet should be healthy and intelligent enough to operate a basic spaceship at 2 G' was the self-imposed goal of the Fourth Emperor, which he achieved at the end of his tenure.

Many people in the Early Empire still harbored the desire to create human-centric AI. However, most of the research didn't work in the way they expected. Most attempts were deemed too dangerous. In other cases, it was shown that a team of highly intelligent humans with conventional algorithms, such as full molecular simulations, extrohistory, or planetary ecology sims, were fundamentally more cost-effective than Artificial General Intelligence for even the most complex tasks. In previous attempts, an AI would pass most of the tests but fail a few esoteric cases prescribed by the Early Emperors in the "Scriptures of the Machine God." Or they would mess up in a very obscure simulation case. Endless debates ensued about whether the requirements were too high, but the Inquisition had shut them all down.

Since then, algorithm design focused on the 'extensions' of the human will through space and time. One way of the extension was 'simulation,' which modeled and predicted specific aspects of reality. Another was 'sub-goal' learning, which was how worker droids picked up skills from supervisors. There existed many contractual algorithms that tracked explicit and implicit promises people made to each other and scored them against objective accomplishments.

Alexander wasn't aiming as high as the previous attempts. He wanted a good soldier, not a general. The code was not that different from a worker AI being aware of hostile wildlife. There were a lot of fail-safes that decreased the Governor's worries substantially. On one hand, messing up the robots would be a massive embarrassment, enough to get onto the wrong side of the history books. On the other hand, if not every precaution was taken against the alien threat, they would likely be dead with no history to speak about.

The Governor thought about the problem of the droid soldier. It was easy to point a rifle somewhere. It was relatively easy to calculate the basic effects of firing it. For example, if the droid was shooting at an alien inside a ship, this would create a hole in the ship's wall and begin to depressurize it. The droid would take into account how disconnected the specific section was from the rest and become aware of the depressurization and the effects it could have on the oxygen content in the ship. That was all doable with existing simulations.

The challenge was, as it has always been, in evaluating the outcomes. Is shooting an alien worth killing two wounded crewmen trapped in the compartment? How much of a ship could be disabled to eliminate a threat? Big explosions inside ships could reduce fighting capacity and ability to fight further threats. How likely is the alien to capture a ship or a part of it? The software could answer all of these questions. It frequently did, and simulation and prediction toolkits were standard parts of crewman space suits, displaying its findings on the suit's visor. However, just as before, one could never properly create a piece of software that figured out reliably whether a specific outcome was better than another.

The Governor reviewed the myriad of algorithmic developments and hoped that something would come to him, some magical insight would reveal itself, just because he needed it to. In all other aspects of his life, solutions to problems would just come to him, like bugs drawn to a campfire.

Nothing came.

The Governor noted that in this situation, he still felt like a child encountering an adult obstacle for the first time. He didn't feel this way about his economic conflict with Idris and the Patriarchs. He didn't feel this way about a potential legitimacy struggle with Albert. He didn't even feel this way about the upcoming alien threat. At some point, the worry about the threat was no longer necessary. You got as ready as you could, and you either won or lost. That was the Way of the Stars.

However, the droid situation, if mishandled, could spin out of control in horrifying ways. Soldiers have a habit of becoming generals, a good quality in people, but a bad one in droids. The Governor allowed himself to see the worst-case scenario of the entirety of system resources taken by machines to kill people in other systems. It was too sad to contemplate.

The Governor stopped his thinking; he had been at this for hours. He went for a walk, hoping the light of the Star would guide him on the proper path.

After a while, it did. He came to the decision and called his subordinates.

"I have decided that the full attempts to create a droid soldier are too dangerous. Let's create a specific extension for the Will of the remote droid operator. A timed pursuit of limited goals in case of disconnection. We have a similar subroutine for the workers. If the worker gets lost inside a cave, and it infers that the operators would have wanted it to get out, it will do so, as long as it takes less time than a pre-specified threshold. In the same way, the droids will continue to fight temporarily. The way it extends human Will is more of a spear than a gun."

"Guns are more powerful than spears," Alexander stated matter-of-factly.

"Still, the test cases we and Albert have created will prove useful to verify even in a limited scenario like this," the Governor said.

"Agree. This is safer than the original design, even if it technically violates the First Law," Ernest spoke. "I will abide by your decision."

"Speaking of Albert, let's give the boy a rematch."

Ernest was surprised, "You know that if you lose, he would challenge Kariel and then claim Governorship of the system after you."

"I plan to win, but I accept whatever fate brings."

Chapter 37

Oaguth

Two challenges that plagued the human condition are: improper control of the money supply and the fact that warriors gloriously falling in battle are unable to reproduce. Theoretically speaking, I have solved both.

The First Emperor addressing his infantrymen after establishing the sacred right of "Oaguth." (Early Unification War)

22.2 MS AA

Albert got ready for his date. It was an important one.

Together, Sheene and Albert walked to a grassy field barely in view of the Academy and lay down. It was gentle grass, specifically engineered to grow not too tall or too short. Occasionally, the nearby bison farm would let its animals graze on the grass to keep it clean. But tonight wasn't the time for that. Many fields on Old Earth or other planets were not cozy enough for one to lay on due to large numbers of bugs. Derev, before humans got to it, had one of the highest densities of insects ever recorded in the Empire. Part of the terraforming challenge was figuring out which bugs were necessary and which ones the biosphere could do without. And then, of course, gene driving the unneeded ones to extinction. Now, only an occasional cicada interrupted the night silence.

The stars shone brightly with not a cloud in the sky. The Academy, like most buildings, kept a "lights out" policy after dark, where only windowless rooms were allowed to have bright illumination. There wasn't an artificial light visible from the small hill they were on.

Just the two of them, the grass and the stars.

Albert's left arm was underneath Sheene's neck. They looked up at the sky.

"Someday," Albert waved his right arm across the millions of visible stars, "this will all be ours."

Sheene turned to him and hugged him, "Damn, you even talk like a citizen now. I am impressed. Also, a decent chunk is already ours."

"Yeah, this general area." Albert traced the human-controlled portion of the Milky Way with his hand.

"I love you"

"I love you too," Albert responded.

"How much do you love me? Would you move the Earth for me?"

"Of course. If I had a massive engine and the approval of the Emperor, then yeah, I would totally move the Earth for you," Albert replied in the same teasing tone.

"OK, boyfriend, you passed some fancy tests before, but I have one for you now," Sheene said.

"My father warned me about women and tests," Albert said, smiling. "I am always ready."

"First, lay down and look at the sky. Now, close your eyes."

Albert closed his eyes.

"To make sure you don't cheat, put this on." Sheene took off her shirt, exposing her bare chest, and tied the shirt over Albert's eyes. She took out a space compass from her pocket.

"Where is Earth?" she asked, touching his left index finger.

"So easy," Albert pointed to the sky.

"Correct. Where is the Corial system?" she asked.

"Another easy one." Albert swung his left hand across his body to the right.

"Where is Lyra M56?" she asked.

This was a harder one. Albert hadn't memorized this particular system. He visualized the starry sky in his mind, focusing on the key local stars, and rotated the map to match the Lyra constellation. He didn't know which one was M56, so he moved his left hand leftward as if looking for a clue. As he began outlining the constellation, his hand touched Sheene's naked chest.

"It's around this general direction," he said, moving his hand around her left breast a few times. "But if I had to guess, it's in a straight line from your heart to mine."

She kissed him with her shirt still covering his face.

Albert unblindfolded himself and looked at Sheene, "I will protect you." He put his hand on her bare chest.

She smiled but was a little shy for a second. She put her shirt back on and playfully said, "My assignment is ground control for our House asset defenses around Will of the Star and in orbit. So, maybe, I will protect you." She sat very upright and changed her tone. "You seem different now. You walk upright, you speak with authority, you take me fully. The ceremony did a number on you. In a good way."

Albert looked her in the eye. He hesitated about how to proceed.

Should he tell her about his past life? Is it wrong to keep such secrets from a loved one? Or would the situation change too much? Would she feel compelled to stay with him for the wrong reasons? He had to tell her. He started a little slow, "It has been said to us that our Blood Memory is our business, unless significant enough to impact the entire planet."

"You don't have to tell me, it's ok," she said unconvincingly.

"But mine was already discussed by the higher-ups even before the ceremony. So I don't want to keep you in the dark."

"Wait, why?"

Albert told her the full story: his previous life as the Fifth Emperor, his claim to the Governorship, his desire to challenge the Governor and Kariel in an official match, "I hope this doesn't change much about the future of our relationship."

"Um, this kinda changes things," Sheene said, her jaw wide open. Albert looked a little worried. She continued, "But in a good way. Like I always knew you were special; it's nice to be proven right." She smiled at him, "But there's something I don't get. Why do you want to challenge Kariel? Do you really want to be a Governor? Change things up at this uncertain time?"

Albert nodded. It was a good question, "I know deep in my heart that I can do more for this planet. That being a captain of a small ship is a good start, but I can command more than that. An entire task force or even a fleet. I have the skills to do it. But I don't want you or anyone to take my word for it. I want to prove it."

Sheene nodded, "A challenge like that, you need a team and a plan."

"I have a team," Albert said, putting his hand on her shoulder. "And I do have a plan. I came up with it right before meeting you. I finally know what the Principal meant about 'seeing at a glance'."

Sheene and Albert discussed the plan before she wanted to take a break to admire the stars.

"I love you," she said. "Fifth Emperor or not, you will still be my favorite person to study next to in the library."

"That's sweet," he said.

Sheene suddenly turned a little sad, "It's a great time being here with you. I just feel sad about the uncertain times. It comes and goes."

Albert straightened himself. He wanted to say that it will be ok, but he could not promise that at this moment. Instead, he went back to reminiscing about his ancestry, "Blood memory awakening is not about just seeing the past. One sees the karmic flow and the turning of the Great Wheel. One sees the pivotal acts of history around which the ripples of destiny form both backward and forward like water from a dropped pebble."

Sheene wiped a single tear and asked, "You see the future? You know what is going to happen with the battle?"

"Not exactly. I don't know what will happen with the First Fleet. Or with me. But I know this: my bloodline will survive. No matter what happens in orbit or on the ground. The karmic flows do not point to this life being my last incarnation," Albert said.

Sheene seemed both cheerful and confused, "Do you mean the genetic backup or something else?"

Albert shook his head, "No."

Sheene's eyes widened. She knew what he was about to say, and she began to feel tremendous nervousness.

"Sheene? Will you be my oaguth?" Albert looked at her.

Human marriage became a more complex construct as life expectancy increased. Standard 'till death do us part' marriage was still a common practice of elites on Border Worlds. Many commoners or even long-lived elites on Mid Worlds practiced 'temporary marriages' which expired in 1 to 5 gigaseconds [~30-150 Earth years]. Generational spaceships had their own marriage customs. Many started with with strict pairbonding while the kids were growing up, but then followed by some 'loosening' of rules afterwards.

However, there was one type of unbreakable marriage bond.

Available only during wartime to warriors of the Empire.

A battle death was no excuse for ending it.

The sacred right of 'Oaguth.'

Bound for life.

At least.

She looked at him as tears streamed down both of her cheeks.

"Yes," she answered.

They held their hands in silence.

Unknown to Albert, but not entirely unexpected, Ken, Max, and Sunnak all had the same idea. The four oaguth ceremonies for them were held at the Emperor's Judgment. Many of the families normally present were too occupied with war preparations and called in through a 300-meter-long holo-presence auditorium that still maintained a strong illusion of a large crowd.

Bishakha was the only one who cried during the ceremony.

Chapter 38

Rematch (Part 1)

We could use a morale boosting event. How about a video game tournament?

The First Emperor addressing leaders of Human Nations after the debate on how to avoid future wars.

22.3 MS AA

Albert was now competing on the Admiral's ladder and climbing the 1v1 ranks. His most recent victory over both Idris and Kariel had certainly earned him a measure of respect in the Governor's eyes.

But this was a team battle. On one side, the Governor with Alexander, Ernest, Idris, Deepak, Tong, Mencius and Kariel. On another, Albert, with Ken, Max, Sunnak, Sheene, Diana, Yezi and Bishakha. Only Sheene knew the true purpose of the match. The rest of the team was told the partial truth that this was the early start of their competition against adults, normally reserved till after the Academy.

This was the most unpredictable pure battle format. Instead of predefined fleets, players were given a pool of points to spend. They could 'purchase' conventional ships or design their own: a combination of armor, shields, lasers, missiles, and railguns that had never been built. It was less complicated than 'full planetary control,' however this sim type was considered the key determinant of Governorship legitimacy. Advisors could help you with planetary control given enough time, real-time battles could never be properly outsourced.

The Governor trusted the standard designs. He knew Albert was not book-savvy, so he would rely on stealth and unconventional engagement tactics. The Governor decided to splurge some points to prepare for this eventuality. He acquired a large neutrino sensor station, capable of detecting basic stealth fleets. He also invested in sophisticated stealth of his own: two octozi frigates. They were equipped with a few expensive missiles carrying titanium-eating nano-weapons. The Governor also added a "dual drive" for his corvettes, enabling them to fire engine exhaust from both front and back, and even gimbal the drives for a very fast in-place spin. It cost a few points, but he liked that this gave him a certain very interesting option for close-quarter combat.

The rest of his fleet was standard. Two carriers and lots of railcruisers for the capital ships, along with a line of laser-based destroyers and point-defense guns on the corvettes.

As the battle started, the strangeness began right away. The sensors picked up Albert's fleet, and the Governor quickly noticed that it was smaller than expected. The visible points looked close to 40% of the total points. The Governor expected some shenanigans, such as Albert probably having stealth ships. But 60% of one's fleet being stealth was a bit much of a surprise.

The second surprise was Albert's fleet composition. It was ENTIRELY railcruisers and a single carrier.

The third surprise was that the railcruisers lacked the typical weapons loadout. Most of them had only two railguns and two torpedo bays, instead of the standard 8 of each. They had only 8 micro railgun point defenses, instead of the conventional 32 chemical gun-based point defenses.

There wasn't a single laser visible in the fleet.

Many thoughts raced through the Governor's mind. Does Albert's fleet carry lasers anywhere? If the answer is yes, they must either be in the stealth fleet or on the drones in the carrier. If the answer is no, then Albert expects a purely long-range engagement. The Governor considered the possibility of doing a hard burn on an intercept course. He could re-order the formation for close-quarter combat, shield his destroyers, and devastate Albert at point-blank range.

"Maybe he is baiting me into a hard burn, and this is a trap," the Governor thought. He looked at the neutrino detector, which would have been able to see basic stealth if it was unobstructed by line of sight.

The neutrino detector found no stealth ships. The stealth fleet must have been blocked from being seen by the detector by the visible fleet's formation. Doing this meant Albert expected a neutrino detector. This was unnerving.

The Governor wanted to wait for a couple of seconds after the battle start to fully come to the decision of what to do with against the strange fleet of entirely under-weaponed railcruisers.

Then, to his shock, Albert's entire fleet began doing a hard burn TOWARDS him.

This was extremely weird for a number of reasons.

The first and most obvious reason was that Albert's visible fleet was smaller than the Governor's, both in terms of raw ship mass and certainly in terms of weaponry. This could be mitigated by a second stealth fleet attempting a flanking maneuver. However, stealth fleets had to use a slow 0K drive and would need time for a favorable flanking spot. The composition of both stealth and non-stealth ships would either burn away from the enemy, coast, or feint.

The second reason was the weapon composition of Albert's fleet. The Governor's fleet had few lasers, but it was more than zero. Both fleets had reasonable point defense coverage, and in close quarters, missiles had no space to accelerate and lost much of their effectiveness. In the absence of lasers, a close-quarters engagement would almost always be decided by who had more railguns. In this case, the Governor had a lot more. Albert should have known this.

The third reason was the speed of the approach. The fleet was burning at 5G, which was too slow if the goal was to close in as quickly as possible but a little too fast for efficient running or feints.

The fourth reason was ship directionality. Approaching an enemy fleet in orbit would require reducing orbital velocity to shift to a lower orbit, colloquially known as 'slowing down to catch up'. This required facing the enemy at a fairly unfavorable angle and taking many measures to counteract that.

Never mind the last reason. Albert's ship design had multiple engine exhaust ports, including directing exhaust at any angle from the front of the ship. This was an expensive design that cost him a few points, but it allowed an approach 'nose towards the enemy' while executing burns in any direction.

The Governor began tasking his team with firing assignments. Alexander on the railguns, Deepak on the missiles. The initial target priority was Albert's drives and reactors. The initial missile volley from the Governor failed almost completely. Albert's fleet, while lacking conventional point defense, used several of his missiles with flak warheads. They sent shrapnel forward in front of his ships, creating an effective flak debris field. Albert's ships also carried "flares," small rockets with chemical power and chemical payload, which were used to both confuse and intercept the Governor's missiles.

Albert was defensive on the approach, sacrificing forward firepower for safeguarding his ships.

However, after an initial volley of the Governor's railguns with a few connections, an observational droid remarked, "Low probability ship movement detected."

The battle computer assistant kept basic track of assumptions both it and the fleet commander made during the battle. A 'low probability' event was a signal that an assumption had been violated. In this particular case, the assumption that a clean railgun hit at a specific place on one of Albert's ships would result in the loss of reactor power. Instead, Albert's ship coasted for a few seconds and then re-joined the flight towards the Governor's fleet.

This was bad news, but the Governor expected some bad news, and this specific bad news was only a little bad, updating his overall estimate of "total bad" downwards.

Albert's fleet had redundancies in the drive design of each ship. This wasn't the standard battle doctrine of using redundancies across ships, but this wasn't too uncommon either. Due to flares and redundant front-back drives, it did seem that the number of points spent on the visible fleet was higher than the Governor initially anticipated.

The initial targeting of the drives was a mistake. The Governor re-tasked the targeting towards enemy railguns.

Albert's fleet used some of its railguns and non-defensive missiles to attack the Governor's fleet. The Governor noted the target priority. Albert focus-fired the destroyers in the fleet, specifically their laser turrets. This made perfect sense as part of the approach. Destroyers were the second line of the formation, behind the corvettes. They were more vulnerable than capital ships to missile fire since they had fewer overlapping point-defense systems. If the approach was meant to take the fleet into close quarter battle, those lasers would be the most devastating weapon under 100 km. Though this aspect of Albert's strategy made sense, the entire strategy didn't. If this was any other student in the Academy, the Governor would have expected simply an uncommon formation without a fully thought-out plan. However, this was the reincarnation of the Fifth Emperor, and the Governor had to pay some respect.

In the meantime, the Governor reorganized his team and fleet into four equal-sized task groups, giving special contingency orders, "If needed, prepare for an orthogonal cross-split maneuver, including an out-of-plane burn. Prep, but don't execute line-of-sight defense. Ready the 'spin-torch' protocols."

Idris smirked, "And you expect him to pull the lasers out of... where exactly?"

A cross-split maneuver was a desperate measure to burn parts of the fleet into different directions, in case the enemy not only got inside the rectangle capital-ship formation, but also had the laser advantage at that point. The line-of-sight defense would line up ships in a single line facing the enemy formation. Line of sight made the fleet significantly more vulnerable to railguns since they could now hit multiple ships, but less vulnerable to lasers since the first ship screened off the others. The orders would only make sense if Albert had lasers.

The Governor responded, "Somewhere. Maybe the carrier. This is an order."

Idris responded back," "Yes, sir," and began preparing for the contingency.

The Governor looked at the approaching fleet. The carrier looked like the centerpiece. It lagged a little behind the very center of the railcruiser rectangle, heavily defended by its point defense and flare rockets. What could it be carrying? A fleet of laser drones? This would do some serious damage, but his fleet could likely finish them off in time. A full loadout of nano-rockets? A very high-risk, high-reward play. A single nanobot rocket connection could destroy an entire capital ship, but they would also be easily shut down on the approach. Something more exotic?

The Governor briefly considered focus-firing the carrier but decided against it. It was too obvious of a target. He did task a few railguns to poke at it; there were a few connections, which probably damaged whatever it was carrying, but the carrier itself plowed ahead as before. He decided the carrier would be the proper target for his own sneaky preparation. The Governor plotted a course for a close approach of an octozi ship into the pathway of the carrier if it was going to come as close as 80 km.

The Governor did note that, despite his team's railgun superiority, the execution of the approach from Albert's side was nearly flawless. His missile volleys were the perfect size to neither be shot down fully nor cause overkill on the destroyers. Albert's railgun volleys arrived in a flawless grid that made dodging every single shot impossible. Albert's dodging was also well-timed. His team was pulling their weight, given the unusual circumstances.

The Governor's message alerts were encouraging:

"Enemy railgun destroyed by railgun fire."

"Friendly destroyer destroyed by triple missile hit."

"Enemy railgun destroyed by railgun fire. (x3)" x3 meant the same message repeated 3 times.

On the surface, the fire exchange on the approach was going well. The Governor's destroyers were all lost. His laser-drone carrier was destroyed as well, able to launch only a portion of the drone payload, which was not useful yet. However, Albert's railguns were getting pulverized and on track to all being destroyed when the fleets converged into CQB.

Another surprise was that a couple of Albert's railcruisers had been hit with multiple railgun and missile impacts around the center of the ship, breaking said ship in half. However, due to the drive redundancies, both ship pieces were able to re-orient and still fly. Even though one or both pieces of it completely lacked weapons, they could be used for... something. This was a known pattern used with over-redundant ships, it just was not the meta-game the Governor had seen recently.

Ernest and Idris were cheerful. Alexander and The Governor were not.

As one of the key break points of 100 km approached, a computer announcer spoke, "Enemy fleet flipping."

The relative speed of the fleets at this point was 2 km /s, but the new flip and burn had put Albert's fleet on a direct collision course. The maneuver dropped the fleets to nearly 0 relative speed as it would arrive inside the Governor's formation.

"Low probability explosion detected," the AI voice spoke, but its tone of voice was that of extreme concern. Battle assistants used human voice tones to convey tricky information quickly.

The Governor looked at the screen, "Low probability explosion detected (x30)"

All the explosions were inside Albert's ships.

Huh? A lucky missile hit? Secondary explosions? A neutrino chain reaction from defensive torps flying too close?

He didn't quite have time to finish that thought because a number of other messages came onto the screen.

"Friendly railgun destroyed by laser"

"Enemy destroyers decelerating at 15G"

"Friendly railgun destroyed by laser(x7)"

"Perform cross-split," the Governor said, running on pure instinct before the conscious thought caught up to him.

There was only so much information that even an elite human mind could theoretically process in a short time frame of a couple of seconds. From the moment of seeing the messages on the screen, the Governor's mind pushed very close to this limit.

The enemy fleet in front of him had lasers.

A lot of lasers.

Unseen.

Hidden until now.

In plain sight.

Inside 'railcruisers.'

In a singular moment, as the words giving the order left the Governor's mouth, he came to many realizations regarding the battle at hand. He understood exactly how Albert's points were allocated. Albert's fleet had no stealth ships. Instead, each ship was a railcruiser look-alike shell that housed 2 to 3 destroyers inside it. The explosions were a 'split-ship' maneuver separating the destroyers into four task groups that began to flow towards the likely means of escape via a cross-split. The railguns and the missile tubes were a diversion. And now the Governor was facing a maxed-out laser fleet in CQB.

The instinctual pre-conscious order to cross-split was the correct decision.

The shock wore off and the Governor re-focused on the battle.

For the first time in a gigasecond, he was close to losing in a space simulator.

As Albert's hand was revealed, the time for the Governor's own tricks had come.

Chapter 39

Rematch (Part 2)

The Foundation of a Stable Society is a clean movement of power from the old elites to the new ones. The conflict must be fought in a positive-sum manner. Or, at least, in an objectively measurable one.

The First Emperor discussing philosophy (time unknown)

22.3 MS AA

Albert's plan worked. Sort of. He had lost more ships on the approach than he expected. The Governor didn't take the bait of focus-firing the carrier. While this could have been a good thing, as the carrier arrived undamaged, shortly after the laser reveal, Albert got the message, "Carrier hit by nanobots. Full destruction in two minutes."

The nanobots came from a rocket fired by a tier-2 stealth octozi frigate. It came from an angle behind the carrier, completely uncovered by point defenses. The frigate being revealed meant lasers easily dispatched it. But the carrier armor and hull were being eaten by the nanobots, which used the raw materials to make more of themselves and eat the armor and hull even faster.

'Carrier, all launch now,' Albert said. 'Target the neutrino detector.'

The carrier payload was another one of Albert's tricks. Instead of loading up on laser drones or expensive nano-torpedoes, Albert loaded up on escape pods, which were extremely cheap short-range shuttles filled with droids. It was one of the ways to spend as few points on the carrier as possible. Given the recent allowance of droids to perform rudimentary in-ship combat roles, these escape pods were now boarding craft. The neutrino detector's command and control section had already been melted off, preventing the overload of the reactor core and a self-destruct.

Instead of targeting one of the rapidly escaping capital ships, he commanded Bishakha to use the droid fleet to take control of the slow neutrino detector. If the Governor brought one stealth ship, he could have brought others. And the Governor's assets could now be used against him. The neutrino detector's point defense guns had already been melted off by now, and the boarding craft was barreling towards it unopposed.

In the meantime, the Governor's fleet split into five groups, burning as far away from each other as possible. This was expected given the laser threat, but Albert was still surprised by how quickly the split happened. Four of the groups rapidly arranged into a line-of-sight blocking formation.

The Governor was certainly fast.

Albert also split his destroyers into five groups to press on the pursuit. He tasked Max, Ken, Sunnak, and Sheene to take control of the other four. Four of the Governor's groups burned perpendicular to the approach vector, with two of them going out-of-plane-of-battle. The fifth group burned directly away from Albert's fleet. Given that a few of Albert's ships hadn't slowed down yet, the group burning away was the easiest to catch.

'They are flipping for beams,' Sunnak reported with his group. 'Shields going up.'

Another sharp response by the Governor, though only with one of the groups. Electron and proton beam weapons were a drive/weapon mix mounted on the front of the ship. Unlike most turreted weapons, beams could only fire in the direction the ship was pointing.

'They are turning, reason unknown,' Max reported about the group he was pursuing.

'Same,' responded Sheene and Ken.

However, a number of messages rapidly came onto the screen:

'Friendly destroyer damaged by exhaust'

'Shield ripped by railgun (x3)'

'Friendly destroyer damaged by exhaust'

"Shit, shit, shit," Sunnak said.

All five groups of the Governor's fleet simultaneously flipped and fired a cacophony of weapons. The corvettes in the fifth group that were behind Albert's fleet were now spinning in place, using their main drives with exhausts mounted in both front and back as weapons. The group Sunnak was pursuing activated proton beams. And the other three groups used whatever remaining railguns were not already melted off. All were aimed at Sunnak's group and flawlessly timed.

The focus fire continued. Railgun hits ripped the shield generators from their diamond screw mounts, and the beams melted right through the armor.

As Sunnak's group was focus-fired, the rest of Albert's team could catch the groups they were pursuing and do their butcher's work. Laser melting off outside weapons, radiators and sealing the engines of the Governor's fleet. The Governor made a trade. Save one group at the cost of the rest of the fleet.

Bishakha then reported, 'Neutrino detector lost.'

Fuck. It wasn't her fault, though. The Governor had directed many missiles at his own neutrino detector. And while all were shut down on approach, two corvettes slipped through and crashed right into the station. Point defending a neutral ship that could not move was too tricky an affair.

However, this action confirmed that the Governor still had a stealth ship, likely armed with nano-torpedoes.

The surviving group of the Governor's ships now flipped once again and began a full-strength 15 G burn away from the battle.

They were in the endgame now. Albert's midgame surprise did it's work, but what looked like a victory was slipping away. Albert faced a difficult choice.

Endgames of simulated space battles were situations with few ships, where most firepower on both sides was concentrated within a single weapon type. At this moment, the missiles of the Governor's fleet were either already spent or remained inside already disabled ships. Albert had lasers; the Governor's fleet had railguns. Nominally Albert outnumbered the tonnage by a factor of 4 to 1.

It was a well-understood endgame. Combat computers were better at analyzing endgame situations than ones with a bigger variety of weapons. They gave Albert a 65% chance of winning, without taking into account a stealth ship in the case of two equally matched opponents. However, the Governor held the edge over everyone in the system specifically because of his control in such endgames. Conditioned on the Governor being his opponent, the computer gave him a 0% chance of winning. 0 isn't something the probability computer had ever output. The display rounded the probability to the nearest 0.001%. Probably.

There were standard measures and countermeasures that Albert could undertake. If Albert managed to once again get even one-sixth of his fleet into laser range, he would be able to disable the remaining weapons of the group. However, the four-way split had worked to put some range between Albert's fleet and the Governor's. Albert could charge forward at the fleet, but the Governor would simply run away and kite the fleet at the edge of the railgun effective range.

Albert could attempt a pincer maneuver, flying around the formation with multiple fleets outside railgun range until it was time. Creating and evading orbital laser pincers is the kind of thing the Governor had done thousands of times. His team was no doubt starting to drift into the optimal orbit soon. The more space there was between fleets initially, the harder the pincer was to pull off.

The window of opportunity was closing, so Albert had to once again invent something unorthodox.

"Max, Ken, Sheene, prepare a pincer. Sheene, go high; Ken, go straight; Max, go inside the atmosphere."

"The ... what?" Max asked incredulously.

"Burn inside the atmosphere. Radiators in. Ionize the pathway with beams and shields up," Albert ordered him to use the emergency procedure for crash-landing a high-speed ship through an atmosphere. It was to fire an ionizing beam of electrons forwards and then wait for it to gain charge so that the shield could repel them.

"Obviously, keep decel at 12 G at most," Albert stated the obvious. Moving too fast through the atmosphere with engines off created deceleration. And having too much time above 12 G would mean the simulation considered the crew to be damaged or dead/

"Ships don't all have intact shield, armor, or plating." Max responded.

"Take the ones that do. Separate the rest into Ken's and Sheene's groups." Albert commanded back. He kind of expected Max to solve this, but being in charge meant micromanaging sometimes.

The move through the atmosphere created one jaw of the pincer. In doing so, it protected the ships from railgun shots, as the fast-moving slugs melted themselves in the atmosphere. It was also a surprise, one that would not have been on the Governor's short list of contingencies to prepare for.

Albert tasked Diana to find the most likely position of the stealth ships. It was a near-impossible task, but he knew that even though her regular command was subpar, she occasionally pulled off the impossible.

The Governor's fleet made the predictable move, beginning to shift to a higher orbit, hoping to avoid Max's pincer and moving to strike one of the other two groups. However, this allowed Max to cut through the atmosphere unopposed, emerging behind the Governor's fleet.

As the Governor's fleet and the three groups began to engage in a dance of trying to stay outside the railgun effective range but vectoring close enough for a quick burn. Of course, they still exchanged fire. The Governor fired railguns, and Albert's fleets carefully dodged them. Albert also used lasers at a far distance. Their damage output was pitifully low, but scoring even a small hit on a radiator meant that ship cooling would become an ever-increasing problem.

Diana gave Albert her best probability estimate about the stealth ship. It was a smaller area around the original battle site than Albert thought. She managed to isolate some inconsistencies in the Governor's railgun attack patterns that suggested he was avoiding a certain area of space. This put a very good estimate on at least which line the stealth ship could have been at a point in the past.

"That's... good girl," Albert exclaimed. He was about to exclaim "That's my girl" but stopped himself. Sheene and Max both gave him slightly weird looks anyway.

With the understanding that the stealth ship was somewhat far away, Albert decided that he could afford to wait to readjust his groups for a perfect 'collapse' onto the Governor's group.

What followed for the next several kiloseconds was an extremely precise game of cat and mouse as the fleets postured against each other, breaking into various formations. The Governor fired off railgun shots, and Albert dodged them. Albert tried to close in, and the Governor moved out-of-plane. Albert followed and readjusted the plane. Tens of thousands of railgun slugs were orbiting the planet, presenting a small danger of a stray hit.

The stealth ship had not revealed itself yet, and all of the conventional methods of detection Albert had available didn't seem to work. A low-power laser sweep of likely locations didn't turn anything up. A couple of escape pods of droids collected some of the debris, turned it into powdered dust, and sent it into orbits around the likely trajectories. They also found nothing. Albert even dug into the simulation code and ran a parallel simulation of the battle on his private server. He would compare response latencies rendering specific parts of space between the two. It still shocked Max to see such exploits even in official matches, but he mumbled something about 'I guess it's important to learn how to cheat.' However, the exploit also found nothing. This suggested, but did not prove that the stealth ship was not using its drive.

Albert gave up on the stealth idea for a little. It was very likely not flying next to the Governor's remaining fleet, since the fleet moved too quickly. He gave Diana the task of figuring out if any ships in the Governor's fleet had an unusual mass profile, indicating a ship attached using a tether. However, after checking the mass, taking into account every missile, exhaust plume, and railgun slug, as well as having good estimates of pieces of ships blown off from getting hit, the tether idea was proven false.

After another back and forth, it was once again time to converge Albert's fleet onto the Governor's. As the three groups entered railgun range and began losing ships, the Governor once again split his remaining forces into two. Every split presented a challenge, as you had to perfectly allocate pursuing craft. Give too few to a group, and it will escape, raining railgun slugs at its pursuers. However, the two railcruiser groups could pick and choose which ships they targeted, making reallocation more and more tricky.

Albert gave control of Ken's group to Sunnak. Ken was re-tasked onto salvage operations, such as supervising droids in moving pieces of broken apart ships from both fleets to patch up still functional ones. Broken-off radiators from railcruisers were a little too big for destroyers, but with enough welding and reprogramming the ship's turn thrusters, Ken made it work.

Ken's salvages were one of the few times the computer estimate of their chances slightly rose. At other times, they were slowly dropping and now stood at a 57% chance of winning.

At the final approach vector, only one-eighth of Albert's mid-game fleet remained. He thought it was enough. The final railgun turrets were burned off. But the time to relax hadn't yet come. The handful of missiles that the Governor was saving now flew at Albert's fleet. At its original size, point defense would make short work of such a volley, but now, with a lot fewer ships and them being spread out, the volley looked like it was going to devastate the remaining fleet.

"Max, time to do the piloting," Albert said. Max had been assuring him that he could outdodge the volley, and after an epic flight of manual thrusters and an even more epic point defense re-targeting by Sunnak, Max proved himself correct. They survived the last volley.

Barely.

Albert had four total ships remaining. Two destroyers, each with only one laser turret and one point defense gun remaining that participated in the final assault, and two salvage ships commanded by Ken. They were no longer easily classified as being in a particular class, since they contained frame pieces from both destroyers and railcruisers. All were heavily damaged.

Albert looked at the Governor's fleet. All the ships had either disabled guns or drives or both. He was waiting for the victory screen. Their local computer gave them a "probability of win: unknown," which meant that the only ship remaining was still in stealth.

'Nano-torps on approach,' Ken and the computer spoke together at once.

The two salvage ships barely had a moment to react, shooting down part of the nano-volley. It took a little longer than normal for nanobots to eat the ships. Ken's unusual shenanigans in ship construction altered alloy composition in between armor panels. The delay in ship destruction let Albert take manual control of the ships and fill the likely location of the stealth ship with all the firepower available. He managed to nick it with a few bits of a flak torpedo, increasing the ship's temperature just above the background.

This confirmed it was a tier-2 stealth octozi frigate. The good news was that it only carried six nano-torpedoes, and four were already used up. The bad news was that it could re-stealth faster than the two destroyers could get back to the original battle site.

Albert sent his team into a huddle as they decided on what to do next.

They shifted to a higher orbit, extended radiators and solar panels, and put lasers into a low-energy sweep mode. Nothing could get as close as 50 km without being illuminated. Two point defense guns could handle two nano-torpedoes. Ken got going on fixing whatever parts of the ship he could.

They were defended, but they had no way of attacking.

After about a kilosecond [~17 Earth minutes] of flying, while scratching their heads about the next steps, the Principal came in to call the game.

"I am calling it a draw, unless anyone objects."

Albert looked around the room. Everyone, especially the guys were slumped in their chairs, the stress visible in their bodies. Albert looked at Sheene. She gave him a look back. He knew what she wanted. What was the right thing to do. There was no point in pushing his friends further for his ego.

"Draw it is," Albert said. "The stars favored both of us today."

The Governor came in to congratulate Albert. They exchanged looks of respect.

The Governor spoke to him and the Principal in private. "This was impressive. From the perspective of Governorship legitimacy, a draw is not sufficient to challenge me or Kariel for the Governorship. Though you are welcome to try again in 2 gigaseconds [~63 Earth years]. In the meantime, I am giving you 4 stars on your uniform and tactical command of the student frigate group, if the Principal agrees."

Ken and Sunnak would have 1 star, as the lowest level crewmen, Max would have 2 as a pilot. Captains of most ships would have 3. 4 was reserved for the Patriarchs as commanders of House fleets.

The Principal nodded, "Most certainly."

The student frigate group consisted of eight frigates comprised of both first and second-year Academy students. The Principal had strategic command. However, as he was no longer able to handle 12 G flights, the Principal remained in the nearby hangar bay rather than fly as part of the group. Should decisions be made that required faster processing of local information, they fell to the tactical commander.

"It is a great honor," Albert said.

He meant it. There were moments when reaching as high as possible was the way of his life. But not now. Now he felt content. Win or lose, the legitimacy system was working properly. The Will of the Stars had revealed itself.

"Where was the stealth ship all this time?" he asked the Governor. Albert could find out by watching the recording, now available for all Space Force personnel. But he wanted to see the Governor's reaction during his answer.

"The second frigate was hiding inside the carrier wreckage," the Governor answered. "You aren't the only clever boy around."

The Governor smiled in a way that made Albert realize that they had certainly met in their past lives, but he could not immediately narrow down where and when.

After the students got on the plane back, Max hugged Diana and then patted Albert on the back. 'Massages for everyone, my treat,' he said, 'already picked out the spot in Plasch.' He showed a hologram of eight lovely massage ladies to the group.

'I like the new Max,' Albert said. 'Good work, everyone.'

Chapter 40

The First Fleet

More than 4 billion people, 90% of Earth's population, have demanded my Ascension. This is The One True Election. To end all further elections.

The First Emperor of Mankind issuing a re-organization of the Human Security Council and Becoming The First Emperor Of Mankind

23 MS AA

The Fleet train relay gathered the Noble House naval personell from all over the planet. On the central open-air platform, Idris and the Governor met and shook hands, their crews behind them.

Idris asked the Governor, "Do you think we have enough ships?"

There were 1024 ships in the First Fleet. 400 corvettes, 170 destroyers, 320 Cruisers, 85 railships, 44 railcruisers, 1 dreadnought, and 4 carriers, totaling over 400 million tons. Fully fueled and armed to capacity. More ships were being added to the Second and Third fleets every day.

"No," the Governor looked at Idris. "There are never enough ships." He smiled, somewhat sadly, "Do you think we have built enough bunkers?"

Over 300 million people, 60% of the population, could fit in the existing bunkers, while more capacity still being added. Those who could fit would be housed and supplied for 100s of megaseconds in nuclear-powered and armed fortresses. Every citizen of every House and many House-affiliated civilians made the cut. Plasch was the only major city without a corresponding bunker.

"We are a fortress world now. First of its kind. But no," Idris said, mimicking the same smile, "there are never enough bunkers."

The two men raised their palms towards one another, elbows bent, and exchanged an arm-wrestle handshake. They separated and went back to their respective crews.

The Governor walked up to his podium to deliver a speech, watched in person by the crews and broadcast across the star system.

"All civilizations in this galaxy sector are aware of at least one other. One, whose appetite for expansion is only matched by its skill in warfare.

Ours.

The Empire of Man.

Every generation from the founding of the Empire of Man until now had a choice. One choice was to stay home and embrace the comfort of a settled planet. Another was to fly into the unknown. When some did go further, their children faced the same dilemma. Many of those children settled further still, claiming the next lifeless rock, the next unusual star, the next hostile atmosphere.

As our ancestors reached into the void, they found they were not alone. The void reached back.

At that moment, did they turn away? Did they let others claim the open stars? They did not, sometimes working with the bare minimum of faith, titanium, and nukes.

As the our distance from Earth grew, there were bloodlines who always chose the unknown. Over and and over again, one generation after the next. Who stands at the end of this multi-terasecond chain of generations, unbroken by void, alien, or promises of comfort?

We do.

Today, we sail into the unknown one MORE TIME. And as we forge our fate, remember that we trained for this. We were selected for this. The stars chose US."

The crews cheered.

The Governor's speech presented a theory of history that was not fully accurate. Most claims to the open stars happened by 'default,' with one civilization arriving a full gigasecond earlier than another. Occasionally, they were decided through basic negotiations where humans sent information about their empire size and warship acceleration to nearby civilizations. But this wasn't the time for nuance.

Albert, watching the speech in an auditorium inside the Space Academy, cheered as well.

"The Governor has a way with words," Albert thought.

The Governor continued, "This is not the first challenge that I have faced throughout space, time and souls. As an incarnation of the Sixth Emperor, I have solved many problems that kept humanity from taking the next step or reaching the next star."

Albert leaned in and then leaned out. How could he have not known? A cacophony of past lives flashed past his eyes. Out in the distance of time, he remembered the warm embrace that he shared with the Sixth Emperor as he transferred power to his son.

The Governor continued, "And now, as a genetic reincarnation of the Sixth Emperor and the power vested in me by the honor of simulations, I am taking command of the First Fleet as the Commander."

He was no longer the Governor. The Commander handed over the House seal, which bore an image of grass, to Kariel, who as of this moment, let go of his name in the eyes of others and thus himself. Now Kariel was the New Governor.

After the speech, the Commander came to embrace Camina one last time. She was sitting in a private booth where neither the onlookers nor the cameras could see her cry. She has already said goodbye to two of her sons and five of her grandsons who were members of the Commanders' or other crews.

The Commander embraced her.

"Come back," she said with her head on his chest.

"I will do whatever it takes," he responded.

The speech riled him up as well, and served as a distraction from the gripping sadness of the situation, however embracing Camina brought it back. There was a logical sense from which he knew that his bloodline was not in danger of being extinct. He had many cousins on Corial, his genetic backups were flying into nearby systems. But the emotion of going to battle with one's kin tended to override the more logical mind.

He let go of her and walked to the boosted 'orbital plane' staying on the train tracks. His crew walked behind him in a V-formation with the XO on the right side, the pilot on the left side, and the rest behind them according to ship rank. The other crews and onlookers stood quietly as the 42-person railcruiser crew loaded into the orbital plane.

A boosted orbital plane is one of the most efficient methods of getting to orbit with a minimal amount of Gs. The plane started on a set of train tracks, which took it from a standstill to 10 times the speed of sound in 300 gentle seconds of 1g. From there, the plane took off, traveling at an angle not too far from horizontal. The atmospheric jets accelerated the plane forward until the planet curved away underneath them. As the horizontal pathway inside the atmosphere turned into an orbital pathway, the rocket engine fired to allow the plane to rendezvous with the railcruiser already in orbit.

The other crews took their planes up and in several kiloseconds the First Fleet began its journey towards Zeun. The plan to move the fleet from regular operation to 'dark running' had many steps.

23.1 MS AA - 37 MS AA

Shortly before the burn, the Governor called Albert. They exchanged warm nods. The Governor started, "You probably wonder why I didn't come to catch up with you sooner."

Albert said, "you seem pretty busy."

"Yes, but I was worried about you. A young mind, even as strong as yours, can handle only so much wisdom being imparted at once."

"Well, there will always be time for bonding after you get back," Albert said.

"Indeed," the Governor smiled. Despite all of Albert's challenge shenanigans, the warmth of past lives still guided their way. His worry was genuine and Albert's hope for him to come back was as well.

The first step was a 5G burn for a kilosecond to gain speed for the journey. The second was a coasting period. The initial megasecond [~11 Earth days] of coasting was done with fully extended radiators dumping the heat generated by the initial burn.

However, as the Enemy approached and the heat stabilized, the extended radiators gave way to directional radiators, which dumped heat using a laser in a direction unseen by either Enemy fleet. Some heat was retained in the ship to keep the crew comfortable.

The crew spent most of their time 'chilling,' a technical term for cryo-meditation, which consisted of sitting on an ice block doing specialized breathing exercises. This prepared their bodies for the extremes of cold required in the next steps. During his cryo-meditation, the Commander noticed he still harbored some tension around the finality of their actions. There was always a slim chance that after seeing the Greeter station, the Enemy fleet would attempt a peaceful First Contact and send a copy of a radio signal repeating back, 'We exist in peace.'

He wanted to let go of this tension but could not do so, despite his extensive mental training.

The third step was a 0K drive deceleration. Providing only around 0.1g of thrust, the 0K drive was hopefully unseen by the Enemy. So far, neither of the Enemy fleets seemed to have altered trajectory since the start of the First Fleet's flight, and this was all the more reason to keep the low-energy stealth protocols.

Requiring low energy usage meant that crew activities were kept to a minimum. Most cabins were illuminated extremely dimly, and only the bare minimum of computers were on. 'Running dark' was more than just a euphemism.

The fourth step was the 'final heat dump' and a final burn to enter Zeun's orbit. The entirety of the ship's residual heat, even that which was used for life support, had to be dumped in the direction of the planet at that point. Reactors were offline, and the fleet ran on batteries.

Everything was cold.

The coffee was cold, the air was cold, and the seats were cold. The panel displays emitted the smallest possible amount of light that provided minimal heat. Even the acknowledging glances the crew gave to each other felt cold.

Many parts of the ship close to the armor were cooled down to only 5 degrees above absolute zero. They were depressurized as well. There was no point in keeping the air in those spaces just to have it turn liquid. The living quarters were kept at a more human-manageable -40 C.

The crew wrapped themselves in layers. Layer after layer, layer after layer.

Trained human resistance to cold was not as revered as that of certain deep-ocean-born alien species like the octozi. Or as feared as the human resistance to high-G. But it was still respectable enough to maintain stealth at key points of warfare. After the final heat dump, the crew nicknamed the fleet 'The Column of Winter.'

The final step was the wait. The ship stopped dumping heat to the outside to remain unseen. The minimal life support system began to slowly warm up the ship. It was still going to be cold enough to handle the initial engagement without extending radiators. Communication between ships was limited. Radio was too likely to be noticed, even in the presence of noise-generating civilian stations. Instead, the ship's exteriors had analog monitors, which changed shape without emitting light. Illuminated by the light reflected off the planet, the messages were read by the other ships.

37 MS AA

The intergalactic fleet was expected to reach Zeun in 600 kiloseconds [~7 Earth days]. The Browly Enemy fleet had decelerated to 1% of the speed of light and was continuing to decelerate. It was coming up on the 'Greeter' observation station in 10 kiloseconds [~2.8 Earth hours] and would reach Zeun 100 kiloseconds [~28 Earth hours] after the intergalactic fleet.

The Commander fixated his attention on the outcome of the first meeting with a new civilization. Pilot Brod reported, "Several small entities on approach vector from the Enemy fleet to the observation station. No deceleration. Size around 10 centimeters each."

The Commander sighed. Not that he still held any illusion about the Enemy. A friendly fleet would have decelerated faster. Those were simple kinetics moving in the direction of the observation station. The intention was clear. At 1% the speed of light, an impact of several 10-centimeter objects is enough to destroy the station.

Another station next to the Greeter was also destroyed, thought it took two Enemy volleys due to the automated point defense shutting down the first one. The second station used EMF coated paint, but was not cooled to absolue zero. Everyone already expected the Enemy to have subtle heat-detection capabilities, the station was there to try and fool the Enemy into thinking humans had only low-tech stealth options.

The Commander asked his crew, "Can we detect the EMF signature of whatever fired the ordinance?"

"Negative on any EMF signature. The relative speed of the ordinance leaving the enemy craft was less than 50 m/s," Brod reported and jokingly added, "They just tossed it out the window."

"I can already feel the disrespect," the Commander joked back. "Ordinance composition?" The Commander wasn't expecting any breakthroughs.

"Too complicated to analyze without spinning up a computer," Brod responded. "I advise against starting one on the ship or calling the planet."

The Commander shook his head, "Don't bother with either. Kariel will know what to look for. If the data is meant to alter our battle plan, he'll call us."

Brod said, "Acknowledged"

The Enemy hadn't altered trajectory ever since the First Fleet started its flight. This could be a simple fact of them not noticing the First Fleet. Zeun's orbit still hosted many scooper stations. Cargo freighters were operating as before, except flown entirely by droids. As the station was destroyed, all the cargo freighters began to burn starward. The humans wanted to give the appearance of being surprised by the aliens' hostile intentions. The appearance of wanting to move as far away from the Enemy fleets as possible.

It's possible the Enemy fell for the appearance. It's also possible that the First Fleet was entirely visible on the Enemy's scopes, who were laughing at human attempts to remain hidden. Were humans like a child who plays hide and seek behind a one-way mirror. It's possible that the Enemy already modeled the battle as being easily won.

The Commander reminded himself not to overthink this.

Chapter 41

The Third Fleet

You have endured much in the past, but you have earned an honor rarely achieved by people of mankind. You now have the Right to an Orderly society, the Right to be governed by Good men.

The First Emperor of Mankind addressing the citizens and civilians of the newly formed Empire of Man.

37 MS AA

The students practiced several configs of their ship and toured similar frames. However, they had only a few kiloseconds to examine their ship before it joined the Third Fleet. Albert's ship was called 'Novel Strike,' a standard non-stealth frigate. The ship looked like a large model of a vanguard corvette. It had a cross-section that was halfway between a triangle and a hexagon, allowing for proper surfaces with its 3 pairs of point defense guns: frontal double-turreted laser, middle conventional 40 mm Gatlings, and a pair of small railguns capable of firing ten 2 g bullets per second. It also carried an armament of missiles.

"Got that new ship smell," Max cheered. "Too bad it's only rated 12 G, I could totally pass the test at 15." He approached the box of unloaded warheads.

"Let's see the missile specs here," Ken said, picking up a piece of paper on top of the box, which described there were 30 of them, 50-kiloton uranium warheads each.

"What?" Max was shocked. "Did it just say KILO-TON? What else do we have? A little gun that shoots a piece of paper with 'booo' on it? These are like little flashlights in space."

Albert chucked at the image.

The Principal stated matter-of-factly, "Deuterium production has not kept up with demand and it has been rationed primarily to capital ships. Besides, smaller missiles will be safer to use closer to the planet, where we will be stationed."

"I didn't even know we had much uranium left," Albert was also surprised.

"We didn't," the Principal responded. "It's all in orbit now, inside one of these or as igniters for thermonukes."

"You're telling me that despite the boy genius here and his great work on the deuterium production, our ship doesn't get any," Max waved at Albert.

"The old money kid here has a point," Albert returned the half-compliment.

They nodded at each other.

"I know the big bad adults don't let you play with the nice toys, but you have to trust the plan," the Principal went back to teaching mode.

"In addition to being an only 12 G cramped frigate, we are practically unarmed. Unbelievable," Max shook his head. "I spent nearly 30 megaseconds training [~1 Earth year]. Where is the trust?"

The Principal and Albert let this question go unanswered.

Ken walked past them all onto the ship, "Ladies, feel free to chat, your mechanic has some exploring to do."

After a few kiloseconds, Ken scoured the ship from top to bottom and emerged, his forehead dark from grease, "All the screws are where they are supposed to be."

Max boarded the ship, carrying his personal belongings in a heavy backpack, "Isn't this what droids are for?"

Ken smirked back, "Never rely on droids completely."

The nearby droid shrugged its robotic shoulders as if to indicate that Ken's attitude was the prevailing wisdom.

Albert observed the nearby solar collector. It was a massive 40 km frame, covered with basic solar panels and a very thick cord connecting its power to the shipyard. Some pieces of infrastructure were so ubiquitous as to almost blend into the background. Yet, since the Blood Memory awakening, Albert had been practicing noticing. The importance of paying attention to the mundane was a piece of wisdom that his ancestors learned the hard way at times.

Before the maiden flight of the ship, the crewmen had a moment to call their oaguths. Bishakha and Yezi were both stationed at the Academy itself. Bishakha received her assignment for the planet crew in charge of the temple air defense. Yezi was part of the Academy Preserve "Defense and Relations." Both were pretty upset about being given roles that were not nearly as prestigious as Diana's stay in the Governor's bunker or even Sheene's House asset space defense.

The Principal joined Albert's ship for the trip to their next orbital location next to heligun 3. The flight was 8 kiloseconds [~2 Earth hours] long and used a few brisk 3 G bursts. The Principal then flew on a shuttle to the nearby immobile hangar station.

Most of the vessels in the Third Fleet were former civilian craft. Many of them moved moved crews and ordinance between different orbits. 9000 of the others occupied a 60,000 km high orbit around Derev. Many used to be small asteroid mining rigs, supply haulers and even entertainment vessels.

There was a 300-meter-long pink yacht ship 'Little Pony,' meant as an Academy graduation present for Jei, Diana's 1.3 gigasecond old cousin [~40 Earth years] and a Princess of the House Darien. The ship displayed a Pony on the side, spun around its axis creating gravity, and used to host to swimming pools and luxurious gardens. The princess was now inside it reviewing mini railgun placements and point defense coverage along with 2 of her assistants and a hundred worker droids with basic combat capacities

There was a 500-meter-long gas hauler, captained by Nimi, which was now mostly empty except for fuel, four laser turrets, and four conventional bullet point defense guns, half the armament of a standard destroyer.

There were two multi-generational ships, nearly 4 km in length, too bulky for backup protocols, now reconverted into hangar bays.

The entire civilian fleet in that orbit was bait.

The bulk of Third Fleet's actual firepower was in the stationary heliguns, hangar bays, and mobile ships protecting them, in orbit 10,000 km below them.

Putting the Third Fleet into position wasn't strictly necessary from an immediate military perspective. The Browly Enemy Armada was approaching the Greeter station and decelerating towards Zeun. However, moving served both as a functional exercise and preparation for the contingency of movement to support the First Fleet.

The frigate 'Novel Strike' made its way towards its assigned spot. Afterwards Albert went on a brief spacewalk, attached to the outside of the ship with both magnetic boots and a tether. He wanted to stretch his legs and marvel at the magnificence of heligun 3, a standard 1.5 km in length, and only 500 meters away from them.

The heligun is a marvel of human engineering and a testament to the Human drive toward technological perfection. Combining a coilgun and railgun in one, it moves a massive slug along a long barrel, achieving speeds for weights too tricky for either design to handle individually. The engineering of its components had to be flawless.

Just like a normal coilgun, the sections of the coils had to only be turned on as the slug was moving forward through the section. If they didn't turn off in time, the magnetic force would begin to pull the slug backward. However, at those speeds, the residual electricity of simple circuits would linger for far too long. This problem was solved through a mix of adjustable resistors that moved electricity in line with the ordinance, laser-based electric shutdowns, and cooling as well as nanosecond level responsive computer.

The stress on the rails was much substantial than that of the normal railgun and caused deformation after every shot. This was solved by building the rails out of a liquhard metal alloy that would crystallize for the duration of the shot, turn liquid, and re-crystallize afterward, effectively healing the rail damage.

The acceleration of the ordinance was over 300,000 Gs, which deformed many materials over time, further complicating the calculations predicting its location inside the barrel. Even subtle changes in the ordinance and heligun alignment from internal stresses meant that an onboard computer had to model every shot at nearly a molecular level to ensure the smooth flow of electricity through both the rails and coils.

Derev orbital heliguns shot a 500 kg slug with an exit velocity of 100 km/s, 3 times faster than the escape velocity necessary to leave the system at that point. A slug impact was less damaging than a missile, but the fleet had ten times as many slugs as missiles.

The feeling of observing heligun 3 filled Albert with an almost religious fervor. Parts of the circular coils exposed themselves to the vacuum of space to radiate heat. The railgun barrel reinforcers peeked through them. It dwarfed the already impressive ships that flew nearby. Just like looking at an Imperial Temple, it was something that would take a while to get used to. He wanted to simply lie on the side of the ship and pray. Yet the spacewalk was over.

It was time to be ready to receive data from the 'Greeter' station and wait for further orders. Albert stepped back into the airlock, removed the spacewalk suit, and got back into the G-suit.

The flight cabin was in the center of the ship towards the top. The ceiling faced the front of the ship, the floor faced the engine. It was a standard arrangement to create gravity in the downward direction during engine burns. The crew sat around a circular computer table facing each other. The arrangement improved eye contact and made bursts of gravity in an unexpected spin easier to handle. Unlike in capital ships, the captain sat at one of the seats at the table.

The Principal and the students under Albert's command started an inter-ship call watching the latest development from the alien fleet.

"So, you think we'll see combat?" Ken sighed. "Do you think we can make a difference?"

"We'll crush as many aliens as we can!" Max responded.

"Well, one option is that the First Fleet destroys both the Enemy fleets and goes home. We don't need to do anything.

Another option is the First Fleet getting completely crushed, in which case we will too," Albert sighed. "The range of possibilities for us to make a difference seems rather small."

"We have already made a difference," the Principal disagreed. "Just by being here, we allow the First Fleet some leeway in how they engage, where they run off to, whether they pursue splinter fleets coming to us."

Albert nodded. It was good to have some optimism in the cabin.

The light delay between Derev and Zeun was slightly more than four kiloseconds [>1 Earth hour]. The light delay between Derev and an outlying station at the outer edge of the system was around 20 kiloseconds [~5.5 Earth hours]. To human intuition, untrained by understanding of the speed of causality, the event had already happened. After the Browly fleet destroyed the station, Albert let out a heavy sigh.

"As if there was ever any doubt," Max said.

They waited for a short time. Ivan, the Commander of the Third Fleet, broadcasted a wideband message that no repositioning was required. The boys got out of the G-suits and walked around the ship again.

"Alright, I got the basic telemetry from the station before it blew up. Gonna task some Academy computers for a molecular-level analysis to suggest what the ordinance was made out of," Albert said.

"Did I miss some order that was given?" Max asked.

"There is no order, but it needs to be done. We have planetside computers standing by without a task," Albert responded.

"Are we just not following orders now?" Max was raising his eyebrow.

"The First Fleet is in deep stealth mode; they would not issue unnecessary radio transmissions. May our Will to Act be as strong as the Emperor's," Albert expected Max to protest, so he prepared his answer in advance.

They made another call to the Principal, and he confirmed, "Albert is right, the data needs to be analyzed. I will alert Kariel you are onto this, and he'll compare your findings with the other teams."

"What do you expect to find?" Max's protest was less loud than expected.

Albert was already getting deep into the received data, "Something is weird even with a basic mass/volume spectrometry. The ordinance is only 5% more dense than water."

Ken and Sunnak turned to him. "That is weird," Ken sounded puzzled. "What does it mean?"

Albert continued typing code, "We are going to find out."

Chapter 42

Alpha Strike

The Eternal Question is: "Which Beings are to Be and which Beings are not to Be?". The time for debate is over. This Question of Being will be decided by the valor of our Space Marines, the production capacity of our Manufactoriums, and the accuracy of our Railguns.

The First Emperor after his Men won the First Space Victory for the Human Coalition against the Cyborg Theocracy and Traitor Nations in the Unification War

37.6 MS AA

The analysis of the visual spectrometry of slugs that hit the station matched that of the Enemy ship's armor. That meant the enemy armor was less dense, but thicker than previously supposed. Low-density railgun iron slugs and shaped charge tips could be just as effective as tungsten ones. The Commander got this information from the radio relay obscured by purposefully generated "noise." He ordered a re-configuration of some warheads, but kept the rest of the plan the same.

The intergalactic enemy fleet was decelerating towards the ecliptic. The deceleration parameters had not changed since the flight of the First Fleet began. As far as they knew, the Enemy was not aware of them. The Commander felt fully at peace with battle, like a calm eye of the intergalactic storm.

"Begin the alpha strike," The Commander relayed the order on fleetwide comms.

6000 missiles with thermonuclear warheads had already been dislodged from their tubes and flying in front of the First Fleet in the same orbit several days prior. They were coated in EMF-absorbing extra-dark paint that didn't reflect a single photon of light. And now they began their flight forward.

The initial burn to alter orbit was done where the planet obscured the heat signature from the line of sight of both Enemy fleets. Nano coolant and internal rocket heat sinks were functional enough solutions to trap the heat from the initial burn. Once the heat turned inward, the missiles were no longer visible on any human detector. As the dark running missiles followed their orbital path, they eventually "turned the corner" around the planet and faded from the First Fleet's direct line of sight.

The intergalactic enemy fleet was still decelerating, needing to shed around 120 km/s of its speed relative to the ecliptic. That added to the initial burn and Zeun's orbit created a relative speed of 200 km/s between the missiles and the Enemy fleet.

The missiles approached the Enemy from roughly the direction of the engine exhausts. Given the large amount of reaction mass ejected from the Enemy engines, the line of sight from the Enemy to the missiles would have to pass through a region of space with a higher density of fast-moving particles, which confused the sensors ever so slightly. However, they did not approach the exact exhaust vector to avoid being accidentally illuminated by the exhaust rays. The trajectory was also carefully calculated to avoid crossing a straight line between the Enemy Fleet and any bright background stars.

"Volley on approach. 600 seconds to contact. No reaction from the enemy." The chief weapons officer of the Commander's ship noted.

At that speed, "600 seconds to contact" meant a distance of 120,000 km, 10 times the diameter of Earth. Detecting EMF-coated, light-absorbing, heat-non-dissipating objects at that distance could be a trivial task for an advanced civilization. Or it could be an impossible one if they didn't have a proper micro-particle detector tuned and ready to go.

"Everyone strapped. Fleetwide. Helmets ready." Commander relayed on intercom.

Every crew member was now strapped into a crash-padded chair. They placed their g-suit helmets in arm's reach, attached to a nearby surface. In battle, most of the ship would depressurize to avoid losing oxygen when holes began appearing in the outlying armor.

"50 to contact; enemy is reacting," Brod announced.

The Commander adjusted himself in the chair. The reaction at a distance of 10,000 km indicated that stealth detection of the

Enemy was reasonably good, but imperfect. The stealthening, the Alpha strike, the first step of the plan. It partially worked.

"Now is the time for light and fire," The Commander spoke to his cabin only.

Spotting the volley was the first miracle; preventing the impacts was another matter. It meant understanding the trajectory of every single missile, deciding on an interception plan, firing an appropriate weapon, and waiting for it to properly converge into each missile.

Hundreds of thousands of objects of varying sizes and speeds attempted to intercept the volley. Many looked like basic kinetics similar to the ones that destroyed the "Greeter" station, many had exhausts and behaved like rockets. Others looked more complex with computers still working out proper classification.

Within 10 seconds of the first reaction, 500 missiles noticed there were attempts to intercept them and activated thrusters dodging side to side. They also activated variable schedule forward drives, specifically designed to make their position hard to predict. Every half-second, the onboard missile computer altered its trajectory to guide itself away from the attempted interceptions. Within 20 seconds, the entire volley was noticed, but only a few missiles were shut down.

"Kinetic and rocket interceptors only so far," Brod reported after 30 seconds of their volley being spotted.

The Commander wasn't sure what to make of that. He expected lasers to start firing as soon as the kinetics. At 200 km/s relative speed, a standard destroyer laser would have only half a second of firing. It would be enough to melt an already hot railgun barrel, but not enough to damage a colder, more armored and better sloped missile. However, the Enemy should not know the exact composition of the missile armor. From the Enemy's perspective, lasers could be worth using even at 12,000km to try to get a lucky hit at the rocket optics or other sensitive parts.

The Commander was a little surprised. If the enemy fleet had no lasers, it meant they had more kinetics and rockets than he expected. Good thing he brought point-defense. The Enemy would be worse at fighting up close, but getting up close to this many ships was clearly suicidal. The Commander thought about his battle with Albert staining his perfect record with a draw. Lasers could be inside enemy ships, and decided to not rule things out too hastily. The absence of shields wasn't as surprising. Fast-moving missiles would tear any shield generator apart and the Enemy interceptors might function better with shields off. It's possible that their shields could not be detected from this distance.

The computer finished classifying the complex objects that attempted to intercept the volley and determined they were 'drones.'

"Low probability momentum transfer," an automatic voice reported.

"Low probability" events were the most feared alerts. The Governor got a tingle of fear, quickly pulling up the information. Two of the Enemy ships closest to the missiles collided with each other and then cleanly separated with an unexpected gain in momentum, thus dodging one of the missiles. Human ships could theoretically do this maneuver using their shields, but since it would destroy both of the ship's shield generators, it would be a one-time act. The Governor was relieved once he saw what had happened. A desperate last-ditch attempt to avoid a missile that they failed to intercept wasn't something he had spare brain cycles to worry about, even if it had used a technology not fully understood by the combat analyzer.

"Max dodge 1G, Capital dot 4G," Brod reported.

The entire cabin let out a huge sigh of relief. Finally, some good news! The Enemy ships were slow, just as he expected. The largest ships tried to dodge by accelerating at only 0.4 g. None had gone into complex spins. The option to kite was still there, the option to close in was still there, the option to run away... The Commander stopped this train of thought. Too early to think about this.

"First explosion. 10 meters d," Brod reported. "D" in this context meant distance from enemy ship.

The Commander clenched his fist in excitement. Even allowing any of their ordinance to detonate so close to the enemy ship meant their gambit had worked at least in some way.

Several other explosion reports came on his screen:

'0.8 ExaJ 20 m d'

'1 ExaJ 3 m d'

"If we can surprise it, we can kill it," The Commander spoke to the radio. Morale is worth keeping up. "Put the first explosion on screen."

The Commander's screen showed a blurry image of a 0.4 Exajoule [~100 megaton of TNT] warhead bathing a 500-meter-long Enemy space vessel with gamma rays. After the flash disappeared, debris began to emanate from the zone; the Enemy vessel remained, with its engine turned off and its shape slightly changed.

Before fully understanding how little damage the warhead did, the Commander triumphantly declared, "It breaks!"